SHE HEL
DIAPHA

"But Alex, how ever did you guess the size?" Yolanda asked, blushing.

Alex watched her intently from beside the bed, his eyes narrowing as he spoke. "I didn't have to guess. I took your lingerie with me to the shop."

Yolanda giggled wickedly, burying her face in the softness of a lavishly laced satin teddy. She looked at Alex again. His expression was unreadable, but a tiny nerve ticked beside his eye.

Then Yolanda did something she never dreamed she'd be wanton enough to do. She stood up slowly, gracefully removing every stitch of her clothing. Smiling provocatively, she tried on everything he'd bought her, her nakedness even more apparent under the flimsy garments.

"You see, Alex?" she said softly, turning her body this way and that. "I told you I'd teach you to spend your money wisely."

ABOUT THE AUTHOR

A British Columbian native, Bobby Hutchinson chose that province as the setting for her second Superromance, *Meeting Place*. She and her husband, both motorcycle enthusiasts, live in Vancouver, B.C., with their five children. Bobby is an award-winning short story writer as well as a novelist.

Books by Bobby Hutchinson

HARLEQUIN SUPERROMANCE
166—SHELTERING BRIDGES

HARLEQUIN AMERICAN ROMANCE
147—WHEREVER YOU GO

These books may be available at your local bookseller.

Don't miss any of our special offers. Write to us at the following address for information on our newest releases.

Harlequin Reader Service
901 Fuhrmann Blvd., P.O. Box 1397, Buffalo, NY 14240
Canadian address: P.O. Box 603,
Fort Erie, Ont. L2A 9Z9

Bobby Hutchinson

MEETING PLACE

Harlequin Books

TORONTO • NEW YORK • LONDON
AMSTERDAM • PARIS • SYDNEY • HAMBURG
STOCKHOLM • ATHENS • TOKYO • MILAN

Published September 1986

First printing July 1986

ISBN 0-373-70229-9

Printed in Canada

For Nel and Al Hutchinson, my parents-in-law,
for giving me their love and their son.

My deepest thanks to Adele
for sharing her knowledge of Czechoslovakia.

CHAPTER ONE

"I DON'T CARE if she's a dead ringer for Miss Europe. I'm still not getting railroaded into this preposterous scheme you two have cooked up for me."

Still, Alexander Caine couldn't resist looking at the tiny snapshot he held so gingerly between his fingers. He stared curiously at the face of the girl-woman. No, he corrected himself, twenty-nine is definitely a woman. And it was this woman his father and Uncle Barney wanted him to marry. The woman they'd badgered him about for weeks. The picture showed only her face, a serious face. Her gaze was forthright and faintly imploring, or was that only his guilty imagination? Her cheekbones were slavic, wide and high, and the forehead was broad beneath the crown of dark, luxuriously thick braids.

An attractive face, not pretty but arresting. Her coloring surprised Alex. Instead of the blond Prussian coloring he would have expected with such deep blue eyes, her hair seemed almost black in the photo, her skin tawny and clear.

"She doesn't look like Aunt Sophia at all," he commented absently, studying the slightly exotic tilt to the eyes, the full, clearly defined lips. There was a tiny round mole beside her mouth.

Barney shook his head, and a fond expression crossed his face.

"No, she doesn't take after my Sophia. She's more like old Anna, Sophia's mother."

Alex heaved a sigh of frustration, giving the photo one more cursory glance. So this was the notorious Yolanda Belankova, the woman he was being pressured to marry.

No beauty, he concluded again. Features too strong. Exotic looking, maybe. Unusual eyes. Wide set, thick lashed. Questioning. Accusing? *Forget it, Yolanda. My armor's too rusty for rescuing damsels these days.*

Across the desk, Robert and Barney Caine watched Alex intently, their narrowed glances speculative and cautious. The brothers were slouched in comfortable leather chairs in Alex's inner office, and in the corridors beyond the closed door the everyday business of the Parliament Buildings continued, muted and ordinary despite the grandeur of the setting.

The resemblance between the three men was subtle, transcending the generation between the two older men and the younger. All three shared a certain cragginess of facial lines, a sense imprinted physically of a civilized veneer thinly disguising an almost primitive urge to inflict their will on the world. They had tall, muscular frames more suited to rough woolen shirts and jeans than the carefully tailored expensive suits all three wore. And there was a similarity in the set of jaw, the stubborn expressions on all three faces evinced by a slight tightening of muscles, a flaring of handsome nostrils that hinted these were powerful men who were used to having their own way, one way or the other. By force, if necessary.

"There has to be another solution," Alex stated flatly, tossing the photo down amongst the clutter on his wide oak desk. It landed among reports stamped Ministry of International Trade and Investment, reports Alex should be studying right this minute, instead of having this recurring, insane conversation. Which one of these two had dreamed

up the damned scheme in the first place? Not that it mattered once they'd made up their minds.

"You have to think of an alternative, because I'm absolutely not marrying some woman I've never met just to get
her out from behind the iron curtain. I'm thirty-nine years
old, damn it. I got over wanting to be James Bond years
ago." If only Barney and Robert had, Alex reflected.

Alex deliberately folded his arms across his chest in defi-
ance, straining the back shoulder seams of his tweed jacket.
"There has to be another way," he growled again stubbornly.

"Well, I'm telling you there isn't." Uncle Barney's voice
was booming and aggressive. A narrowing of his nephew's
green eyes made him clear his throat and consciously mod-
ulate his tone before he went on.

"We've battled, fair means and foul, for five years now.
You know that, Alex." Barney Caine lifted his massive
shoulders in a gesture of frustration and defeat and scowled
at his nephew. "We've tried bribery, we've applied repeatedly for visitor's permits, and we've even looked into
smuggling her across the border. That's so bloody dangerous it has to be a last resort. Which we're gonna have to start
planning by the look of things, if you won't listen to reason." This time he met Alex's quelling glare with a narrow-
eyed stubbornness, refusing to be silenced.

"Look, this kid started out way behind. When she was
twelve, her father was shot over that Dubček thing, so her
background leaves her under suspicion to start with, and
now she's in the soup over some stupid interview. Lost her
job, demoted to sewing dresses in a factory, for God's sake.
It's driving Sophie nuts." A look of concern and tenderness crossed the big man's face at the mention of his wife's
name.

"Sophie's not sleeping at night, worrying about this girl. Yolanda's her only niece. The kid has no other relatives except old Anna, her grandma. Her mother died soon after Josef was shot. Sophie tried to get old Anna out years ago when it was easier, but she wouldn't come." Barney shrugged, his massive hands held out, palms up.

"So fair enough, home's home. But Yolanda, well, the way I see it, she never had a choice. She's Sophie's only brother's kid, and if she'd married like most of them do over there, if she weren't so hardheaded and outspoken, it wouldn't be as dangerous. But in a place like Czechoslovakia, she's heading straight for a lot of harassment, possibly even a prison term. Fast."

His gaze swung out the window to the hazy gray rain of a Victoria winter. The street outside the Parliament Buildings bustled with gaily colored umbrellas, rain-coated people hurrying about their Monday morning business, the reassuring everyday normal patterns of life in a free country.

"I saw a group of women prisoners the last time I was over. Two years ago, when the company had that foul-up at the pulp and paper plant outside of Prague." His soft dark eyes caught Alex's clear green gaze, and his gruff voice was flat and hard, remembering. "It was early in the morning, wintertime. There were maybe twenty prisoners, with one woman guard. She was dressed in a warm coat. Their clothing was shabby, warm enough, I guess. They all looked old, sixty, seventy. They were carrying picks, and they started to break up the pile of rubble on a side street. One of them caught my eye . . . maybe she was younger than the rest—I don't know. She'd been pretty once, you could tell. Anyhow, she glanced up, and her eyes were empty. Nobody home. Her body was there, but whoever she'd once been was long gone." His face twisted, and he slammed a fist down on the hard oak desk. "Damn it, Alex, what a miserable waste. Those women should have been like my Sophie, plump and busy, cooking, smiling. Loving some old coot like me. Anything but what they were doing. I asked one of the Czech engineers later what the hell they might have done to be imprisoned, and you know what he said?" Barney's voice had grown progressively louder again, and he sat on the edge of his chair, hands clenched into futile fists, punctuating his words with impotent downward thrusts.

"He said they'd probably been critical of the system. They'd probably had the audacity to tell their kids that life hadn't always been that way, that they remembered a better time, before the Russians took over. And for that, they were doing a life sentence?" His booming voice filled the quiet room, and his fist crashed down on the desk, sending papers drifting to the gray carpet. Then he sank back in his chair, breathing heavily. The lines in his face drooped, and Alex studied him, a frown beetling his heavy dark brows. Uncle Barney looked older than his sixty-four years.

"Uncle Barney, calm down. You'll have a heart attack, carrying on this way."

But Barney ignored the words, instead locking Alex's concerned gaze with his own zealous glare.

"You know I worked over there for four years, off and on, Alex, when the industry made the deal with the Russians to send our engineers over to start the pulp project and teach them to operate it. Sophie was an interpreter, like Yolanda. You remember me telling you how I met her, how scared she was to even be friendly. And that was years ago, before things got really bad. Before Dubček." He shook his head, and his thick fine white hair slowly settled back into its customary haphazard order.

"Czechoslovakia is a beautiful country, physically. Politically, I'm not exaggerating the way it is. I feel damned lucky to have met Sophie there, and even luckier to have gotten her out. Even then, marriage to a Westerner was the only sure way. I loved Sophie, so that part was easy." Barney took a huge gulp of his coffee, and his hand trembled slightly when he put the cup down.

"Damn it, Alex, I understand how Sophia feels about Yolanda. Hell, you're my only nephew. What if the situation was reversed, and you were the one trapped in the Eastern bloc, the one I might never see again? Don't you think I'd move heaven and earth to get you over here, give you a chance for a decent life? Just the way Sophie wants to do for Yolanda?"

Barney was capable of dramatics if the occasion called for it. Alex had watched him orchestrate scenes worthy of Academy Awards when an important business issue was at stake.

But somehow Alex doubted this impassioned speech was one of his uncle's calculated performances. The man was sincere. This was hard for him, this favor he was asking. Barney Caine was usually on the giving end of favors, Alex mused uncomfortably.

So was Aunt Sophia. Alex visualized her mischievous smile, the caring warmth she seemed to radiate. More times than he could count or even remember, all during the difficult teenage years when these two well-meaning but rough men roared and ordered and disciplined the motherless Alex in their blundering, loving fashion, Sophie had quietly managed to make him feel she loved him, cared what happened to him, really listened to him.

Barney and Sophia had been there in the past whenever he needed them.

All during the awful year after Dixie's death, they'd insisted he and Tracey join them for dinner twice every week, in spite of the fact that Sophia worked and maintained a busy social schedule.

They'd invited his difficult daughter along on holidays, giving Alex precious time to himself. They'd even had Tracey to stay with them last summer, when Dixie's mother was ill and couldn't care for the girl, and his job had necessitated a trip to Norway. Tracey loved them both, and now she often stayed at their apartment when she was home from school, and Alex had to go away on business. Although lately he was uncomfortably aware that Tracey was neither an easy, nor a pleasant, guest.

No doubt, he owed his aunt and uncle more than he could easily repay, he realized with growing discomfort. Sophia had taken the place of the mother he didn't remember, adding a much needed balance to the "tough love" his father and Barney had employed in raising him. If she seemed as much at a loss in dealing with Tracey as he himself was, it certainly wasn't Sophia's fault.

He shifted restlessly in his seat, and reached to pour more coffee into the thick brown mugs, then added a stiff shot of brandy to each from the bottle of Courvoisier half buried on the desk top.

"Wouldn't it look suspicious, me racing over there and marrying her?" he queried abruptly. "I've never met the damned woman," he added, his stomach sinking when he caught the sudden flash of hope on Barney's face, and the glance he shot at Robert. Both older men were giving him that "atta boy" approving look they'd perfected years ago.

"What could they do about it, son?" Robert Caine spoke for the first time, his quietly reasonable voice a counterpoint to Barney's bluster.

"The girl isn't in prison, at least not yet. Your position with the government here lends you a great deal of credibility and respect, and our company's plant outside of Prague does need attention, so there's a valid reason for the trip. You're single, and your papers are all in order."

Alex felt a wrenching dismay in his gut. Not only was he single, he was absolutely determined to remain single. One marriage, for better or worse, was enough. He wasn't good at marriage.

Barney was saying eagerly, "They'll run us through the usual amount of red tape, but I can't see them being able to block us. Robert and I'll take care of all that. All you have to do is fly over, marry her and bring her home on a visitor's visa. We've checked with immigration, and they have a special policy for immigrants from Communist countries. They bend the rules a little. Once she's here, we'll get her permit extended until she receives landed immigrant status. That'll take about six or eight months. As your wife, they can't stop her from leaving Czechoslovakia, either."

Robert held up a hand, anticipating the query his son was about to make. "I know, you're wondering how long you'd have to stay married to her. For sure until she gets her landed immigrant status; then there'd be a discreet annulment as soon as possible—marriage not consummated and all that." He cleared his throat, a bit embarrassed. "Maybe a year, probably less." He met his son's gaze squarely. "There's nobody here you're serious about, is there, son? Nobody going to be heartbroken about a marriage like this? No breach of promise suits?"

It was the one sure way Alex could have ducked out of this whole thing honorably. The foxy old devils. Although they never openly discussed it, Robert knew Alex avoided serious entanglements, just as Robert himself did.

Annoyance mixed with humor quirked the younger man's mouth into an ironic half grin. They both knew he dated Carrie Russell from time to time. They probably guessed he'd spent the odd night at her luxury town house.

But they probably also knew that the ambitious journalist was more of a friend than a serious love interest. Carrie was a career woman, through and through, and the possibility of Alex's marrying her never arose. Which was why he went on taking her out.

"No, Dad. I wouldn't be facing a breach of promise suit."

The only promise he'd break was the one to himself, the one about living the remainder of his life alone.

In his deepest soul, Alex was still married to Dixie, despite the fact that she'd been dead four years this July. How could he explain that the bottom line in the string of objections he had to this preposterous scheme was really that one plain fact? The illogical but very real feeling that he couldn't marry because he was still married.

He carried the emotional impact of that first, long marriage buried deep in his soul. He remembered Dixie vividly, despite the fact that his wife was dead, had been dead for long enough that everyone but him had begun to forget.

Even their daughter. Even Tracey was slowly forgetting. She never mentioned her mother to Alex. It was probably healthy, this ability in the young to leave the baggage of the past behind. He couldn't seem to do it.

And that was the very reason he couldn't do this, either. He drew in a deep breath, preparing to refuse one more time, definitely and finally this time. *Spare me from aging warriors on a search-and-rescue mission,* he thought. *Especially tough and wily specimens like these two.*

But when he glanced up, he saw clearly that the two men he loved most in all the world were actually growing old. Their eyes had deep wrinkles at the corners, their hands, though still strong, were veined and stained with brown marks of age. And on each lined face was the single-minded conviction that they weren't too old yet, by God. Maybe they might still right one more injustice, rescue one more fair damsel from distress.

Two aging knights with a reluctant apprentice. How long or how short a time before men grew old and ineffectual? A line from Dylan Thomas sprang into his mind. "Do not go gentle into that dark night . . . Rage, rage against the dying of the light."

These frustrating, infuriating, beloved men were raging.

Alex slumped in defeat, squeezing his eyes shut in horror at what he heard himself saying.

"Okay, damn it. I'll do it. I'll do it. I'll marry her. Make the arrangements."

CHAPTER TWO

"Tu PRITOMNĪ, ALEXANDER THOMAS CAINE, *chcete si vzit dobrovolne la—*"

"Do you, Alexander Thomas Caine, take this woman," the nervous voice of the male interpreter echoed the fibrous Slovak in accented English, "to be—"

Repeating the words twice seemed to make this farcical marriage doubly binding, Alex thought ironically. The town hall in the tiny village of Votice, fifty kilometers south of Prague, was crammed to the rafters, and the person conducting the ceremony—Yolanda had assured him the man was a Communist official in good standing with the Party—had now fixed Alex with a piercing gaze, waiting for his response.

"I do," Alex said hastily, and the interpreter faithfully reproduced, in Slovak, his exact tone.

Alex gazed beyond the imposing official to the tapestry that adorned the wall. It was maroon velvet, trimmed in gold tassels, a colorful country scene of trees and brook and bridge. Two golden candelabra stood on the floor, and although it was still afternoon, the candles were lit. Ten candles in all, he counted, adding their golden glow to the afternoon sunshine filtering through the high window.

Yolanda was now making her response, her pleasantly husky voice faltering only a little. "I do," she said in English, and Alex glanced at her. Surely this was as difficult for her as it was for him, this charade of a wedding to a person she'd just met and spoken with perhaps half a dozen times in the past week. She seemed remarkably composed.

SHE'D BEEN THERE to meet him at the airport in Prague. He'd submitted to the passport checks, the rigid currency exchange—so many koruna for each day the visitor remained in the country—then verification and another passport check, luggage retrieval and the thorough inspection of his bags by still another official.

His first impression was of a politically oriented, rigidly controlled country in which one should obey the rules to the letter.

"Papers, please."

The lavish numbers of dark blue uniformed policemen, carrying guns and accompanied by dogs, as well as the imposing presence of numerous army personnel reinforced the impression in Alex's mind. This was a regime that took itself very seriously, indeed, and all of Sophie and Barney's descriptions paled before the harsh and sobering reality of the actual experience.

"Papers, please."

After what seemed hours, he was finally approved, passport stamped, nodded to, papers stamped, peered at and dismissed. Grasping his single large leather suitcase, he strode across the building, wondering irritably where he could rent a car.

She came from behind him, laying a hesitant hand on his arm for just an instant before shyly withdrawing it.

"Alex Caine?" She was taller than he'd imagined, perhaps five eight, and generally bigger than her picture had indicated. Not fat, exactly, but plump and tall.

She wore a scrupulously pressed and outdated two-piece blue suit with a paler blue blouse underneath, revealing luxuriously voluptuous contours beneath the outfit's prim facade. For all her weight, she was well proportioned.

"Excuse me, you are Alex Caine? I am Yolanda. Welcome to Prague."

He noticed both her voice and her eyes. The voice was faintly husky, with a slight break now and then, giving it an enchanting cadence. She called him "A-lexx."

Her eyes, thickly lashed with curling, dusky lashes, were the most amazing shade of sapphire, and seemed somehow translucent. She had absolutely beautiful eyes, and the realization confounded him. He hadn't expected to find her beautiful. He stared at her for long seconds before he said, "Yes, of course, how do you do, Yolanda?"

He extended a hand, grasped her strong fingers in his own, smiled at her, and she was able, with a great deal of effort, finally, to return the smile.

She was intimidated by Alex. Tall, handsome, foreign; he seemed so suave and sophisticated in this echoing place that he might have come from another planet. The pictures Aunt Sophie had sent had done nothing to prepare her for him. He'd looked simply agreeably attractive in them. Nothing had hinted at his size or the force of the animal magnetism he seemed to exude. Broad-shouldered, powerful-looking, he took her hand, and she wondered despairingly why she couldn't have met this man under different circumstances, had a chance to know him in a situation other than this awkward charade.

How ironic, to be so instantly attracted to him. And how dangerous.

THE OFFICIAL, to Alex's surprise, was adding a stern admonition to the legal proceedings of the wedding. The old bird was waxing poetic.

"Your pathways in life have intersected, and of your own free will. You are now man and wife. You must love each other and work hard at making a good life together." He fixed Alex with his gray-blue stare, and Alex held the gaze evenly until the man's eyes dropped. He indicated with a brusque wave that they should sign the register on the small table behind him.

Then, to Alex's relief, the mood altered. A bottle of red wine was produced, and glasses were filled for the official, Yolanda and Alex. There were toasts, and a young woman recited a poem that sounded highly romantic.

Alex's eyes met the clear, translucent blue of Yolanda's, and she swallowed hard at the despair she read there. He hated this performance. Well, so did she. Clearly he wanted to be anywhere but here.

It showed plainly in the tight hard set of his mouth, the slight tick beside his left eye, and irrationally, she felt hurt.

There was still the reception to get through, prepared by *babička* and the village women, sure to last most of the night. Yolanda tried to give Alex a reassuring smile, but her lips felt stiff and dry, and a peculiar sad ache began somewhere in her chest. This was her wedding day.

THE RECEPTION HAD BEEN GOING ON for what seemed forever to Alex.

He and Yolanda had been swept from the town hall by the noisy, laughing crowd, escorted down the narrow street in the first blush of summer evening to this reception hall. The crowd had marched them inside, singing merrily, *"The people from the wedding are coming; the bridal group is coming."* Yolanda, her arm through his, had translated breathlessly.

Then, when all were inside, there had been an odd little ceremony with salt and bread. Alex and Yolanda had placed token bits in each other's mouths, and Yolanda then had taken the plate holding the offerings and smashed it at their feet. Alex was given a broom, and he'd swept up the broken glass to the sound of cheering and laughter.

"It is a symbol," Yolanda explained, "of how two married people, they support one another." She didn't meet his gaze as she said the words.

Next he had to swoop Yolanda into his arms and carry her to the gaily decorated banquet tables set all around the periphery of the room.

He saw the trapped reluctance in her face, and in an effort to console her, he caught her eye and winked. There was simply no way to get through this easily. Alex looped an arm under her knees, careful to encompass the heavy satin of her gown, and swept her into his arms.

She was warm and fragrant and trembling, and not as heavy as he'd feared. She put an arm shyly around his neck, and he saw the long lashes shielding her eyes from his glance.

He felt a stab of remorse for her, for this elaborate and special ceremony that should be a romantic rhapsody and wasn't. He gave her a small reassuring hug before setting her down.

Then, there was the feast. Thin ham rolled around cheese, beef broth with homemade noodles, schnitzel with potato salad. And in front of every single guest, a large bottle of vodka and one of mineral water.

Alex welcomed the vodka and its inevitable blessed blunting of his senses drawing him onward through this dantesque inferno of noise and heat and strangeness.

When the food was done, the lights in the hall dimmed, and dozens of candles were lit. Music began—a four-piece band; guitar, accordion, violin and piano.

"We must dance, in the center," Yolanda explained, "the dance of the bridegroom. Then, the women will pay to dance with you, the men with me."

"Pay?"

"Yes, they will give the money to the master of ceremonies, Rudi, over there. It is the custom," she added anxiously, and he nodded reluctantly.

Well, he would quietly make an anonymous donation to the town tomorrow to make up for what had to be hurtful generosity. These people didn't have much, and yet they were going to pay to dance with him? A sense of despair had been growing stronger in Alex with each passing moment. Memories of another wedding, years before, kept surfacing inside him, and with them, a steadily increasing sense of urgency that this be over, soon.

Yolanda Belankova—Mrs. Alexander Caine, Yolanda Caine, she corrected herself silently, covertly watched the tall stranger she'd married. Despite wide shoulders and a deep chest, his large body was svelte and slim in the elegant dark suit, his ash-brown wavy hair expertly cut to complement the rather craggy face with its slightly crooked nose and square, strong chin. Clean-shaven and tanned, his was a foreign face, guarded and expert at hiding true emotions. Almost a frightening face, with the green eyes cold and unresponsive, the strangely sensual mouth set in polite and disdainful grimace.

No wonder he stood out, with such a remote expression as that amidst the broad, open countenances of her countrymen, the farmers from this village who'd watched her grow up, and her more recent close friends from Prague. They too knew the secrets of subterfuge, perhaps even better than he, but somehow he made them look clumsy.

Alex raised an eyebrow at her questioningly. He thought of her, living with him, in Canada.

Home. It was sane and quiet and predictable. The way he'd been, one short week ago. What in blue hell was a respectable politician from Victoria doing at a wedding—his own wedding—in a village hall in Votice? Barney and Robert Caine would pay for putting him through this, Alex resolved, gritting his teeth, smiling as a bridesmaid, an extremely large and toothy blonde named Ludmilla, claimed him for what had to be her fifth dance.

Across the room, Yolanda studied him as she'd done all day, covertly, trying to discover the reason for the conflicting and disturbing emotions he stirred within her.

Was it something about the way he moved, she wondered, the smooth, gliding motions, precise and understated, yet giving an impression of leashed strength?

Now he bowed and smiled politely, his face a mask above Ludmilla's blond braids. He'd smiled in that same strained way, his eyes a flat and frigid green, when the official had married them this afternoon.

He'd slipped the plain gold band on her third finger as if he were performing a duty. She had no ring for him, believing the marriage too much of a falsehood to emphasize the deceit further.

He's doing his duty, what more do you ask of him? she demanded silently. *This marriage is a farce, whether or not babička believes it.*

One of the matrons nearby, Jenda Jaraskova, neighbor and longtime friend of *babička*'s, chose that moment to joke loudly, "He's a handsome one, Yolanda's foreigner. I shouldn't mind taking her place tonight in the feather bed, with one who looks like him. Think he'd notice the difference?" she inquired archly of the appreciative cluster of women busying themselves for the second banquet, which would take place at eleven.

Although Alex was too far away to hear the women' ribaldry, it was still fortunate he understood almost nothing that was said.

Yolanda's nerves tensed, and the blood rushed to her face as she imagined his reaction to such remarks and the many others to come during the late dinner, when everyone would be relaxed and loose-tongued from vodka and dancing.

Yolanda fervently hoped that no one would attempt translation for him. Alex Caine provoked enough reactions in her without the added humiliation of sexual innuendo.

The truth was that Yolanda felt bone tired and more than a little disoriented and unsettled ever since the dance she'd shared with Alex.

If only this celebration hadn't been necessary. Their wedding was, after all, only a formality. The feelings he stirred in her must be suppressed for he must never know what ridiculous fantasies she'd entertained in his arms.

She brushed absently at the filmy ivory veil floating around her shoulders, Grandma's wedding veil, ancient handmade gossamer lace. Her dress was a rich silvery satin that Yolanda had painstakingly cut and fitted and shaped into her wedding gown.

She slid a hand over the fabric's richness, loving the slippery weight of the expensive material, the feel of it against her skin. She had spent nearly all her meager savings on this gown, this celebration, this…counterfeit union. If only her wedding was the triumphant happy occasion it pretended to be, instead of a mockery. If only she were marrying the way she'd dreamed of when she was still a romantic young girl, marrying a handsome man who loved her. Someone familiar, whom she understood. A man who would be her friend.

She straightened her shoulders in a typically determined gesture. Romance was an indulgence few could afford. At twenty-nine, she wasn't a girl any longer, she reminded herself stoutly, and nowadays, nightmares were far more common than dreams. Nightmares of soldiers and guns and prison. She forced the specters of her sleep away, but her eyes automatically scanned the crowd and found the deceptively innocent face of the woman who pretended to be her friend. Katya Krajinkova undoubtedly was making mental notes this very minute, to report as soon as possible to the authorities everything that was said, done, eaten, insinuated here tonight.

An old anger surfaced, and rebellion tightened her lips. Let them suspect. They could prove nothing, for all their snooping. Sophie and Barney had been scrupulously thorough in their groundwork for this marriage of convenience, just as Yolanda herself had been.

But Katya's presence forcibly reminded Yolanda of the true purpose of the seemingly joyful festivity.

This wedding was as it had to be—a means to an end, a route to the freedom she'd almost given up hoping for, a way out of the country she hated and adored. Czechoslovakia. Her prison, her joy, her despair.

She raised her chin stubbornly, defiantly, her confused emotions focused on her new husband.

Smile, she entreated him silently. *Really smile at me, with warmth in those gold-flecked green eyes instead of ice!*

Her eyes seemed to gravitate to him, picking him instantly out of the crowd. The eerie awareness he created inside her drew her eyes toward him. Again, the illogical hurt. Obviously the awareness was totally one-sided.

He was bowing politely to Ludmilla, and Yolanda's pulse leaped, alive with excitement she couldn't explain or control, for now he was approaching, moving in that graceful fluid fashion toward her.

"I understand we're supposed to sit down, Yolanda. Come."

Rudi must have prepared him. It was time for another ceremony.

Alex and Yolanda sat side by side, arms entwined, holding glasses of wine. The strong young men of the village grasped the wooden chairs they sat on and raised them high over everyone's head.

"For luck and happiness," Yolanda whispered in explanation.

There was nowhere to look except into Alex's eyes. He met her glance for half a second, then hastily sipped from the stemmed glass she held. She did the same, and the glasses were tossed to the floor, the bridal couple lowered unsteadily by the singing crowd.

With a quick impatient gesture, Alex loosened the burgundy silk necktie threatening to choke off what little air there was in this press of sweating bodies. He lost count of the number of tiny glasses of fiery vodka he assured himself he was obliged to swallow, the number of indecipherable toasts he saluted with the endless glasses of the excellent local wine, unaware that at some point he had stopped pretending and actually started to relax.

The noisy raucous merriment spilled out the open doors, over the humble cottages of the village, or *vesnice* as it was known here. The sound tumbled over the fields of newly planted potatoes and turnips and cabbage, losing velocity as it rose through the clear night air, disappearing entirely long before it reached the heights of the mountains that ringed the village, or the countries that ringed the landlocked borders of this nation of Czechoslovakia, this beleaguered tiny area long known as the geographical heart of all Europe.

Even the stars were gone when the hall finally emptied. Gray tendrils of dawn stroked the inky eastern sky, and the clear heady air struck Alex like a hammer, intensifying the effect of the potent alcohol, underlining the exhaustion he felt. He forced his aching shoulders back, forced himself to walk straight and tall down the earthen path. The dark blue Skoda he'd rented was parked where he'd left it that morning outside Yolanda's grandmother's cottage and acted as a beacon in the semidarkness.

He'd suggested driving back to Prague right after the celebration, and now he could only be fuzzily grateful that Anna Belankova had quietly but firmly insisted they stay there with her in her cottage for the night.

Alex, touched by the old woman's obvious devotion to Yolanda, had reluctantly agreed to the plan. What did it matter where he spent one more night in this godforsaken country? Tomorrow he would leave Prague for four days of business meetings, touring the pulp and paper plants set up by the Canadian Trade Commission, and then he would return to Prague, collect Yolanda, then head for home.

Once in Canada, Yolanda would be Barney and Sophie's responsibility, Alex told himself. That's all this heightened awareness of her probably amounted to, just an overdone sense of responsibility. He had to deliver her safely to Barney, and then he would be free to more or less forget about her.

Tonight, this moment, it was increasingly difficult to think that far ahead, anyhow. He longed only for a bed somewhere—anywhere—and sleep, for whatever remained of the night. His wedding night, the second wedding night of his life.

He'd fought the memories all day. After all, there was no comparison between that long-ago day and this, no similarities except in the solemnity of the two ceremonies. But by some quirk of irony, the differences made him remember far more poignantly than likenesses would have. Every difference brought painful memories of that other time.

Yolanda was the antithesis of his first wife. Dixie had been slender as a reed that day, laughing and flirting coyly with him, always touching him, holding his hand, stroking his arm, those seventeen years before. He was twenty-two, and Dixie was eighteen. A girl.

This somber woman had probably never flirted in her life. He cast a quick glance sideways at her. Certainly she didn't make any effort to touch him. She walked beside him, keeping distance between them, and he glanced at her now and then, at the lush ripeness of her. She moved a bit ahead on the narrow path, and Alex watched the unstudied grace of her movements, the proud tilt of her head. The traditional white satin she wore emphasized her breasts, her ample hips. She was... he searched for a word, forcing his muzzy brain to cooperate. She was... erotic. She had flawless skin, golden skin that had tanned a glowing copper shade in the early June sun. And those oval jewellike eyes, with their exotic tilt! The luxurious coils of thick soft dark hair—Dixie's hair had been a pixie cap of red gold curls, her eyes dark brown.

Dixie had been all that was delicate, almost childlike, ultrafeminine, coquettish.

No, this sturdy creature striding along at his side was no Dixie, he reminded himself bitterly.

But he'd married Dixie believing he loved her. And even with that depth of emotion as a firm beginning, his marriage had somehow gone awry.

Yolanda? Yolanda, he reminded himself, was strictly duty. Family duty. He'd do well to remember that. The vodka was to blame for that embarrassing response in his body when they'd danced; the liquor created the ache deep in his groin.

By the time he'd reached Anna Belankova's cottage, the iron discipline he exerted over his limbs in order to make them obey was fast disappearing, and the quantities of vodka and wine he'd consumed had torn down the barriers he usually used to block the loneliness in his soul.

He'd had too much to drink. He was a hairsbreadth away from maudlin. Cautiously he climbed the steep narrow staircase to the bedroom the old woman had shown him to earlier that afternoon.

He closed the bedroom door behind him, sighing with relief to find himself alone at last. He located the light's string after a bumbling search, and the single bulb swinging on the cord harshly lit the tiny area under the eaves, making him dizzy with its swaying.

There was cold water and a fresh cotton towel on a small washstand in a corner. He drank deeply from a glass, then tipped the yellow china pitcher over the basin. He doused his hot face, fastidiously washed away the sweat from his body and smacked his head on the ceiling when he stood upright.

Rubbing the spot, he cursed under his breath and wondered where the hell to dump the water from the basin. He finally found the bucket tucked discreetly under the washstand and cautiously poured out the soapy water.

At the foot of the stairs, Yolanda heard the bang as he knocked his head. She winced for him, and then the bedsprings creaked, the sliver of light under the door at the top of the steps went out. Taking a deep, weary breath, she tried once again, the Slovak words tumbling one on top of the other.

"But *babička*, you know this is not a real marriage, you know the reasons for..." Yolanda's whispering almost hurt her throat with its intensity, but Anna Belankova was adamant. Her leathery skin was like a roadmap, creased and lined and proudly advertising her seventy-nine difficult years of life. Yolanda didn't recognize the stubborn set of the older woman's chin or the narrowing of the faded blue eyes with their slight tilt as a mirror image of the determined expression her own features wore.

The words spurted from Anna's lips. "A marriage is a marriage. You were knotted in the sight of God. It's only right you join your husband on your wedding eve."

"Grandma, he's not really my husband. He married me only because of Aunt Sophie...please try and understand—"

The stubborn expression in the old eyes changed to one of cunning.

"What's to understand? You married him, with witnesses, but words are not enough. A marriage must be consummated, my darling, or it is no marriage. This union more than usual. What are words, with no physical joining? Pshaw!" The work-worn hands spread, the shoulders lifted and dropped in a graphic gesture. "The marriage can be annulled—he feels no responsibility for you. After all, he has done his duty by simply coming here. But lovemaking, ahhh." She nodded wisely, a reminiscent smile making the thin old lips softer, younger.

"The flesh forms a stronger bond than even the words of God or man. Go to him, Yolanda—I order you."

Yolanda's arms were folded across her breasts, partly to ward off the chill air of near-dawn in the unheated kitchen, partly to help buttress herself against Anna's inflexible will. There was no reasoning with Anna when she made up her mind like this. Patiently Yolanda tried, anyway.

"There isn't any love, *babička*. He married me only because his uncle asked him to, because of Aunt Sophia. To...to get me out. You know that. It would be obscene to...I would feel humiliated if..."

"Enough." The fierce outrage, the fiery anger in Anna's face silenced Yolanda. The old woman had raised her, and that expression, coupled with the single word, had always stilled Yolanda's outbursts of rebellion.

"Marriage is not only love and happiness, the way you young fools think. Marriage is much greater. It isn't meant to be happy at first: you struggle together, you fight the world to make a life, and you grow to really know each other, then you fall in love afterward."

"Is that another one of your Gypsy sayings, Anna Belankova?" Yolanda teased tiredly, gently, hoping to deflect Anna's purpose.

"So what if it is? Do as I tell you, Landa. Please, for your old grandma. I will die soon, and I want to know you are safe and happy before I go."

Her voice quavered slightly, and the suddenly weakened mouth and chin trembled. The drama, the tragic passion in the lined face delighted Yolanda. *Babička* should have been a dramatic actress. *Babička* was a dramatic actress, she decided. A tiny smile tilted her full lips.

"Try to wait until you harvest all those potatoes we planted—it would be a shame for them to go to waste."

"What have I done, to raise such a bonehead, such an ungrateful child," Anna moaned, but there was a flicker of amusement now in the shrewd old gaze, although not the slightest weakening of intent. "I will stand here all night if I must, an old woman deprived of her rightful rest, to make sure you do as I ask, Yolanda Belan—Yolanda Caine." The unfamiliar name came with difficulty, but Anna emphasized it, her gaze boring into the young flushed face inches above her own. "Go to your husband, as a proper wife should. Go," she whispered. An almost frantic note came into the old woman's tone. "Sometimes even in our own homes, the state has eyes and ears. This is your chance, my darling. Please, for me, make certain it succeeds." All trace of acting was gone now. Anna was pleading, and with an angry, defeated flick of her satin skirt and an irritated exclamation, Yolanda started up the steps. After all, where else *was* there to spend the night? The man was asleep, unlikely to awaken. Her very bones ached with weariness, and the chairs in the kitchen were meant for sitting upright. There were only two tiny bedrooms, the one on the right, the room Yolanda had occupied since she came, orphaned and bereft, to live with her grandmother sixteen years before. Where Alex now slept. The other was Anna's. There really wasn't anywhere else to go, with Anna guarding the kitchen like a bulldog.

He would be sound asleep, anyway, she repeated to reassure herself as she halted near the top of the steps. Her heart pounded with nervousness, and she silently turned the knob and slipped through the bedroom door.

Sure enough, deep, even breathing filled the little bedroom. It was dark; the heavy curtains at the window blocked what little dawn light there might be. Yolanda knew every inch of the cottage, and she crept silently over to the wooden hook on the wall where she knew Anna had hung a freshly laundered nightdress, an embroidered white gown of bleached soft linen. She was more aware each second of the mounded form of Alex on the bed, the alien male odors of leather and some sort of citrus after shave, overlaid with a totally undefinable scent she'd noted when he danced with her earlier, the intimate body scent of a clean, perspiring man.

With shaking hands she stripped off her gown. Alex cleared his throat, heaved half over. Yolanda froze, then raced to hang the satin gown on its hanger on the peg and to tug off her long taffeta slip and sturdy white bra. She yanked the voluminous folds of the nightgown over her dark head, fighting a wild panic when a small button caught in the strands of her loosened hair and her body was half exposed in only white panties for agonizing seconds.

But the man on the bed still slept, his breathing the deep, even sighs of exhaustion. After a moment's hesitation Yolanda slipped the panties down and off.

Planning every slightest move before she made it, she poured icy water, drop by nervous drop, into the china basin. Using a cloth to wash away the light traces of lipstick and powder she'd worn, she then laved her underarms and breasts, her stomach and legs, as best she could beneath the folds of the sweet-smelling gown, still redolent of the sachet of herbs and flowers *babička* used in her closets and drawers. With every movement, she listened to the sounds of the man on the bed for signs of wakefulness, but there were none. Silently, stealthily, trying not to disturb the goose-down quilt or touch her sleeping husband in any way, she crawled into her marriage bed.

Her feet were freezing, and every nerve in her body felt as if it were vibrating. In contrast, the body inches from her own was sending out soothing waves of warmth, like the stove downstairs when Yolanda stoked it with coal on winter morning weekends.

Slowly, inch by inch and limb by limb, that comforting warmth and her weariness took over, and she relaxed, still not moving, but gradually slipping uncontrollably into the deep sleep her tired body craved.

HIS DREAM WAS SENSUAL, permeated by a lingering old-fashioned odor of mingling flowers and spice, an elusive, compelling scent that intrigued and excited him unbearably, reminding him of simpler times and forgotten, innocent passions.

Perhaps the softness surrounding him and the evocative summer smell convinced him that he was carefree again, a man with his life still before him, strong and proud of this primeval pulsing urgency in his loins. There was a woman in his fantasy. She wasn't Dixie.

This woman's full breast was lush and comforting in his palm, her nipple responding instantly to his touch, erect and echoing his own fullness. He exulted in his strength and her response, his hardness and her supple yielding, the potency of their desire. He was both intrigued and driven to madness by the softly modest coverings his beloved dream companion wore.

He knew her to be a creature of his subconscious imaginings, soft and all-encompassing, sweet smelling, and best of all, his own companion. His need was almost pain now, and he craved the sweet release he knew he'd find if only he could penetrate these folds of cloth. His tumescence slid unerringly up a newly naked satiny thigh. There was some reason that he should awake, and he fought it with considerable will, desperately denying any return to consciousness. Then, the battle lost, he penetrated the hot soft flesh at last.

She pulsed and burned and drew him irresistibly. She held him tight, luring him into a spiraling ecstasy so intense that he convulsed immediately and moaned. With his final uncontrollable surge of release, he flew upwards from the red and heated wetness of somnolent delight into the grayed and stark images of reality.

The groan he'd emitted from ecstasy swiftly became a choked exclamation of concern as he disentangled himself from Yolanda. The dawn light was enough to reveal her, hazy with sleep and confusion, blinking up at him, and it took only seconds for the full impact of what he'd done to penetrate the numbed, delicious lassitude of sexual tranquility still shivering through his long form.

His curse was graphic, and Yolanda hadn't ever heard that particular expression in English. He rolled off and away from her, burying a fist viciously into the soft enveloping feather tick that covered them both.

"Why didn't you stop me?" he ground out, and she felt her body contract with humiliation at the unleashed fury of his tone. She swallowed hard, and then prayed he hadn't heard the clumsy gulping sound she'd made.

"You . . . you are my husband," she whispered, so softly he barely could make out the accented words for the huskiness of her tone. "I was asleep."

She could see him in the gray light, his wavy hair disheveled, the rough bristles of his morning beard apparent on his cheeks and chin. Her face and neck still tingled from the evidence of that beard where his head had rested in the crook of her shoulder short moments before, his breathing stertorous and uneven and sweet in her nostrils. Her heart hammered so loud she imagined she could feel the bed shaking from it.

She'd been drugged with sleep. He was already moving languorously against her body before she started to wake, and the delicious feelings he generated seemed to be a continuation of her dream.

One of his large hands was cupping her breast, circling lazily, gently, making her nipple curl and bud in response, sending sleepy spirals of delightful sensation through her.

She came fully awake then, immobile with shock, and almost immediately felt him enter her, a slow certain entry that took advantage of the unconscious way her tired limbs had sprawled in sleep.

Her body reacted with all the suppressed response he'd generated in her from the moment they'd met. She welcomed him, moist and convulsive.

Her action had been instinctive and totally natural, and her face burned now at the recollection.

Without hesitation, she'd made it easier for him, despite the involuntary tensing of her inexperienced flesh. It had been so many years since . . . But before she could join him, he'd stiffened and moaned against her, before she could adjust and respond to the exquisite sense of fullness and heat sending delicious undulations through her thighs and belly.

That quickly, it was done, and she was truly the wife of Alexander Thomas Caine. His seed trickled in a warm stream down her thigh. Trembling uncontrollably, she listened to the low, steady stream of cursing from the man beside her. He rubbed an agitated hand through his hair, and his amber-flecked guilty eyes collided with her quietly furious stare.

"I am twenty-nine years—I am no child," she stated, her voice as steady as she could make it. She desperately hoped he hadn't been able to sense her inexperience. Surely Western women were more sophisticated in these matters.

"If you find me so, so, disagreeable . . ." What did he expect of her now? Her stomach twisted with uncertainty and hurt, but she proudly refused to look away from him. He met her gaze with his own burning green glare in charged silence, his broad chest with the mat of curly hair exposed above the puffy eiderdown. His arms were strongly muscled under the tanned skin, and his hands were large and veined, clenched into fists. Yolanda's own hands were callused, her nails short and stained from planting.

Self-consciously, she kept them under the covers and averted her gaze. The awakening memory of his hand so sweetly on her breast was vibrant and painfully intense.

"Disagreeable? Hell, no. Just the opposite," he burst out, miserable, angry with himself, not able to distance himself yet from that moment of utter bliss he'd known in her arms. He reached out a hand, absently tucked a long strand of silky fine hair back from her cheek, and she wanted to turn her face into his palm, sniff at the skin smell of him.

"I'm furious with myself. I had no intention, I . . . What are you doing sleeping here, anyway? I was . . . I never thought for one minute you'd actually crawl in beside me. Hell, Yolanda, surely you know enough about men—" He stopped abruptly. What was he doing, blaming her? The responsibility was his.

"Sorry, it sure as blazes isn't your fault," he growled shortly. "I apologize."

Her face was burning, and she could only hope that her tanned skin would hide her embarrassment. With all the dignity she could summon, she said, "There are only two beds in the cottage. Grandmother—she's old fashioned— she insists we're married, and I was tired."

How to explain Anna's insistence, her devious reasoning? Translating from Slovak to English in her head was hard enough without the convolutions of Anna's reasoning. Yolanda gave up with a discouraged sigh.

Alex sank slowly back down on the pillows. He felt as though he was sinking deeper and still deeper into this bizarre plot his father and Barney had engineered, and far from simply being a crucial but uninvolved bit player, he had, by his actions of the past half hour, suddenly entangled his life with that of the woman at his side. He didn't want to be involved with her, at least not more than he'd planned. He didn't want to feel this tenderness for her, this insane urge to take her in his arms and replay what had happened in sleep. She was so lovely. . . .

Enough. But against his will, he remembered the delight of his dream, and he shuddered.

How could he have guessed his body would betray him?

CHAPTER THREE

YOLANDA LAY IMMOBILE, waiting for Alex to make the next move. Getting out of bed, sharing the intimate morning rituals of washing and dressing in front of him seemed unthinkable.

How ridiculous, she chided herself, to feel shy with him. Especially now.

The first tentative cheeping came from birds outside, picked up rapidly by others until the chorus was constant. Gradually, too, more light filtered gently through the blue curtains. It was a fine morning. *Babička* would be awake soon.

"What time does everyone get up?" His voice was neutral, devoid of the intensity of the past half hour. He'd bent his arms at the elbow, folding them under his head, staring up at the ceiling. If she turned her own head the slightest bit, her forehead would touch his underarm. She could see his armpit with its curling nest of light hair and the light blue tracing of veins under the skin. His leg, rough with hair, brushed against her ankle.

"Anna is usually up at dawn. If I'm home and it's cold, I always light the stove for her." She drew her legs carefully away from him. "Before, as a translator, I had more days off. Now, as a seamstress, only Sunday," she said matter-of-factly.

"Why didn't you apply for work as a translator some-where else when they fired you?" he queried. "With your training, it seems a waste to be stuck in a factory, sewing."

She gave her head a single decisive shake. Her blue eyes had grown dark, and her lips pressed firmly together. "If I try to change jobs, my work permit will be revoked, or I will be sent miles away to some remote place. I'm a dissident, you see."

"But your language skills, don't you speak—what, four or five languages fluently?" Alex remembered one of Bar-ney's sales pitches about Yolanda. "Czech, Slovak, Ger-man, Russian, French, English," he recalled, slightly awed again by her linguistic abilities. He'd barely mastered French in university.

"Yes, I speak them, some more than others, but of course the work permit determines what job one does." *And how well you obey their rules,* she added silently. She was much better at languages than rules.

"I'm thankful, at least, still I am in Prague. I might have been assigned anywhere. The factory is close enough; I can come home."

He didn't understand her acquiescence at all. He propped himself up on one elbow, studying her curiously. "What did you do, exactly, to lose your job?" Barney had said some-thing about a journalist, an article in the French newsma-gazine.

"There was a group of French tourists. One man kept on talking about how fortunate Czech women were, free to have careers, all of us working. Liberated, he kept saying. I was, I think the word is, indiscreet. I was critical of our so-called freedom, saying that what most women have are two full-time jobs, that even though a woman is pregnant and sick, she must still be at work at 6:00 a.m., put in eight hours, go home and cook and clean." The vehemence in

Yolanda's voice surprised him. She caught his expression, and her voice trailed off. "I didn't know he was a journalist, you understand."

Alex frowned and lay back on the pillows. Harsh punishment for what sounded insignificant. But her words reminded him of a new subject he'd have to broach.

The silence hummed awkwardly. Her stomach rumbled, and her hands flew down to try and quiet it. Beside her, he moved restlessly.

"Yolanda?"

"Yes, what?"

"I don't suppose, ah, you're using, er, birth control?"

She started to answer and had to clear her throat before speaking.

"No. It has not been necessary for me. There have been no men." The words were so simple, spoken with dignity, revealing more of her than he'd expected to learn. She was touchingly naive in her blunt honesty.

"Well. I wanted to tell you that it's, well, that it's highly unlikely there'll be any problem." After two desperate years of trying with Dixie, they had adopted Tracey. Unlikely, indeed, that one dreamy encounter would produce what prayers and youth and love had been unable to create, although it had never been proven that the fault was his alone.

"I believe the—the timing is not—" She groped for the proper expression, desperately translating in her head. "The cycle, it is not appropriate," she finally managed. "So there is not needs for concern."

He did his best not to smile at her mangled syntax, and a frown creased her smooth forehead. This conversation was infinitely worse than any awkwardness involved in getting up with Alex watching.

She slid out of bed, tugging the high-necked gown down around her ankles, scooping up her underwear. Her everyday clothing was in the armoire in the corner, and she hurriedly grabbed the first thing her hand landed on, a printed polyester dress with buttons down the front. Her hair floating like a shawl down her back, she literally tore out of the room, banging the door behind her. Drawing a deep, quivering breath of chill air into her lungs, Yolanda escaped down the stairs.

When Alex entered the kitchen half an hour later, she had already lit the huge blue-and-white tiled stove that dominated the small room, and its crackling and sparking was sending out welcome rays of warmth.

Her face was glowing from a recent scrubbing, devoid of any makeup, but wholesomely fresh and cheerful. Her purple-and-pink printed dress was buttoned sedately to her neck. The shining black hair lay coiled on her neck in a bun, and she wore the incongruous combination he'd seen often in this country—nylon anklets, which Western women wore with slacks, combined with sensible medium-heeled black pumps. An expanse of bare unshaven leg stretched between the skirt hem and the nylon sock top. The most disturbing discovery, for Alex, was that the leg was also curvaceously long and well shaped.

"Coffee?" she inquired, deftly moving a speckled enamel coffeepot to one side on the stove top. With a miniature shovel she stoked the fire with chunky lumps of brown coal, then replaced the lid before any smoke could escape into the low-ceilinged room. Her movements were swift and economical, born of long habit and familiarity.

She poured a mug for him. "Cream, sugar?"

"Black." Even bending to tie his shoes upstairs had been a rash act, swelling his skull to bursting with reminders of excess. "You wouldn't have a couple of aspirin?" he inquired sheepishly, and she flashed him an understanding, almost teasing glance before producing two white tablets and a tall glass of water, which he downed with a sigh of gratitude.

He sat down at the wooden table and watched her prepare a small tray with coffee and a generous slice of fruit-filled bun.

"Kolatchi," she identified it. "For *babička*. She won't admit it, but she loves having coffee and *kolatchi* in bed, if ever I can beat her to the kitchen. I will be only a moment." She climbed up the stairs, and Alex heard Yolanda's cheerful greeting and Anna's chiding tones before the door shut.

It would be hard for Yolanda... leaving Votice, leaving Anna, Alex mused. He hadn't considered her feelings much before. Now, watching this little ritual, he remembered the radiant warmth, the generosity and family feeling the villagers had generated at the wedding celebration. Uneasily Alex thought of his own casual family in Victoria. They undoubtedly cared about one another, but the demands of modern living left little time for family socializing. Yolanda would miss all this closeness.

Well, it was a vastly different culture, and she would have to learn to adapt. Still, he felt a tender sympathy stir within him; then he reminded himself sternly that it was her choice to come to Canada.

Yolanda was back quickly, and without asking, set about boiling him eggs, setting out peach preserves, toasted chunks of golden-crusted peasant bread and cherry-filled *kolatchi* atop a snowy linen cloth she spread over the table. She was careful never to meet his eyes, however, and he watched her preparations in silence, thankfully sipping the potent coffee and feeling his head gradually clear.

The kitchen had scrubbed wooden floors, scattered with brightly colored braided rag rugs. The stove Yolanda worked at was ornate, one large flat oval set atop a second, with a row of shiny pots hung above it, an attached reservoir to heat water and several roomy baking ovens. Everything gleamed with cleanliness, but not one modern appliance was in evidence—no toaster, mixer, electric oven or microwave. He might have journeyed into a peasant kitchen in a past century.

The walls of the house were at least three feet thick, and morning sunshine filtered through the several small blue-curtained windows. Hand-carved brown wooden plates, varnished and intricately inlaid with detail were hung on the whitewashed walls, and near the table were several stern-looking yellowed photographs in wooden frames. A gray furry cat purred and wound sinuously around Yolanda's ankles as she worked, and she spoke to it absently in Slovak.

At last everything was ready. Pouring coffee for herself, and refilling his, Yolanda sat across from him, aware that he was inspecting the pictures.

"My father, Josef Belan."

She indicated an imposing young giant in a smart military uniform, with a swooping handlebar moustache and the burning eyes of a zealot, staring fiercely into the camera's lens.

"He was a handsome man," Alex commented.

Yolanda stared up at the photo, her full lips pressed into a tight line. "He was a fool," she stated flatly, contemptuously. "He was a supporter of Alexander Dubček, and because he never learned to compromise, he died in a silly, useless uprising when I was twelve. Within a year my mother caught influenza and she also died. Of course you know the story of Dubček and our liberation?" The sarcasm underlining the word was unmistakable.

Alex remembered well, but he wanted her to go on talking to him in this unself-conscious way. Her voice was passionate, with that beguiling break coming unexpectedly every now and then. The kitchen was a comforting place to be. The aspirin had dulled his headache; the coffee was strong.

"Tell me, anyway," he demanded, watching curiously as she neatly arranged her breakfast before her, adding cream to her cup, breaking the toast into tidy chunks, deftly cutting the top off an egg.

"Alexander Dubček was elected first secretary by the Czechoslovak Communist Party in January, 1968," she recited like a good student. "He tried to combine Communist ideology with democratic rights. For eight months, there was an open window to the West." Yolanda kept her recital dispassionate, concentrating on her food and trying to avoid eye contact with the man whose knees grazed her own disconcertingly beneath the small table.

"Then, in August, Russian tanks rolled into Prague." Her eyes flew to her father's photograph, remembering the last time she'd seen him, her mother weeping hysterically, the quiet determination he'd radiated that fateful morning, and again she felt the anger inside her that always flared when she remembered him. His had been such a pathetic, useless sacrifice.

Hadn't he considered his family, his gentle wife, his daughter? Why hadn't he put them first? Weren't they important to him; wasn't she, Yolanda, important to him? She subdued the old pain, controlling her voice.

"My father was there—he'd gone to school with Dubček. Regrettably he died in the liberation, but Dubček lived. We, the people of Czechoslovakia, benefited. We were set free by the Russian army. Fortunate, yes?"

The slight catch in her voice, the irony of her tone, were all that stamped the words with bitterness and changed their surface meaning. "It was too bad my father chose to die in such a misguided manner, because as his daughter, I am suspect, and will always be under this regime.''

He glanced keenly at her, and then busied himself with his breakfast.

She made her features impassive, as she'd learned to do over the years, had to learn in order to survive. Inside, emotions boiled and surged, frustration and anger churning through her. With the kaleidoscope of bitterness a new flicker of hope stirred, as well. Perhaps she could learn to forget. In the new country, perhaps she could stop remembering.

This morning was different, she reminded herself. The past was the same, and its effect on her. The cottage, the village, her homeland, Czechoslovakia, were just the way they'd always been. Her eyes ventured past the curtains at the window, seeing the small carefully tilled field where she and Anna had planted potatoes and turnips.

The difference this morning was that before it was time to harvest, she would be gone. She would be in Canada. For so long, she hadn't dared even to dream, despite the determination and confidence of her Aunt Sophia. It was ironic that now, with the dream becoming reality, she was a hundred, no a thousand times more frightened than ever before. She was afraid of going to Canada with this disturbing man.

What did she really know about his country, or him? All of Aunt Sophie's attempts to describe Alex had fallen far short of reality. Yolanda could only suspect her information about Canada would be just as inadequate. What kind of country could produce a man like Alex?

Yet some things between men and women were universal. Her gaze lifted shyly to him, busy with his egg and toast. Her mind vividly replayed the moment when she'd awakened to find him loving her, and a hot awareness curled through her body.

Those long-fingered hands, occupied now with deftly knocking the end from his egg, had touched her, stroked her expertly, tenderly. She studied his heavy eyebrows, the way they tufted up at the ends, the definite bump where his nose had been broken, the way his mouth and eyes had tiny wrinkles at the corners. Worry? Humor?

He glanced up and caught her staring and quickly lowered one eyelid at her in a teasing wink, so her embarrassment became a smile.

Babička had been right after all; there was now a tenuous bond between them. He no longer seemed as remote and unknowable to Yolanda. He'd pressed himself into her urgently, wetly, needing her terribly. They had shared intimacy, and with that sharing barriers had crumbled. It was possible this morning to ask questions about his country, his life, his job, which she had been much too shy to ask yesterday. Hesitantly she began to question him.

"Please, I know you're a politician; could you explain for me your system of government?" she asked tentatively. And, for the next hour, the night's intimacies, the awkwardness of their situation, even the tiny kitchen was forgotten as two minds and cultures exchanged ideas. She forgot her shyness, intrigued and stimulated by his concise and seemingly open responses to her ten million questions, each couched in careful textbook English, answered in his deep-timbred Canadian accent.

Several times his laugh rang out full and pleasantly masculine when some remark she had made amused him, and she found herself waiting for those responses, intrigued by the warmth that kindled in his amber-flecked eyes.

She already knew much about his life, thanks to Aunt Sophie. She wondered if he realized that fact, if he would be angry to learn that Sophie gossiped fondly about him in her letters.

Regardless, it was enthralling to have him tell her himself, give life to the sterile truths she knew about him.

"My grandfather was a lumberjack," he explained at one point. "Grandpa had dreams of his own timber company, and he started small, but he succeeded. He named the firm Western Forest Industries, and by the time Barney and Dad were adults, the whole thing had become big business. Timber is one of B.C.'s major resources, along with mining and fishing. Like everything else, you don't just go out and cut trees anymore and sell them. It's much more complicated than that."

Yolanda sat, her chin cupped in her palms, nodding when a response was required. She noticed the timbre of his voice, the way a slight frown came and went between his heavy eyebrows.

"Barney became involved first with international sales, and that led to setting up pulp and paper plants in other countries. Dad still manages the company from offices in Vancouver and Victoria, but the whole operation has become pretty sophisticated." His gaze turned to the window, but Yolanda could see he was looking inward.

"And you, Alex? What is your profession?" Aunt Sophia had said only that he worked for the provincial government in British Columbia.

His name came easily to her lips this morning, and he responded with a half grin, again enjoying the way she'd posed her question.

"I was sent to university to study forestry and ended up with a degree in trade and commerce instead, and an avid interest in politics. I'm an international lumber buyer by profession, appointed by the deputy minister of International Trade and Investment in B.C., as an advisor to the department. Although my title is assistant deputy minister, I'm not an elected representative. It's an appointed position."

She knew about such positions and the underhanded benefits they provided. A wave of disappointment overwhelmed her. She had so wanted him to be that rarest of specimens, an honorable man. But she should have known that politics and the resultant payoffs were universal. West and East were similar that way, obviously. Bile rose in her throat, and her next words were harsher than she'd meant them to sound.

"Such a position must greatly benefit your family business." The sarcasm was obvious, and to her amazement, he threw back his head and laughed heartily.

"You sound exactly like one of our backbench politicians who regularly accuse the entire cabinet of pork-barreling." Her totally confused expression also amused him, and he explained, "Pork-barreling is using a position to further one's own interests. It's a shoddy practice, not unheard of in Western politics, but fatal to the politician caught red-handed. Because of my family's business, I'm extremely careful never to breach confidentiality or release privileged information. You see, Yolanda," he said, suddenly earnest, "it's not as if I campaigned for office—I simply had expertise in an area helpful to our present government. Curtis Blackstone, the man I work for, is an elected member. He knew of my interest in both timber and trade and asked me to work with him as an assistant deputy minister during his term in office. I'm not an elected politician. In fact, I'm not at all sure I'd want to be. I'm sort of a . . . well, a hired hand, you might say."

Anna joined them just then, and Alex rose politely to greet her. Anna Belankova's smug delight in the spectacle of Yolanda sitting at ease, talking comfortably with Alex, shone in her faded blue eyes and it was obvious in the grin she shot her granddaughter. "I told you sharing a bed was a good beginning," her triumphant expression seemed to say. A fiery blush burned its way up Yolanda's neck and suffused her face, and she scowled horribly at the smug old woman.

Now it was Alex whose face registered confusion. He knew there was an undercurrent between the women, but the silent communication baffled him.

THEIR DRIVE BACK TO PRAGUE later that morning was more relaxed than Yolanda had anticipated. She'd dreaded spending this time alone with him in the car for fifty kilometers after the tense silence and painful politeness of yesterday's trip, but the lengthy discussion over breakfast had already made it possible to talk to him. He, too, was more at ease, driving with a one-handed ease that both frightened and thrilled Yolanda.

He wore brown cord pants and an open-necked short-sleeved shirt the color of fresh cream. In the strong sunlight she could detect an underlay of silver in his ash-brown hair, but instead of aging him, it simply made the strong planes of his face seem even younger. He was thirty-nine, Sophie had said. She wondered how and when he'd broken his nose, and then swiftly turned her head to the window when he glanced her way.

"The countryside here is magnificent," he commented. "It changes so quickly from flat cultivated fields to these wooded areas. What kind of trees are those? I recognize maple, oak and fir, but what's that?" He pointed at a copse.

She said, "Acacia, and some basswood."

Hilly fields of rich loamy soil, newly planted, were punctuated by wooded glens resplendent with every shade of new spring green. They drove through a tiny hamlet, passing

faded red-tiled roofs and crumbling plaster houses. Each
yard had a vegetable garden and a stand of poppies, not, as
she explained to Alex, for decoration, but to supply the
poppy seeds that were ground and used for filling in cakes
and buns. The hamlet looked as it must have looked for
centuries, and this morning, she saw through his eyes.

Once again in the countryside, Alex said, "It's not unlike British Columbia. We have higher mountains but the
same sort of rugged terrain as this. But of course we also
have the ocean."

He pulled out to pass a wide wooden cart pulled by two
gray horses, and Yolanda shut her eyes. But they were safely
past, and he went on talking as though he'd hardly noticed
the near-accident, a trace of nostalgia in his voice.

"My family home, Rockwoods, is situated on a grassy
knoll overlooking the ocean, outside the city of Victoria. It's
quite isolated, with trees sheltering it on three sides and a
view of the water on the fourth."

"You . . . you live there, in this house?"

Yolanda was sure that Sophia had told her he lived in an
apartment in the city, a short distance from Sophia and
Barney. But perhaps she'd gotten it wrong. Aunt Sophia
was, unfortunately, inclined to be vague.

"I lived there with my wife and daughter, but after my
wife's death, the house has been empty. It's more convenient for me to live in the city," he explained stiffly, and she
felt reproved for asking.

He kept his eyes on the road and added, "You knew I was
married—" the next word stuck in his throat, and he cleared
it before he went on "—before? And that I have a fifteen-
year-old daughter, Tracey?"

Yolanda nodded and said softly, "Yes, Aunt Sophia has
told me these things."

Alex seemed to need to tell her himself. He continued talking as if she hadn't spoken.

"Dixie and I were married for thirteen years. She died four years ago of an illness nobody suspected she had. She was thirty-one."

He'd stopped believing that he should have known or could have done something to save her. The doctors had emphasized that it was nothing anyone could have prevented or even diagnosed, and finally, he'd accepted their conclusions. Four years had accomplished that, at least.

"We adopted Tracey as a newborn baby. She knows she was adopted, but it's never bothered her. She's not at home much. Her school is in Vancouver, and she often stays there with her maternal grandparents."

What could he say about his difficult daughter? That she'd been suspended from the strict Catholic boarding school last winter for smoking marijuana, and he'd had to practically beg them to take her back? That she'd run away three times? That she made him feel helpless and hopeless and useless as a father? That he was terrified she was heading for a life of ruin, and that he didn't know how to prevent it?

His knuckles were white on the wheel, and he consciously relaxed them as an oxcart plodded over the next hill. He rapidly steered a course around it without diminishing speed, missing Yolanda's wide-eyed gulp and clenched hands at the maneuver.

"Tracey's at camp just now, but you'll probably meet her before the summer's over."

He felt an uncomfortable sense of relief, knowing Tracey was at camp for six weeks.

His attention was on the highway, and again she watched his rugged profile unobserved. He had sideburns trimmed

low around well-shaped ears, and the line of his strong jaw
was angular and clearly drawn.

"Where will I...where can I live in Canada? I mean,
where will it be convenient? Of course, later, I will find an
apartment if that is possible, but at first..." Where she'd
live was a problem she'd worried about for weeks.

Alex had discussed that issue thoroughly with Barney. It
had been a loud and lengthy discussion, and in the end, Alex
had bowed to logic with little grace or hospitality. It had
begun to seem as if one concession—agreeing reluctantly to
marry Yolanda—had simply led to more and more disrup-
tion in his well-ordered existence.

"You'll stay with Barney and Sophia, and then at my
apartment. It's better if there's no suspicion about our
marriage being anything but legitimate."

Yolanda noticed the sudden aloofness in his tone, and
embarrassment twisted her stomach into a fist.

He'd fought the arrangement tooth and nail, but Barney
had insisted that until her waiting period for citizenship was
over, the facade was necessary.

"We'll help you find a place of your own, of course, as
soon as possible." *The very instant it's possible,* he revised
mentally, feeling angry with himself all over again, remembering the previous night. Should he reassure her on that
score? He needed reassurance himself. What would happen
with the two of them living in close proximity at the apartment?

Confusion made him frown. Damn it, what unholy demon had made him act so stupidly? If only they could both
forget it had ever happened.

He glanced over at her. She was quietly watching the
countryside slip past, the strong lines of her face almost
somber. Her profile was arresting, clearly drawn and powerful. Beautiful? Not quite, but definitely attractive, and

again he felt the captivating sensuous aura she exuded, and he frowned and looked again at the road.

She really wasn't what he'd expected, not at all. She had an impressive mind, quick and incisive, and she was amusing. She'd never make a fashion model with those clothes, and yet she had an offbeat beauty. Her eyes made him feel as if he could peer into her soul.

They were entering Prague. The afternoon streets were again all but empty of cars, a fact that had astonished Alex when he'd arrived. No rush-hour traffic here. People simply had no money for cars, Yolanda had explained matter-of-factly.

This part of the city, one of Europe's oldest and most historical, looked as though it was slowly slipping into a gray decay. Piles of rubble littered the pavement.

Newer construction seemed invariably to be cement block, utilitarian but absolutely devoid of aesthetic appeal. Even now, in the first June glory of a European summer, the only color discernable in the streets they drove through were the red flowers planted around the prominent and numerous sculptures of the hammer and sickle, with their two doves and inscription.

"What does it say?" Alex asked curiously.

"Thank you for forty years of freedom," Yolanda translated in a flat and uninflected tone. Alex snorted inelegantly, and she shot him a startled look, then she, too, dared to smile at the irony.

An ominous and heavy atmosphere of life reduced to the most functional denominator—work for all, luxury for none—pervaded the somber city, and yet he knew Yolanda had friends here, had made a life for herself and didn't see the bleakness the way he did. He was, after all, comparing this country to his homeland. She had no comparison.

At her instruction, he stopped the car in front of her apartment in an older, despairingly down-at-the-heels area, where grayness lay like a leaden skin over the littered streets and the crumbling stone. He was now pressed for time—he had appointments Barney had deemed urgent with the Canadian engineers employed by his family's company. Yet strangely, he was reluctant to drop Yolanda there and disappear, even for the three days before their flight to Canada.

As a precaution he'd given her the plane ticket, duplicates of the documents in triplicate translated by Berlitz identifying him by birth, marriage, job, age, character, income. There were copies of everything he'd had to submit to the police: the wedding license, the documents identifying her as Mrs. Alexander Caine—her life, her hope, her future, all contained in a large brown manila envelope.

"No need to come in with me," she insisted. He'd seen her apartment the day she brought him there after meeting him at the airport. It was cramped—an eight by ten foot galley kitchen with a tiny fridge and gas stove, a modest living room, and the smallest bathroom he'd ever been in. The miniscule sink was perched over the equally tiny tub. The plumbing was rusted tin.

The amazing thing was the hominess she'd somehow created: the cheap, colorful pictures carefully tacked to the walls, the green plants, many in bloom, flourishing everywhere, the gaily embroidered pillows and bright curtains over windows hiding a dismal view of a children's muddy playground.

"Please," she'd said to him, "be at home."

And the strangest thing had happened. He'd relaxed. She had the ability to put people totally at ease.

But now he wanted to be on his way, wanted time away from her to think over the events of the past day and night.

At the last moment, as she slid out of the car, he took a thick roll of dollars from his eelskin wallet and pressed them into her hand. When she shook her head in proud dismay, trying to hand them back, he insisted, "Use this money to buy something for Anna, at the Tuzex store you pointed out to me."

She'd shown him the government-operated wonderland of a store where, with this magical Western currency, one could purchase vouchers that would buy almost any necessity or luxury.

"What sort of things?" he'd asked curiously, and she'd shrugged.

"Almost anything, a hot-water tank, soup, soap, a summer cottage," she'd elaborated. "It's an effort on the part of the government to attract valuable foreign dollars into the country."

She'd shrugged again with fatalistic acceptance and added, "Of course, the ordinary citizen never has dollars and never goes there."

He firmly opened her clenched fingers and closed them again over the money insistently. "Buy Anna something from both of us, please," he pleaded. It was the "both of us" that surprised her into keeping the roll of bills. *Both of us* sounded so . . . married.

Then he hurriedly shook her hand. She had strong, slender hands, he noticed. He climbed into the Skoda, impatiently forcing it into life. "Goodbye," he called, and she stepped back as the car began to move.

"Good luck," he said quietly, watching her tall, sturdy figure grow smaller in the rearview mirror, alone on a side street in the afternoon sunshine.

He wished fervently that the Skoda had a radio, for he needed something to distract him from the confusion of his thoughts.

Yolanda. He didn't want this depth of compassion for her, this awareness of her as a woman.

He braked to let a chain of hand-holding kindergarten children cross the street. All of them were in uniform, red sweaters and blue pants, with serious little faces, and he pictured Tracey as she had been at that age. He fervently wished she still was a sunny child in kindergarten. It was infinitely preferable to the intractable, sullen girl she had become.

"Thank you for our freedom."

Another inscription flashed boldly past on yet another monument, and Alex found himself also wondering again how being introduced to real freedom in the days and weeks ahead would affect the woman he'd married yesterday.

Would Yolanda feel just as alien in Canada as he felt here?

TWO DAYS LATER, Yolanda lined up at midmorning to catch the bus for Votice, attracting curious stares from the few old people and children also waiting to board, partly because of the heavy box she carried but mostly because it was a workday and it was unusual for a young woman to be away from her place of employment. The prickling uneasiness, the nameless anxiety of going against the system, of doing something to draw attention to herself made her sit uncomfortably tense, staring out the window. She avoided meeting anyone's eyes. The bus left the city behind.

In Votice, Yolanda climbed carefully down the high step of the bus, balancing her box. Her arms ached by the time she reached the lane to the cottage, but her heart leaped with the joy of coming home. Today was the last time she would walk up the lane this way, but she wouldn't think of that.

Anna was on her knees in the garden, weeding the rows of budding cabbages.

"Babička," Yolanda called impulsively from far up the lane. Anna raised her head, and she wiped her hands on the grubby apron covering her skirt. Stiffly, she slowly got to her feet, still rubbing her hands up and down to cleanse them, then waved eagerly to Yolanda and hurried to meet her, her stride vigorous and forceful.

Anna's face was tanned almost mahogany, making the blueness of her eyes, the faded echo of Yolanda's sapphire, youthful and vivid amidst the wrinkles.

Yolanda set the box down in the grass and wrapped her arms tightly around Anna, smelling the musty, sun-scented hair, the slight odor of mothballs and strong soap that always clung to the old woman.

"So, you've come, have you? I thought you'd come today. And what do you have there?" Anna asked briskly, leading the way to the open door of the cottage, shooing away the gray cat weaving itself around her ankles. "About time, too. I was beginning to believe you'd grown so fond of that new husband that you'd forgotten your old grandmother. What is that there in the box, Landa? So it's tomorrow you go, child. Is your clothing all washed? Did you do as I told you and pack your winter underwear? Sophia has told me this Canada is wet and cold. You know how you take a chill, Landa."

She busied herself at the stove, adding meager bits of coal to boil the water for tea and stirring the thick soup she'd started that morning—Yolanda's favorite. She kept her back carefully turned to Yolanda despite the smoke screen of words and tugged a corner of her apron up, surreptitiously wiping her eyes now and again.

Birds trilled outside the open door, and a dog barked somewhere nearby. The kettle bubbled on the stove. Yolanda looked at the peaceful room with eyes that devoured each item she'd always taken for granted, desperately mem-

ɔrizing color. scent, shape, like someone about to be
blinded. Why had she never really seen that delicate embroidery *babička* had done on the throw? It must have been
years that it had covered the back of the sofa, yet it seemed
she saw it for the first time.

"Tomorrow we leave on the plane in the early morning,
Grandma. The arrangements are complete. I phoned to
Aunt Sophia as she directed. She sent you her dearest love."

"And your husband? Did you also speak with him?"

"Yes, he phoned last night. He will pick me up in the
morning to go to the airport." She lifted the box from the
floor to a small table.

"He gave me money for the Tuzex store and told me to
buy this for you, *babička*."

Proudly Yolanda removed the tiny television and set it up
on a small table, grateful that the cottage had been wired for
electricity. Even so, she was relieved she'd bought the long
extension cord—there was only one plug here.

Anna eyed the set greedily, her tears forgotten for the time
being.

"Jenda Durchnakova's daughter has one just like this, so
small. I watched it all one evening. Surely, Landa, this man
of yours has more money than sense, sending you to buy a
television for me," she scolded, but her attention was caught
immediately when the set flickered into life showing a group
of Russian folk singers. With a pang Yolanda realized what
they were singing.

"Co to za veselie?" the song asked. "What kind of gaiety
is this?" It was one of the songs that had been sung at her
wedding reception, and the words had struck her then as ridiculously inappropriate and ironic. Here they were ludi-
crous, with the time of parting hanging like a storm cloud
over the cottage.

Nevertheless, Anna sat still, totally entranced, for fifteen minutes.

"Well," she said with a sigh when the music ended, "I can't wait to see Jenda Durchnakova's face when she finds out I have one of these." The smug delight in her voice told Yolanda how perfect the gift had been, and she felt a rush of warmth for Alex's kindness.

Anna set out large dishes of soup, a loaf of heavy bread, pastries and a cucumber salad with vinegar and sour cream.

"Babička?"

Anna was spooning up the savory broth, dunking a thick slice of bread to soften it, but still didn't meet Yolanda's eyes directly.

"Afterward, after I am settled with a job in Canada, if I send for you, please, will you come?" Yolanda had hardly touched the food, and now the words tumbled out between them, voicing the request she'd never dared to make during the long time since Sophia's visit, the beginning of the campaign to get Yolanda out.

"You know that older people can leave freely—there are no restrictions like the young encounter," Yolanda added.

Anna sighed dramatically. "Why do young people make things so hard for themselves? New countries are for the young, Landa. What would I do there? I don't even speak the language. Here I have my pension, my home, my cat, my garden." She nodded her head at the television. "Now, even that." She paused to chew, drink steaming tea. "I am Slovak, Landa. No matter what they do to my country, I am Slovak, with, of course, a touch of Gypsy. This is my home, and I will stay here till I die. It's easier that way when one is old."

"But it would be so simple for you to leave. I will send the tickets . . . I could get us an apartment?" Yolanda heard the note of frantic pleading in her voice and was helpless to contain it.

Anna shook her head slowly. "Landa, no. You know I grew up not far from here, in the high Tatra mountains. Your grandfather, Karel Belan, came there one summer to work at the haying. My father saw he was a strong young man—our family was only five girls—and Karel looked at me more than the others . . . a marriage was arranged." The blue eyes softened with recollection, and Yolanda felt a poignant tenderness for the older woman. The story was a familiar one, related often, yet always fascinating for Yolanda. It was her history, the way she'd come to be.

"My marriage was not unlike yours, dearest. Arranged, but Karel and I learned to be happy together. We had Sophia, then no more babies came for so long. Ten years, before I was pregnant again with your father, my Josef. His birth was hard, and after him I couldn't have more babies. It was a sadness for Karel. He wanted many sons." Her gaze strayed to the portrait of her son on the wall. "How they quarreled, those two. One a farmer, one a dreamer, father and only son. After their arguments Karel would rage at me, say it was my fault, my wild Gypsy blood that made Josef so." Mischief lifted her mouth into a secret grin. "Always, though, he would make up later. He liked me as I was, Gypsy blood and all, your grandfather."

Yolanda sat still, listening intently, knowing Anna was imprinting these verbal memories as a heritage for Yolanda to carry with her to the new land.

"I was always glad Karel died before his son, before the Dubček thing. He couldn't have stood losing his only son, you know. Men are not as strong as women when it comes to such matters, Landa." Anna reached to refill her mug with tea, absently nibbling a pastry oozing apricot jam. "Karel died when your father was still at the university. He wanted his son and daughter to have a better life than him, to have education. Sophia, she had this gift of languages, and she was an easy child. But your father, was he a bone-head!'' Anna clicked her tongue, her head tipped to the side. ''It was always politics, politics, and he and his father would argue. Poor Josef. And Karel, too. They never understood each other. Now Sophia, she was lucky, always a gentle, happy girl, easygoing. Funny, she was like my own mother, ladylike always. Perhaps a bit scatterbrained. But you, Landa, *oi yoi yoi*.'' Blue eyes met blue, and both mouths quirked ruefully.

''Yes, you are like me, I'm afraid. A little wild, a little crazy. Never able to swallow your words.'' Anna paused, then caught up the thread of her story again.

''Your Aunt Sophia, sweet as she was, still was too fussy when it came to marriage. Truly, I believed she would never marry—she already was in her thirties. Then, after all, she did so well, when those Canadians came. Although she never had children, I was always sorry for that. You know, when she left, she, too, asked me to go with her to Canada, but in those days we believed it would get better here. And afterward when you came to me after your mother died, taking you out would have been hard.'' Anna shrugged. ''Well, it is all for the best. 'The worse, the better.' ''

She quoted the widespread slogan automatically, and Yolanda felt the helpless rage she always experienced when she heard it. ''The worse, the better,'' indeed! To her, the words were a confession of helplessness and utter impo-tence instead of the brave stubborn maxim they purported to be.

''Landa, I want to live the remainder of my days here, be buried close to my Karel and my son, here in my homeland. Not in some strange country far away, with customs I don't even know. The only traveling I will do is maybe back to the valley where I grew up, before I die. Up in the Tatras, where the snow covers the tops of the mountains all year. Then again, maybe not . . . I don't know. I'm getting to be an old woman, you know."

"Yes, *babička*, I know, but only because you tell me often enough." Yolanda smiled, but the usual bantering was hollow today.

They cleared away the food and washed the dishes with hot water from the reservoir on the stove. Each familiar routine became achingly special for Yolanda. Would she ever stoke this fire again, sweep this floor, gaze out this deep-set window at the tiny *vesnice*?

When the afternoon began slipping into evening, Yolanda and Anna sang together the wild Gypsy melodies and the lilting folk songs Anna had taught her. The hours marched so swiftly. Far too soon, they walked up the lane to the wooden bench where the last bus stopped for the trip back to the city. If only the bus would be late, as usual. There must be a million things they'd forgotten to discuss . . .

The bus came wheezing up almost immediately, and Anna's roughened hand trembled suddenly on Yolanda's. She groped in the pocket of her skirt, drew out a small paper-wrapped box tied with string and tucked it into Yolanda's purse. "It's your father's wedding ring; your mother left it for me to give to you." Her tearful voice strengthened suddenly, and her words had a desperate intensity. "Give it to the one you love, and always remember, my darling," she implored, reaching up to cup her granddaughter's face between her rough palms, "Remember always you are not just Slovak or Canadian. You are also one-quarter Gypsy, and for the Gypsy, all the world is home." Her steely control broke then, and her face dissolved into a crumpled mask of tears.

"Go safely, my Landa. Be happy—don't concern your-self over me. I am still a young, strong woman." Anna pulled herself determinedly away from Yolanda's fierce embrace, stepped back and motioned toward the bus where the patient driver waited. "Go, go," she ordered crossly, sniffing back her tears. "I want to show the neighbors the television."

Blindly Yolanda boarded the bus, paid her fare and stumbled into a seat with all her parcels. It became imperative that she watch Anna as the vehicle pulled away. She staggered to her feet, sobbing openly, lurched into the aisle and bent over an irritable middle-aged man reading a paper to watch helplessly through the dusty window as Anna's lonely waving figure, swathed in dark clothing, grew smaller and smaller in the growing dusk.

Then the bus careened around a corner, and Anna and the village were gone. Yolanda collapsed into her seat, and the tears ran unhampered down her face. Despite what Grandma said, this was her home, this place she was leaving. Unbidden, the words of the Czechoslovak national anthem came into her mind.

"Kde domov můj?"

"Where is my home?"

Yolanda understood for the first time why the land of her birth had the only anthem beginning with a question.

CHAPTER FOUR

"THE LARGE WHITE BOATS down there are provincial ferries," Alex explained, raising his voice to be heard over the steady thrumming of the floatplane's motor. The last portion of their interminable journey was in a much smaller craft than the gigantic Lufthansa aircraft that had carried them to Canada, Yolanda thought nervously. She was heartily sick of airplanes, whatever their size.

"The ferries are essential to Vancouver Island, bringing supplies and people back and forth every hour, every day."

What would it be like, living on an island? Yolanda wondered. Alex flashed her a smile before he turned his attention back to the window, the same smile she'd watched for in vain during the long first hours they'd traveled together. It tilted the rather narrow lips up in a crooked line and reached his green eyes, making the amber flecks seem to dance. He was pleased to be nearing his home, she thought.

They were winging their way across the strip of water separating the mainland of British Columbia from its provincial island capital, and Yolanda hesitantly gazed down at the many rugged small islands scattered through the straits, patches of green and violet in the expanse of gray-blue ocean below. She longed for this journey to end, and at the same time, she dreaded it.

The past two days had been an exhausting, stomach-wrenching series of echoing airports, muffled announcements Yolanda couldn't understand, a barrage of hedonistic meals and drinks and solicitous, efficient attention. Who, in her homeland, could ever imagine such opulence, such sophistication? They traveled first-class, and Yolanda watched and listened as Alex competently managed every detail of their journey and sidestepped all her efforts to recapture the warmth they'd seemed to share the day after the wedding. Somewhere during the days he'd spent on business away from her, he'd become an aloof, unapproachable stranger.

Certainly, he was a gentleman, making certain she was warm enough, wasn't hungry or thirsty and that she had stacks of magazines to read. He made sure she understood the route they would follow on the seemingly endless flights, and what landmarks to watch for when the plane landed first in Frankfurt, then briefly in Calgary and finally in Vancouver.

Yet his was a cold, impersonal kind of consideration, and she watched hungrily at first for the smile she remembered from their earlier time together, needing the reassurance of its warmth, wondering anxiously what she could have done to anger him.

Those first hours, he'd never smiled, never even met her eyes. He'd been silent, his lips pressed together grimly, and he'd avoided looking directly at her. He'd pulled sharply away if he happened to touch her, even during the endless night hours on the flight when they rested tensely side by side, neither of them sleeping.

Yolanda resented this reticence in him, this holding back of himself, the cool polite attention offered as if she were a casual stranger he was accompanying. There was none of the closeness they'd shared driving back to Prague that morning. What could be wrong? she wondered. How had she offended him? The unreal hours passed, and Yolanda struggled to maintain her fragile equilibrium.

The fact was that Alex was exerting a steely control over himself. He'd surreptitiously watched her ingenuous response to the comforts every other seasoned traveler took for granted, and how the predictable airline food delighted her as well as the small, unremarkable services that pleased and surprised her.

He was alarmingly conscious of her beside him. Without having to look, he knew exactly how her deep-set eyes widened at takeoff, how the long dark lashes shadowed the high cheekbones and the full pink lips parted slightly in unconscious awe at the strangeness of flying.

She stirred some deep chord in him, and he felt confused. Vulnerable. Damn it all, he had never wanted to feel vulnerable about a woman again, he reminded himself, and ended up feeling angry.

Alex struggled with his emotions, and the tension his body generated filled the small space between him and Yolanda.

Their exit from Prague had filled her with stark, vivid terror. Even now, countless hours and thousands of miles later, Yolanda felt a renewal of the fear she'd experienced as they'd lined up for official inspection of their documents.

She began to shake uncontrollably as the line shortened, and by the time they were ushered into a tiny private office, she was near panic. Her inbred fear of any sort of uniformed official became impossible to control, even though Alex had explained that every one of her papers was in meticulous order.

He'd walked slightly behind her, his flight bag casually over one shoulder, his briefcase firmly gripped in one hand.

Why couldn't he just touch her this once, take her hand in his free one, she thought wildly, heart beating at triple time as she looked at the grim-faced uniformed official who ad the power to block her exit even now, at this last second.

Alex seemed to exude an invisible aura of wealth and authority and calm, while she could hardly walk for the trembling in her legs.

What she couldn't know was how careful he was not to reveal his own nervousness as the series of officials suspiciously examined her papers. He had faith in Barney, and Barney had masterminded these details, these pink forms in triplicate, these signed authorizations, this all-important green passport for Yolanda. But the sense of isolation from the outside world that Czechoslovakia inspired in him made him anxious.

Who knew what could go wrong?

Alex felt dampness grow and spread in his armpits beneath the soft blue cotton shirt, and then a wild surge of relief coursed through him as he watched the papers slowly receive officially stamped approval.

Everything was fine. He drew in a huge, relaxing breath. They were free to board their flight.

With every step she expected them to be called back. Finally she whispered to Alex, "That's all? We are free to go?" Her voice as well as her hands were now shaking as if she had palsy. Alex gave her a cool glance. "Of course," he said casually. "I told you there'd be no problem."

Her feet carried her along while she absorbed his words. He was acting as if she was on a holiday trip, and he was the cultural guide appointed to accompany her.

Somehow, in a blur of conflicting emotion she didn't care to remember, she boarded the plane to freedom.

But the farther she came west, the more she was aware that she was entering unknown territory. The responsibility for adapting was hers alone, and she'd never been more frightened or felt more insecure.

Frankfurt was busy confusion. An indefinable light-hearted aura pervaded even the airport. Soon they were back on the plane for the longest leg of the journey.

Half a globe and endless hours later, they landed in Calgary.

"You must deplane," the friendly stewardess announced, "and wait in the area provided for international passengers, as you will be clearing customs in Vancouver."

The area was clean, new-smelling, sterile and cold. Outside the windows there were no trees. Everything was flat and arid, and beyond the airport runways rows of identical houses lined up like soldiers on parade with nothing to alleviate the tedium of the horizon. Disappointment surged inside Yolanda, and her spirits sank as she walked slowly from window to window. The day was overcast and dull.

"What do you think of Canada?" Alex queried impersonally.

"There is not much here, is there?" she finally said weakly.

Everything, even the rest room Alex directed her to was different, totally alien, neatly confirming her feeling that she was absolutely stupid and gauche.

How could he, this foreigner, understand that she mourned the loss of her green homeland, of all that was dear and familiar, even as she welcomed the opportunity to escape?

How could he know that she hadn't been able to find the ridiculous button hidden on the floor in the bathroom, the button that flushed the toilet, and she'd been forced to ask a motherly woman with blue hair, who'd then acted as if Yolanda were mentally deficient, taking her by the hand with awful, stupid patience and making her push the button several times?

This indignity, plus Alex's coldness suddenly became too much to bear. She longed desperately for a warm glance, a friendly touch, a word to indicate he knew how she felt, some sign to show her he sympathized. It became more and more important to her with every step she took into this strange country that he accord her some human recognition, a response beyond the duty he performed.

Shaken, she returned to the waiting room and quietly sat down in a chair beside him. He was engrossed in a newspaper.

Her nerves, her confidence in herself, were shattered. She started to weep noisily, floods of burning tears pouring down her cheeks in a torrent she couldn't control, and she was much too miserable to even notice the electrifying effect it had on her companion.

"What the hell? Yolanda, what's wrong? What's happened?"

Feminine tears had always terrified Alex. There had been times in the distant past when he'd suspected Dixie had used them to her advantage, but his reaction never varied. Women crying made him feel responsible, ineffectual. This torrent of tears coming as it did from Yolanda, a woman whom he saw as being incredibly strong and stalwart, reduced him to a state approaching panic.

"Don't cry, Yolanda, for God's sake, don't cry."

The trace of impatience in his tone masked his alarm. She heard it, misunderstood and sobbed harder. Then she got up, stumbled, hardly caring if she fell, knowing only that the tears were uncontrollable, and she must get away from him.

What am I going to do with her? Alex wondered frantically. He took her arm and guided her back to a seat. People were looking sympathetically toward them, and Alex scowled viciously at a heavy man a few feet away who insisted on staring. The man flushed and looked away.

Alex groped in his jacket for tissues, clumsily mopped her satiny tanned skin free of tears, aware of its texture against the roughened tips of his fingers, its poreless natural beauty. He held her chin with two fingers, tipping her face up to his rough ministrations.

"Can you tell me what's wrong?"

Her eyes were brimming, seeming to swallow her other features with their mute expression of primitive hurt. A desperate appeal for human comfort, for tenderness, signaled nakedly in their depths.

He met that gaze with his own, and he couldn't stand it.

"Landa, honey, please don't cry like that." With a deep groan, Alex gathered her close against his chest, the way he'd held his tiny daughter years ago when she hurt herself, when she still turned instinctively to him for comfort.

Yolanda collapsed in an orgy of weeping then, at the endearment, the affectionate shortened version of her name that *babička* had always used, and at the senseless desire to have him go on holding her forever.

He rocked her back and forth, ignoring the onlookers, mumbling meaningless phrases and holding her tightly against him, and he remembered clearly the other time he'd held her, in the dreamy gray dawn in that village far away. The memory stirred feelings that were anything but fatherly, and Yolanda felt him shudder before he drew abruptly away from her.

But this time, the quizzical smile he gave her was warm, driving out some of the cold loneliness in her heart.

"Stay right here, and I'll bring you coffee. And don't cry anymore; I'm flat out of tissues."

The command was gentle, and she sniffed and nodded. She'd stay anywhere, if only he went on talking to her in that gruff, caring way.

A final bumbling swipe at her face with a sodden Kleenex, and he'd hurried off, his tall form disappearing in the wasteland of plastic and chrome and disembodied announcements.

What if he never returned? New panic threatened to overwhelm her for an instant.

But already Yolanda knew that Alex kept the promises he made, and in a few minutes she saw him slowly coming toward her, balancing plastic cups in his large hand, with pastries in the other. After that, Yolanda's desperation had eased.

Now, as this final segment of the journey drew to a close, the plane made a swooping circle above the crowded inner harbor of Victoria, bumped hard, then glided to a smooth, watery landing. Alex half turned to her.

"Welcome home, Landa," he said in the sudden quiet as the motor died. "I see the family is all on the wharf, waiting to greet you."

As she clambered, awkward and suddenly bashful, onto the floating walkway, Yolanda found herself enveloped in the arms of a joyously weeping Sophia, whose gauzy peach dress and firmly plump body sent wafts of lavender up Yolanda's nostrils. Next, she was nearly smothered by the rib-cracking bear hugs of an exuberantly triumphant Barney and hugged by a quietly elated Robert. Both men smelled of fresh sea air, pipe tobacco and spicy after-shave, and both had suspiciously wet cheeks against her own. *They cared,* she thought dazedly. Openly, they were showing her they cared. How big these men were, how reassuring, how welcoming.

"Hi, darlin', glad you got here safely," said Uncle Barney.

"Hello, Yolanda, great to meet you, welcome to Canada," said Robert, Alex's father, so much like Alex, so handsome...

"Darling, I'm delighted you're here at last. How was the... Barney, where are the flowers? Where did I... Alex, dear, over there, I laid them on the bench. I got so excited when I saw the plane. Oh, Alex, thank you for bringing her. My dearest Yolanda, I can hardly believe you've come. I couldn't sleep last night... I was so... oh, dear, do let's go home, Barney. The poor child's probably..."

Everyone seemed to be talking at once, asking and answering questions, the older men avidly pumping Alex for every official detail, Sophia's gentle voice twittering, filling the pauses in conversation as she patted her eyes with a tiny lace-trimmed handkerchief and slid one braceleted arm around her niece.

Somehow, the delicate bouquet of baby's breath and miniature pink and golden roses was retrieved and presented to Yolanda, who buried her nose in it and fought back tears of her own. The cornflowers and daisies had been blooming at *babička*'s cottage too, only three days ago.

With a sense of unreality Yolanda raised her head and slowly looked around, allowing the sights and sounds and smells of this new country to penetrate her senses. Her first blurred impression had been of color, of carefully groomed lushness, and next, the smell of sea air.

The protected harbor was in the heart of the city, full of brightly colored yachts and bobbing float planes. Sidewalks were dotted with ornate lamp standards. From the lamps hung chained baskets of variegated flowers spilling lavishly out of pristine white pots. There was color everywhere.

Was it a holiday? Everything looked so festive. Everywhere she looked, there were people, carefree, chattering, arm in arm. The couples strolling by looked relaxed, happy, beautifully and expensively dressed. Young people in casual blue jeans and T-shirts lounged on a nearby lawn. In the near distance rose a towering ancient gray castle with turrets and graceful lines, and many windows twinkling in the warm afternoon sunshine.

"Our Provincial Parliament Buildings," Sophia explained proudly.

Overhead, sea gulls swooped and cried, their raucous voices joining the swelling chorus of traffic noise, voices, music, and the gentle undertone of the waves slapping against the cement abutments.

"The car's parked over this way, come, dearest Landa," her aunt beckoned.

Yolanda walked with Sophie as if in a dream. The entire city had a gay, holiday feeling, a character so lighthearted that she could hardly begin to absorb its significance.

Happy. This place seemed happy. Could a city exude an emotion?

Yolanda slowed, stopped and turned in a full circle, her hands clasping the flowers Sophia had given her, and Alex, glancing at her from where he stood flanked by his father and uncle, noted the bedazzled look in her wide blue eyes.

He, too, reexamined the lighthearted landscape he'd always taken for granted. Remembering Prague, he knew exactly why Yolanda looked bewildered, and he wanted to reach out to her, touch her arm and whisper, "I understand."

But he couldn't. His rescue mission was over, and it was time to let the others assume responsibility for her. So why didn't he feel more relieved?

The group loaded into a silver-gray car, with Barney at the wheel, Alex beside him, and Yolanda nestled protectively in the back between Robert and Sophia.

Barney pulled the car into traffic with the flourish of a man who loves good machinery, and Alex quietly asked his uncle, "Have you heard how Tracey's doing at camp?"

Barney glanced sympathetically at his nephew and sighed.

"She's not at camp, Alex. She's back at the apartment, waiting for us. She didn't want to come along, and I thought it was better not to make a scene."

Alex cursed softly. "What the hell happened? I paid a King's ransom to send her to that place. What'd she do this time?"

Barney deftly maneuvered the big car through afternoon traffic, and under the excited mixture of Sophie's Slovak and English, he explained, "We got a call from the police. Seems Tracey and another girl took off in the dead of night from that camp, and the cops picked them up trying to hitch a ride into Vancouver. I went down and got her, phoned the camp counselor and straightened it all out." He glanced over at his nephew. "Don't be too tough on her, Alex. She's just a kid. There's no real harm done."

Alex shuddered. Thank God there was no real harm. Fifteen, female, hitchhiking at night. His daughter. Dixie's daughter. Where had they gone wrong? And what was he going to do with her for the next three weeks? He had to attend that conference in London, which meant leaving here no later than Tuesday. He glanced down at the date on the gold watch on his wrist. Three days from now. He'd figured that at least the problem of what to do with Tracey's summer was taken care of. Camp Kelsey had assured him that the "young ladies" they accepted had a wonderful time for two full months. His head ached, and he rubbed a weary hand across the back of his neck.

Yolanda noticed the gesture as she allowed Sophia's voice to wash over her, childishly grateful for her aunt's soft small hand firmly clasping her own, and for Robert's protective arm extended like a benediction across the seat behind her. Somehow these two instinctively guessed how much she needed their physical assurance, and both gave it freely. Perversely, it was Alex's arm Yolanda longed to have resting behind her. What new phase would their strange relationship enter now?

They pulled into the underground parking area of a modern hotel apartment, and within minutes Yolanda found herself whisked to the twenty-fourth floor, down a silent corridor, and into Barney and Sophie's home, the first Western home she'd ever seen.

Its opulence intimidated her. Everything looked new, and luxuriously appointed. She sat gingerly on the patterned brown velvet sofa, nervous about even walking on the thick ginger pile of the rug that stretched throughout the entire area. One entire window wall afforded a magnificent view of the ocean, with a balcony where glass topped tables and brightly flowered lawn chairs shared space with tubs of scarlet geraniums.

Yolanda glanced toward the hallway where the bedrooms must be, and her eyes met the frankly hostile glare of a gray-eyed girl, hovering in the doorway. Before Yolanda could do more than smile hesitantly at the slender blue-jeaned figure whose long braid of auburn hair hung over one shoulder, Alex entered and distracted the girl.

"Tracey, come here," he ordered sternly, motioning her fully into the sun-drenched room. Tracey squared her shoulders resentfully, and her heavily lipsticked mouth pulled into a petulant pout as she slowly came to stand before her father. He slid his hands to his hips, pushing back his sports jacket in a vaguely belligerent fashion, narrowing his eyes. The girl crossed her arms over her chest protectively.

"Tracey, I'd like you to meet Yolanda. As I explained before I left, Yolanda is, um—" he hesitated, clearing his throat "—Yolanda and I are married," he concluded.

"Yolanda, this is my daughter, Tracey." He made the introduction without taking his eyes from the girl, an unspoken warning evident in his expression.

Yolanda stood up uncertainly, smiling and extending her hand. Tracey ignored her.

"You told me it wasn't for real, Daddy. So she's not my stepmother, is she?" The young voice was husky and belligerent, with nasty inflections on key words.

Alex moved a threatening half step toward her, but the girl stood her ground, her chin jutted out stubbornly.

"Tracey." Her father's voice was low and steely. "You're already in a good deal of trouble, young lady. I'd suggest you remember your manners before I forget mine. We're going to have a talk about this camp business right after dinner. Now, I expect you to be polite."

He held her eyes with his furious gaze, and after a second of consideration, Tracey relented.

"Sorry," she mumbled. "How'd ya do." The words were aimed generally in Yolanda's direction. The narrow shoulders sagged.

"I am happy to meet you, Tracey," Yolanda lied, eyeing the girl warily. She was profoundly shocked at Tracey's rudeness. She'd never met any young person the least bit like Tracey. She'd expected a shy child, hovering uncertainly on the brink of adulthood, as Yolanda herself had been at fifteen—polite, serious, keeping her true feelings secret. This girl was of another species entirely. This one was *trāpenī*—big trouble.

"Come now, Tracey, help your old auntie with the food," Sophie said gently, and the tension was dissipated when she took Tracey's hand and led her off to the kitchen. But Yolanda saw the resentful glare the young girl shot at her as she passed, and she felt the palpable hostility surround her like glacial air. She shuddered.

Alex had turned his back to the room, staring out the window, his shoulders slumped.

"C'mon, Alex, sit down here and have a beer," Barney invited, sidling into the room with a tray full of bottles and mugs. Robert followed and brought Yolanda a tall cool glass with a slice of lime in its lip. Sitting down beside her, he gave her a warm smile and a pat on her arm.

"You're probably exhausted, my dear. You're going to need a couple of weeks just to get used to being here. Don't worry if everything seems strange at first," he remarked quietly to her. "Try to relax. We want you to feel at home, look around, take the time to get to know us all." He sipped his beer, and Yolanda smiled at him.

"I am very grateful to you. There is no way for me to thank you for what you have done." Yolanda fervently wished the words didn't sound so stilted and formal, because every syllable came from her heart.

Warmth began to replace the strangeness of everything when he gave her a mischievous grin and a half bow, and said, "Believe me, it was our pleasure. Old men like Barney and me don't get the chance to rescue beautiful young damsels often." She flushed, pleased at the courtly compliment.

Barney, talking quietly with Alex, overheard the comment and warned Yolanda loudly, "Honey, you watch that old silver-tongued devil beside you. He's always been a rogue with the ladies."

The good-natured, affectionate joshing that followed was fascinating to Yolanda. Even though whole phrases escaped her at times—her command of formal English might be excellent, but she was fast realizing there were many idiomatic words and phrases she missed—there was no mistaking the warmth between these giants. Barney, Robert, Alex: these men seemed larger than life, with hearts to match.

Before his death, her father had been away a great deal, although she could vividly recall the excitement that had flooded over her whenever he'd come home unexpectedly. She had still believed, then, that she and her quiet, gentle mother were foremost in his life. How stupid she'd been!

After her parents died and she had gone to live with *babička*, the household was feminine. She knew only the farming men of Votice until she went off to university. She'd never known men such as these, men who seemed to fill a room with their presence, men who laughed with great good humor, who teased each other, whose kindness glowed from mischievous eyes.

No wonder Alex had that air of power and authority, possessed as he was of such a big-boned muscular frame, such a strong, handsome face. He'd inherited his green eyes from Robert, she noticed.

However, there was an intensity, an undercurrent of sadness in Alex that was missing in the older men, and each time his daughter sullenly passed the trays of delicious hors d'ouevres Sophie had prepared, Yolanda noticed that he watched Tracey, his brows knitted into an unconscious frown.

He didn't smile as easily as either Barney or Robert. Barney was vocal, big and blustering, balding on top, with dark, twinkling eyes that nearly disappeared in a network of wrinkles when he laughed, which was often. Robert was quieter, more distinguished, his mane of silver hair becomingly long on his neck and above his ears.

Sophie buzzed in and out of the room, unable to contain her delight at Yolanda's presence.

"Alex, somebody wants you on the phone," she announced now. "Take it in the study. Tracey, go hang up the kitchen extension."

Delicious smells had been emanating from the kitchen, which she wouldn't allow Yolanda to enter, and Sophie stood in the doorway, her face flushed rosy pink, a frilly organdy apron over her dress.

Her aunt was lovely, Yolanda decided. It had been four years since Sophie's last trip to Czechoslovakia, yet she seemed to have aged hardly at all. Petite, with hair like dandelion fluff, she had blue eyes that were several shades lighter than Yolanda's, and her skin was delicate, her dainty hands well tended.

Now, she gestured to her niece, and ordered the men around like a diminutive general. "Yolanda, darling, there's just time to freshen up before we eat, if you want. Barney, come and carve this roast. And Robert, would you see to the wine? Tracey, show Yolanda where the guest bedroom is. I had Alex put her suitcase in there."

Tracey, her back stiff and shoulders swinging defiantly, led the way down a long central hallway to a lilac bedroom with a deeper lilac rug, a tilting white-framed mirror, puffy lace-edged duvet and matching frilly pillow covers. Yolanda's eyes roved over the room, astonished at such lushness, such decadent comfort. Her gaze fell on her own reflection in the mirror. Her blue suit was creased and she looked rumpled. There was a small stain on the white blouse. Her hair was beginning to escape from its chignon. The shoes that she'd thought smart in Prague looked chunky and clumsy here.

She looked foreign, as if she didn't belong in such a luxurious setting. Obviously Tracey agreed. The girl stood behind her, and Yolanda read the contemptuous expression in Tracey's hard gray gaze.

Sauntering over to a closet, Tracey threw open the folding wooden doors with rather more force than was necessary.

"You can hang your clothes in here, I moved all mine out. It doesn't look as if you've got many, anyhow," she spat out venomously. Her eyes were hard as gray agates, holding Yolanda's stunned gaze without flinching. "You managed to trick my father into marrying you—you might as well have my bedroom, as well."

CHAPTER FIVE

YOLANDA STARED SPEECHLESSLY at the angry girl for several moments, and the harsh words echoed between them. Yolanda felt astonished, hurt and defensive at the unprovoked attack. Most of all, she was uncertain how to respond to this kitten with fangs.

"This, this is your room?" Yolanda asked as she crossed the room to Tracey's side, and impulsively put a hand on the girl's shoulder.

"Please, Tracey, I have no wish to take your bedroom. I will tell Sophia—"

Tracey jerked away, crossed her arms over her thin chest and turned her back. Yolanda recognized the action; Alex had done exactly the same thing in the living room, not an hour ago.

Watching the girl, Yolanda was at a loss. Was this brat of a Western teenager as tough as she seemed, or was her behavior simply the cocky bravado of a lonely child? Yolanda studied the tense back, the narrow, childish hips in the tight jeans. The last thing she wanted was to cause a rift between Alex and his daughter, she thought wearily.

"Tracey," Yolanda started hesitantly, "what you said about the marriage of your father and me."

"I," Tracey corrected condescendingly. "Your English isn't very good, is it?"

Yolanda subdued her irritation. "The marriage of your father and I. There was no trick, as you call it. It was a kind gesture on your father's part, and you must know, as he told you, it was a formality only." A wrenching knot of sadness twisted her insides at the admission. Relentlessly she made herself continue.

"As you said, I am not really your stepmother. Your father, your uncles, they are such kind men; they have made it possible for me to come here to your so beautiful country. And dear Aunt Sophia. But it would be . . ." Yolanda paused, lost for words for a second, intimidated by the girl's stance. Was Tracey even listening? After taking a deep breath, she began once more, the difficult words tumbling over themselves this time in an effort to make her listener understand.

"There is no reason for you to like me, of course. I think it's a big mistake for me to take this room which is yours, most . . . unfair." Yolanda's tired brain groped for the proper words. "Just as it would be a big mistake for you to think I want to divide your father from you. I did not come here to make trouble for anyone. You understand, Tracey?"

The stiffness of the girl's shoulders held for another long moment, and dejectedly Yolanda decided she had failed. But then Tracey turned. The serious gray eyes met Yolanda's blue ones with less hostility.

"What should I call you, then? I can't go around saying Mrs. Caine—that was my mother. And I can't say 'hey, you,' can I?" The resentment was still plain, but there was less anger now. The question was guarded, testing.

"If you are Tracey, then I am just Yolanda, of course." Yolanda knelt and flipped open the top of her suitcase. "In here, somewhere, I have small gift for you if you will accept. . . ." She finally unearthed a box, carefully wrapped in tissue paper, and held it out to Tracey with a smile and inner misgivings. It seemed like blatant bribery, yet she didn't know what else to do.

Would the girl like it? Would she even accept it? The gift suddenly seemed pathetically insignificant when viewed beside the opulence of this apartment.

Tracey hesitated only a moment before stiffly accepting the box and unwrapping it with her narrow hands. The girls nails were bitten almost to the quick.

The wrapping fell away. Inside was a blouse, fine white cotton, covered with delicate hand-stitched embroidery. The garment was an ornate peasant style, with red, blue, yellow and green intricate patterns worked round the neck, and red trim on the three-quarter sleeves.

Tracey was still child enough to be delighted with a gift. She drew the garment out, and at last her mouth curved into a spontaneous, sweet smile. "Hey, it's sort of funky. Peasant is in right now, too."

Yolanda drew a relieved breath and smiled back, explaining, "*Babička*, my grandmother, she made this for you. The pattern of the design is supposed to bring the wearer good luck—it is Gypsy custom."

"Gypsies? Is your grandma a Gypsy?" Tracey's tone was eager now, curious. "Aunt Sophia never told me that."

"Not full Gypsy, you understand. Only half. It was *babička*'s mother who had full Gypsy blood. So *babička* has half, Sophia—what? One-quarter, and me, only one-eighth, isn't that correct?"

Yolanda's voice was even, but she felt close to tears. It hurt unbearably to speak of Anna and to fully realize how far away she was. "As long as you wear this blouse, no harm can come to you, Tracey."

She made an attempt at lightheartedness, and Tracey held the colorful cotton up against herself, preening in the mirror.

"I better put it on, then," the girl said with a drawn-out sigh. "Because my dad is going to kill me for sure, right after dinner." Now Tracey's voice quavered alarmingly.

Yolanda translated silently, and frowned in confusion.

"This is a joke, yes?"

"Uh-uh." Tracey shook her head and slid cross-legged onto the rug, one hand fondling the blouse. "Daddy's raving mad at me because I ran away from that stupid damn camp, and I just know he's probably gonna make me go back." Her clear voice took on a note of desperation. "I'll run away again, first chance I get. I hate it there. They give you makeup lessons, and play stupid games, and show movies everybody saw ages ago, and call one another silly nicknames. I absolutely hate it. I'll...I'll kill myself if I have to go back."

She sounded as if she was on the verge of tears. Yolanda abandoned the suitcase. Her clothing could wait. She sat down on a chair, facing Tracey.

"Your father is very understanding," she fibbed hesitantly. Alex lacked a bit in that area, if she was to be truthful. "If you explain how you feel about this camp, then I am certain—"

Tracey shook her head from side to side, making her braid swing. Her chin quivered. "He won't listen," she stated with weary conviction. "I've tried to talk to him before. It's just hopeless."

These sudden confidences were just as hard to handle as Tracey's earlier animosity so Yolanda felt a great surge of relief when Sophia appeared in the doorway, scolding them because dinner was ready and Yolanda wasn't.

Tracey whispered urgently to Yolanda, "Don't say anything about the bedroom; it's fine with me, honest. I'm in the one just down the hall, anyhow. Actually, I like it better. It's no big deal."

From the bathroom Yolanda heard Tracey a moment later saying cheerfully, "Look, Auntie. Your mother made it. The pattern's a gypsy design. Yolanda brought it for me. Neat, eh? How come you never told me about your mother being part Gypsy?"

As she stripped off the tired blue suit and used a terry facecloth thick and soft as sponge cake to quickly wash, Yolanda marveled at Tracey's mercurial changes in mood. Sunny, stormy, sunny again.

She shook her head at the mirror reflection of her tired face: lavender smudges inked under the glassy blue eyes, clear skin looking sallow under its tan. Such a face would never do for a celebration. Ruthlessly she doused with cold water and rubbed with the terry towel until she'd created a hint of color in her cheeks. The desire for sleep was overwhelming her. If only she could stay awake during dinner.

It was hard, but she kept her smile intact and her eyes wide open during the next several hours, only to find that when at last she lay between the silky, scented sheets in the fairy-tale bedroom, aching with fatigue, she was, ironically, unable to sleep.

Beneath her chaste white cotton nightgown, her skin had trapped the fragrance of the exotic bath oils and powders her thoughtful aunt had given her for the long, blissful soak in the strange blue tub. She smelled like the delicate lily of the valley plant that grew wild on the banks of the stream running through Votice, and the gown still echoed the fresh air and sunshine of her home, half a world away.

But this was Victoria. Canada. North America. A new and different world, with only fragrance to echo the old.

The cool night air blew the window drapes in and out in a peaceful rhythm, and Yolanda's brain replayed the events of the evening, snippets of information about this family she'd joined. Some things still puzzled her.

For instance, it had gradually become obvious that the family's gathering together for dinner was not a frequent event.

"We have to do this oftener. It's a damn shame when people get too busy to spend time together," Barney had declared. "Is it that way in Czechoslovakia, Yolanda?" he'd asked, and she'd found herself trying to explain the long hours of work contrasted with the joy people took in being together whenever they could.

"Grandma and I had no real family in Votice, but the neighbors always included us." How could it be otherwise? she wondered. Didn't people here get together to enjoy the simple pleasures of conversation, a glass of wine at the end of the day?

Pleasure welled up in her when Alex described the wedding celebration people had given them. "They were so welcoming, so full of emotion." His deep voice was pleasingly resonant, and Yolanda, seated across from him, was electrically aware of his every nuance of expression, every glance he sent her way. His hair looked tousled, for it had been finger-combed absently until it had tumbled forward in an unruly wave on his forehead. The chandelier overhead caught the planes of his face, shadowing the rough contours and emphasizing the crooked nose, the strong, square chin. He lifted an eyebrow in silent query when he caught her intense stare, and she quickly looked away.

Conversation turned to the trip Alex would make the following week, and a sense of depression overwhelmed Yolanda as she realized he would be gone for several weeks.

She really must fight her attraction for him, she decided, reject the feelings he aroused in her. It was undoubtedly only the result of having traveled together, of relying on him for everything during the past days. Then a shiver swept over her, and she remembered the wedding night, the weight of his body on her, the burning delight of having him inside her. Her face flamed. Her thoughts had wandered far from the conversation around her.

"We must visit the Parliament Buildings, the Provincial Museum, have tea at the Empress, and of course, drive out and see Butchart Gardens...." Yolanda became conscious of her surroundings with an uneasy start. Sophie was cataloging alarmingly busy plans for Yolanda's first weeks in Victoria.

"Dear Aunt Sophia, this is not necessary." The last thing Yolanda wanted to do for the next few days was to become a tourist, hurrying here and there.

But Sophie was making still more detailed plans. "First, we'll go sight-seeing, and then maybe we'll take a trip over to Vancouver."

Yolanda felt her spirits sink with the idea of such a busy itinerary. She desperately needed a quiet time, a period in which she could begin to adjust slowly, and at her own pace, to her new country. Sophie's plans sounded as if she was about to be captured by a whirlwind.

It was Tracey who rescued Yolanda. Alex had been alternately watching the expressions flit across Yolanda's arresting features and puzzling over his daughter's suspiciously quiet, impeccably correct behavior.

Now, carefully pouring hot coffee to accompany the rich chocolate torte Sophia was serving, Tracey inquired ingenuously, "That's going to take all summer, and I thought you only got two weeks off, Aunt Sophia." Her eyes were wide and innocent. "Meals on Wheels depend on you, don't they?"

Sophie's brow puckered slightly, and she cast a worried frown at Tracey, and made a motion to be quiet with her hand.

"I told them I needed more time off—I'm certain it will be fine. But one of the other drivers has to go into the hospital for tests, and they're short. Of all times! But they're trying." She'd told Yolanda enthusiastically about her volunteer work, driving all over the city to take hot meals to old people who were unable to care properly for themselves. It was evident Sophie adored her job, and Yolanda felt appalled that her aunt would consider neglecting it simply to entertain her. Barney had also wistfully mentioned a trip through the Rockies, jokingly asking if Sophie could fit him into her busy schedule. Yolanda shuddered at the idea of being a burden to her aunt.

In her entire life, she'd never had more than a week of idleness. She wanted to learn to make her own way in Canada as soon as possible, just as she'd always done. "Please, I am grateful for your plans, but it is not necessary...."

Halfway through her stammered objection and Sophie's adamant rebuttal, Tracey suggested smoothly, "This whole thing is crazy. Auntie, you're busy, and so is everybody else except me. I have all summer off and not one thing to do." She carefully avoided Alex's sharp glance. "Why couldn't I show Yolanda around? I know all the places she'd like to see, and I've got nothing to do on my holidays."

Alex's face was unreadable as he studied her thoughtfully.

Tracey's voice grew cajoling when he didn't immediately object. "We could stay at Rockwoods, Daddy. Yolanda would love it there." She drew in a quick breath, and her words tumbled out. "You'll just adore it, Yolanda, there's a beach and everything. We could ride bikes, and I could show you around Victoria on the bus. We could sort of keep each other company."

Although very well aware that the plot was cleverly presented to benefit Tracey herself, this alternative was vastly better than the prospect of being a burden, regardless how welcome or beloved, to Sophie. Yolanda nodded eagerly at Tracey, and then shot a glance at Alex. Ultimately, it would be his decision.

"Before you run ripshod over Yolanda with this scheme, Tracey, remember that you and I still have the matter of camp to discuss." Alex's tone was quiet but implacable. Tracey opened her mouth to argue, then shut it again.

Everyone covertly watched the interplay between Alex and his daughter and tried to fill the nervous silence that fell when the two disappeared into Barney's study directly after dessert. When they emerged three-quarters of a long hour later, Tracey flew across the room and grabbed Yolanda's hand with impulsive glee.

"Daddy says we can stay at Rockwoods if you don't mind chaperoning me. Yolanda, please say you will?" she gasped breathlessly.

Yolanda of course agreed.

Lying in bed later, however, she wasn't at all confident about her ability to be a chaperone for Tracey. The idea frankly frightened her.

As if she were focusing her mind on a mantra, Yolanda concentrated instead on a mental picture of Alex as she willed her body to relax. He'd taken her hand in his tonight as he left to go to his apartment, his strong, long fingers encompassing her own momentarily with firm, friendly pressure, sending messages through her nerve endings that she was sure were unintentional.

His eyes had flicked over her features in that odd way he had of looking at her, as if each feature deserved concentrated scrutiny. He'd centered finally on her lips, and she had the strangest feeling he might have kissed her if the others hadn't been there.

"I'll come by late tomorrow morning," he'd promised. "We'll see about getting you and Tracey settled." He'd given his daughter a light kiss on her forehead, and left. Tracey had remained with Barney and Sophia, and Alex hadn't seemed to even consider that his daughter should be with him.

He and Tracey were like strangers, groping for common ground.

What a strange land, where families don't gather regularly together, thought Yolanda, marveling that Sophia, although she'd grown up and been a part of that other life in Votice, was now totally Canadian in thought and manner. Even though she'd been even older than Yolanda when she'd come here as a bride. She'd adapted to the West totally.

Yolanda, too, was here as a bride. But the difference was that Barney loved Sophia. Did a man's love make it easier to adapt?

She fought a sudden overwhelming feeling of desolation until exhaustion overcame her, and she slept.

THE NEXT MORNING, Alex turned the key in the lock and pushed the heavy cedar door at Rockwoods inward. It creaked, just as it always had, and opened into the wide front hallway. A delicate table stood under a gilt-edged mirror, and an antique coat stand stood huffily at attention to the right of the door.

How long was it since he'd last been here? That one long weekend last fall, at Tracey's insistence. He'd been too busy to come at Christmas. The business trip to Japan had interfered with the holiday, and she'd sullenly stayed with Dixie's parents in Vancouver.

He knew he'd been avoiding Rockwoods the past four years, despite Tracey's love for the place. The smell of an unused house washed over Alex; clean, cold, faintly musty and redolent of memories of the past. Rockwoods. Dixie. She'd chosen that mirror and hung that pastel watercolor over there.

Her girlish presence was so real to him here, where they'd spent most of their marriage. He stared blindly at the three curving stairs leading up into the living room, his arm stretched across the opening, unthinkingly blocking the doorway.

"Daddy?" Tracey's impatient voice came from behind him, where she and Yolanda stood in the morning sunshine, waiting for him to move.

Yolanda wasn't watching Alex. She was staring out over the grounds, the immaculately groomed wide lawns with their careful flower beds stretching in an undulating green carpet to meet the thick woodlot that isolated Rockwoods estate from the road. *So much grass, over an acre. Where were the vegetable gardens?* She turned in a slow circle. Perhaps behind the house? But the house seemed to perch almost on the edge of a short steep embankment, and beyond the sandy beach at the bottom stretched the ocean.

The woods, thick and dappled with every shade of emerald, curved to either side, forming a pocket for the house and lawns. Outbuildings larger than most of the cottages in Votice were gathered in neat groupings a discreet distance away. She couldn't see another house anywhere, and the treed lane effectively blocked out traffic noise. Yolanda pursed her lips and expelled her breath in awe at such opulence.

"Daddy, move, please. This bag's getting heavy." Tracey juggled the oversize sport bag she carried, and Alex quickly led the way into the high-ceilinged entrance hall. Mouse-brown carpeting cushioned their footsteps, and sand-colored walls stretched up to a vaulted ceiling. The stairs led gracefully up to a large L-shaped room, whose interior wall was dominated by an immense fireplace with a raised stone hearth.

Light spilled through the window wall facing the ocean, muted by beige draperies. Yolanda drew them aside and caught her breath, overwhelmed by the panoramic view. Perched near the edge of a low cliff, the house seemed to float above miles of sparkling water, and the wall of glass acted as a frame for the seascape outside, water and sky, boats and faraway islands. The curtain fell back over the window, and the glory was gone.

Tracey, impervious to the view, rubbed her bare arms.

"Brrr. It's chilly, Daddy. I'm going back outside, down to the beach. Why don't we have a fire in here? It smells damp." She skipped across the carpet, and a moment later the door slammed behind her.

Alex moved to the fireplace. "She's right; it is cold in here. Agnes comes in once a month when the place is empty, to air it and dust. I phoned her this morning, and starting Monday, she'll come every day. Agnes Witherspoon. Tracey knows her; she's been our housekeeper here for years."

Alex spoke as if his attention was elsewhere, and Yolanda paused in her scrutiny of the room to eye him curiously.

Why would he think two able-bodied women like her and Tracey needed a housekeeper? she wondered. Perhaps he didn't quite trust her with his daughter or his house? A sense of hurt came over her, but then she reminded herself stoutly that Alex could hardly know if she were reliable or not. He'd met—and married—her in the space of several weeks.

Still. She felt she knew Alex, a strange sense of familiarity, as if she'd somehow always known him. How could that be?

She watched him kneel before the natural stone fireplace, crumple paper, add kindling. He wore casual gray cords with a navy cotton pullover, running shoes with sport socks, and the long line of his back tapered gracefully into a narrow waist as he crouched on one knee, his trousers pulled tight on his long thighs and trim buttocks. His hair curled down his neck, and the muscles bulged across his shoulders. He was—she searched for a satisfactory description, and several graphic, earthy phrases in her native tongue ran through her mind.

Strange. She'd never really understood their meaning before meeting Alex.

A wave of pure sensuality tingled like moths' wings in her stomach, and a glowing surge of desire warmed her. They were alone. If only this marriage was more than just paper. She'd move behind him, stroke her hand down his hair and into the neck of his shirt where the smooth brown skin felt warm and smelled like pinecones.

Nervous tingles made goose bumps rise on her arms, and she reproached herself for being fanciful. Legal or not, there was no real marriage between them, and she must remember that. Homesickness was undoubtedly playing tricks with her emotions.

She forced her attention to a row of photographs precisely arranged on top of the rough cedar mantel, and like a physical blow to the pit of her stomach, she recognized framed snapshots of Alex and his dead wife. His first, his real wife. Dixie Caine. Yolanda's eyes were riveted to the face of the woman Alex had loved. She was tiny, pixielike, beguiling, childlike. She had a delicate figure and wide, innocent eyes. Alex's arm was around her…Alex's head close to hers…Alex was holding her hand.

Yolanda's throat constricted, and she gulped involuntarily. It was stupid, she chided herself, to let the photos affect her. This had been their home together, after all.

Alex held a match to the carefully stacked wood and absently watched as it flared and caught fire. He fed more chips into the blaze, his mind far away, but strangely, it wasn't Dixie's memory that haunted him at the moment. It was last night's phone call from Carrie Russell.

He'd closed the door to Barney's study the previous evening and picked up the receiver.

"Welcome home, Alex. I thought I'd be the first to congratulate you on your wedding." The silky voice was open, friendly, sincere, and Alex felt himself tense. The red-haired reporter was at her most dangerous when she appeared the most ingenuous. It was a trait that had often amused him when he read her interviews with fellow politicians, because he understood exactly how the unfortunate subject had been lured into making the controversial comments that had been quoted. Carrie made verbal indiscretion absurdly simple. Her flamboyant looks, her hearty good nature, charmed then captivated her victims.

Invariably, the subjects of her interviews grew relaxed and expansive, lulled by her easygoing questions, her quick wit, until suddenly they found themselves discussing some issue they had no intention of even mentioning.

Like the matter of his marriage to Yolanda. There was no point speculating how Carrie had found out about it this quickly. The question was, what would she do with the information?

He shuddered at what she could say in her column, considering the press's interest in the Eastern bloc countries, Alex's position with the government, the family's interests in Czechoslovakia.

And Carrie's personal interest in Alex? He grimaced. The redhead had never made a secret of her attraction to him, despite the casual nature of their relationship.

"Hello, Carrie." He'd carefully avoided saying more than that, and after a second she'd laughed softly.

"Just 'hello, Carrie'? You're a cautious man, Alex Caine. You sure don't sound like an ebullient bridegroom on his honeymoon. Haven't you got a few romantic remarks I could quote to my faithful readers? It's not every day one of our most eligible political figures secretly marries 'Anna Karenina' and spirits her home to Canada."

He'd managed to chuckle. "That lurid imagination of yours is working overtime."

"I must admit I'd imagined an entirely different lurid scenario for you and I. It would have been nice of you to warn me, Alex." As if she'd pressed a button, the hint of wistfulness in her tone disappeared, and her voice became businesslike.

"Just so I get the facts straight, can you tell me your wife's name, where you met, and how long you were engaged? Either this was a whirlwind romance, my boy, or you kept it pretty quiet."

The steely undertone was almost indiscernible, but Alex caught it.

"I seem to remember having a drink with you not six weeks ago, and nary a word was said about an upcoming wedding."

Alex cursed silently. Aloud, he tried for casual ease. "These things happen pretty fast sometimes. I'm sure one romance is much the same as the next. Hardly material for a political column, I'd think."

"Then you'd think wrong, my friend. My faithful readers will be fascinated to hear all about West marries East, especially when it involves an assistant deputy minister. But I wouldn't want to get the details wrong, so...?" The satin voice muffled a threat.

He tersely gave Yolanda's name, and the bare facts that he knew Carrie could dig up, anyway. But he knew better than to hope she'd let the matter go at that. He shook his head in frustration. The last thing an assistant deputy minister wanted or needed was undue interest in his private affairs. Would this marriage bring exactly that, thanks to Carrie?

The fire was crackling and the chill in the room began to disappear. He got up, dusted off his knees and realized Yolanda had been quietly watching him, and he'd been ignoring her. He rubbed a hand across the back of his neck and met her intense blue stare.

The exotically high Slavic cheekbones, the tiny mole beside her generously curved lips registered sensually in a subliminal part of him, and his gaze roved unconsciously over the lush fullness of her breasts then went back up to the wide, honest eyes.

"You are troubled, Alex? If you worry about Tracey, I promise you I will take the best of care with her." Her husky voice was pleasingly soft and earnest, and Alex smiled warmly at her. The complications in his life weren't limited to his marriage, after all.

"I haven't the slightest doubt you will. What concerns me more is what kind of merry chase my daughter might lead you. She's not the easiest child in the world, and I'm afraid that for the past few years..." He paused.

"I think maybe Tracey and I will be friends," Yolanda stated with a reassuring confidence she was far from feeling.

"I hope so," he said fervently. The house was suddenly warmer, his spirits inexplicably lighter, and the quizzical grin she gave him sparked an answering smile. He reached impulsively for her hand and grasped it firmly, liking the feel of her palm against his own.

"C'mon, I'll give you a guided tour of Rockwoods."

Her heart was beating furiously, as if the strong hand capturing hers carried an electrical current straight to her heart. He seemed unaware of her reaction, tugging her along in a playful manner she'd not yet seen in him.

"This place is a mutation, new improvements grafted on to the best of the old. Dad and Barney grew up here. My mother died when I was a baby, and Dad and I and Barney lived here together. Now, we all seem too busy to live outside the city." He gestured to a portrait over the mantel. The old photo was sepia-toned, ornately framed, a posed study of a broad-shouldered, roughly handsome man who looked uncomfortable in his tight white collar and vested suit.

Vividly, uncomfortably, Alex remembered losing his temper with Dixie the day she'd taken the picture down. He'd retrieved it immediately from the attic and rehung it where it belonged. She'd wept prettily, but for once he hadn't given in.

"That's Grandpa Caine, the lumberjack," he said hastily, fighting the flashes of haunting memories with words. "He had foresight, old Gramps. Instead of just drinking and gambling like most lumberjacks are likely to do when they make money, he bought land. Huge tracts of forest nobody wanted. By the time Dad and Barney were young men, lumber had become one of B.C.'s major resources, and because of Gramps's investments, the Caine family was well on the way to being financially solid."

Rich, Yolanda translated. This family was undoubtedly rich.

Without giving her time to absorb details, Alex whisked her through a dining room with a highly polished table, spindly chairs, gleaming silver precisely arranged on a sideboard.

All the furniture was elaborate and looked new, unused. The curious thing was that the delicate French provincial lines seemed unsuited to the ruggedness of open beams and wood, brick fireplaces and window walls. Only the heavy-framed old picture suited the architecture.

Like the living room, where every piece of frail furniture, every tiny satin pillow, every expensive figurine was precisely arranged, the dining room and small study were meticulously ordered. The rooms looked as if no one dared live in them. Here, too, formal frilled draperies covered the windows. It was all Yolanda could do not to draw them rudely aside and let nature in.

He drew her finally into a modern kitchen painted pale green, with a flowered cloth in a deeper shade of green covering a cozy table set in front of another wide window covered in frills. A back door, also with a half window, gave access to a path that curved down to the beach.

Yolanda suddenly felt more relaxed. A kitchen was a kitchen, although it was doubtful that anyone had ever whipped up a messy batch of anything here. She turned to the window and pulled back the curtains, rearranging the hooks so the window was clear.

"Does every room look out over the ocean?" she asked. The view intrigued her. She'd never lived beside a large body of water before.

"The house was designed around the view, by a practical architect Gramps hired." Alex's eyes twinkled mischievously. "Wait'll you see the bedrooms. The guy was definitely ahead of his time, and I've always figured Gramps must have had a wide streak of hedonism under his red long johns to agree to the design. C'mon."

He recaptured his hold on her hand, and he whisked her rapidly along until she tugged him to an abrupt stop.

"What is this hedonism under long johns?" Yolanda's brow furrowed in charming confusion, and Alex had to laugh at the question even as he noted the length of the naturally thick dark eyelashes shading her eyes.

"Long johns. Men's winter underwear." He laughed again, shared laughter as she nodded in understanding. "Hedonism isn't as easily defined. It's the belief that pleasure is the most important thing in life. Enjoying life's comforts to the fullest." He decided to tease her a bit.

"I suspect you'd call it decadence, Yolanda."

"Like Aunt Sophia's bathroom?" she immediately retorted.

He shrugged, puzzled. He'd never really noticed Sophia's bathroom, when it came right down to it.

"She has perfumed soaps and lotions and powders. I think this hedonism is not such a bad thing," she declared decisively, and Alex loved her smug tone of voice and made a mental note to pay more attention the next time he visited the facilities in his uncle's apartment.

They climbed the wide curving staircase to the second floor, and Alex pondered, not for the first time, what there was about Yolanda that created this tangible rapport between them—and also created the unsettling current of acute sensual hunger her presence stirred in him.

Ever since the night of their wedding, Alex persistently thought about the compelling way her most intimate curves had cradled him, the softness and heat of her luxuriant breasts cupped in his hands, the elusive, wildflower scent of her body. He wasn't proud of his actions that night, but neither could he forget the ecstasy he'd found in her arms.

She paused at the round porthole window set in the landing.

"Alex, look there, so many birds. Are they sea gulls?" His body brushed against hers as he peered out, and desire stirred.

"Yes, sea gulls. They nest on the cliffs."

Despite the sense of ease he enjoyed in her company, this other, spontaneous response didn't exactly promote relaxation. Even holding her hand stirred emotions he wasn't ready to examine. He released her fingers abruptly and moved ahead to throw open the first door leading off the hallway, turning so he could see her face.

"This room is yours, if you want it," Alex told her. "That door leads to a bathroom, shared by Tracey. Her room is next door."

He watched Yolanda, and her unaffected pleasure delighted him. How stimulating to introduce her to Canada. Seeing Rockwoods through her unsophisticated eyes was a new experience, one that he savored. Dixie had never really liked it here.

He found himself suddenly envying Tracey, wishing he could be the one to show Yolanda around Victoria.

"Ahhh." Her breath escaped in an unconscious sigh, and she hesitantly stepped through the door and into liquid sunlight.

The room was golden, its warm honey-colored rug stretching to meet walls of buttercup yellow. A pale lemon ceiling took on the texture of variegated silk where the reflection of sun on water flowed through the by now familiar window wall, rippling, re-forming, like an ever-changing kaleidoscope. She'd never been in a room that felt this... giddy... before.

One interior wall supported a tumbled stone fireplace, and louvered doors led to wide closets along another. A long low window seat cushioned in soft, worn amber corduroy lounged invitingly below the expanse of glass. Here, nothing looked new or stiff. There were no swathing draperies choking off the view. The room had obviously escaped the fussy decoration lavished on the downstairs.

"We never used this bedroom."

"We." Alex and Dixie and Tracey. Yolanda's delight in the beautiful room faded a trifle. Everywhere at Rockwoods, it seemed, the ghost of the lovely Dixie lingered.

"Your room is also on this level?" she blurted, and then cursed herself for asking the gauche question.

Alex shook his head. "Upstairs," he said gruffly, pointing to where a narrower set of spiral stairs curved upward. "It used to be an attic. Now it's the master bedroom," he added, not offering to show her, and effectively breaking the delicate thread that had woven a knot between them.

"Hey, where are you guys? I'm hungry—can we have the picnic Auntie Sophia sent along?" The cheerful tones changed dramatically as Tracey came charging up the steps and into the yellow room.

"Oh, here you are. What are you doing up here, anyway?" Her gray eyes flickered suspiciously from her father to Yolanda, instinctively sensing an intimacy in both the setting and the charged atmosphere of the room. Her face stiffened, tightening into hard lines.

It wasn't hard for Yolanda to identify the feminine jealousy Tracey was feeling, but the animosity she radiated was chilling.

"I think the basket of food is still in the car," Yolanda improvised. "I'll get it." It was a relief to escape, to leave Tracey alone with her father.

Lunch was uncomfortable for Yolanda. Tracey jealously excluded her from the conversation, drawing Alex into reminiscences Yolanda couldn't share. The ham sandwiches and fruit salad lodged in Yolanda's throat. She could understand Tracey's insecurity, but that didn't help the feeling of isolation such intimacies produced, or make it easier to field the triumphantly venomous looks the girl shot at her when her father wasn't looking.

Alex, annoyingly oblivious to his daughter's ploys, answered all her questions absently. His thoughts were far away—lost in memories of the wife he'd lost? Yolanda wondered. His distractedness only made Tracey doubly determined to attract his attention.

"I think I will take a walk along the beach," Yolanda announced as soon as the plates and glasses were loaded in the dishwasher. Tracey had condescendingly instructed Yolanda in the process.

"You mean you've never used a dishwasher before?" she'd asked. "Man, I can't believe it. That's straight out of the dark ages. You can't put that in; it's too big. You really don't know, do you?"

Yolanda longed to get away, to escape the hard-eyed glances Tracey shot at her and the thinly veiled sarcasm. Had the friendliness of the night before been only an act, a show of good behavior calculated to get the girl out of going back to the camp she hated? What was it going to be like, Yolanda wondered apprehensively, to spend the next weeks being responsible for so devious a girl? Yolanda's knowledge of teenagers was sketchy at best.

"We have to drive back in about an hour," Alex announced unexpectedly, finally emerging from his reverie. "There's a meeting this afternoon I have to attend."

Tracey's face immediately lost its expression of sly triumph at Yolanda's retreat, and her attention was fully on her father.

"But I thought we'd stay here all day," she wailed. "How come we have to start back so soon?"

"I told you, I have to go to a meeting. It's a briefing on the trip next week, and I can't miss it." Tracey's whining tone annoyed Alex, and his answer was curt.

"Then I'm coming to the apartment with you, Daddy. I don't want to stay at Uncle Barney's." The look she shot Yolanda silently added, *"with her."* "You and I could go to a movie later, okay?"

"That's not possible, honey. I won't be home till late."

"I'm not a baby, Daddy. I can stay home alone."

"I said no, Tracey. I'm too busy, and I want you at Barney and Sophia's until Sunday. Then I'll drive you and Yolanda out here."

Tracey was standing near the sink, slouching against the counter. She straightened suddenly, her face crumpling.

"Go to your stupid meeting, then," she shouted. "See if I care. You never want me around, anyhow." Tears shone in her eyes, but she turned them to anger, grabbing the first thing her hand touched on the drainboard, a heavy glass bowl Yolanda had put the fruit in.

Before Alex or Yolanda could move, Tracey flung the bowl as hard as she could against the opposite wall. It shattered, and glass shards flew across the room. Alex and Yolanda instinctively put their hands up to shield their faces against the splinters.

Tracey raced to the back door, wrenched it open and slammed it behind her with a crash that shook the house.

For an instant Yolanda and Alex stared dumbfounded at the glass, then at each other. Alex was the first to move. He cursed, and strode out after Tracey, rage evident in his face and his rigidly held shoulders, his balled fists.

The door slammed behind him, and Yolanda let out the breath she'd been holding in a long sigh. Then she found a broom and carefully cleaned up the glass. She smiled wryly as she imagined what *babička* would say and do with one like Tracey. The smile faded rapidly.

What was she going to do with Tracey? She was responsible for her, beginning Monday.

CHAPTER SIX

ALEX LEFT, RELUCTANTLY bidding goodbye to Tracey and Yolanda at Rockwoods. After the drama of that first visit to the estate, Tracey had been morose, sullen and withdrawn.

Barney, Robert, and Sophie were anxious and hesitant with her, as if they didn't know how to deal with her moody silences, her bursts of tears and dramatic exits to her bedroom. Yolanda watched the teenager manipulate her older relatives with ease, watched them pamper and coax her to no avail.

Her moodiness lasted until she and Yolanda were alone at Rockwoods on Sunday evening, and everyone had gone.

Then, like a chameleon, she'd dramatically switched to sunny good behavior. Yolanda eyed her warily, wondering when the other Tracey would again emerge.

"I've told her in no uncertain terms," Alex had related privately to Yolanda, "that she either behaves herself, or she goes back to the camp. At the first sign of trouble with her, I want you to phone either Dad or Barney. If they aren't available for any reason, call this number. It's my hotel in London."

So far, Tracey was fine. The housekeeper whom Alex had promised, Agnes Witherspoon, arrived at nine Monday morning, and it was she who set Yolanda's teeth on edge, not Tracey.

"You Alex's new missus?"

Tracey was still asleep, and Yolanda had been enjoying a quiet cup of coffee at the kitchen table when Agnes let herself in the back door. Tall, with a round face, small eyes and yellow skin, Agnes wore her sparse gray hair drawn into a nubbin on the top of her head. She pulled her wool sweater closer around her concave chest and advanced on Yolanda.

Uncertain as to how one treated a housekeeper, Yolanda stood up and smiled hesitantly. Agnes's beady eyes insolently assessed Yolanda's face and figure.

"Humph. You sure ain't nothin' like Mrs. Dixie, I'll say that. She was the sweetest little thing, bless her heart."

After several more syrupy testimonies to the marvels of Mrs. Dixie, Agnes set to work, and soon the entire house, which Yolanda had thought scrupulously clean to start with, was subjected to latherings of bleach, lemon oil and detergent, interspersed with aggrieved comments from Agnes.

"That girl had better get up. Never seen such laziness."

"That tray don't go there, missis. We keep it up here."

"Miss Tracey, you didn't scrub out the bath the way you're supposed to—what would your mother say?"

Yolanda, and Tracey, too, finally escaped outside.

"Miserable old thing," Tracey commented petulantly. "She's always hated me, even when Mum was here. She was always sickly sweet with her, though."

Although Yolanda suspected that Tracey exaggerated the number of people whom she insisted "hated" her, their mutual dislike of Agnes spun a momentary bond between them.

Tracey soon wheeled two bikes from the garage and suggested they go for a ride. Yolanda enthusiastically agreed. Back in Votice, her battered bike had been the major form of transportation, and she missed cycling.

"This one belonged to my mum," Tracey announced, mounting the yellow cycle. "But I don't think she ever rode it. I used to wish she'd come riding with me. It's great to ride bikes with somebody, don't you think?''

Tracey's references to her mother interested Yolanda. It was perfectly natural for Tracey to want to talk about Dixie but Yolanda suspected that the girl had learned not to mention her mother often to Alex.

"Don't you think this is great, Yolanda?'' Tracey persisted.

Yolanda gave her a wide smile.

"This is good idea, yes,'' she commented gratefully, preparing to climb on the shiny green bike.

"A good idea. You have to use 'a.' Are you really riding in that dress?'' Tracey's tone was a blend of astonishment and disbelief. Yolanda looked down at herself, puzzled.

"Of course, yes,'' she confirmed. Her pink nylon dress had buttons down the front and a flared skirt. She could ride in it easily.

Tracey's strong features screwed into a grimace.

"Don't you have any jeans? Like, nobody rides a bike in a dress.''

It was gradually becoming apparent to Yolanda that what women wore here in Victoria was vastly different from clothing styles back home. Yesterday, Tracey had staunchly vetoed the short nylon anklets Yolanda was accustomed to wearing with dresses.

"That's gross,'' she'd groaned, and then succinctly interpreted gross, using as a further example Yolanda's unshaven legs, then offering dainty pink razors she'd unearthed from a bathroom drawer to remedy the situation.

Yolanda accepted the criticism gratefully. After all, how was she to discern "gross'' from "not gross'' unless someone told her, she'd assured Tracey.

Evidently a dress on a bike was also gross. Yolanda shrugged and, taking care to avoid Agnes, quickly changed into her only pair of slacks—navy polyester.

Tracey looked her over and reluctantly nodded.

"I guess that'll have to do. But I'm gonna tell Auntie Sophie we need to take you shopping," she muttered, mounting her bike. With Yolanda close behind, they pedaled down the winding drive.

It was overhung with blossoms from ivory-pink Japanese plum trees, and the surrounding woods were redolent of moss and wetness, with salt-scented ocean and burgeoning growth. Rockwoods smelled of summer, and a sudden bird song sent an unbearable ache zigzagging through Yolanda's heart.

Just so were the birds singing in Votice right now. *Babička* would be weeding her garden. Sometimes homesickness clutched at her chest and made it hard to breathe.

The lane snaked through dense woods before it deposited them on Beach Drive, which wound its way along the shoreline and into Victoria.

Yolanda let her mind wander as she followed Tracey's erratic fast-slow-fast pattern.

The past days had given little time for thinking, as Sophie and Barney and Robert showered her with attention and kindness, guiding her around their city, pointing out attractions and landmarks until her mind felt stuffed to overflowing with details, and with beauty. Victoria and the island it was on made Yolanda feel she was in a fairyland at first, a frothy confection of beauty and charm where everything was pleasant and prosperous.

Then Yolanda began to look beneath the surface, beginning to sense the deeper, more profound differences between this culture and that of her homeland, and she saw that not everything was perfect. There was poverty here, and other social ills. For some reason, such inequities made her more comfortable with Canada.

She was eager to learn, to adapt. Most important, she was striving to understand Alex, to know what influences had shaped and molded him. He was seldom out of her thoughts. In fact, thoughts of him pervaded her days and haunted her confusing dreams. As she looked and listened and analyzed, Yolanda compared everything with Czechoslovakia. The Pacific Ocean here, the mighty Vltava River there. More cars here, more bikes there. Here, not as many birds. She especially missed the cuckoos, and the small villages full of kitchen gardens, each cottage with its few chickens or geese.

Those gardens. She steered around a corner, momentarily losing sight of Tracey. "People here must eat grass; they have no gardens," she'd commented to Barney, and he'd laughed uproariously. Wealth probably made the difference, she concluded, pedaling hard.

She was beginning to sweat. Tracey was setting a furiously fast pace, and Yolanda's hair tumbled loose as she recklessly let the bike run free down a hill, her heart-stopping descent uncontrolled and thrillingly dangerous, and she pulled up sharply at the bottom. Tracey was wildly exuberant.

"Way to go. Let's ride into the city, and have lunch at McDonald's. You'll love it, Yolanda."

That meant Tracey would love it.

"Is it expensive, this place?"

Tracey giggled at the question. Yolanda's extreme caution with money both puzzled and amused her.

"It's fast food. Fast food is never very expensive, silly. Besides, we've got the money Dad left. He never asks me for any back when he goes away like this," she said complacently.

Alex had left enough cash to keep four Czech families for a month, Yolanda estimated. It was a shocking excess, she thought.

"How can I know how much it will be if I don't ask?"

In the next hours, Tracey guided her through a more practical introduction to Victoria than Yolanda had yet had. Among other things, she learned where one could get the biggest doughnuts in town, which rock star was appearing in person, and what theaters would let underage teens in to see adult-rated movies. It was an education that left Yolanda's head reeling and convinced her more than ever that Tracey was in serious need of supervision.

The girl had become giddy, chatting boastfully about her independence. In the process, Yolanda accidentally learned several things that horrified her about the exclusive boarding school Tracey attended in Vancouver. Smoking, sneaking out, meeting boys. Surely fifteen was too young for such things even in Canada?

"Why not attend school here in Victoria?" Yolanda asked. They were having hamburgers, fries and Cokes—Tracey had ordered for both of them—and Yolanda decided that this "fast food" was delicious. She dunked her french fries in ketchup the way Tracey instructed and savored the taste of some kind of sauce on the hamburger.

"Nobody has time to have me around much. Aunt Sophia works and plays bridge a lot, Grampa and Uncle Barney go to their office most days. Besides, they're all old. Dad's just never home. There's nobody around, so it's easier if I board."

She looked pensive, and she said defensively, "My dad has a real important job, you know. He has to travel lots."

"I'm sure he would prefer to spend more time with you if he could manage it," Yolanda said.

Tracey shrugged but focused her eyes on the Styrofoam holder the food had come in.

"Nana and Papa Mitchell, my mother's parents, live over in Vancouver, so I see them a lot."

Yolanda sensed that caution was in order. Tracey was flippant, as if none of this mattered, but she wasn't wolfing down her lunch as she had been only a moment before. One forefinger went unconsciously to her mouth, and she bit the short nail viciously, tearing it off.

Yolanda said casually, "My *babička*, my father's mother, raised me. My father and mother died when I was twelve."

Tracey's eyes widened. "Hey, that's how old I was when..." She stopped.

Yolanda seized on common ground. "Sometimes it was very difficult, because to me my *babička* seemed—" Yolanda searched for the word "—old-mannered."

Tracey's gray gaze was intent on Yolanda's face.

"Old-fashioned," she corrected. "Boy, you got that right. Nana and Papa are nice to me, but man, it drives me nuts. They give all my friends the third degree, and they don't approve of jeans or makeup, and they talk about what a saint my mother was all the time." Realizing what she'd blurted out, Tracey looked appalled, and her words rushed out in a torrent.

"Like, Mother really was something; I know they're right about that. She never got into trouble, or made anybody mad, or anything. She was tiny and pretty and really smart. There's still some of the same teachers at school—it's the same school she went to. They tell me all the time how nice she acted. But I don't figure they know I was adopted. Like, it's not the same if you're adopted, you're not like your mother then, see?"

The wistful plea in the young voice unexpectedly wrung Yolanda's heart, and she had a flash of inspiration. "*Ba-*

bička always wanted me to act just like my Aunt Sophia,''
she confided. Tracey's eyes once again flew to Yolanda's
face.

"Yes, the same Aunt Sophia you know." Yolanda nodded. "When I was a girl, all I heard in the village school was
how brilliant Aunt Sophia had been, how polite, how clean,
how quiet."

She had Tracey's undivided attention, and Yolanda nodded again, making her eyes wide.

"Truly. The whole time I was growing, *babička* told me
also, at least twice a day, how well-behaved Sophia had
been, how hard she worked, how good-tempered she was
compared to me."

She pressed a hand dramatically to her forehead. "I used
to run from the house, way into the fields, and I would stand
there and shout, 'Aunt Sophia, I hate you, I hate you, do
you hear? I hate you, perfect Sophia.'" Tracey's mouth
hung open with amazement. Yolanda took another big bite
of her food and chewed thoughtfully. "Afterward I felt
better. And Sophia, way over here, never heard me once.
Fortunately, neither did *babička*." Yolanda winked at Tracey.

Over the clutter of disposable containers, mischievous
blue eyes met uncertain gray ones, and Tracey let out a tiny
squeak of a giggle. In another moment, both were laughing, and by the time they left, Yolanda felt the most tenuous of bonds beginning to form between herself and the
fifteen-year-old girl, a bond as fragile as a spider's web on
a summer morning and just as easily broken.

"Can we go now to the museum?"

Sophia had insisted that Yolanda visit the Provincial
Museum near the Parliament Buildings.

"I wish I had time to take you, because, more than anything," Sophia had assured her, "it will give you a feeling

for this beautiful province." It had a massive totem pole outside, and beautiful glass, timber and gray granite architecture.

Tracey gave the mandatory groan, but she led the way.

Yolanda stepped through the museum's doors, and stood enthralled.

A larger than life dugout canoe—carved of cedar and peopled with naked Haida Indians hunting a whale—was screened behind a realistic waterfall. It was so lifelike, the expressions on the fierce handsome faces so evocative that she shivered with the message it conveyed of another time, of people adapted to their environment.

She followed Tracey up an escalator, gaped at a wooly mammoth and told Tracey that she felt she could actually smell the ocean from a lifelike beach where sea lions cavorted.

"You can," Tracey said smugly. "This place uses smells and sounds to make you think you're really there."

On the next level they entered a turn of the century British Columbia town. There was a train station, and the old steam train could be heard approaching just down the tracks. On each side of the boardwalk, shops offered glimpses through windows and half-open Dutch doors, and an eerie feeling came over Yolanda. Tracey was right. The sounds and odors made her feel she was actually in the old town.

"Neat, eh, Landa?" Tracey asked, obviously enjoying her role of tour guide. She moved impatiently to the next half-open door, and the scene caught at Yolanda's heart and brought tears stinging her eyes.

It was only a kitchen, an old-fashioned kitchen, like the one in *babička*'s cottage in Votice. A wood-burning cook stove had a tea kettle steaming on its surface. A soiled bib hung carelessly from a high chair, and a wooden table held pie pastry half rolled out. A hand pump stood beside a sink, and above it, red gingham curtains blew gently in and out at the open window. Just outside, a dog barked, horses' hooves clattered up the lane, voices called cheery greetings. The smell of cinnamon pervaded the room.

Warmth, love, family—the room embodied the spirit of home.

Instantly, Yolanda was back in Votice. In another moment, *babička* would walk in and make the tea. Yolanda stepped forward, drawn irresistibly, but the half door banged against her thighs, and Tracey tugged impatiently at her arm. "C'mon, let's go. Hey, are you crying?" She gazed at Yolanda in alarm. "It's only a kitchen, for gosh sakes."

Only a kitchen. Yolanda allowed herself to be drawn away, but before she left the museum, she slipped down once more to stand in the kitchen doorway. This room was important to her. It spoke to her soul, to her loneliness, to her sense of displacement. Somehow, it drew Votice and Victoria together in her heart.

Outside again, Tracey led the way to a shopping mall.

"What're stores like where you come from?" Tracey asked as she efficiently locked their bikes in the rack provided for bikers.

Yolanda was staring with awe at the racks of seedlings and plants casually laid out on the pavement.

"Nothing is displayed like this," she said, and when they entered the wide doors she felt dumbfounded at the magnificent array of goods, the shoppers with their carts, the abundance everyone around her seemed to accept unquestioningly.

She struggled to draw a picture of the stores in Prague for Tracey as they wandered along the aisles.

"The grocery stores. *Potravini*, we call them. Small, neat. Rows of preserves in glass jars. Pickles, sauerkraut, peas, beets. Coffee, rice, sugar, flour."

Yolanda gazed around, and in her arose a sudden awareness that the life she'd known and lived till now was over. She'd been transplanted, like a young tree, and she was suffering root shock. The soil was alien, but she must adapt.

They were passing a display of fruit, and to Yolanda's horror, Tracey calmly reached out and ate a green grape, then two purple ones. Next, she picked up a mushroom, casually wiped it off, and ate that, as well.

Reacting instinctively, Yolanda landed a sharp slap on the girl's fingers as she reached for more.

"What'ya think you're doing? I'm only having a grape, for god's sake."

The camaraderie of the day disappeared as they glared at each other.

"You are stealing," Yolanda hissed, looking around and praying no one had seen. "This is a very bad thing, and your father made me responsible. What would we say to the owner if he saw you doing such a thing?" Yolanda was scandalized.

"Calm down, nobody cares about it. What's a few grapes, anyway? The girls from my school do it all the time. It's called grazing."

"Grazing? Like cows, eating grass?"

Tracey nodded.

"This is not your grass to graze upon. You are forbidden to do this thing anymore, do you understand, Tracey? There are some rules that are universal, and stealing is the same everywhere."

Tracey mumbled sullenly for the time it took to leave the store, but Yolanda was relieved to see that there was a certain amount of embarrassment evident on the girl's face as she unlocked her bike with sharp, angry movements.

"You can go ahead and tell my father; I don't care," she spat out at Yolanda.

"Why should I do that? This thing is between you and me, a private matter," Yolanda said reasonably, struggling with her own lock. "And now it's over," she added. "Tracey, this lock. Show me, please, how it works."

There was a pause, and Yolanda held her breath. Would the girl simply ride away without her? Yolanda waited, and waited.

Nimble fingers with torn, chewed nails took the chain from Yolanda's fingers.

"It's a combination, see, 41-6-18." The lock sprung open, and Tracey handed it casually to Yolanda. She climbed on her bike and balanced for an instant.

"Everybody else always tells my father on me," she said, and then she was pedaling furiously across the parking lot.

"Hurry up," she hollered back to Yolanda. "Aunt Sophia will be home by now, and I'll bet she'll make us some sandwiches when we stop by. I'm starving."

The rest of the afternoon passed pleasantly, and Agnes Witherspoon was gone by the time they stowed the bikes wearily in the shed at quarter to six that evening. Sophie had taken Tracey's complaints that Yolanda had no "decent" clothing in which to ride bikes seriously, insisting they go shopping that very afternoon.

Ignoring Yolanda's panicked objections, the other two had marched her to a store near Sophie's apartment.

Now, the pants she'd worn were in a bag, and she had on a pair of new-smelling, stiff-feeling blue jeans and a fluffy pink T-shirt. She wore deeper pink canvas runners on her feet. She felt weak thinking how much they had cost her—

she'd adamantly refused Sophie's offers to pay, and scrupulously avoided using any of Alex's money, either.

Yolanda's small hoarded savings had disappeared like smoke with the purchases, but a purely feminine delight bubbled inside her as she caught a glimpse of herself in the hallway mirror at Rockwoods. She looked almost... Western.

It had been a shock, though, to see herself in the triple mirrors at that store. For the first time she'd impersonally evaluated the undeniably plump figure in the mirror, the snug fit of the jeans over her ample hips and backside.

Subconsciously, she'd been comparing herself all day to the women she saw on the streets; casually dressed, incredibly thin, sophisticated women, looking so elegantly beautiful.

She studied her hips and rounded stomach as objectively as she could, and then pulled on the T-shirt thoughtfully.

Well, it covered that roll of fat at her waist, at least. The shell-pink color suited her well enough. But there was all this spare flesh. Sticking her head out of the dressing room, she impulsively called Sophie and Tracey inside and candidly pulled the shirt up, exposing her midriff.

"Here," she pointed, frowning at her waist, "and here," she said, indicating her hips, "and here." They giggled as she cupped her behind. "There is too much of me in these places," she announced. Sophie, tactfully loving, started to object, but Tracey had no such delicacy.

"You need to lose a few pounds, fer sure," she declared candidly, giving Yolanda's figure an assessing once-over. "You don't actually look bad in those jeans, and your boobs are great, but ten or fifteen pounds less would make a difference, all right."

"I joined a diet group, years ago," Sophie announced unexpectedly. "I know I kept all the booklets. It was a good, sensible diet, too. I'll find them when we go home."

She had, and for the rest of the afternoon, they'd mapped out a sensible diet for Yolanda.

"If you're going to seriously diet, we have to find that scale," Tracey fretted that evening. They'd looked in the bathroom on the main floor, and now in their own.

"I know, I'll bet it's in Dad's bathroom." Tracey leaped up the stairs.

"C'mon, Yolanda, have you been up here yet?"

Her heart began to beat a fast tattoo. It was probably unforgivable of her to enter Alex's private rooms without his express invitation. But her curiosity, and the relentless desire burning within her to know all there was to know about him, overwhelmed Yolanda. She slowly climbed the curving iron staircase.

The spacious area had been reclaimed from a high attic, and open beams gave the sensation of airiness, with the inevitable breathtaking vista out of one block of triangular window, which was curtainless.

Deep, rich navy blue carpet stretched from wall to wall, and the furniture was solidly masculine. A terry robe lay tossed carelessly across the deep blue spread. Did it still hold the body scent of Alex?

"Isn't it neat up here? Like a tree house," Tracey chattered, disappearing into the adjoining bathroom on her search for the scale.

"Dad changed the furniture here two summers ago."

So he hadn't slept in this bed with Dixie. But beside the bed, on a table, a studio portrait of her smiled toward the empty pillows. Yolanda swallowed hard. A hopeless, nameless yearning came over her, and a sense of dread. Alex went to sleep each night with that picture next to his bed, with Dixie's memory alive in his heart.

"Come in here, Yolanda. I found the scale."

Tracey was pulling it from a cupboard under the wide sink in the huge bathroom. What drew Yolanda's eyes was the array of crystal bottles, elegant boxes of powder, vials of exotic perfume, eerily aligned on the dressing table. Downstairs, too, she'd found evidence of Dixie's silent presence, but nowhere else had it affected her as deeply as here, in Alex's private bathroom.

He bathed and shaved and dressed with this constant, mute reminder of Dixie all around him. Perspiration broke out on Yolanda's brow, and a sickness rose in her stomach. What a fool she was, to half dream that there might be a future for her and Alex. How could there be, when Alex was irrevocably wedded to the past?

They were hardly downstairs again before the phone rang. Tracey answered, and Yolanda heard her sing exuberantly, "Hi, daddy. You sound awfully far away."

Several minutes passed, with giggles and rapid comments from Tracey. Then Tracey called, "Yolanda, Daddy wants to speak to you."

With her pulse beating heavy and slow, and her hands trembling, Yolanda hesitantly took the phone.

"Yes, hello?" The simple words stuck in her throat. All she could think of was the photo beside the bed upstairs, the endless reminders of Dixie all around her at Rockwoods, and the transient nature of her own relationship with the man on the other end of the line.

"Yolanda, hello." Alex sounded weary across the humming wires, and his voice held a vulnerable note she'd never noticed before. Against her will, she anxiously wondered if he was eating properly, if he was getting sick.

In London it was early morning, hardly dawn. Alex hadn't slept well and finally left the rumpled bedroom and the twisted sheets for the adjoining living area. He had to be at meetings, difficult meetings, all day long, and he felt tired before they even started. Jet lag had caught up with a vengeance, and his body ached. He slumped on the ridiculously hard chair beside the phone.

Outside, a gray drizzle pattered on the hotel's dusty window, and Alex knew a moment's longing for the scene he could see in his mind's eye of Rockwoods, of late evening over the ocean and flags of pink and violet cloud spreading across the gentle silver sky.

Tracey's prattling tale of bike riding and shopping brought a smile to his lips, and a sense of relief from the anxiety he felt about leaving her for Yolanda to cope with. It was obvious that Tracey, at least, was happy and content for once. What about Yolanda?

Her rich, gentle tones with their charming accent made him suddenly close his eyes, creating a vivid picture of her standing with the phone pressed to her ear, her head with its crown of dusky hair tilted quizzically to one side, the way she held herself when she was listening intently or was puzzled about something. When had he noticed that?

"Is, ahm, everything is fine, I take it? Tracey sounds great. Do you need anything? Has Dad been over yet?"

The contained, husky tones of her voice gave the requisite answers, and when he caught himself asking about the weather, he realized it wasn't her answers he wanted. It was the soothing, lilting sound of her voice. For the first time since he'd arrived, he felt unreasonably happy.

What the hell kind of nonsense was this, anyway? Confused, slightly disgruntled, he ended the call abruptly.

"I'll be in touch in a day or so. Goodbye for now."

"Alex?" The accented word came hesitantly over the miles.

"Yes, I'm still here. What is it?"

"Could Tracey and I perhaps have a garden, do you think?" The breathless query came in a rush, and for a second he couldn't make sense of it. A garden? He squinted at the picture on the wall, his eyebrows meeting in puzzlement. The photo was called "The Hunt." He studied the details absently.

"If you want one, of course you can. I told you to make Rockwoods your home, to feel free to do whatever you want. Get Ian Cameron to help you dig it. He's the old gardener who does the lawns—Tracey knows him."

"Ian Cameron? Thank you, Alex. Thank you very much. I'm happy you don't mind if we do this thing. Goodbye."

She was gone abruptly. Alex hung up and decided to go down and see if breakfast was a possibility this early. He needed to shake off the tension that had inexplicably built up during his talk with Yolanda. For a fleeting moment he frowned over the turn the conversation had taken.

A garden seemed a strange thing for a woman to want. It was a new one on him, he mused. It was probably a small flower garden she wanted, an area to grow roses or daffodils or some such thing. She was—he searched for the proper words—an earthy woman, Yolanda.

Well, Ian would manage it. He'd forgotten to warn Yolanda that Ian Cameron didn't exactly see eye-to-eye with Agnes Witherspoon, though. He headed for the bathroom, and the three weeks of his stay hung like an albatross around his neck. For the first time in four years, he wanted to be at home. And he didn't particularly want to examine why.

He suddenly found himself desperately trying to remember what kind of flowers Dixie had liked best. Violets, that was it. He was sure it was violets.

Yolanda undoubtedly preferred sunflowers, but when he found a shop selling bath supplies, he bought gardenia for her. In everything.

"YOLANDA, SHOULD WE PUT the tomato plants here or over there?"

The morning was hot, and Tracey's nose was as red as the tomatoes they planned to grow. She wore an old pair of cutoffs, and her knees were black from kneeling in the earth. Her torn nails were now dirt-encrusted, and a smudge made her look as if she had a black eye. She crouched in the rich loam they'd sweated to prepare for the seedlings they'd bought that morning, and her eyes sparkled with excitement.

Yolanda was just as sweaty, dirty, and excited as Tracey.

"Ian Cameron, didn't you say they needed plenty of sun?" she called out to the gnarled little man raking the soil at the far end of the garden.

"Aye, they like the sun, those." The man's thick Scots brogue was almost another language to Yolanda. She deciphered it, and nodded.

Yolanda studied the garden plot, a trace of unease undermining her pleasure at the destruction of such a large part of Rockwood's front lawn. With a machine called a Rototiller, Ian had efficiently carved the "waste" of front lawn into rather more of a garden than Yolanda had envisioned, putting an extraordinary amount of enthusiasm into the task.

"If it's a wee bit more than ye wanted, plant potatoes in what's over," he'd shouted at her, turning over more and still more lawn.

"Agnes was some mad when she saw our garden," Tracey commented apprehensively. "She said she's phoning Grandpa on us this morning."

Yolanda shrugged with a lot more nonchalance than she felt.

"I asked your father, and he gave permission. Agnes is perhaps just in a bad temper today."

That was putting it mildly. The woman had seemed on the verge of apoplexy when she arrived an hour before and saw what had been the lawn. None of them had dared venture into the house for anything since her outraged retreat. This was silly, Yolanda finally decided. They could all use a drink of water, and she'd love a cup of coffee.

"I'll bring a tray out," she promised the other two bravely.

"A Coke for me, please," Tracey requested. "If the dragon doesn't eat you," she added softly, and Yolanda couldn't bring herself to reprimand the girl. Agnes *was* a dragon.

The kitchen was empty when Yolanda ventured in the back door, and she reached for the coffeepot she'd left half filled at breakfast. It was empty, scoured out, and it had been doggedly replaced on the shelf.

Annoyed at Agnes's fanaticism, Yolanda impatiently re-filled the pot and set it to perk just as she heard Agnes approaching.

"I just finished those floors," Agnes immediately barked, "and now look at the dirt you tracked in. I must say, you sure ain't like Mrs. Dixie, always so fresh and clean she was. Dainty," she huffed, glancing pointedly at Yolanda's less than dainty shorts and sweaty cotton shirt.

"I just cleaned out that coffeepot, too," she grumbled. Agnes shot a sly look at Yolanda. "Mr. Robert is coming by to look at the yard. Don't know what that old fool Ian thinks he's doing out there, but I'll bet he's gonna lose his job, the way he ought to have years since. Rude, he is, and dirty. I've been here lots longer than him, that's a fact, and

I'll be here after he's gone. Mrs. Dixie hired me, and I'll be here after the likes of him.''

And you as well, the statement implied.

"Ian Cameron is following my directions," Yolanda stated coolly.

"Humph. Mrs. Dixie sure never went around giving directions like that. She wouldn't have dreamed of doing such things on her own."

Yolanda felt a surge of fury, and she levelled a cool stare at Agnes.

"But I am not Mrs. Dixie, am I, Agnes Witherspoon? Mrs. Dixie is dead, and I am Yolanda," she said deliberately and turned to pour the bubbling coffee into the cups. Then she added slowly and succinctly, "This garden, it is mine. I want to hear no more of it, do you understand?" Her hands trembled.

"Well, I never," Agnes choked as Yolanda balanced the tray on one hip and propped open the door. "Don't you take that tone with me, you, you, furriner. Don't even talk the Queen's English, you don't. I don't have to work here, you know. There's plenty asking all the time for good housekeepers."

"Then you should leave." The words were out before Yolanda fully considered their implications.

Shocked, icy silence followed her exit.

Robert Caine arrived after lunch. He pulled his battered truck into Rockwoods' graciously winding driveway with a flourish, braking to a stop close to where Yolanda and Tracey were finishing a row of tiny lettuce plants.

For several long moments he simply sat, and Yolanda could see his snowy hair but not the expression on his face. Would he be angry? All of a sudden she had misgivings. Time seemed to stretch like elastic until Tracey got to her feet.

"Hi, Grandpa," she hollered exuberantly. "Come and see what we've done. We're gonna grow enough stuff here for everybody."

Robert got out slowly, and Yolanda and Tracey walked to meet him. He studied them, their sunburned faces, soil-stained knees and hands. His gaze lingered on Tracey's happy, dirty face, and then his features broke into a wide grin.

His green eyes alight, he declared, "Well, this is one hell of a good idea. Hell of an idea. Used to have to cut that lawn when I was a boy, and I always detested it. Never thought of turning it into a garden, though." The gnawing anxiety Yolanda had tried to subdue all morning disappeared like smoke, and Robert draped one arm around her shoulder, one around Tracey's, oblivious to the danger of dirt on his sport jacket.

Yolanda happened to glance toward the house in time to see a curtain in the upstairs hall fall back into place. Agnes had been watching.

The next morning, the time came and passed when the housekeeper usually appeared. Yolanda and Tracey waited nervously. At midmorning the phone rang, and Sophia's worried tones announced that Agnes had given her "a piece of her mind," and resigned. Sophia tactfully avoided exactly what the "piece" had consisted of.

Yolanda frantically rejected the suggestion of a replacement. "Surely we can take care of ourselves. It will be good training for Tracey, and I will feel better with some work to do."

At last Sophia reluctantly agreed, adding that she and Barney would drop by that afternoon.

Tracey had been eavesdropping shamelessly.

"The dragon's gone, hurray, hurray—" she shouted.

She was a bit less exuberant when Yolanda laid out a strict routine for keeping the house tidy, allotting chores to each of them and suggesting they share the cooking.

"I can't cook," Tracey said, as if that ended that.

"You will learn easily. I will teach you," Yolanda promised.

Within a week Rockwoods had relaxed into comfortable hominess. Best of all, the plants in the garden took hold and began to grow, casting a pale sprinkling of emerald over the rich umber soil, just as they would have done in Votice.

During the next two weeks, Rockwoods was slowly transformed even more.

Cycling beside Tracey down a willow-lined country lane one morning, miles from Rockwoods, Yolanda saw a nanny goat with a broken tether around its neck, trotting jauntily toward them down the middle of the road.

She retrieved the broken leather strap and patted the little animal, scratching its head and chattering to it in Slovak. It was a sweet little doe, and badly in need of milking, Yolanda pointed out to Tracey.

They spent an hour locating the owner, and finally knocked on the door of a dilapidated house trailer set in the middle of a field. A laconic young woman with a baby on her hip and a toddler clinging to her jeans looked out at them, and at the goat.

"Oh," she said disinterestedly, "You found Cinnamon." Then she simply stood there. The little goat butted its head against Tracey's legs, and the woman sighed and said, "I guess I better tie her up again." She set the baby on the floor where it immediately began to howl.

"Show us where you want her, and we'll tie her for you," Yolanda suggested, smiling at the diapered toddler who had his thumb in his mouth.

"She needs milking. I will do it for you if you want."

"I never use the milk, anyway. This trailer's sold, and I'm going to Vancouver to live with my folks," the woman explained listlessly. "But there's that goat and the geese down by the shed." She shrugged. "I'm leaving tomorrow. I guess I can't just leave them here...."

"They'll starve." The horror in Tracey's voice echoed Yolanda's own reaction to the callous suggestion. They exchanged telling glances, and a small amount of money changed hands.

Now Rockwoods had a resident goat named Cinnamon, and two geese Tracey named One and Two.

The tempo of daily life speeded up. The goat needed milking, and it was unthinkable to let the milk spoil. Yolanda made cottage cheese and yogurt, teaching Tracey how to, using well-remembered methods *babička* had taught her. They fed the excess milk to the geese. One and Two were invaluable as scavengers in the garden, eating the bugs and weeds, not touching the thriving plants.

Ian Cameron seemed gleeful at the changes in Rockwoods, and he stopped by daily. He turned an empty toolshed into a pen for the geese, and fenced off half the huge cement garage as a home for Cinnamon.

Yolanda had anxious moments when she also wondered what Alex's reaction would be to all this. But, she reminded herself stoutly, he'd told her repeatedly to do what she wanted at Rockwoods.

And no one could mistake the changes in Tracey. Gone were the sulks, the whining, the sad face. The girl was tanned, lithe and healthy-looking, and if she still complained now and then, the complaints were centered around vacuuming or dusting instead of life in general.

"I can't wait to show Daddy what a good cook I'm getting to be," she repeated over and over. She was learning, as fast as Yolanda could teach her, all the old recipes Yolanda kept stored in her head from her own tutelage under *babička*, and many new efforts they tried together from cookbooks.

"Mother hated cooking," Tracey commented once.

It was Ian who brought the chickens one afternoon. He had one clucking hen under each arm as he ambled down the drive. He never did say where he acquired them.

"There's a fine market hereabout for eggs, and these two are Rhode Island Reds," he declared. "I thought Tracey could earn a wee bit of pocket money," he said innocently when Yolanda made halfhearted objections to these new additions. But chickens meant fresh eggs, and Yolanda soon relented. Tracey was thrilled.

"They'll be good company for One and Two," she assured Yolanda.

The chickens joined the geese and the goat.

Yolanda made manure tea for the garden. Tracey applauded each egg as if she'd laid it herself, and she grew adept at milking Cinnamon.

"Doesn't it smell wonderful?" Tracey sniffed the earthy odors tempered by fresh sea air. Yolanda nodded. It was like home, to listen to the medley of chickens clucking, geese honking, goat bleating.

And, best of all, Alex would return in two more days.

CHAPTER SEVEN

"YES, HELLO?"

The phone had rung just as Yolanda stepped into the house. She'd gone for a walk after dinner, wandering along the windswept shore below the house. Tracey had taken her bike and ridden over to Ian's to borrow a book he'd promised her, a story written by a woman veterinarian. Tracey had confided she wanted to be a vet, adding in typical Tracey fashion that her father probably wouldn't let her. Remembering the remark, Yolanda smiled and shook her head as she picked up the phone.

"Is this Mrs. Caine? Hello, my name is Carrie Russell. I'm an old friend of Alex's, and I just wanted to welcome you to Canada. Yes, I know Alex is out of town just now, that's why I thought it would be nice to introduce myself. It must be a bit difficult, getting used to a new country and not having Alex around to introduce you to anyone."

Yolanda felt both bewildered by the rapid flow of words and intensely curious about this woman with the silky voice who was Alex's old friend. Accustomed as she was to *babička*'s friends and neighbors popping in and out, Rockwoods often seemed isolated and lonely.

Besides, Yolanda told herself she needed to make other contacts. She must soon think about a job, an apartment, a life on her own. The idea made a hard knot of apprehension twist her insides. She must keep reminding herself that she was only a temporary resident here at Rockwoods. And in Alex's life.

Disquieting thoughts flitted through her mind as she listened to Carrie's voice rush on, hardly waiting for Yolanda's answers.

"I understand you're from Czechoslovakia? I'd love to meet you. Perhaps we could have coffee together? Would you like to come into the city, or should I come out there? Oh, yes, of course I know where Rockwoods is. Tomorrow at, say, ten? Great. Fine. I'm looking forward to it. Bye now."

Yolanda slowly hung up the phone. Meeting Carrie Russell was one more way of knowing Alex. Her feminine curiosity had been stirred, and maybe another emotion as well, one she didn't want to examine. What sort of "good friends" were they? Something seemed to stick in Yolanda's throat, and she swallowed hard. Maybe she didn't want to meet this woman, after all. Well, it was too late now. Her practical nature asserted itself. What would she serve for coffee?

Briskly she set to work sifting flour, beating eggs. She would make *babička*'s special coffee cake, and sweet bread with raisins. There were the tender stalks of pale green rhubarb Ian had brought that morning. She'd stew them. There was freshly curded cottage cheese from Cinnamon's milk, and she could make a custard with all those eggs.

It was soothing to mix, beat, and measure in the ancient rituals taught her by Anna, taught Anna by her mother, rituals handed down to daughters like a precious legacy over the centuries from women ingenious at using whatever was at hand to create food for their families and friends. Would she ever have her own small daughter to teach, as *babička* had taught her, as she was teaching Tracey?

Yolanda's floury hands paused over the mixing bowl. During the past few years, her immediate future had been too uncertain to allow the luxury of dreams. Getting through each day had taken all her energy, and the nights had been haunted by fearful images and nightmares.

Thoughtfully she kneaded the sweet dough, rolling it backward and forward between her strong hands on the smooth surface. There hadn't been time to think much about love, or husbands, or children.

Her hands stilled. She wanted children. Small, rough-neck boys and girls, chasing chickens and trying to ride the goat. The hard lump in her throat nearly choked her this time, and she had to fight back tears. With something like anguish, she leaned over the counter and closed her eyes, facing fully the truth she'd managed to avoid till now.

She wanted love, the love a man and a woman shared. And not just any man. Alex. From the moment she'd first met him, her subconscious had recognized the truth. She'd known it on the day of their wedding. She loved him, and she longed for his love in return. She wanted to have his children—if she were to have any children at all. Already she was nearly thirty. Time was speeding her past the most fruitful years. Babies would have to come soon, or not at all.

Then, there was Tracey. She wanted to watch Tracey's growth into womanhood.

Ironically, she'd fallen hopelessly in love with her husband, and, she reminded herself harshly, her husband wasn't really her husband. He still belonged to the memory of his first wife.

The back door slammed, and Tracey's cheery voice rang out.

''Hi, Landa. I'm home.'' The girl bounced over to the table. She'd ridden into Victoria and had her hair cut the day before, and the result had brought Slovak exclamations of horror from Yolanda.

"They have sculpted you," she gasped.

"Scalped," Tracey blithely corrected. "I told them to; it's the style. It's hot."

Hot or not, Yolanda had to get used to the change every time she looked at Tracey. She couldn't imagine what Alex would say, but after all, as Tracey insisted, it was her hair. Actually, she looked like a beguiling nymph, Yolanda decided fondly.

"What're you making?" Tracey asked.

Yolanda managed a wide smile and injected a light tone into her voice.

"Wash your hands, and come here, beside me. I will teach you to make bread, just the way *babička* taught me."

Everything was ready long before Carrie arrived the next morning.

Yolanda dressed nervously, ignoring Tracey's suggestion that she wear her jeans. She slid on the gray skirt she'd chosen to wear. It slid off her waist, and barely held over her hips.

"Tracey," she called in amazement. "Come look at this."

The girl ambled in from her room. Together they viewed Yolanda's reflection in the wall mirror, and Tracey held her thumb up in her familiar salute. "*Awwright!* That diet really worked. But you sure can't wear that skirt. It's hot out. Haven't you got a summer dress?"

Yolanda, at Tracey's urging, took the panty hose and slip off and settled on a green-flowered cotton with a belt she could cinch in, a simple shirtwaist she'd made herself the summer before.

"Our feet are almost the same size," Tracey noted. "I've got some sandals I never wear; they'll be better than those clumpy shoes of yours." She brought them, and Yolanda buckled them on. A glance in the mirror confirmed that the strappy leather sandals suited the casual dress.

Staring at herself, Yolanda saw a stranger with a familiar face. She didn't quite look like the thin, elegant women she'd admired on the streets of Victoria. Her wide, high cheekbones were more pronounced since she'd dieted, and her blue eyes looked larger. There was a quality in her face that would always mark her as foreign, a look that Grandma had labeled "Gypsy wild."

She didn't look Canadian, whatever that was. But neither did she look entirely Czechoslovakian any more. Would she ever be entirely one thing or the other? She shrugged and went to make the coffee.

"YOU SPEAK ENGLISH very well, Mrs. Caine."

"Alex's daughter, Tracey, she is helping me with idiom, thank you, Carrie Russell. Please, call me Yolanda."

Yolanda felt more than a little intimidated by Carrie Russell. A flaming redhead, Carrie's hair was as flamboyant as the woman herself. Shorter than Yolanda, she was reed-slim, and she moved as if an electric current coursed through her. Her movements were quick and almost awkward, punctuated by dramatic motions of her narrow hands, which boasted a flashing ring on nearly every finger. She had intelligent dark brown eyes. Her straight hair was expertly cut, with a fringe that played up her milky skin and the faint dusting of freckles across the diminutive nose.

Carrie picked up one of the framed photos of Alex and Dixie from the mantelpiece, but to Yolanda's relief, she didn't comment. Instead, she stared at it for a moment with the snappy eyes that seemed to miss nothing, and then put it firmly back in place.

She wore tailored gray slacks and a wisp of a silk blouse in a burgundy rose shade that should have been absolutely wrong with her hair, but instead was exactly right, making Yolanda conscious of her own homemade dress and bare legs.

As if by magic, within ten minutes Carrie's pleasing soft voice and stream of artless conversation had set Yolanda at ease.

Tracey had appeared, said a brief hello in response to Carrie's easy greeting, and then excused herself to feed the animals.

"I had no idea Alex was into farming," Carrie remarked, surprise and amusement in her voice. "That's some garden out there."

"It's not really farming," Yolanda tried to explain. "We have the garden, the chickens and geese. And the goat."

"A goat?" Carrie's voice held a strangled note of disbelief.

"Of course, yes," Yolanda replied. "Cinnamon supplies us with milk, and cottage cheese, and that helps feed the chickens, and the geese keep the garden free of bugs and weeds. And later, we will have roast goose."

Carrie blinked, and nodded weakly.

"I guess there aren't any bylaws out here to worry about," she murmured. For the first time, she seemed to run out of friendly patter, so Yolanda suggested they have their coffee.

The table was set under the window in the kitchen, bathed in morning sunshine and laid with a bright yellow cloth. There was thinly sliced and buttered sweet bread, coffee cake oozing melted sugar and plums, a clear glass dish with darkly pink stewed rhubarb waiting to be topped with the soft curds of freshly made cottage cheese sweetened with honey.

"My God, it's a feast," Carrie breathed, slipping into the chair Yolanda indicated. "And it's all homemade. Fantastic. How'd you know I skipped breakfast this morning?"

She attacked the food with the same energy she applied to everything else, and Yolanda nibbled. If Carrie was an indication of how thin Alex liked women, it was probably a lost cause to even try to diet, she mourned silently. She poured more coffee, urging her guest to try another piece of cake.

They talked easily and superficially at first, about clothing styles in East and West, of Yolanda's pleasure in cooking. Carrie admitted she could barely manage to open packaged bread, never mind bake it.

Then Carrie casually asked, "What work did you do before you came here?"

"I worked in a factory, as seamstress," Yolanda replied simply, deciding not to reveal the problems that led to that particular job. "Days off, I worked with *bab*—with my grandmother. She had a small plot of land. We grew vegetables—smaller than this garden, however."

Carrie laughed. "Alex's garden looks as if he's going to give up politics and start truck farming," she joked.

Yolanda protested earnestly, "Oh, no, I think not. But it helps with expenses, growing enough food for a family."

Carrie shot her a curious glance, one thin eyebrow tilting assessingly above her chocolate eyes.

"I wouldn't have guessed that finances were a problem for the Caines?"

"Every family should be self-sufficient in the matter of food," Yolanda insisted stubbornly. "Here, I have seen people on the television, standing in line for groceries. Yet everywhere are unused acres of land which could be cultivated, like here. It is big mistake to waste in this manner; it surprises me."

Carrie listened. Then she asked casually, "What other things have you seen here that surprise you?"

Yolanda looked sharply at the other woman, and a warning bell sounded.

She said simply, "Why do you ask this?"

The redhead looked away, and a faint stain rose in her cheeks.

Then she said reluctantly, "I have to admit, Yolanda, that I did have an ulterior motive in wanting to meet you. You see, I write a column in one of Vancouver's two daily papers, a column read by a great many women who are always curious about other women, what their lives are like. I wondered if you'd mind my quoting some of your impressions of Canada, of Victoria, just the ordinary things we've talked about here today?"

The woman's admission made Yolanda's stomach clench painfully. It was because of indiscriminate remarks made to a journalist that she'd lost her interpreter's job in Prague. Why hadn't she thought of asking what Carrie's job was?

She'd begun to enjoy their conversation, and she felt acute disappointment at the other woman's disclosure, and a sense of betrayal.

Meeting Carrie's eyes with a forthright look, she said deliberately, "I think you have misled me, Carrie Russell. I welcomed you here as friend of my husband, not as a journalist."

Carrie had the grace to blush deeply, but she held Yolanda's gaze steadily this time.

"And that's exactly what I am, a friend of Alex's. I'd like to be a friend of yours, as well. But you must understand what writers are like. We have to use everything available for inspiration."

She lifted her cup and sipped at the coffee. "Alex, whether he likes it or not, is a public figure. Publicity and politics go hand in hand; he has to accept that. Better that publicity comes from a friend who knows the situation than from a news-hungry stranger. Don't you agree?''

With each passing moment, Yolanda felt more and more that she'd been duped into the meeting, and worse still, that she wasn't at all sure how to handle it. The last thing she wanted or needed was attention paid to her marriage, to the circumstances under which she'd become Mrs. Caine.

"I don't believe Alex's and my private life would be of interest for your readers," she said evenly.

"On the contrary, anything about the colorful Caine family is always interesting. Especially such an exotic marriage as yours. You wouldn't care to tell me how you met…any romantic details of your wedding?" Carrie hadn't gotten her column by being reticent.

"I would not, no," Yolanda stated firmly. She got up. Her body felt stiff.

"I think perhaps we have talked enough," she said with all the dignity she could muster. "You should speak to Alex about this. He will be home tomorrow afternoon."

Carrie rose unhurriedly and thanked Yolanda for the refreshments as if nothing untoward had happened at all. In a few moments Yolanda heard Carrie roar off down the lane in her sporty red car.

Yolanda drew a deep breath. She tried to shake off the ominous feeling that she'd made a bad mistake in talking to Carrie Russell at all, yet when she reviewed their conversation word by word, she couldn't for the life of her recall anything that would cause trouble for Alex. She cleared away the dishes, put on a pair of shorts and headed for the garden.

The tiny lettuce leaves already needed thinning, and as always, the hot sun and the feel of the earth between her fingers calmed and comforted her.

Tracey pedaled up the lane in another hour and skipped over to Yolanda. "That lady left, huh?" she inquired cynically. "Bet she just wanted to see who got to marry my dad." Tracey snorted rudely. "Broads like her don't fool me any. They just pretend to like me because they think that will make Daddy like them. Boy, I'm glad I never got one like her for a stepmother."

Anxious that Yolanda not misunderstand, Tracey added hastily, "Some of the girls at school have stepparents, and they hardly ever get along with them like you and I do, Landa. But you're not really my stepmother, so that's probably why," she finished guilelessly, racing off to check on Cinnamon. The little goat was showing an amazing ability to chew through any tether and escape, sometimes onto the low roof of one of the outbuildings.

Yolanda stared after Tracey's retreating back. It was pretty certain that Carrie's visit was exactly what the girl said . . . a desire to see who had married Alex. Yolanda felt her forehead crease into a frown. Just exactly how many "broads" had pretended to like Tracey, anyway?

ALEX ARRIVED AT THE AIRPORT late the following afternoon, feeling a deep sense of relief at coming home. Even first-class accommodation didn't really allow ample room for his long legs, and this flight had seemed endless.

Robert met him at the airport outside of Victoria.

"I'm sick to death of hotels, of restaurant food," Alex commented as they collected the last of the luggage and loaded it into the back of Robert's battered blue half-ton truck.

He'd resisted the impulse to phone Yolanda each day. There really was no logical reason for him to call apart from the crazy pleasure he felt at hearing her husky voice saying his name.

"Want me to take you straight out to Rockwoods?" his father inquired.

Alex shook his head and reflected that he'd heard men went slightly berserk at forty. Well, he was thirty-nine. There seemed no other logical explanation for the way he was feeling lately, this burning need to get home to Rockwoods. To see her.

"I have to check in at the apartment first, Dad," Alex heard himself saying. For some reason he couldn't explain, he wanted to arrive at Rockwoods alone. He felt strange about seeing Yolanda again, as if in some ridiculous fashion she would know about her persistent presence in his dreams over the past weeks. Erotic dreams, at that.

Robert seemed a bit preoccupied. He slid behind the wheel and then said emphatically, "That Yolanda's a fine woman, son. Salt of the earth. Hell, Tracey isn't the same kid she was when you left—you'll see."

For God's sake, could even Robert pick up his thoughts about Yolanda? Alex slammed the truck door and fussed with the seat belt.

"I'm glad to hear that, because I was ready to strangle Tracey the day I left. Anything's got to be an improvement."

"She's a different girl. I have to admit I was dubious about all the changes at first, but now..."

"I see you're still driving this old wreck, Dad," Alex interrupted, deliberately avoiding the path Robert's conversation seemed to be taking. He didn't feel ready for a lengthy discussion about Tracey, which would lead naturally to Yolanda. He didn't want to talk about her with his father. His thoughts and feelings were far too confused for that.

"What're you doing, keeping the Rolls as an ornament?"

Robert's white Silver Shadow had become a family joke. It sat, gleaming and exquisite, under cover in the garage of Robert's apartment. No occasion ever seemed suitably momentous to drive the magnificent vehicle. Consequently, Robert went everywhere in this battered Chevy truck.

The older Caine chuckled good-naturedly as the faithful motor roared into life. "Reason I like this old truck, son, is that it matches me. Getting old, but still plenty of mileage left in both of us. The Rolls is too much like some women, elegant as hell to look at, but not much use when the going gets tough."

Alex gave his father a wary glance. What had prompted that analogy? Could it be Yolanda again?

"Well, this one's upholstery leaves a bit to be desired, but I guess you're right," Alex agreed lightly.

They were companionably quiet for several miles.

"You know Agnes Witherspoon resigned?" Robert said next.

Alex nodded. "Barney phoned. Did Sophie manage to find somebody?" Privately Alex thought Agnes was no great loss. Dixie had hired her, and he'd never gotten around to firing the woman. Dixie had insisted on having everything hospital-clean and in order at all times. It was one of the things she'd been unreasonable about, in Alex's opinion, and one of the few things they openly disagreed upon.

"Yolanda insisted that she and Tracey could take care of the house themselves, and damned if it isn't a pleasure to be able to spill a few ashes around when I visit, without that martinet of an Agnes glaring at me. Never liked that woman."

Alex slouched comfortably, letting his father's words flow over and around him, not paying too much attention to the details.

It was good to be home. He couldn't remember when he'd so appreciated the lush fields, the grazing animals on the small farms bordering the highway, the distant view of mountains. He couldn't remember, either, when he'd last been so eager to get to Rockwoods.

Robert dropped him at the apartment, refusing Alex's halfhearted invitation for a drink. Within half an hour, Alex was showered and changed, and ten minutes after that, he'd hurried down to the parking garage and into his cherished silver Porsche.

Humming along with the car radio, he drove swiftly along Beach Drive. Sunglasses shaded his eyes, and anticipation made the miles seem longer than he remembered, despite the vista of sparkling ocean.

He approached Seaview Road, and finally the weathered wooden sign, 45 Rockwoods, which signaled the tree-shaded winding lane. Exuberantly, Alex made the turn, screeching the tires and peeling his glasses off, wanting to relish his first glimpse of house and gracious lawn and far-flung ocean without distortion.

The sun was in his eyes as the car burst from the foliage, and all he could distinguish at first were the shining wide windows of the house. Then, the light shifted; the scene unfolded.

"Son of a—" Alex slammed on the brakes without thinking, and the car jolted to a jerky halt halfway down the drive. Momentarily he wondered if he might have mistaken his own address and turned into the wrong driveway.

The car idled, and he automatically turned off the ignition, wrapping both hands around the wheel, leaning forward in the seat and gaping at the scene before him.

Fully half an acre of raw, plowed earth gaped like an open wound on his right, where a carpet of green had spread until it met the wall of encircling forest. Alex blinked, shut his eyes, looked again.

To his left, a goat—a goat?—was tied by a length of rope to the apple tree, busily munching grass in an ever widening circle. Removed from the house, but plainly visible from where he sat, a shed encircled by chicken wire held—two chickens? As his eyes returned in dumb amazement to the garden, he spotted geese happily pecking between planted hillocks.

Chickens. Geese. A goat. *Rockwoods?*

Before he could even begin to absorb it all, Tracey was flying like an ungainly colt up the driveway, all long, slender arms and legs.

"Daddy," she was shouting like a banshee. "Daddy, you're home, you're home." When she reached the car, she stopped all of a sudden, becoming bashful as he opened the door and climbed out.

"Hi, Daddy. Welcome back," she said demurely.

When had she last raced to meet him this way? Not for years, not since she was a plump little thing in a lacy dress. What had happened to...

Alex could only stare at her just as he'd stared at Rockwoods a few seconds earlier. Tracey, too, had undergone a metamorphosis. She was taller. The stooped shoulders were held straight, and what had been long, auburn hair was cut in... Alex swallowed hard. Did they still call that a brush cut?

The sullen expression he'd come to expect was replaced by a wide, crooked grin.

"So what d'ya think, Dad?"

This gamin of a girl radiated tanned good health and high spirits. For the first time he could see the embryonic woman in her waiting to break free, and he had to swallow again, this time because of an awkward lump in his throat.

He reached out and gathered his daughter into a bear hug, then tousled what was left of her hair.

"I used to call you pumpkin, but I better switch to onion now," he managed to say, rubbing a hand over the bristle on her head.

"Oh, gross," she wailed, but her arms were like clamps around his middle, and he realized she'd been tensely waiting for his reaction. "Wait'll you see everything Yolanda and I did while you were gone," she enthused, grabbing his hand and tugging him along the drive.

"You mean there's more?" he muttered, taking another incredulous look to the right and left.

"Where is Yolanda, anyway?" A peculiar tightness accompanied the words, a tension of anticipation.

"She went to gather seaweed for the garden. It's good fertilizer, you know, Daddy. I'll go get her." Tracey dashed away.

Yolanda had just clambered up the beach path, dragging a load of seaweed in a canvas sling, when she had spotted Alex's car pulling into the driveway. Her hair was blown by the wind, and her hands were stained from the green weed. He mustn't see her like this, Yolanda thought, panic-stricken. She ran pell-mell for the house, ducking in the back door.

In a frenzy, she washed her hands at the kitchen sink, smoothed her hair, patted her cheeks with cold water, muttering under her breath like one demented. Her face burned as if she had a fever. She hurried to the front door, jerking it open, and there on the other side was—Alex.

Alex. The nervousness stilled, and her whole being became quiet. She heard her own voice saying something, but the silent words inside drowned out the spoken words, and she was uncertain what she actually said.

I love this man. I am in love with you, Alex. Can you see?

She drank in the sight of him, from the tumbled ash-brown hair with its underlay of silver, the endearingly crooked nose, to the way his thick eyebrows lifted as if he were asking her something.

She'd forgotten he was this tall, this broad. Her head came just past his chin. Her eyes were on a level with his mouth.

Those narrow, hard, sensual lips. She stared at them, unable to look away. A slow, unbearable tension began to grow between them.

Alex had turned for another disbelieving glimpse of what had once been the lawns just as the door was flung open. Turning quickly to Yolanda, he started to say hello, but the word died before he could get it out.

The woman in the doorway was, technically, the same woman he'd married five weeks ago. Yet, like everything else at Rockwoods, this was a vastly different Yolanda than he'd remembered.

"Hello, Alex," she greeted him with a tentative smile. "Welcome home."

The same luminous tilted eyes, startlingly blue, thickly curtained with gold-tipped lashes. Full, slightly parted lips in a face somehow made starkly dramatic, cheekbones carving it into sculptured lines. Mole by the mouth. Curving, slender neck below a cleanly drawn jawline. Husky, accented voice. Golden copper skin. Tendrils of silky dark hair escaping from a thick club of heavy braid hanging over one shoulder—these were more or less the same.

"Hello, Yolanda."

What was it that had changed, then? She was thinner, that was it. High, rounded breasts were outlined under the thin cotton of a white T-shirt, tapering into a narrow waist and delicately flaring hips encased in snug blue jeans. Strength and delicacy melded into total femininity, enhanced by the trace of shyness that brought color creeping up her neck and into her cheeks.

She was less than she had been, yet so much more.

Her eyes seemed to center on his lips like an invitation. His reaction was automatic. He took a half step forward and put his arm around her. When she tipped her head back to give him a startled look, he kissed her, his mouth drawn irresistibly to taste the full, provocative lips, and he knew what it was he'd been hungry for these past weeks.

She was staring up at him when his arms came around her, and his face blurred. Just before she felt his kiss, she touched his face hesitantly. His hands slid around her, spanning her waist and pulling her fiercely tight against him, and she shuddered.

His smell was familiar; a clean, sweet essence of Alex. She remembered the sensation of slightly abrasive male skin against the softness of her cheek.

He nibbled gently for an instant, and Yolanda felt surging excitement and eagerness spring to life within her, trapping her breath in her lungs. She wanted him to kiss her properly. If he released her now, she couldn't bear it.

His lips hovered over hers for less than a heartbeat, and then he claimed her.

His mouth moved on hers, thirsty, exploring, talented and hungry, and a wild elation sprang to life within her. Instinctively her lips opened for him, and his tongue's hard tip memorized their shape, tracing the bow, the full lower lip.

His tongue slipped inside. Her body tingled as small shocks of pleasure touched hidden places within, teasing, hinting of more and yet more. His arms tightened around her, and hers around him.

He made a sound deep in his throat, of wonder and aching need, and her lower body instinctively undulated against the heat of his hardness.

His hand rose, captured the single long braid and tipped her head back so his mouth could explore the long, curving line of her neck, his tongue echoing the pulse that thundered at its base, hot and wet against her skin.

She wanted an unnameable more. With a rushing, pulsing heat in her loins and up into every pore of her body, she wanted his loving. The small sound welling up in her throat was an invitation, a provocative question, totally female and wanting and wordless.

He was the one to remember time and place, to tighten his embrace like a promise and then release her in a tortured effort at control.

He took her chin between his thumb and finger, gazing down at her.

"Yolanda? Landa, is it really you?"

The rough tenderness in his voice was amazement, question, hunger.

Her voice was drowned by delight. All she could do was nod. Whatever he wanted of her, she would give. She loved him.

He looked into her eyes, and a frown came and went on his forehead.

He felt again as if he were gazing down into her soul. Never before had he met a woman this open, a woman so devoid of subterfuge. She could be hurt so easily. She seemed to have no defenses. It threw all the responsibility on him, and he fought the feelings she roused in him, resenting both her and himself. He wanted to throw her down, here in the hall, and make love to every inch of her. He also wanted to turn away, get in his car and leave before he hurt her.

He groaned, drew her roughly against him once more to cradle her in his arms, and they stood silently, trying to recover from what had happened between them, both weak, breathless, throbbingly alive.

"Yolanda? Yolanda, where are you?" The voice was Tracey's. The kitchen door slammed, and there was the sound of hurrying feet pounding across the tile.

They sprang apart, like guilty children caught in mischief. Yolanda tried to steady her breathing, erratic and rough.

"I'm here, Tracey," she finally managed to say, and Alex turned and climbed the entrance stairs to meet his daughter as she burst into the living room, and to protectively shield Yolanda for a moment behind him.

"Where were you? I looked all over," she said accusingly, her gray eyes flitting from one to the other suspiciously. But the desire to show off for her father overcame her momentary doubts.

"C'mon, Dad. I want you to meet Cinnamon, and One and Two, and the chickens. And wait till I show you our garden."

His head turned, and he looked at Yolanda questioningly.

"Go with her, and I'll make dinner. Go."

She was still shaky, and she needed solitude for a time. She'd known the word *desire* in five languages, but obviously she'd never suspected its meaning till now.

It was a power to be reckoned with.

Today, for the first time, she also knew that Alex felt something for her. Was it love? Or was it only the natural need of a man for a woman, the same need with which he'd held her on their wedding night? Would he allow his need to overcome him again? She didn't know.

Her natural practicality refused to agonize over it. He'd held her and passionately kissed her. It was enough. It was a beginning.

But it wasn't at all simple. If her relationship with Alex should ever become intimate, what of Tracey? They couldn't always leap apart the way they just had, hiding perfectly normal emotions from the girl.

Yolanda had come to know Tracey in the past weeks, and she was deeply concerned about her. Somehow, in the midst of all the moneyed luxury surrounding the Caine family, the child had gotten lost. Perhaps when her mother had died, perhaps even earlier. When it had happened didn't matter.

What did matter was that the happiness on Tracey's face remain there, grow stronger and more certain. The girl would never feel an outsider again, Yolanda decided firmly. Not if it could be prevented.

Her hands busied themselves with spreading a freshly ironed cloth, putting out the pretty willow-patterned china, fresh yeast buns, the trays of simple vegetables and fruit she'd disciplined herself to eat, and had even grown to like. There was the fragrant fresh cheese from Cinnamon's milk and the hearty stew she'd made earlier. Preparing food was the same everywhere, and the task always brought her peace. She smiled a little sadly.

How often *babička*'s hands had followed these same patterns, serving food.

And the patterns of the heart. Were they universal, as well? Would she ever find the happiness *babička* had known with her Karel?

There had been only one man in Anna Belankova's long life.

"For some women, that's how it is," Anna had once declared.

That's how it was and would be for Yolanda Caine.

CHAPTER EIGHT

"WHAT'S GOING TO BECOME of the animals when you go back to Vancouver to school, Tracey? You know there's no one here at Rockwoods most of the time, and there's only five weeks of school vacation left."

Alex had avoided the subject until dinner was over, but it had nagged at him as he listened to his daughter chatter excitedly. Yolanda had been quiet during the meal, meeting Alex's eyes squarely, but allowing Tracey to do the talking. The girl's gaze flew to Yolanda now.

"There's a high school near here, one I could ride to on my bike."

Her voice quavered. "Yolanda said to talk to you about it."

Unreasonable resentment stirred in Alex. "Your mother wanted you to graduate from Duncan House," he stated firmly, adding cream to the coffee Yolanda poured for him. She stood poised with the coffeepot still in her hand, her eyes going from Alex to Tracey and back again.

"My mother is dead," Tracey said slowly and distinctly. "Even if she weren't, I'd want to go to school here. I hate Duncan House, Daddy." Tracey's fists were balled into tight knots, one on each side of her plate. Yolanda could see how agitated she was becoming, and she moved to put a calming hand on Tracey's shoulder.

Alex shot Yolanda a glance. He angrily suspected she was aligning herself with Tracey and that she had unwittingly brought this scene about with her garden and animals and God knew what else. "You're going back to Vancouver, back to school at Duncan House, and that's that," he ordered, feeling like a tyrant as soon as he'd said it, baffled anew at his inability to deal with Tracey.

He dealt with politicians, foreign diplomats, touchy international traders, and yet he couldn't carry on a reasonable conversation for longer than five minutes with this child.

The rest of the scene was predictable. She'd throw something, scream and cry, run out . . . He tensed expectantly.

Tracey's lips trembled, and there were tears in her eyes, but Yolanda's quiet voice intervened.

"Ian wanted you to ride over this evening, Tracey. His grandson is coming to stay for the summer, remember? Why don't you go now, and I'll clean the dishes this time?"

Jerkily, without another word, Tracey got up, not looking at her father, and walked stiffly out. She banged the door, but not as badly as she might have.

Alex expelled his pent-up breath in a slow, tired sigh. Now he'd have to try and explain to Yolanda why it was wrong to encourage Tracey's rebellious attitudes about school. Damn it all, this being the father of a teenaged girl was beyond him.

Two minutes, pregnant with silence, had gone by before the door exploded open, and with eyes round and horrified, Tracey hollered, "Cinnamon got loose, and she's on top of your car, Daddy."

Galvanized into action, Yolanda and Alex flew out the door.

Sure enough, the saucy goat was planted firmly on top of Alex's sporty silver car, her chewed roap dangling from her neck, her sharp hooves making dents in the gleaming paint.

he bleated at them, prancing a little, creating new scratches
ith every movement.

Alex cursed in a steady stream, reached up and lifted the
nimal down, setting her none too gently on the ground and
oving the tattered rope into Tracey's hands.

He studied the damage. The hood would need extensive
odywork and the whole car would require a new paint job.
e used a basic Anglo-Saxon expletive.

"Lock this animal up before I wring her bloody neck,"
e gritted.

Tracey gave him a wounded, outraged glare before she led
innamon away, and Alex rounded on Yolanda.

"Alex, I'm sorry. She chews through her rope, the ras-
al..." Yolanda began, but nothing would calm him, for the
oat had simply provided the vehicle for the maelstrom of
onflicting emotions that had warred in him since his ar-
val.

They erupted now in a burst of illogical fury, fueled by the
onfusion of his emotions toward her, the intense sexual
esponse and consequent frustration she stirred in him, as
ell as the recent scene with his daughter.

He jammed his hands deep into his pockets and stepped
oser to Yolanda, disturbingly close. He was formidable,
ith his green eyes cold and narrowed, his voice snarling at
er.

"What the hell did you think you were doing, digging up
alf the estate, filling it with all these damn geese and
ickens, and that infernal bloody goat?"

Her answer was deceptively quiet, and she stood proudly,
er newly slender body held straight and tall. She would not
llow him to intimidate her.

Even in his anger he was disturbingly aware of every tan-
lizing curve.

"I was doing what you said I should do, Alex. You said I should treat Rockwoods as my home. At first it seemed to me some fancy hotel, not a home at all. I asked you about the garden; you told me to go ahead. I should have discussed the animals first with you, but Tracey loved them, and I was caring for Tracey."

She was quiet, reasonable and right. It infuriated him.

He abandoned that attack for another.

"You had no business encouraging Tracey in this ridiculous idea she has about changing schools. You don't understand the first damn thing about the problems I've had with her."

He knew it was grossly unfair and that his troubles with Tracey certainly weren't Yolanda's fault. He felt ashamed as soon as he'd spoken.

"Perhaps not. But the past is over, and what I understand now is that Tracey feels unhappy and lonely in this school. She has told me things about it which concern me, Alex."

"What things?" He'd been about to apologize, but now he felt on the defensive again. How had Yolanda won his daughter's trust in such a short time, while he was unable to communicate with her?

"The details are a confidence between her and me. But I assure you, this place you are sending her is not good for Tracey." Unconsciously she folded her arms across her chest.

Alex glared at her, but she refused to flinch.

"Are you telling me," he said, his voice low now and silkily lethal, "that in three short weeks you think you know more about what's good for my daughter than I do?"

Yolanda felt that if she released her arms from their grip on each other, she'd fall in a heap on the ground. What was she doing, defying him this way? But Tracey couldn't talk to him and make him understand. Robert, Barney, Sophia—they were older, involved in their own busy lives. Who did that leave to fight for the girl? Someone had to make him understand. She stood her ground.

"Yes," she said bravely. "I do believe that, Alex."

Even when he was furious, he stirred her. His hair was rumpled, the green eyes had darkened to a stormy shade, and the fists in his pockets pulled the casual cords tight across lean hips. The memory of his kisses made her catch her breath.

But this was war, not love. She tilted her chin even higher.

Utter astonishment paralleled his outrage at her words. In the course of his whole married life, he couldn't remember one single confrontation during which Dixie had stood with her arms crossed and outright defied him like this.

Sometimes Dixie had cried, making him feel like a heel. Then there were pouts and long silences to get through uncomfortably. He thrust that memory aside. At other times, she'd wheedled charmingly, and if the issue weren't too important, he gave her what she wanted. But this? Yolanda's blue eyes were icy. She was taking him on, toe to toe, her chin tilted defiantly.

Grudging respect for her stirred in him, but he was at a loss as to how to deal with her.

He resorted to tactics that were effective in the legislature debates when a member was being attacked.

"Exactly what do you mean, Yolanda? Explain yourself."

(Does the honorable member have facts to back up his imaginings?)

She looked around, aware of the incongruity of standing in the middle of the yard and quarreling, while birds twittered and a soft evening breeze rustled the arbutus trees. Besides, Tracey might come back and hear them out here.

"Perhaps we should go in the house to discuss this further?" she suggested coolly, proud that she was able to keep her voice from quavering.

A delaying measure. Aha, she was wily. Fine.

He nodded curtly, stalking off ahead of her, holding the door politely for her to slip past, his face hard and impassive, his body rigid.

He was doing his best to ignore the powerful images of holding her here in his arms, the way she'd felt and smelled and tasted. Against his will, his nostrils drew in the faint flowery fragrance she exuded as she hurried up the steps into the living room. His eyes were on her provocative behind as she gracefully climbed the stairs.

Yolanda felt that if she didn't sit down soon her trembling legs would give way. By doing this, she was destroying every chance there might have been for joy with him. What was it in her that made her unable to curb her tongue and ensure her own survival?

She sat on a hard-backed chair. He took a similar chair a few yards away. They faced each other warily. How could she say what she had to, without making him hate and resent her?

"When I was a child, I attended the village school in Votice, and I was happy there. But as I grew beyond it," she began slowly, "I had to board in Prague to go to school, live in a dormitory with other girls. It was not a good experience for me. I was a private child, needing to be alone a lot. Groups of young people are the same everywhere, I think. Either you join them, or you become the enemy. Tracey knows this."

She gazed out over the calming vista of water and clouds and distant islands beyond the window, her blue eyes stormy with memories.

"I was fortunate. I had *babička* to return to every weekend, to help me set a course for myself. To give me courage not to join the crowd when I didn't want to. Tracey doesn't have *babička*, Alex." She met his eyes squarely, deliberately aiming for the heart, feeling desolate as she did it.

"She doesn't even have you at home every weekend. You aren't there for her when she needs you."

He shot to his feet and color rose in his lean cheeks. His jaw was set so the strong bones showed through the skin.

"Her grandparents dote on her, and she stays with them whenever she chooses," he said hotly. "Sophia and Barney keep a room for her."

Her words were stirring a dreadful guilt inside him, a guilt he'd known was buried, but one he hadn't had the courage to drag out and examine. It hurt to do so now.

"Sophia, Barney, her grandparents—they all love her, undoubtedly, but they aren't giving her what she needs: guidance, firm discipline." Yolanda was relentless. "Only you can give her that. When you were a boy, Alex, who was there to talk with you? I remember you said you grew up here at Rockwoods, with Barney and your father. You must remember how secure that made you feel, those strong, wise men to rely on. Tracey needs you, just as you did them."

He stalked to the window, his back to her. Pride made him hide the effect of her words, the awful realization she was forcing him into.

Of course he remembered. There had always been his father, his uncle Barney. And Rockwoods. The school he'd attended was in Victoria, and he'd come home, here, every night. His eyes swept around the familiar room.

In those days there'd been the mounted head of a moose above the mantel...right there, and a huge old rocking chair, his grandfather's, had sat here. Dixie had had the place redone, with flower prints and drapes to cover the windows, and this light, spindly furniture. All the old pieces were up in the attic.

He'd accepted the changes, but secretly he'd liked the old place the way it had been, masculine-looking, relaxed.

Home. With Robert and Barney always there to listen. Blast this woman. What right had she to dredge up all his misgivings this way?

"Tracey is a girl. She needs to learn things I can't teach her."

It was a line of last defense, and he recognized that.

"She needs you. She needs more than occasional visits with you. Tracey needs a full-time father." Yolanda was implacable, but it was costing her dearly to see the anguish she stirred in him. She despised hurting him, ached to rush over and cradle him in her arms, yet she felt angry, too, for Tracey's sake.

When he turned toward her, his tone and his eyes were icy and remote, and he'd erected a wall between them. "You've made your point. Now, if you don't mind, I prefer not to discuss the matter any further."

He strode from the room, and she felt as if she'd been physically beaten. Every muscle hurt from the tension between them. What had she accomplished, except to make him furious with her? Tears burned behind her eyes, but she refused to let them fall. In this instance, tears solved absolutely nothing.

Instead she went briskly to the kitchen and washed and polished, cursing pithy, satisfying Slovak curses as she scrubbed things she normally never noticed. When everything was gleaming so that even Agnes Witherspoon would have approved, she escaped to the beach and walked miles along the rocky shore until it was so dark that she had to feel her way back up the path.

She could hear Alex and Tracey talking in the library, and she crept like a burglar up the steps to her room.

A nightmare she'd had in Czechoslovakia came back that night, a dreadful, formless terror of running for her life, with dogs and men with guns behind her. There was no one to help, no one to care if she escaped or died, and that knowledge was infinitely worse than the danger.

When finally she woke, she lay trembling, ice-cold and afraid to move in the silent darkness. The faint sound of the ocean, the conscious knowledge that she was safe at Rock-woods were of no comfort, because she was still alone. It seemed hours before she slept again.

Still tired when she entered the kitchen the next morning, she was surprised and wary to find Alex already there and the coffee already made. He poured a steaming mugful for her as if he'd been waiting. Her heart pounded at the sight of him, and her throat felt dry.

He wore jeans, and his long, narrow feet were bare. He had the feet of an aristocrat, she thought, glancing at them. His denim shirt was carelessly open, revealing the mat of light brown curls across his chest.

Was he still angry? His green eyes had lost their icy edge, but she couldn't be certain.

"Good morning," he greeted her, pleasantly enough, and his eyes swept over her deep blue flared cotton skirt and faded T-shirt, both Tracey's comfortable hand-me-downs. The girl had delved out an armload of clothing from her immense closets and insisted Yolanda wear whatever she liked.

His eyes took in the early morning freshness of Yolanda, her face shining from a recent scrubbing, her hair braided neatly into a single plait and hanging casually down her back. He studied her closely. He still wasn't used to this slender, graceful creature being the Yolanda whom he'd married.

This bloody-minded, black-determined, stubborn, slender creature, he corrected himself, remembering the quarrel the evening before, the restless night he'd just spent. There was no doubt Yolanda had won the first battle.

His conscience was alive and well, unfortunately. "This matter of Tracey's schooling."

Yolanda tightened her grip on the cup she held, and tension made her knuckles whiten.

"I've thought it over, and last night I had a long talk with Tracey." He was still amazed that the hour he'd spent with his daughter had actually resulted in a productive conversation, accompanied by no tears, no door slamming.

"I think you're right," he said briskly. "She'd be better off over here in a public school. It poses certain problems, however." He was finding it damned hard to admit he was wrong. It wasn't something he'd had to do often, at least in recent years. His lips twisted in ironic amusement. Good for your pompous soul, Caine, he chided himself.

The next part was harder still, because he was aware he wanted her to agree for reasons that had nothing to do with Tracey whatsoever.

"I have to travel a fair amount, as you know. Tracey can't stay here alone, either now or after school begins." Unconsciously he rubbed a hand over his beard-rough chin. He hadn't shaved yet that morning, and Yolanda heard the faint rasping sound. A shiver coursed through her. She'd like to rub her cheek against his, feel that roughness on her skin. Prickles ran up and down her arms and legs.

"I know we'd talked about your getting an apartment soon. Instead, would you consider staying on here at Rockwoods? You'd be perfectly free to take a job in the city, if that's what you wanted. I'll find a cleaning service so you aren't saddled with all the household chores." He did his best to inject a light tone into his words. "I'm not sure I can find one who does chickens and goats, but I'll certainly give it a try."

It was ironic that when Barney and Robert had suggested that she should live with him for a period of time, he'd raged. Now he waited for her to answer with his gut tied in knots. He wanted her here, close to him, of her own free will, more than he'd wanted anything for a long time.

He deliberately avoided putting a time limit on her stay, and he watched her expression closely for a reaction to his words.

There could be no sidestepping with Yolanda.

"Is this what you want, Alex, or only for Tracey?" She held herself absolutely still, steeling herself for his response. It would tell her a great deal she had to know before she could give him an answer.

He let his breath out in a slow sigh. She didn't make anything easy.

"It's what I want. I thought of you while I was away, and I'd like us to spend some time together, get to know each other." He met her eyes squarely, and his voice was slightly harsher when he added, "We'll go slow, Landa. More than that, I can't say."

He was honest. It was all she asked, and more. Her smile flashed and was reflected in her eyes, making him catch his breath.

"Yes," she said matter-of-factly, "I'll stay here with you gladly."

His grin was boyish, lightening the traces of fatigue that lingered on the lines of his face, and a bolt of pure happiness shot through her as she realized how tensely he'd been waiting for her answer. It had been important to him, then, having her agree. *Wonderful.*

"What would you like for breakfast?" she asked, and the hominess of the question pleased her, just as it pleased her intensely to be here with him, in the intimacy of early morning, making his meal.

"Surprise me," he suggested, wishing he had the freedom to swoop her into his arms, carry her up to his bedroom under the eaves, strip her with excruciating slowness and enjoy the breakfast his body insisted it wanted. If Tracey weren't upstairs sleeping, he would have.

How would she taste? How would those lovely breasts feel, cupped in his hands? Like the first time he'd loved her back in Votice? The next time would be slow, he vowed. The next time he'd make damn certain it was good for her; he'd control himself instead of acting like some randy teenager. He'd make her want him, again and again....

With amazement he realized that this was the first time since Dixie's death that he'd acutely desired one particular woman, wanting not a carefully orchestrated physical release with a temporary partner, but true spontaneous love-making, the kind where there was a morning like this after a night before, spent eating breakfast, sharing mundane small talk, going back to a rumpled bed... He drew himself up short.

Was he ready to risk loving again? His eyes settled on a photo in the glass cabinet in the corner. Dixie smiled out at him, and not for the first time since her death, he felt uneasy with her memory.

Yolanda hummed under her breath, breaking eggs into a heavy black skillet, slicing fresh bread for toast. With her back to him, she was unaware of his intense scrutiny. His eyes moved from flesh and blood to the photograph.

He'd been a faithful husband to Dixie. He'd liked having a dainty, pretty wife, a purpose to his life beyond his work. She'd stayed at home, sometimes taking courses in china painting or some other womanly thing that interested her. Often, she traveled with him. When she didn't, she'd always been waiting for him, it seemed. Had he disappointed her as often as he thought?

There'd been rough patches in their marriage, particularly before they adopted Tracey. That had been one of the few times she'd really fought with him, too.

Alex hadn't wanted to adopt a child. At times the responsibility for Dixie's happiness and well-being weighed heavily on him, and he was secretly relieved no babies came. But Dixie was adamant about parenthood, and eventually he'd given in, and then fallen in love with the engaging bundle of energy and charm that Tracey had been as a child.

But somehow it had gone bad. Marriage was something he'd done once, and hadn't planned on doing again. His reasons for that decision were hazy. It was an emotional response more than an intellectual one.

Now he was married again—more or less accidentally, to Yolanda—and it was causing him a great deal of confusion, this marriage of convenience. What was he going to do about it?

Yolanda turned and caught the pensive look on his face, not entirely certain of the reason for it, but instinctively aware that it concerned her, and aware, too, that it wasn't something he'd talk about with her. So she used an immediate diversionary tactic.

She set a plate loaded with toast and eggs and small sausages on the placemat in front of him. Her lovely apricot skin was flushed with the heat from the stove.

"Eat," she suggested. "You look hungry."

Her earthy solution lightened his mood, and in another moment they were laughing together as she related one of Ian's dour witticisms.

That light conversation and laughter marked the pattern for the day, and Alex relaxed and enjoyed himself. When the morning's misgivings appeared like shadows in his thoughts, he dismissed them determinedly. He'd think his way through them another time.

Bashfully he gave Yolanda the huge bag of bath salts, oils, powders and soaps he'd brought her, and her delighted reaction made him ridiculously happy.

"Hedonism," she instantly declared. "Now I need only the long johns."

"Winter's coming; that can be arranged," he quipped, and the smile on her lips and in her eyes was radiant.

Robert arrived in the early afternoon, wearing comfortable old jeans and a tattered sweater. Everyone was outside when he drove up. Alex had just completed another guided tour, and he'd been forced by Tracey to comment on and admire every single plant in the monstrous garden.

"What's planted here?" he had just demanded obligingly for what seemed the billionth time, gesturing to a large area where numerous green shoots were appearing, looking for all the world exactly like all the other green shoots he'd gazed at for the past hour.

"Cabbages. Red and green both. Daddy, can't you tell?"

Several times he'd caught Yolanda's knowingly amused eyes on him, and he'd widened his own at her in mock horror as Tracey blithely moved inch by painful inch along the garden rows.

He admired the cabbages, endlessly grateful for his father's arrival and grateful, too, that Yolanda had made Robert feel comfortable enough to wear clothing Alex remembered from years before. Besides, Alex had wanted a cold beer for the past forty minutes. Tracey greeted her grandfather warmly, and then announced, "Grampa, look what Cinnamon did to Dad's car yesterday." She obviously wanted a second opinion on the gravity of Cinnamon's crime.

Yolanda sneaked an anxious glance at Alex. She realized that she didn't know him well enough to predict his reactions to such matters.

Robert took one look at the damage and burst into laughter. His hearty chuckles were contagious, and in another second Alex found himself laughing, too, somewhat sheepishly.

"This'll teach you to get a sensible vehicle, like my old truck there, son. Farmers don't drive fancy cars."

The day turned into one of those unplanned, wonderfully easygoing times. Tracey and Yolanda bullied the men into helping with the dinner, and then they ate casually on the cement patio outside the kitchen, as the sounds of birds and sea gulls' cries punctuated their lazy, idle conversation.

Traitorously Alex recalled that Robert had never relaxed this way during his visits here when Dixie had been alive. Dinners here then had tended to be rare and formal. Entertaining made Dixie nervous, and eventually they'd done most of their socializing in Victoria's more sophisticated restaurants.

He dismissed the memory and suggested a walk on the beach to watch the sunset just beginning over the western ocean.

ALEX HAD TO GO TO HIS OFFICE the next day. For the first time in years, he would rather have stayed at home, but despite that, he felt great. He'd whistled to himself during the drive in, and the morning was splendidly sunny.

"Good morning, Ruth," he greeted cheerfully, wondering again if Ruth Prentiss had any life outside these walls. She was always here, no matter how early he arrived, and she was usually still at work when he left, prim, proper, correct. He relied on her to keep things running.

He breezed into his pleasant office, went to the window and looked down on the early morning traffic on Government Street. It was good to be back.

He heard Ruth come in behind him.

"Have you seen the morning paper?"

When he shook his head, she laid the paper and a cup of coffee on his desk and went out. He'd missed having breakfast with Yolanda this morning, as he'd left just as she was coming downstairs. The truth was that he'd lingered until he'd heard her, wanting to have her smile good-morning to him.

He cradled the mug, glancing idly at the morning section.

The paper was folded open to Carrie's column "The Way It Is."

Alex shook his head and smiled fondly. What ingenious mayhem was Carrie's typewriter causing today? He started to read.

If you spend any time around the politicians these days, you're bound to hear about recession and inflation. Everything old is new again, you say? Well, there's a bill before the house advocating a substantial raise in our elected members' salaries. What else is new? Their income just won't match their expenditures, they complain, a problem with which many of us ordinary mortals are all too familiar. However, one of our politicians has a solution that doesn't involve hikes in pay—just good-old fashioned honest labor.

Alex had a nasty premonition. His grip tightened on the paper, and his gaze flew, skimming the remainder of the article, reading it again in disbelief and with a growing sense of outrage.

> During a recent visit to Rockwoods, the lovely Caine estate built by the lumber baron Thomas Caine back in 1901, this reporter was astounded to discover that the elegant grounds had been converted to what must be the largest garden plot in Victoria. The spacious double garages have been converted to pens for goats, chickens and geese. Yolanda Caine, newly acquired wife of Assistant Deputy Minister Alex Caine, volunteered the information that these changes are helping the family make ends meet in the face of the economy's belt-tightening. Mrs. Caine believes that if other estates were converted similarly to small farms, Canadian food banks would be out of business.
>
> Well, elected representatives? Man your spades. "The Way It Is," the taxpayers are doing all the digging. With a little help from the Caines.

In stunned disbelief, Alex finished, and just as he read the last word, his phone began to ring ominously.

"Alex, welcome back." It was the bluff, hearty voice of Curtis Blackstone. He asked about the trip and its business results, and then he added innocently, "Say, could you use a load of manure on that farm of yours? I hear the Opposition has a great supply."

It was the opening sally in a barrage of similar comments and queries. Alex's friends thought it hilarious. His adversaries considered the article ammunition. Some of the members regarded it as little short of treason. By four in the afternoon, Alex decided that if one more person whistled "Old MacDonald Had a Farm" one more time, he was going to drive that person's teeth straight down his throat and enjoy watching the blood sully the hallowed marble floors of parliament.

To top it all, he'd forgotten till now that he had to take the goat-damaged car to the garage and try and explain why the roof was covered with hoof prints.

EVERY MORNING YOLANDA read the paper front to back. It was a window on her new world, a way to gauge the thinking of Canadians, a way to discover the character of the people. But this morning, Anna's letter had taken precedence over the news.

Yolanda sat hunched over the thin air-mail sheets with their colorful Czech stamps, reading *babička*'s letter over and over, trying to hear the voice of the old woman in them. Why couldn't Anna write the way she talked, instead of these stilted, formal words that didn't even sound like her?

Tracey's voice interrupted her reverie, sounding shrill and outraged.

"Landa, you absolutely won't believe this. Remember I told you that broad was nothing but a snoop?" She handed Yolanda the paper.

Yolanda scanned Carrie's column quickly, and then re-read it slowly, digesting every twisted inference, her hands trembling with outrage. She felt betrayed, patronized. She felt terrified and helplessly angry.

She felt exactly the way she'd felt in Prague on the day when she'd lost her interpreter's job because of the article in the French journal. A thought so dreadful that it made her gasp leaped into her head.

Alex. This was terrible. Would Alex lose his position in the government because of her? It became more probable the longer she considered it. Remorse and anguish swept through her like a windstorm. Carrie's column would hurt him, humiliate him. He would despise her for being so stupid, and she deserved his contempt.

Tracey, involved in her plans for the day, had already dismissed the whole thing. "Ian invited me over to help him and Victor make a new pen for the pigs today; that new sow is coming tomorrow."

"Victor?" Yolanda felt as if her voice was coming from a great distance away.

"Victor, Ian's grandson, Victor. Jeez, Landa, I've told you his name a dozen times already. Victor Martinos. His Dad's Italian. Anyway, as soon as I finish with the animals, I'm gone . . . if that's okay with you. See you at suppertime."

With a blithe wave, she left.

Like an automaton, Yolanda went about her daily chores. Her imagination fueled her apprehension.

Unbelievable as it was, this time she had even more to lose than the last time she'd been careless with her tongue. After he read this today in the paper, Alex would probably send her away. Who would want her around, making such stupid comments? She debated packing her things and leaving immediately, not going through the pain and humiliation of a scene with him, but she couldn't run away. She'd have to face him. And then there was Tracey. She wanted to explain what had happened to Tracey.

Oh, the thing got worse the more she thought about it.

She couldn't eat. Her stomach cramped and ached with tension. Trying to maintain fragile control, she showered and dressed carefully as the time approached when Alex would arrive. But it was another full hour and a half before she heard his car in the driveway.

Then the door slammed, and she heard him enter the house. She began to shake. It wasn't his anger she feared. He had every right to be angry. It was the loss of the tenuous bond she'd sensed growing between them. That, and her own pain and shame at having hurt him after everything he'd done to help her.

"Yolanda?" His deep voice seemed to echo through the house, full of portent. Slowly she walked to meet him, feeling as if she were dying a little inside with every step.

CHAPTER NINE

"YOLANDA?" Alex's tone was openly impatient.

He stood in the entrance hall, his tan jacket slung over a shoulder, his tie loose, the buttons at his shirt neck undone. He looked hot, rumpled, casually urbane. He scowled up at her.

"Why didn't you tell me you talked to Carrie Russell?" He strode up the entrance stairwell, taking the steps two at a time, and moved past her into the living room. He tossed his suit coat carelessly on a chair as he passed, shrugging his shoulders as if to ease the tension from them.

She wet her lips and straightened her shoulders.

"Alex," she began. He was standing with his back to her, staring out over the sunlit ocean, his hands casually propped on his hips.

She had trouble getting her breath, and her voice was thin and unnaturally high. She wrapped her arms around her waist.

"Nothing I can say will correct this..." she said, choking the words out. "But I want you to know I apologize. I will leave tonight. I feel terrible to have caused you this trouble, this disgrace, after everything you've done for me."

Feeling utterly miserable, she couldn't seem to stop talking once she'd begun, and she heard herself babbling. "It was ignorance, of course, I am unbelievably stupid. It was a big mistake to talk with this Carrie Russell, but she said she was your friend. I didn't at first know she was a reporter," she continued painfully, barely able now to keep the tears at bay, balling her hands into fists.

He'd turned toward her, but she couldn't see his face or his expression. The late afternoon sun filtered through the window behind him, silhouetting him against the brilliant light.

She stood frozen in place, waiting. Why, oh why didn't he say something, rage at her, accuse her? The tension in the room became unbearable, and she whirled around and half ran, heading for the staircase to her room.

But as she passed Alex, he reached out and grabbed her arm, turning her toward him and anchoring her with his hand on her other shoulder.

"Hold it," he commanded. "Slow down, and let's go over this again."

His hands were firm, his grip far too strong to struggle against. She looked up at him, and all the anguish she felt was reflected in her tear-flooded eyes. She drew in a half sob, and blurted, "I cannot. I cannot talk about it anymore. I feel too ashamed, to have said such things. But you must understand; that wasn't really what I did say. I did say these things, but not in this way, you understand. Please, Alex let me go," she begged, on the verge of tears.

Alex was shocked to realize how upset she really was. He'd felt out of sorts, annoyed with both the good-natured joshing and the more pointed remarks he'd had to endure all day. Certainly, he was irritated by Carrie's damned column, but it wasn't the end of the world.

He looked at her drawn face, recognized the panic in her voice. Her body was trembling. Lord, did she think he was going to beat her? Alex reacted instinctively, drawing Yolanda into his embrace, enfolding her tightly in his arms.

"Calm down, now," he soothed. He forgot his own chagrin, forgot the barbs of the day as he pressed her dark, silky head to his chest, stroking the fat knot of hair pinned at her nape.

"Your job, Alex. Will you lose your job because of me?" Even her voice was trembling. She forced herself to ask the question, her body a knot of tension as she waited for his answer.

"Lose my job?" His tone was incredulous. "Of course I won't lose my job. Just because of a . . ."

Suddenly he remembered. She'd told him so matter-of-factly on that morning in Votice, about the journalist, the reprimands, the loss of her job as interpreter. Perhaps because of that remarkable restraint of hers, her matter-of-fact acceptance of absolute censorship and the harsh penalties imposed in her native country for breaking any rules, he'd never given a single thought to how she'd feel today.

His lack of consideration appalled him. Instead of being so damned caught up in the loss of a little dignity, why hadn't he guessed what a calamity Carrie's words would appear to Yolanda?

With a smothered oath for his insular pride, he drew them both over to the sofa, gathering her onto his lap in a crumpled heap of gauzy rose cotton dress and long tanned limbs.

"Now, what's all this about leaving? I'd never blame you for the press and what they consider news. Anyway, that article is only a minor annoyance. It's Carrie's rather perverted version of humor, that's all. People here don't lose jobs that easily."

Convulsively her arms locked tightly around his chest and back, and she burrowed into him. Expecting the worst, preparing herself for his wrath all day, and now being in his arms instead strained her emotions past their limit. Giving up the struggle for control with a smothered whimper deep in her throat, she began to cry, wetting the front of his shirt with hot, copious tears.

He patted her, murmuring comforting phrases, while he thought about the complex woman he held.

The contrast between the defiant, outspoken Yolanda challenging him over Tracey's schooling, and this huddled, soft ball of misery on his lap forced him to examine her vulnerability.

She fought fearlessly for those she loved, and over the past days he'd understood that she'd come to love Tracey. In her convictions as to what was best for the girl, Yolanda was maddeningly confident and infuriatingly secure.

Yet curiously in other ways she was painfully insecure. There had been the tearful scene in the airport at Calgary. She'd had every reason to be terrified during that exit from Czechoslovakia, yet she'd been calm. And then she'd fallen apart because she'd felt that he was indifferent to her, unaware of her feelings, unwilling to talk. "You won't even touch my hand," she'd accused tearfully.

Even now, it wasn't herself she was concerned about, the remote chance this article might raise questions about her application for Canadian citizenship. Instead, it was him, his job, his reaction to her error, his censure of her that had triggered her collapse of serenity.

Her presence made further analysis impossible. He found he was enjoying having her on his knee, with her arms around him. Her newly slender hips were tantalizingly curved and firm. She felt both fragile and strong to the touch.

"Hold still." Following an impulse he didn't even try to curb, he moved one hand up and carefully removed the pins holding her hair in a pristine knot. It cascaded like dusky smoke over his forearm, and he lowered his head to bury his face in its fragrant softness. Flowers. She always smelled of flowers.

Desire didn't come slowly. It surged through him, instantly tightening his body into a hard, aching urgency, and he had to grit his teeth at the sweet agony even her slight movements caused him.

She tilted her wet face questioningly up at him, and of course there was no hiding his pulsing need for her. He groaned and claimed her lips, still tangy with tears, delicately circling them with the tip of his tongue, then drinking deeply.

Alex wanted her. She felt the pounding of his heart against her cheek, the throbbing message of his arousal beneath her hip, and her love for him ignited an answering fire in her body. She let her head fall to his shoulder, and his lips and teeth nipped up and down her throat, sending tiny jolts into her abdomen. Then, with a ferocity he'd controlled until now, he kissed her lips again, ravaging them with his own, silently illustrating with his tongue exactly what he wanted to do to her body.

He was breathing heavily and his uninhibited movements drove her mad with longing. Every part of her seemed to slowly fill with need.

He kissed her, moving his lips down her throat, sliding his hands up and down her body, finding the swelling tautness of her nipples and knowing exactly how to fondle their hard tips so that she uttered a small cry of ecstasy. There could be no question of denying Alex; the thought never crossed her mind.

Small, eager whimpers came from her throat as he touched her, his hand stroking her leg, impatiently pushing aside the folds of her dress, finding her bare inner thigh and slowly, painfully slowly, touching that part of her needing his clever touch so desperately, rubbing gently and persuasively through the flimsy panties she wore, then slipping underneath, alternating rhythms, bringing a panting exclamation from her swollen lips.

"Please, yes, like so, like so . . ."

She writhed, and his own desire surged with her movements. His mouth suckled her nipple, relaying the pattern of her response down to his fingers, back to his lips. He controlled his own craving for release.

"Landa, lovely Landa."

His voice was rough, thick with desire for her, and he wasn't quite sure what he wanted her to answer, only that he needed contact on every level possible with the women he held. Her reply was immediate. "Yes, Alex. Please," she whispered. "You must teach me, tell me what I should do—I know little about this."

Her beautiful simplicity thrilled him. She was completely innocent of the small, coquettish games other women had played when he first made love to them. She demanded nothing more than what he was so eager to give, asked for nothing beyond the moment, no promises about tomorrow, no assurances.

"Where's Tracey?" he asked cautiously.

She had to draw air into her lungs with a shuddering gasp, forcibly pull herself back from the realms of sensation he was creating.

"Ian has invited her to dinner, and later, a movie."

He nodded and lifted her easily from his lap. The flimsy sofa tilted as he moved them to the thickly carpeted floor. The sight of her passion-clouded, starry gaze, her distended nipples poking through the flimsy cloth, her disheveled dress, tumbled high around her thighs, enflamed him.

"Let's get this off you."

He grasped the hem of the garment, clumsily catching handfuls of it as he drew it up over her hips and breasts, freeing her long hair with one hand as he finally pulled the dress off and tossed it aside. His heart thundered as he devoured the sight of her.

She wore a simple white cotton bra, brief flowered panties.

"You're so beautiful," he breathed, and for that moment, she believed him. She felt beautiful with his hands on her, his touch warm and sensitive, fiendishly adept at finding places that made her gasp.

She watched him, drugged with delight. A wave of his hair hung forward nearly into his eyes, and his face was flushed, the amber-flecked eyes half shut.

Reaching up, she shyly slipped his tie over his head, unbuttoned the silky shirt so she could place her palms on his chest and gauge the hammering of his heart against the way her own hot blood pounded in her veins.

He tantalized her, running his tongue from the thundering pulse point in her throat down to her engorged breasts, then stripping the bra away and cupping the fullness in his hands, flicking the hardened tips with his thumbnails and soothing them immediately with his mouth.

"Landa, I ache to make love each time I'm near you," he muttered, sliding a hand down over her satin skin, exploring the downy nest of soft dark curls hidden just under her panties.

He could hardly control his own rush of elation at her indrawn breath, her rhythmic, uncontrollable responses to his sure touch.

He wanted to give her pleasure. The memory of their wedding night haunted him, as well as the burden of his own selfishness. More than anything, he wanted to bring her fulfillment, wanted to watch her writhe, hear her moan as a result of his caresses. She was so moist, so hot beneath his fingers, velvety, liquid, urgent.

He was close to demanding fulfillment himself, dangerously so. There was a primeval sensuality in her that stirred him, excited him as no other woman ever had. He felt tender and passionate and ravenously curious about her.

The pulsing agony of longing grew in her until nothing existed except Alex, his smell and taste and touch pulling her into an upward spiral she couldn't control, didn't want to control. She wanted it never to end, she wanted to rush him to its end.

She cried out, teetering on the brink of release yet holding back, fearful of being so helplessly outside of herself.

"Easy, I'm here, holding you. Now, Landa. Let it happen now." His whisper was both a command and an entreaty.

The release that he controlled intensified, crested and exploded within her. Her arms clasped him convulsively, and his choked whispers were echoed by her low song of wild fulfillment.

After an endless pause, the involuntary writhing ceased, and she collapsed, drowned with satiation, lassitude, peaceful happiness and wonder.

She opened her eyes when he stood up, watching him strip off his clothing with heedless efficiency, his tall form graceful and muscularly firm, swollen with the virile need she'd stirred in him. And then his weight was on her, delightfully heavy.

Her trembling thighs parted to him, and with a single thrust he entered her, pausing to allow her time to adjust, to become familiar with their joining flesh.

His teeth were clenched with the effort of withholding his instinctive drive for fulfillment, and the face above her own took on a savage urgency as he adjusted his motions to the hesitant response he felt her inner muscles giving him, the quivering beginnings of her renewed desire.

He went slowly. She wound her body around his, her arms tight around his neck, her legs entwining him like silken vines, and she marveled at the quickening inside her.

He encouraged her, whispering all the things he wanted to do, watching her face intently to time the moment of her release to coincide with the bursting explosion he suddenly could restrain no longer. He shut his eyes, shuddering with pleasure. The cry that he uttered was guttural and ancient, the sound of a man claiming his mate, and when his cry subsided, hers began.

Afterward, they clung together in sated peace, content at first to hold and be held, gloriously naked and wrapped in each other's arms as twilight fell.

"Alex?" Her voice was warm, thick and sleepy. He held her head pillowed on his chest, one hand in her hair, the other flat on her abdomen, feeling the rich pulsing diminish slowly under the satin skin. Her body held a fascination for him, slender but voluptuous, quivering at his touch.

"Alex," she repeated calmly. "I am in love with you."

The words, the way she said them, demanded nothing of him. Her confession was a random, comfortable truth she felt like telling him in this intimacy of afterlove.

He moved his hand away from her stomach as if he'd been burned. His body tensed, and he had to consciously control his voice. He felt deeply, inexplicably disturbed.

"That's flattering coming from such a beautiful woman, but you don't really know me well enough to love me, Yolanda."

He sounded as if he were reprimanding her, damn it. He didn't want to sound like that. But he didn't want the added responsibility of her love. He had to say something more, to try to make her understand.

"I know it's ridiculous, but I'm still not over the death of my wife. Can you understand that, Landa?" He couldn't see the picture of him and Dixie from where he lay, but suddenly he was aware of it, up there on the mantel.

She sat up and looked down at him, allowing her hand now to stroke back the hair on his forehead, linger on the planes of his cheek. She was aware her words had upset him. How stupid of her, to blurt it out that way, spoiling this miracle between them. But a tiny part of her was hurt and angry and betrayed.

"You're right, of course. It's much too soon to know you." Her fingers strayed into the curls on his broad chest, and she made her voice teasingly light, deliberately ignoring the other half of what he'd said.

"I think you're an excellent teacher, Alex Caine."

He brought her face down to his and kissed her gratefully. The awkward moment was gone. She buried the hurt of his rejection, telling herself it was her own fault she was in pain for once again saying too much.

"We need to have supper," she said practically. "Are you hungry?"

"Starved," he confessed, getting to his feet and pulling her up easily. "But you're not cooking tonight, Landa." He picked her rose dress up from the floor and held it up. The cotton gauze was hopelessly creased.

"I've pretty well wrecked this one. Go put on another dress, and I'll take you out to dinner."

She scooped up her underthings and hurried naked to her yellow bedroom to shower. She heard Alex go to his suite under the eaves. She visualized him looking at the picture beside his bed, the collection of powders and creams in his bathroom, the silent but ominous reminders everywhere in this house of the woman who had been Dixie, and she slammed her fist down on the soft eiderdown of her bed. How could anyone compete with a ghost?

After washing, she dried and dressed in a flowered cotton wrap skirt patterned with huge cabbage roses—one of Tracey's offerings again—and the pink T-shirt she'd bought.

She brushed her tangled hair and decided to leave it loose, tied with a scarf at the nape of her neck.

Alex had said Yolanda didn't really know him. Certainly, she hadn't known Dixie. How could she? It would help to find out what kind of life Alex had lived with the first Mrs. Caine. Yolanda suspected it would reveal a great deal about Alex.

Perhaps she should just openly ask Alex about his former wife, and see what he said.

A small, wry grin twisted her lips as she slowly went downstairs. No doubt about it, she had never really learned to keep her mouth shut.

"Is there anywhere you'd especially like to go to eat?" Alex's eyes admired the wholesome beauty she projected.

"I like McDonald's," she said, loving the way he looked at her.

"I think I'd better decide," he remarked dryly, and he caught her long, thick mane in one fist, drew her near, then planted a playful kiss on her lips.

The restaurant he chose for them was called Chez Arnand. It was on Yates Street, in the heart of what Alex called the Old Town. The lighting was dim, and a piano played softly in the background. The menu was written in both French and English.

"Monsieur, madame? Bonsoir."

The maitre d' was suave, a tiny bit haughty, tall and dramatically handsome in his well-tailored suit, with eyes as smooth and softly dark as sable. He had shiny black curly hair, and his body looked as if he worked at keeping it fit.

Quite naturally, Yolanda stated her preference in excellent French. The language unleashed a torrent of words from the man. Smiling at her delightedly, he volunteered the information that he had recently arrived from Quebec with his sister, bought the restaurant and renovated it, and that he loved Victoria but that hearing French spoken so fluently made him feel homesick.

Yolanda smiled back, then complimented him on the decor. He told her of the difficulties he'd had with painters, and inquired about her charming accent. She explained she had recently moved to Victoria and she also was homesick at times, just like him. "Ahh," he purred. "I knew we had a great deal in common."

Alex waited impatiently through all of this, understanding a word here and there, noting irritably the way the man's eyes lingered on Yolanda's long, flowing hair, the way her startling blue gaze responded to the waiter's rapid discourse.

"I am Armand, Armand Mollins," he finally volunteered. He bowed slightly over the hand Yolanda offered, and Alex's smile was only slightly strained as he, too, was belatedly included in the conversation.

But the food was wonderful, delicately prepared and attractively arranged, although, Alex pondered, one would think Armand had more to do than flash that engaging grin at Yolanda all evening.

"My wife would like another cup of coffee."

Yolanda couldn't believe she'd heard Alex correctly. *My wife*. She stared over at him, but he and Armand were silently exchanging an eloquent, masculine look. Armand poured her coffee with a flourish, gave Alex a mischievous, purely Gallic shrug, a wry smile, and left them alone at last.

Alex waited with ill-concealed impatience until her coffee cup was empty.

"Let's get out of here," he half growled, and Yolanda walked to the entrance and waited as he paid the cashier.

"Perhaps you would enjoy meeting my sister, Dominique," Armand suggested. Armand's musical French words came from behind her, and when she turned to him, he handed her a small yellow business card.

"She has this tiny boutique, Foofera, very chic, close to the waterfront. I think you and she would like each other...if ever you are in the vicinity."

He bade her and Alex, who appeared at her elbow just then, an effusive good-night in accented English.

Alex nodded coolly and took Yolanda's hand firmly in his. He seemed thoughtfully quiet as he helped her into the car. He pulled out of the parking lot, turning into the street before he spoke abruptly.

"Shall we drive, or would you rather go to a club for a drink? There are things we need to discuss."

"No club, thank you. Already I feel the wine."

He drove to an area just across the Inner Harbour from the Parliament Buildings, and Yolanda made a small murmur of appreciation for the place he'd chosen. The car engine stopped, and the open windows caught the intermittent salty breeze from the water, carrying the sound of waves lapping on the pleasure craft moored in the inlet. The summer night was balmy, and the sky above the buildings was a deep, almost navy blue with stars scattered across it.

"This is one of my favorite views," Alex confided, and Yolanda nodded in agreement.

The scene was spectacular. The entire facade of the domed buildings gleamed in the night, illuminated by bulbs whose combined golden wattage etched every ornate architectural line in glowing, incandescent light. Windows, doors, spires, cornices were silhouetted both on the central structure as well as the east and west wings.

"I want to talk about our future, Yolanda." His voice was solemn, and her heart seemed to slam against her ribs.

"You are planning a future for us, Alex?" The words were difficult, her voice hardly audible.

"You know everything changed between us tonight, Landa." He turned his body urgently toward her, his arm stretching along the back of the seat, his face shadowed in the reflected light from the water so she couldn't read his eyes or expression.

"It was good, making love to you." He thought about that, and quickly rephrased it. "More than just good, at least for me." He seemed to be waiting and she was grateful for the darkness that hid her hot blush.

"For me also," she whispered.

"Yolanda, we have to make some decisions here. We have to decide whether we want an actual marriage or not. Tonight, well, our lovemaking was certainly unplanned. But from here on, it can't be. I don't intend to go on like this." He sounded almost angry. "It's not as if we're involved in some casual affair. It's the damnedest thing, being already married to you, yet feeling guilty about making love, thinking afterward that I've taken advantage of you, violated the original agreement."

He leaned toward her, and his intensity was obvious.

"You don't feel that, do you, Landa? That I'm taking advantage of you? Believe me, that isn't what I intended." He sounded anxious, and she shook her head vehemently in denial. He was vulnerable, this strong, reliable man. It touched her, and made her tease him gently.

"Perhaps you feel I've taken advantage of you?" she queried softly. "I, too, am a responsible adult, Alex." She turned the tables on him neatly, and after a moment he even laughed a little. Then he was serious again, and his voice became low and passionate, sending shivers through her.

"All the same, I suspect I'm more experienced at seduction than you. The truth is I want you, Landa. I want you in my bed. I realized tonight that subconsciously, ever since that first time in Votice, I've intended to have you again, to feel you move like that under me, the way you were tonight. The softness, the way your eyes get wild... God, I can't seem to get enough of you. Right here, this minute, I'd like to—" He stopped abruptly, and she had the feeling he'd surprised even himself.

Mischievously she pretended to loosen her T-shirt, striving to add a martyred note to her voice, twisting around and looking at the other cars parked nearby, and at the blue-and-white police cruiser slowly driving past.

"If you really must, then I suppose right here is fine, Alex. If you don't mind these other people watching, and the policeman in that car allows it—"

His grin flashed, and he said slowly, "I should call your bluff, crazy Gypsy." He put a restraining hand on hers and linked their fingers.

"But on second thought, I'll take a rain check."

The tension was gone. "Rain check?" She was puzzled.

"A promise for later," he explained huskily, and she shivered at the velvet depth of his voice.

"Besides driving me mad, you're good with Tracey. You understand her better than I do." The admission hurt. He let her hand go, rubbing his distractedly through his already tousled hair.

"I'm making a hell of a botch of this. What do you think, Landa? Should we give this marriage a try? I'm not much better at being a husband than I am at being a father, but I'll do my best."

The admission puzzled her. There was something in his voice; reluctance, bitterness, perhaps? He was a proud man, and it was obviously hard on him to admit his problems with Tracey. But why did he feel he was not a good husband?

Just a few hours ago he'd insisted she didn't know him well enough to love him. She sensed he wanted no more protestations of love from her. Certainly, he was making none. He wouldn't want prying questions, either.

She was acutely aware of what he wasn't saying, of all the romantic promises he wasn't making. He'd married her out of familial duty to Sophie and Barney. Was he going to continue the relationship because of Tracey? She couldn't agree to that, however much she loved him.

As if he'd read her mind, he said next, "I'm not suggesting we stay married for Tracey's sake, if that's what you're thinking. That would never work."

She was sorely tempted to ask, "Then why, Alex? You don't say you love me, only that you want me in your bed. A marriage is full of many things besides lying together in bed."

But for once, she managed to hold her tongue. She wanted what he was offering, wanted this chance to be his wife in every way he would allow.

"Don't turn down half a loaf when you're starving, waiting for a whole." That had been one of *babička*'s folk sayings, and Yolanda was starving.

She snatched the half loaf.

"Yes, please, I want to try this," she said.

He sucked in a deep breath and slowly let it out again. For a brief moment he experienced jubilation at her calm, husky acceptance of his proposal. He'd needed her acceptance, he realized, however reluctant a part of him had been to commit himself to another, real marriage. It was done now.

After all, he reasoned, there was no other way. If he wanted her this ferociously—and he did—then he had to offer her the security of a future. His own ambivalence about being married again would surely fade as time passed. Anyway, he didn't really understand why he felt as he did.

Then she was in his arms. As long as he held her, there was no need for thought. Her breasts seemed to swell, her arms entwined around his neck. Gypsy. The name suited her. She'd cast a spell on him, and he wanted it to last forever.

"About this rain check." Her whisper tickled his ear. "Perhaps you should drive us home, Alex, so we can get this rain check settled?"

CHAPTER TEN

THEY WERE TURNING INTO Rockwoods' driveway when Yolanda noticed the light from the upper hallway shining out of a small window. For one last moment she let herself believe that it was possible to go with Alex to his bedroom and explore the sensuality they craved, then sleep all night in his arms. Then she faced reality. Legally married or not, there was Tracey to consider.

Softly, dejectedly, she told Alex her decision.

"Until we talk with her and explain this change in our marriage, Alex, I think we must go on as we have been. Another rain check, yes?"

Her voice sounded as disappointed and wistful as Alex felt at this new development. All the way home, he'd been lasciviously plotting the rest of the night in his head.

He'd conveniently forgotten he had a teenage child, because he felt like a virile teenager himself just now. He'd driven fast, expertly maneuvering around curves and up hills, with one arm holding Yolanda tight to his side, stroking her hair and her neck as the miles few by. He'd felt like letting loose with a rebel yell out the open window of the car, just from sheer exuberance. He hadn't felt this way since he was sixteen, full of the joy of a speeding car and the feel of a beautiful girl nestled into his shoulder.

His disappointment was keen, but he had to agree with the sense of Yolanda's suggestion. As he parked the car in the quiet yard, apprehension rose in him as he remembered in a rush all the jealous scenes Tracey had concocted at various times in the past, and the careful assurances he'd given her about this not being a real marriage.

Hell. Now that he thought about it, being both Tracey's father and Yolanda's lover was going to require diplomacy he wasn't sure he possessed.

He kissed her, and the kiss was full and deep and hungry; then she went to her yellow room reluctantly.

Alex spent the remainder of the night figuring out the best way to break the news to his daughter, and feeling grumpily deprived. His brain knew all the reasons for circumspection, but his body insisted that if he was going to have a wife, damn it, he wanted her beside him. Now.

He rose early and out of sorts, pulling on a pair of old jeans and quietly descending to the kitchen in his stocking feet to make some coffee.

He sat sipping the hot brew, running his fingers through his hair and frowning as he rehearsed the best way to explain himself to his daughter.

"Tracey, Yolanda and I have decided to sleep in the same room from now on." Nope, that wouldn't do. Too simplistic. Just how much did a fifteen-year-old girl understand about the physical side of adult love? he wondered. Damned little, he decided, absently watching the ocean turn from formless gray to gray-green, and then become molten as the sun appeared.

"Tracey, Yolanda and I are going to live together as man and wife." Was that better? Would she question him about what being man and wife implied? Surely not. He put too much cream into his cup and had to dump it down the sink. He could hear those stupid geese honking in the shed.

Tracey's school was for females, and it was run by nuns. He was pretty certain they taught basic concepts of sexuality, but the actualities of it all—no, she was an innocent child.

What had he known at sixteen? He grimaced. He'd forgotten some of what he thought he knew then, and it was a good thing. But there was no comparison between a girl and a boy, of course.

He rose and paced back and forth, sloshing coffee on the tiled floor, soaking it up with his stockinged foot.

Tracey had never asked him about sex. Hazily he remembered her asking Dixie where babies came from once. Dixie had become prettily flustered, and she'd bought a dainty little book with pictures that weren't exactly misleading, but definitely weren't graphic. If he remembered correctly, the book had turned the whole process into the development of a flower or something.

She'd undoubtedly progressed beyond the flower stage. But how far? Exactly what sort of things would she want to know about him and Yolanda? She wasn't the type of kid to just accept something without asking a million pointed questions. Damn it, why weren't there courses for things like this? He could hear footsteps coming down the stairs. Maybe Yolanda could help him figure this out. His mood lightened at the thought before he realized there were two sets of feet.

"Morning, Daddy."

"Good morning, Alex."

The two females were dressed similarly in cutoffs and T-shirts, their faces clean-scrubbed and glowing. Alex sent one quick, covetous glance at the curvaceous length of Yolanda's legs.

"Morning. What're you two doing up so early?"

"This is the day we clean Cinnamon's pen," Tracey informed him. She popped bread into the toaster with studied casualness, and he shot her a look. Something was coming; he was sure of it.

"You can help us if you like, Dad." There was a pregnant silence. Then, with her back turned to him, she blurted out, "Yolanda says you guys are going to start having a real marriage, Daddy. She explained it all, like about adults needing companionship, and a physical relationship, and you two wanting to be honest with me. I was a little freaked at first, but I see your point. I'm not exactly a child, you know. I know you need somebody your own age to be with. I can relate to that." Still without turning, she added, "Besides, Yolanda understands about my—my...mother. About her still being my mother, even though..." Her voice faltered, and she cleared her throat. "Landa says she and I'll be friends, and naturally, I'm not jealous of my own father. So, no problem," she concluded, smearing toast with half an inch of peanut butter and adding honey. "Everything's cool." She didn't sound as certain as the words indicated, but her response amazed Alex with its brave attempt at reasonable maturity.

Yolanda watched Alex clench his coffee cup with both hands, until she marveled that it didn't shatter. Then his gaze swung from his daughter, now rooting in the fridge for milk, over to Yolanda, and he slowly raised one thumb in Tracey's currently favorite "all right" signal. His approval made her feel warm and delightfully happy, but she also felt slightly uneasy at how relieved he seemed to be. Should she have insisted he talk to the girl himself?

The opportunity had come up spontaneously, with Tracey's appearance in her bedroom earlier, and some instinct had suggested the issue was better handled woman to woman.

Perhaps she'd been right. Her face flamed at the memory of the forthright questions Tracey had asked. Youngsters were sophisticated. It was better, maybe, that Alex wasn't present.

"I guess you and my father want to sleep together, eh?" the girl had demanded sarcastically. "I guess he's forgotten all about my mother by this time, anyway." It had taken a great deal of honesty to help her understand, and Yolanda felt Tracey still had a great deal of thinking to do before she'd feel easy about it.

But the tender, warm look Alex telegraphed across the table made joy bubble inside Yolanda, and her deepening flush now had nothing to do with Tracey.

"Can I go over to the Camerons' later? Vic and I are going riding. Ian's neighbor has horses he's gonna loan us." Tracey obviously felt they'd exhausted the subject of fathers and daughters and stepmothers.

"Who's Vic?" Alex asked.

"Oh, Dad, I told you. Victor is Mr. Cameron's grandson, Victor Martinos. He's staying here for the summer, maybe longer. He might even be going to the same school as me. He's older, though. His mum and dad are divorced."

Fatherly caution made him demand, "How old is this Vic?"

"Sixteen. Mr. Cameron's going to show us how to saddle the horses and everything. I can go, can't I?" she demanded anxiously.

"I'd like to meet Vic sometime soon, but yes, you can go," Alex answered.

"Perhaps we could plan a picnic on the beach, and you could ask Vic and his grandfather," Yolanda suggested.

"Oh, super," Tracey enthused, all signs of the earlier strain disappearing. "Can we do it next weekend, Dad? We can have a bonfire and a corn roast—okay, Dad?"

Alex would have agreed to much more than just a picnic right then.

"That's fine with me," he said. "Now, are you two ladies going to teach me how to clean out a goat pen?"

He was, in short order, extremely sorry he'd asked.

From that moment on, the long hot weekend slid by, the
hours like beads on an abacus used to measure contentment. The garden burgeoned, the animals flourished, and
the people smiled a lot at each other.

There were a few awkward moments when Yolanda
moved her things into Alex's room. She noticed immediately that he'd removed the picture of Dixie that had been
beside his bed. But in the bathroom the perfumes and powders still rested in neat rows. Yolanda found a box and
packed every last one neatly, then carried it into the base-
ment. Upstairs again, she arranged the things Alex had
brought her from England on the wide countertop.

Alex didn't seem to even notice the change.

Plans for the picnic accelerated. Yolanda and Tracey had
expanded the guest list to include Robert, Sophia, and Barney.

"Who else, Alex? Are there friends from work you'd care
to ask?"

He shook his head. During the past years he hadn't encouraged friendships. Being a widower was awkward. There
was Curtis, but a family picnic was the last place a roué like
Curtis would choose to be. Besides, Alex didn't want Curtis lavishing his charm on Yolanda.

"There's my secretary, Ruth. But she'd never come to a
picnic."

"Why not?"

He shrugged. He couldn't imagine Ruth outside of the
office. He told Yolanda that, and she gave him a scathing
look.

"You are being a chauvinist, Alex. I'll phone and invite her myself," she insisted. She did, and Alex was astonished when Ruth promptly accepted.

During the week Alex worked, but the entire parliamentary process slowed down in the summer, and the buildings were all but deserted. His workload was light, and he found himself hurrying home in the early afternoon, eager to change into shorts, drink a beer, even to weed the garden.

Most of all, he looked forward to just being with Yolanda.

"Will you tell me, please, why . . ." she would begin, and he'd find himself having to view a perfectly ordinary situation from a point of view he'd never considered. They talked incessantly. They discussed newspaper articles, political dogma, hairstyles, the weather. They argued frenziedly, and to his amused chagrin, Alex found himself winning only part of the time.

On Wednesday night she insisted on teaching him and Tracey the finer points of making cottage cheese.

"But I don't even like cottage cheese," he objected.

"You must learn to like it, of course," Yolanda stated firmly. "Otherwise what will we do with all this milk?"

Alex very nearly suggested getting rid of the goat. He still had visions of the damned animal's hoofmarks on the roof of his car. Instead he ladled warm curds into cheesecloth and tried not to gag at the smell. He wondered if there were three people who laughed as much.

Until bedtime came, she was a friend. Until they climbed the stairs to his room, and then the true magic between him and Yolanda began.

There he discovered the other Yolanda, the woman he'd labeled "Gypsy." She was amazingly sensual, naturally so, despite her inexperience. He would love her to exhaustion, leaving both of them boneless and sated. And then she would wriggle against him with mock innocence and the satin of her skin, the wildflower scent of her body mixed with the musk of their love, would ignite him, and desire raged until once again he felt her sheathing him, felt the dainty rippling of her innermost pleasure beginning. It drove him to white-hot frenzy and to depths of release and delight he'd never before experienced.

Once in a while he caught himself comparing the tempestuous abandon of their lovemaking with the quiet occasional sex he'd had with Dixie.

When that happened, he felt angry with himself, disloyal. Dixie had never actually refused him, but he'd sensed quite early in their marriage that she didn't share his deeply passionate nature. Oh, she'd always been welcoming and warm. He'd loved her, and because of that, he'd been faithful to her, even though at times he'd been sorely tempted.

He'd grown more and more aware of subtle signals other women gave him during those years, messages that hinted they would be happy to take on the burden of his virility.

He'd turned to sports, soccer, handball, jogging—exhausting physical ways to control an appetite Dixie didn't share.

It was the opposite with Yolanda. He was intrigued with the contrast between her composed, cheerful daytime self and the moaning wanton she became when they made love. Intrigued, and disturbed. She was like a drug to which he was becoming more and more seriously addicted.

There had been women after Dixie's death, far too many of them. He'd needed to purge a lingering insecurity in himself, a deep-seated fear that Dixie's lukewarm responses had been his fault, as a result of his clumsiness or lack of technique.... He'd been lavishly reassured on that point, at least. Repeatedly. And each of his willing partners had been a delight. But none of them had affected him like Yolanda.

His desire for her increased as each day passed. He thought of her at work, reliving details of the previous night. The need to be with her would become so compelling he'd miss portions of conversations, and Ruth had taken to repeating most things several times as well as staring at him strangely at odd moments. Once, she slipped her half-moon glasses farther down her nose and asked loudly, "Are you sure your hearing isn't deteriorating, Alex?"

She was so typically earnest about it that he'd wickedly held a hand behind his ear and bellowed, "Eh? What's that, woman?"

Ruth had snorted, then marched out of the office.

He would leave early in the afternoon, race his sporty car over the hills and along the winding shore road to Rockwoods like a boy let out of school.

That hot week in August, Rockwoods was sunshine, cheerful voices and the smell of bread baking.

There were only two discordant notes to Yolanda's happiness.

Since their lovemaking that first night, Alex had meticulously taken care of protective measures.

"It's unlikely you'd conceive, but I'd rather not take any chances," he'd explained, his voice suddenly harsh as he added, "I'm not much good at being a father. Even though I'm almost certain it wouldn't happen, I'd rather not ever try it again."

The dim light in the bedroom hid the pain Yolanda's face reflected at his words. With Dixie, he had loved enough to adopt a child. With Yolanda, he was unwilling to accept even the remote possibility of having one.

Did he realize that he was making the decision for her, as well as for himself? She struggled with her emotions, and finally her practicality won. She must welcome what he could give and never demand more. After all, she'd known all along there was a vast chasm between the passion Alex felt for her, and the love he'd had for Dixie.

With morning, she'd put such matters determinedly to the back of her mind. She had more of Alex than she'd dared ever dream of having. She'd make it enough.

The other incident was less important, perhaps, but it hurt all the same.

From the first, she'd felt the house was stiff and unwelcoming with its careful groupings of delicate furniture and the precise arrangements of figurines and china. One evening she impulsively suggested, "Let's move that couch over to here, and fill the vases with wildflowers and sweet peas instead of those plastic roses, and take down all the curtains."

She was already planning further changes when she realized Alex wasn't answering. He was standing stiffly, his face half turned away. She caught a glimpse of his expression, and her heart plummeted.

Unthinkingly, she'd made a dreadful mistake. He looked decidedly unhappy, ill at ease, and his gaze went slowly from one area of the room to another, as if he were seeing more than what was there.

His amber-flecked eyes were apologetic and sad. "Let's just leave the room as it is for now, Landa."

Dixie's ghost had won again.

Yolanda did her best to hide her dismay, throwing herself into preparations for the picnic on Friday. But she fretted over the scene, nervously wondering if she would blunder socially, as she'd managed to do privately with Alex.

It was only a party, she reminded herself sternly on Friday afternoon, the same sort of happy get-together that the

villagers planned in Votice after the annual day of mushroom picking. The guests here were mostly family. Still, her
palms felt clammy. She couldn't stop imagining she might
make a fool of herself somehow. Ruth Prentiss had sounded
frighteningly sophisticated when Yolanda had impulsively
phoned and invited her.

Promptly on time, with Victor, his tall grandson, beside
him, Ian Cameron was first to arrive, wrestling his old Jeep
down the driveway.

Tracey quite suddenly became as shy as Yolanda felt, and
she scampered into the house, mumbling about putting
Coke in the fridge.

"C'mon, Gypsy. This was all your idea, remember?"
Alex squeezed Yolanda's hand reassuringly, and his teasing
made her smile. All at once, everything was all right again.

Robert arrived, bumping up in his blue truck, giving Yolanda a warm hug and a fond kiss even before he greeted his
son.

"That's a hell of a garden you're growing, Alex," he
commented, giving in to the urge to tease his son again
about the newspaper column he'd found so hilariously
funny. "Have you had the minister of Food and Agricul-
ture over here to see it? Seems to me this could go a long way
toward solving world famine. Can you drag yourself away
from farming in a couple of weeks to come fishing with
Barney and me, or will we have to take the goat along?"

"Lay off, Dad," Alex warned. He jerked a thumb at Ian,
who did his best to look innocent. "This is the old repro-
bate who's responsible for that damned garden, and for the
chickens, as well. I couldn't even guess what he used for
fertilizer, but I've never had to eat so many fresh vegetables
in my life."

Or endure as many bad jokes. But he could see the humor in the whole thing now, because the garden had gotten

totally out of control, lavishly presenting new tomatoes, zucchini, onions and peas at a rate even Yolanda had trouble dealing with.

Barney and Sophia drove in just then, and right behind them, a bright red motorcycle roared up. Alex's mouth actually dropped open when Ruth Prentiss, smartly dressed in a gray cotton jumpsuit, casually dismounted and removed a shiny red helmet.

From that unlikely moment on, the picnic acquired a personality all its own.

"Ms Prentiss, can we have a look at your bike?" Victor, with a no longer shy Tracey in tow, was eyeing Ruth's machine with religious fervor. "How many cc's? What's the gvw?"

In another few minutes Ruth was demonstrating the gears and braking system and showing them how to start and stop in the driveway. Robert, beer in hand, wandered over to watch, and soon even he was taking short trips up the driveway with a gleeful grin on his face.

Barney asked Yolanda for a tour of the garden and an introduction to the animals, and of course Cinnamon neatly escaped the moment her pen was opened. Ian gave chase, swearing colorfully at the capering goat as it eluded him, and everyone laughed, making outlandish suggestions. Alex brought Sophia a glass of white wine and sank down beside her in a lawn chair, taking a deep swig of his second beer. This was easily the most unusual gathering he'd ever hosted, all right. He was beginning to resign himself to the fact that whatever Yolanda involved him in always ended up just a little out of control.

Sophia prattled on for several minutes and then abruptly said, "Alex, I know men never notice these things, but Yolanda needs a new wardrobe. I tried to buy her several things one day when we were shopping, but she's very proud and independent. She absolutely refused. She insisted on buying herself that very outfit she's wearing. And Tracey told me that when Yolanda lost so much weight and nothing fit her, Tracey gave her some things of hers.'' Sophia frowned. "I know she didn't have much money of her own. If there's some way we could—'' Her voice trailed off uncertainly.

Alex's eyes immediately found Yolanda, slender and girlish looking in her jeans and pink T-shirt, and he suddenly remembered how often she'd worn that exact outfit over the past week.

He cursed himself silently for being a heedless fool and felt ashamed of his insensitivity. Why hadn't he noticed how few clothes she had? Probably because she looked delectable to him in anything she wore. Probably because all he thought of lately was getting whatever she wore off her as quickly as possible.

"I'm glad you mentioned it, Sophia,'' he said evenly, sipping his beer and watching Yolanda, who was laughing now at something Barney was saying. "Don't concern yourself any longer. I'll take care of it." He was furious with himself for not being more observant, but he also felt irritated with Yolanda. He'd made very sure she always had money, but he'd never dream of asking her what she did with it. Why hadn't she been using it for necessities like clothing?

"I didn't think I'd ever have to encourage a woman to buy clothes,'' he joked weakly. "Dixie filled so many closets with things she never wore that I could hardly find room for my suits.''

Sophia put a gentle beringed hand on his arm, and her voice had a serious note despite its bantering tone.

"You mustn't make the mistake of thinking that just because we're female, we women are at all alike, dear, or the slightest bit predictable. For instance, I noticed the expression on your face when Ruth Prentiss arrived on that motorbike. She surprised you, didn't she?''

Horrified would be a better word, he thought, nodding wryly at his aunt. "I just hope Tracey doesn't get any ideas in her head about learning to ride one," he commented.

Sophia gave him a penetrating look and said spiritedly, "I hope she does. Then she could teach me how, as well."

Alex was greatly relieved to have Barney arrive at that moment and demand a refill for his empty glass of Scotch. There had been an undercurrent to his aunt's words that Alex found vaguely disquieting.

"ALEX, IT WAS a very big success, this picnic of ours, wasn't it?"

It was late, almost morning. They were alone in his room under the eaves, wrapped together in a relaxed lover's knot of entwined arms and legs.

"Yeah, it was. It turned out to be the longest picnic I've ever been at," he teased. "For a while there, I thought they were going to stay all night. And I wanted to be here instead, doing this with you."

He stroked a finger down the line of her back, marveling again at how completely she gave herself to him, innocently and honestly taking the physical satisfaction he delighted in bringing her. He'd controlled himself, using his expertise, holding back his own ecstasy just to watch her desire grow, the delight blossom in her exotic eyes, and burst, as it had moments before, scant seconds before his own.

"Alex? I like your Ruth Prentiss. She has invited me for lunch one day next week. And you know, I think your father liked her also." The smug pleasure in her voice amused him, and he laughed.

"Matchmaker. That woman on the motorcycle tonight sure as hell wasn't 'my' Ruth Prentiss. The Ruth Prentiss I know wears dark suits and intimidates strong men on the phone, and yet I could swear she was flirting with Dad. A motorcycle, for God's sake. Now I suppose Tracey's going to want one."

"If she does, is it so terrible, Alex?" The gentle tones reminded him of the conversation with Sophia, and he frowned as Yolanda went on, "Victor wants a motorcycle, of that I'm certain. I heard him telling his grandfather."

The mention of Vic made Alex suddenly uneasy. Meeting the kid had been a shock. Victor was taller, more muscular, more—everything—than Alex had expected. He looked like a man, an extremely handsome man, at that. He probably already shaved. And Tracey was with him practically every day. He remembered, uneasily, his recent memories of sixteen-year-old males.

He drew his arm from under Yolanda's head and rearranged the tumbled pillows restlessly.

"I don't think it's good for him and Tracey to see so much of each other," he blurted, folding his arms under his head and frowning up at the ceiling.

"They are friends, Alex. Ian has also become Tracey's friend. It's hard for you to accept, but Tracey is growing up. I believe she needs this contact with other people."

As she spoke, Yolanda realized vaguely that she, too, needed contact with other people. She'd been living a rather insular existence. It was time to venture beyond Rockwoods, make new friends beyond the family.

"Maybe you should have a talk with Tracey about Vic. Explain things to her," Alex suggested vaguely.

On the edge of sleep, Yolanda felt a tiny pang of apprehension. Alex was placing the responsibility for Tracey's sex education squarely on her.

It was confusing. Alex chatted easily with his daughter about everyday matters. He teased her and listened to her.

But they spoke only about superficial things. When a serious issue arose, an emotional problem, Yolanda found she, instead of Alex, ended up talking to Tracey.

The issue was forgotten as Alex drew the blanket over them, snuggled her into his arms and yawned sleepily.

"Night, beautiful Gypsy. We have to get up and go shopping tomorrow, so go to sleep now."

"Shopping for what, Alex?"

But he pretended to snore rudely, and soon they both slept.

"DON'T MEN IN CZECHOSLOVAKIA buy clothes for their wives?"

Yolanda stood in the expensive boutique, her chin thrust out belligerently, arms folded across her chest. Alex was a bare few feet away, as furiously angry as she'd ever seen him, looking totally out of place and ridiculously masculine in this unlikely setting.

Why hadn't he told her his intentions before they left the house, she thought, so they could have had this quarrel there instead of in this carpeted, perfumed, frightening salon, while the sleek salesperson in her black suit and pearls avidly listened as she pretended politely to arrange a display of lingerie?

"Of course." She shot daggers at him through slitted eyes. "Of course they do. But I am not those women, and I don't want you buying me clothing." It was impossible to explain why, because even she didn't fully understand. It had to do with independence and freedom.

From the first, she'd worried about being a financial burden to him. It mattered not at all that he was obviously wealthy, and ridiculously generous. From the day she'd moved into Rockwoods, she'd kept careful account of all the money he'd given her. He refused to even glance at the neat figures, laughing and teasing her for her thrifty ways.

What mattered desperately was that she maintain at all costs that elusive freedom she'd come here to find. In order to do that, she had to feel she was paying her own way.

So far, she had. By taking over Tracey's care for the summer, she'd spared Alex both worry and expense. The garden and the animals...well, they'd served other purposes besides economics. But what Alex was insisting on now seriously threatened her independence.

He was glaring at her ferociously. Alex Caine was not an easy man to fight with, but she'd had training. She'd learned plenty from *babička*. She squared her shoulders.

Alex scowled. The woman was driving him insane. He felt like a perfect fool, but this time, he refused to let her win. He narrowed his eyes, and revealed his strategy.

"Yolanda, you are my wife. Correct?"

She nodded unwillingly. It wasn't a fair question. He knew as well as she did the status of their peculiar marriage. "That is correct, yes."

"As my wife, you'll be meeting people I know...going out to lunch with Ruth. There are social occasions we'll have to attend." He was getting better as he went along, improvising. He'd make a politician yet, by God.

She listened, expressionless.

"Yolanda, as my wife, you have a certain responsibility to dress well. People will notice what you wear. Your appearance will reflect back on me."

Her deep-set eyes with their long lashes looked a little uncertain now. Good. He was getting somewhere.

"It's important that we maintain a certain standard." If Barney or his father ever heard that pompous statement, they'd choke to death laughing. But Yolanda was nodding slowly. He was winning. Elation swept over him—too soon, however. He should have guessed it wouldn't be quite so easy.

"I understand, Alex. I agree. You must not be made ashamed of me." It touched him strangely that she would even think he'd be ashamed of such beauty. But he hid his reaction, because he needed to win.

"Whatever you spend today is a loan, which I will repay."

He swore in frustration, and the saleslady who'd been listening raised her plucked brows and sniffed. He would do her serious injury if she didn't move the hell away and stop eavesdropping. He gave her one patently furious look, and she finally scuttled off.

"There's no need..." he snapped, but Yolanda's certain tone cut him off.

"Not for you, Alex. But for me, there is need, yes." There was almost panic in her voice, and he was lying in his teeth when he said testily, "Okay, okay, so we'll consider it a loan."

After that, bags and boxes accumulated swiftly. The older clerk whom he'd insulted, huffily refused to wait on them, which was great, because they were helped by a cheery young salesgirl who had an artist's eye for what best suited Yolanda. She carried armloads of whispery finery into the dressing room, and Alex, seated on a ridiculously spindly chair, considered gravely, then nodded or shook his head as Yolanda shyly appeared in one outfit after the other. He was surprised and touched by her absolute trust in his judgment—not once did she protest or argue about his decision. In Alex's experience, that, too, was a first.

She was dazed by the array. She searched furtively for price tags, but there weren't any visible, and when she asked, she got a wink in response.

"The way you look in these, Mrs. Caine, they're a bargain at twice the price." Alex had given the staff strict instructions.

On each giddy trip out of the cubicle, Yolanda repeated, "Alex, this is enough—surely I don't need so many...?"

He nodded at the clerk. The simple scarlet silk dress with the outrageously exaggerated shoulders was added to the pile on the counter.

"I can only handle one shot at this shopping thing, Yolanda," he warned gruffly. "Once a year it is, so go try on those slacks and the jacket, and stop bitching."

His crooked grin took the sting out of his words, because she wasn't complaining, really. She was starting to actually enjoy the experience. What sane woman could resist trying on these soft rainbow-colored silks, the glovelike leather strappy shoes to match, the jewel-toned blouses and sweaters and skirts?

But how much would it all cost?

She shuddered and slid into butter-soft vivid blue suede pants, a wildly patterned crepe shirt, a matching suede jacket with wide lapels and dramatic blousing narrowing in at her slender hipline.

Alex's nod was emphatic.

A deceptively simple emerald green jersey dress that skimmed her body provocatively was modeled next. It was slit high on her thigh, but the neckline was demure, dipped just enough to hold a necklace in the hollow of her throat. The sleeves were full at the top, narrowing into tiny buttoned cuffs. Yolanda's eyes sparkled when she buckled the ridiculously high-heeled sandals the sales girl proffered to complement the dress.

This time Alex's eyes held banked fires when he nodded his approval.

Finally they were done. Yolanda wearily tugged on the serviceable blue skirt and plain blouse she'd worn into the salon, unconsciously comparing their quality with the clothing she'd just tried on. The new garments would undoubtedly cost a fortune. Her fingers trembled, and she shook her head at such extravagance. Well, she would have to find a way to pay him back.

Alex hastily scribbled an astronomical amount on a check, and the clerk hid it away in the cash register's drawer.

When Yolanda emerged, he casually accepted a handwritten bill for a ridiculously lower figure from the bemused clerk. Yolanda held out a hand, and he gave it to her reluctantly.

She was almost afraid to look, but when she did, it wasn't as bad as she'd expected. She sighed deeply, and the impressive stack of boxes and bags and padded hangers with garment bags took several trips to carry to the car.

Fifteen minutes later Alex made two approaches before he found the courage to enter a women's lingerie shop while Yolanda was in the supermarket buying groceries, and he came out with still another embossed bag, with cold sweat on his forehead and shaking hands.

He'd come close to running out of the store. He'd been the only male in the place. And those confusing stacks—bikinis, hipsters, full cut, French cut—he slumped deep into the leather seat of the car and closed his eyes. He'd give anything for a drink, or several drinks.

But any strain he'd felt was worth it to see Yolanda in those clothes, watch her eyes glow. And her body. He swallowed hard, remembering how she'd looked as she anxiously turned before the mirror, clad in soft, floating things, her slender, voluptuous form graceful and seductively curved beneath the clothing.

Sexual urgency flared so powerfully he clenched his teeth.

Savagely he reminded himself that she was his and that they were going home. Tracey was in Vancouver for the weekend, on a reluctant but long overdue visit with her grandparents.

"You are my wife," he'd reminded Yolanda earlier, although the words had made his gut clench in protest.

Why couldn't he allow himself the emotional luxury of loving her? He was obsessed by their lovemaking, and he enjoyed being with her more all the time. Yet whenever he projected the relationship over a span of years, thought of himself as a permanently married man again, a cold dread crept over him.

He'd admitted long before that he hadn't been able to make Dixie happy during the long years of their marriage. Those painful memories were still strong; the impotent sensations of failing someone he loved, of feeling responsible for her happiness and guilty for being unable to provide her with what she needed.

He grimaced and his hands curled around the steering wheel until the knuckles were white.

He wanted Yolanda, but he'd rather not be married to her. He'd rather not be married to anyone. Ever.

"You are, though, Caine," he muttered bitterly. "You sure as hell are. You're about as married as any man can get."

CHAPTER ELEVEN

THE FOLLOWING TUESDAY Ruth phoned Yolanda and confirmed the tentative luncheon she'd suggested at the picnic.

"Is there anywhere special you'd like to go? I usually just bring a brown bag, so I'm not too familiar with restaurants," Ruth explained.

"I know only two, and one is McDonald's. The other was called Chez Armand, and I liked them both."

"I think we'll choose Chez Armand," Ruth said dryly.

Yolanda was excited the next morning, and also a little nervous.

"Come, please, and help me decide what is best to wear to a luncheon," Yolanda asked Tracey as soon as Alex had driven away.

Tracey had seen and approved of Yolanda's new wardrobe as soon as she'd returned from her Vancouver visit. Everything, that is, but the contents of the bag Alex had abruptly produced at bedtime that evening.

"This is for me, Gypsy," he'd warned aggressively. "Before you blow a fuse and get all independent and huffy on me, you get to wear it, but just remember I bought it for myself."

Mystified, she'd emptied the bag's contents on the dark blue bedspread, and then stood, spellbound, afraid to touch the magical wisps of satin and lace lest they disappear.

There were silk bikini panties, so scant she blushed to imagine how little they'd cover. Each dainty pair had a matching bra, gossamer sheer. The sets were ivory, burgundy, palest powder blue and warm peach. What puzzled Yolanda when she dared examine them closely was that the sizes were exactly right.

"But Alex, how did you guess the size?" Alex was watching her intently, his green eyes narrowed as he waited for her response. Fleetingly she thought he seemed almost nervous, but that was so unlike him she'd dismissed it.

"It wasn't a guess. I wrote down the numbers on one of your sets this morning."

The mental picture of him, laboriously copying the confusing numbers from her underwear, made her give a wicked little giggle. By then she was examining the rest of the lingerie, holding them up, pressing her face into their fragile softness. There were three lavishly lace-trimmed one-piece garments called "teddies," in palest apricot, pristine white and wicked black. They were all more lace than fabric.

Lastly, there were four tissue-wrapped diaphanous thigh-length silk nightshirts, indigo blue, dusky rose, peach and pale vanilla.

"I, um, I like the nightgowns you wear. These were the closest they had." He really did sound uncertain this time. Yolanda looked at him closely. His expression was unreadable, but a tiny nerve ticked beside his eye. It slowly dawned on her that he was actually afraid she wouldn't like what he'd chosen.

Instead of saying anything, she did something she'd never dreamed she'd be wanton enough to do. She stood slowly, and with his narrowed eyes tracing her every movement, she gracefully removed every stitch of her clothing. Deliberately then, one by one, smiling provocatively as she did so, she tried on every single garment he'd bought her, slipping them on and off with loving care, her nakedness even more apparent when covered by the garments. She turned her body this way and that, growing more heated with every movement because of his heavy-lidded gaze.

"You see, Alex? They are a perfect fit."

He didn't move. He stood with one leg propped on a chair, his buttocks resting against the low oak dresser across the room from the bed. But she was all too aware of her effect on him, of the heated flush rising in his cheeks, the increased tempo of his breathing.

He let her finish, let her draw last of all, the rich blue silk nightshirt over her nudity, her tumbled dark hair falling loose down her back in disarray. The lamplight behind her outlined her body, her proudly peaked breasts, nipples hardened in awareness, the inward curve of her waist, the womanly flaring of her hips and the long, beautifully shaped legs below the hem.

"You like these, Alex? You will allow me to wear them for you?"

In two strides, he was holding her against him, making her feel his hardness.

"Witch," he breathed. "Teasing witch. Feel what you've done."

She put her fingers gently on his lips before he could kiss her, holding him away so she could tell him with words what she guessed he needed to hear. "Alex," she said softly, "never have I had things so beautiful as these. I know they are your gift for me. I love them, Alex, and I don't know how to thank you."

He'd shuddered, drawing a long, shaky breath before he'd claimed her lips in a burning kiss and tumbled them both back onto the bed. "I can think of several ways, Gypsy," he'd murmured. "Now pay attention while I show you."

The images of that night were strong in Yolanda's mind as she and Tracey climbed the winding stairs to the bedroom she shared with Alex.

"Tell me why you thought I would not like your gifts," she'd asked him hesitantly that night, lying clasped in his arms so tight she could feel his every heartbeat. He'd sighed, a long, shuddering sigh, but he hadn't answered, and she'd been more and more aware that though he clung to her physically, he still kept her at arm's length emotionally.

The morning's brightness poured in through the triangular windows as they entered Alex's bedroom—her bedroom, too, now, she reminded herself stoutly. Why did she always feel so—temporary—here, in Alex's private space?

"Yolanda, do you like being married?"

Her reverie was interrupted by Tracey, and Yolanda recognized immediately the carefree tone the girl used. It usually accompanied questions or comments that were anything but casual.

Tracey had plopped herself down on the neatly made bed, her gray eyes wide and innocent, emphasized by the street-urchin hair.

"I like so much being married to your father, yes, Tracey." Yolanda moved to straighten the books on the long bookshelf, waiting for the rest of the girl's questions. Something warned her this wasn't going to be easy.

"Lots of the girls at school said they weren't ever going to get married, just have affairs and stuff like that."

Yolanda kept her voice neutral.

"How about you, what do you think about it?"

Tracey's shrug was nonchalant.

"Things are different than they were in the olden days, when you were my age. Women are free to have affairs if they decide to." She rubbed her palms back and forth across the furry spread, her head down, and there was only a slight catch in her voice when she added, "That's probably what I'll do, I guess." This time a nervous gulp accompanied her words. "Most of the girls at school that I hung around with had already slept with guys. They didn't think it was any big deal." Her next comment was hurried. "None of those guys were half as neat as Vic is, either."

The smile that had threatened at the term "olden days" faded quickly, but Yolanda went on methodically removing books and replacing them in almost the same order. Her hands were steady, but her thoughts were in turmoil.

Alex, what do I say to her? What do I tell your daughter?

"Do you want to..." She hastily borrowed Tracey's own phrase. "Are you thinking of having this, this—affair—with Victor Martinos?"

Tracey kept her head bent low, so only the auburn sheen of her spiky hair was visible. Her voice was forlorn.

"I do...don't know, for sure. I mean, sometimes I think so, but it...it's kinda scary, you know?"

Yolanda nodded, giving up on the books and sinking down on the bed herself, imitating Tracey's cross-legged pose. She made a quick decision, and she could only hope it was the right thing to do for Tracey. The girl was mature enough to understand, Yolanda was sure of that.

"I do know. This is not a new thing, Tracey, whatever or not you believe. It is a decision all women come to in their lives. I was several years older than you when I myself decided to have an 'affair.'" Yolanda shook her head ruefully. "I don't know for you, but for me, I assure you it was a big mistake."

Tracey's head snapped up, her startled gaze fully on Yolanda.

"You had sex...you slept with...how old were you?"

"I was seventeen, but this is not just a matter of age, Tracey. For women, it might sometimes be right at fifteen." Privately Yolanda doubted her own words, but she felt she was walking on eggshells. "Or, I suspect, it could be wrong at twenty-one."

Tracey's voice was querulous. "I don't see what makes the difference."

"It has to do with how you feel, not how many years you have lived." Yolanda was finding this discussion harder and harder as she went along. "With me, I was curious, impatient, eager for what I felt was adulthood. I wanted to know. It had little to do with the man, and everything to do with myself and my impatient nature." She added slowly, "I think for lovemaking to be good, or right, it has to have everything to do with the other person."

"You mean you have to love him?" Tracey sounded skeptical. "All this junk about love. How does anybody ever know if they're in love or not?"

"If you have no doubts, and what you're doing feels not only right, but inevitable, and you care more about the other person than about yourself, then I would say that is love."

Sweat was beginning to trickle under Yolanda's arms. This conversation was the worst yet, harder even than the morning she'd explained to Tracey about her and Alex sharing this room.

"Is that how you feel about my father? Are you in love with him?"

Yolanda felt her tension ease. This, at least, was easier, and she could smile confidently. "Yes," she said positively. "I do love your father, Tracey."

"Why didn't you . . . what happened to that other guy?"

It took Yolanda a moment to catch on.

"Who . . . oh, Antonin." She was silent a moment, remembering. "He went to the army, and I went on to school. He was glad to leave, I think, and I was glad to see him go. We had become a burden to each other. It happens like that if it's not right, and instead of being friends, you finish never wanting to see each other again." A new thought struck her, and she said awkwardly, "Tracey, this school you went to, they taught you about the body?"

"You mean like ovaries and stuff? Yeah, we had life class, it taught us about venereal disease and—and birth control."

Should she take this any further? Yolanda studied the flushed young face now turning to stare out the window. It was unfair to stop halfway.

"Tracey, if you decide to have this affair, do you have a medical person for birth control?"

The girl shook her head. "Only old Doctor Hanes, and I'd die before I'd go to him. He knew my mother and everything. There's a clinic downtown, but it's kind of scary to go alone." Obviously, Tracey had given the matter a great deal of consideration already.

"Think it over, and if you want, we will go together."

Suddenly the impact of what she was doing fell heavily on Yolanda.

"Perhaps you should talk with your father about this?"

Absolute, unmitigated horror registered on the girl's features.

"I can't, oh, Landa, don't make me, don't tell him. He'd never understand. He'd... you're not going to... he thinks I'm still a baby."

Her distress was so acute that Yolanda put an arm around her and soothed, "No, no, you and I are friends and this is a confidence. Only he is your father, and—"

"I can't talk to him about stuff like this."

Yolanda felt torn between her loyalty to Tracey and her responsibility to Alex. Reluctantly, knowing Tracey would never confide in her again if she violated her trust, Yolanda promised.

Then, enough was enough. Bounding from the bed, Yolanda threw open the closet door. "Now, please, important decisions. What do I wear for this luncheon? I now have so many choices, I don't know where to begin."

"YOU LOOK ABSOLUTELY ELEGANT," Ruth said when she greeted her an hour later, and together they walked the short distance to the little restaurant.

Armand Mollins was again very much in evidence, and he welcomed Yolanda like a compatriot, embarrassing her a little as he rattled on in French, interspersing it with English to explain to Ruth that Madame Caine and he were old acquaintances. He escorted them to a choice table by a window.

Ruth waited until Armand was gone, then raised a well-groomed eyebrow at Yolanda before demanding, "Where did you learn to speak such excellent French? And how did you meet that charming man?" An impish look came over her usually stern features. "I do hope Alex is suitably jealous."

For the next half hour Yolanda found herself volunteering a capsule account of her background, with the exclusion of any details about her marriage, and then she concluded, "So, then I married and came to Canada. Enough about me. Ruth Prentiss, it's your turn for biography now."

Ruth looked distinctly different today than she had at the picnic. She wore a no-nonsense brown striped shirtdress, and her soft brown hair was drawn tightly back in a bun instead of becomingly loose the way it had been the other evening. But her regular features and large brown eyes were quietly attractive, and she nodded agreeably at Yolanda's suggestion.

"Fair enough. My life story is singularly dull, however, compared to yours, Yolanda. I was born and raised here in Victoria. I attended school and business college here as well." She sipped her wine from the long-stemmed glass, staring down at her ringless fingers.

"I didn't marry. I'm forty-seven years old, and I've always lived at home. When my father died seven years ago, my mother became bedridden. I cared for her until she died last October." She sipped her wine again, grimaced at Yolanda and said, "There, see? Just as I said, dull, dull, dull." There was a sadness in the lines of her face as she set down her glass, and the two were quiet while Armand served them small pannikins of golden quiche.

"You've left the interesting parts out," Yolanda accused. "How did you come to buy that machine that Tracey talks of constantly?"

Ruth looked a tiny bit sheepish, and a lovely soft pink shaded her cheeks.

"I woke up one morning feeling that my life had gone by, and I'd never really done anything exciting. I saw an ad in the morning paper for a course in motorcycle training, and I registered." Something came and went in her eyes. "I passed the course, marched out and bought the bike. It's become a passion, I'm afraid."

She raised her wineglass rebelliously. "Here's to passion," she toasted throatily, and they both laughed.

Yolanda drank the toast, enjoying the cheery atmosphere and quiet sense of relaxation in the restaurant. At the other tables were well-dressed groups, eating and talking and laughing together. Yolanda found herself wondering idly who the other women in the restaurant were and what they did to allow them time to idle away the afternoon so pleasantly.

Like a dream that suddenly takes on the aspects of a nightmare, she abruptly saw herself in this setting. She looked like a Canadian here, laughing, talking, drinking wine. She wore expensive, smart clothing. She had time to sit and wile away an afternoon. She had money in her purse, thanks to Alex. Was this why she'd left her homeland, to lead this type of life? Where had her sense of purpose gone? Ruth had a career; she'd earned everything she had.

And herself? She'd become decadent, lavish, useless, her Czechoslovak roots accused, and in the space of a heartbeat, her stomach clenched in the by now familiar agony of homesickness. She would never belong in this country, never feel at peace with her past and her present lives. Fighting nausea, she stared at Ruth. Ruth belonged. She was born here.

Would Yolanda ever belong anywhere again? Slowly she fought the sickness. Slowly she became aware once more of what Ruth was saying about her motorcycle.

"I've met new people because of riding it, and I must admit they're people I'd never have spoken to before. It's made changes in my life," she said thoughtfully. "Good changes, but difficult for me. Half of me keeps wanting to stay in the same old groove, while the other half is out there making things happen." She shrugged. "Sometimes I think that's what life means us to do, change every so often. Look at the changes you've gone through, Yolanda." She flashed a warm smile. "It helps to know other women go through the same sort of thing."

It was eerie, almost as if Ruth were somehow aware of how Yolanda had been feeling for the past few moments and was reassuring her. Their situations, their ages, their backgrounds were vastly different, but underneath, the emotions were probably identical.

Was there a universal pattern among women, a set of experiences besides the usual one of childbirth, which formed a bond despite nationality or culture? Ruth must have been reaching the same conclusion as Yolanda, because she lifted her wineglass again.

"To us," she said. "To women everywhere."

The luncheon was a great success. The tentative warmth the two women sensed between them at the picnic had blossomed today into friendship. They talked and laughed and enjoyed themselves immensely.

"Ruth," Yolanda said hesitantly when the other woman reluctantly rose to leave, "do you mind telling Alex I will meet him at his office later and ride home with him? I think I will stay in town for a few hours."

She would do some exploring. Seeing Armand again had reminded her that she'd never visited his sister's boutique as she'd promised. She'd go there right after her next stop. She pulled out an address she'd scribbled from the phone directory just before she left Rockwoods, the result of the disquieting conversation with Tracey.

Tracey's questions that morning had reminded her uncomfortably that she had allowed Alex to take all the birth control precautions, and that it was unfair of her not to share the responsibility.

She was nervous as she entered the modern building with the Planned Parenthood sign on its window, but forty minutes later, she felt reassured and comforted as she left the clinic. Doctor Mary Carlisle had been caring and easy to talk with, as well as thorough. She'd examined Yolanda and ordered tests done at the downstairs lab, but it was closed when Yolanda tried the door. A sign announced Back in Fifteen.

Should she wait? After fifteen minutes, and with no sign of the returning technician, Yolanda decided to come back another day. After all, the tests were routine, and Dr. Carlisle had given her detailed instructions on a product to use until she could begin birth control pills. And there was another, much more appealing visit she wanted to make this afternoon.

She visited the neighboring pharmacy, purchased exactly what the doctor had recommended, tucked the package into her purse and fished out the cheery yellow Foofera card. She asked the friendly clerk for directions, and the man pointed out the proper bus stop, just down the street.

As Armand had indicated, the address was on the waterfront, in an old part of Victoria where brick warehouses had been converted to trendy shops. Foofera was halfway down a block, its bold yellow sign highly visible among the more subdued stores surrounding it. Yolanda hesitated before going in, admiring the clever and eye-catchingly simple window display.

When she opened the door, she was aware of several customers waiting patiently for service at an oak desk that served as a counter. Classical music was playing softly, but the most prevalent sound was that of a small baby crying frantically. The wriggling blanket-wrapped bundle was clamped incongruously in the left arm of a reed-slender, dark-haired woman with a harried expression, obviously the owner.

"I know, *madame*, I promised the hem would be done. But my assistant, who does these things, is ill, and I myself, well..." she brandished the screaming baby helplessly. "As you can see, right now it is impossible. The baby is hungry, and there is nothing for it, I must feed her."

With that, she sat down in a backless rocking chair, calmly undid her stylish purple smock top and began to nurse. The baby made frantic snorting noises and choked several times, waving tiny flower fists in the air as if she were drowning before she finally calmed. The nursing mother, looking like a high-fashion model posing for a motherhood ad, caught Yolanda's amazed stare and gave a typically Gallic shrug, rolling her eyes dramatically.

She rocked gently, stroking her snuffling baby's cheek with one long, well-manicured finger, an expression of resigned acceptance on her face. Yolanda wanted to giggle; it was all so outrageous.

This woman was undoubtedly Armand's sister, for his classically handsome features were more marked on her face in a way that might have been unfortunate but instead was arrestingly attractive. Her black hair was curly, cut boyishly short to accentuate a well-shaped head.

"Excuse me, Mme. Dominique..." Impulsively, Yolanda introduced herself, using rapid French for privacy and quickly explaining that she'd met Armand and come at his suggestion. Hesitantly she asked if she could help in any way.

"I can't feed the baby, but I do know how to sew," she added. Dominique unleashed a torrent of dramatic, grateful French. An angry wail followed from the baby, who'd lost her place while her mother gestured expressively.

Forty minutes later the baby was tucked back in a wicker bassinet, sprawled sound asleep on her full stomach, contentedly giving an occasional wet burp, and Yolanda had the store under control.

Ten minutes after that, Yolanda dazedly accepted Dominique's offer of a temporary job at Foofera.

Yolanda stroked a finger over baby Lili's downy cheek, made arrangements for hours and wages and hurried to catch the bus to the Parliament Buildings and Alex.

Yolanda felt dazed and frightened and exuberant, all at once. She had a job, her first real job in Canada. And she'd found it all on her own.

Alex wasn't as excited as Yolanda when she burst into his office at five forty-five, breathless from hurrying and flushed with her news. In fact, he was surprised at how negative her announcement made him feel.

"Is this job really what you want?"

She stood just inside the office door, her high-heeled sandals planted apart, the dark, shining head with its smooth coronet tilted to the side, considering his question. Her white slacks discreetly outlined the narrow waist, the gently swelling hips, the intriguing curve of her pelvis.

"For always, no. I should like a job where I could use my training in languages. But for one month, Alex, yes, I will love this job."

He rose from behind his desk and strode over to hold her in his arms for a moment and gave her a quick kiss. He did his best to hide his reaction, reminding himself that in the beginning of their marriage the plan had been for her to find a job as quickly as she could, so that she would become independent and self-sufficient.

It was a shock to find that now he didn't want that at all. He wanted her at Rockwoods, ready to give him all of her attention. He wanted her all to himself, and the discovery made him uncomfortable. What kind of a caveman instinct was that for a modern guy to have?

"Tell me more about this Dominique and the madhouse she operates," he said lightly, grabbing his suit jacket and hooking it on a finger. He led her out of the building with his palm resting on the small of her back.

She did, her husky voice full of animation, her blue eyes deepening as she described her unorthodox employer. Involved in her story, she was unaware of the male heads that discreetly turned to follow her progress down the wide marble stairs, the carpeted hallways. Alex noticed, however, and slid a proprietory arm around her waist. They were in the car when he pulled a gold-engraved invitation from the pocket of his shirt and handed it to her.

"We're invited to the fall garden party at Government House," he explained. "Next Sunday."

She read the ornate printing and demanded, wide-eyed, "This is a big deal, Alex?" She drew the words out dramatically.

He laughed, recognizing one of Tracey's expressions. Several ornate teenisms had creeped into Yolanda's vocabulary, amusing him.

"Yup, you could certainly say that. Everybody gets shaved and showered and suited to stand around making polite noises with a glass of sherry in hand, and it can be boring as hell." She turned toward him, and he saw her eyebrows lift quizzically.

"You would rather not go, Alex?"

"I haven't gone for the past several years."

Yolanda translated that statement to mean "since Dixie's death." She waited for him to continue. He wheeled the silver Porsche out of the parking lot, his arm across the back of the seat as he watched the rear window.

"Everybody watches to see who's there and who isn't. It's a big social event. It's colorful and traditional." The little car darted through the afternoon traffic like a ballet dancer, and he savored the low, powerful thrum of the motor.

"I only wish they served beer instead of sherry," he said plaintively, and Yolanda laughed. Her hand rested lightly on his thigh, and she studied him as he drove, thinking how good he looked. He'd tossed his sport jacket over the seat, and his shirt was rolled up on his forearms. His hair was carelessly rumpled over his forehead. The silver in the brown was increasing.

As the years passed, she mused, Alex would undoubtedly develop a silvery white mane, like his father had, and his leonine handsomeness would only increase, as had Robert's.

What would it be like, growing old with Alex? More to the point, did he plan on spending the years ahead with her? His projections for them were invariably short-term plans, never even extending a few months ahead, let alone years.

They were now free of the city, and his mouth twisted into a smile as he whipped the car around the curves and up the hills, driving expertly, but far too fast. He had a streak of recklessness that showed in his driving.

It also showed in his lovemaking. A tiny secret smile tilted Yolanda's lips. Alex made love to her with an intensity almost shocking, a passionate power that left her senses imprinted with his touch. Looking at him like this was enough to remind her of the previous night and make her anticipate the one to come. He was a mysterious combination of wild and gentle lover.

Then, as they turned into Rockwoods, she thought of the visit to the doctor, the package in her purse. A vivid image of Dominique's baby came into her mind's eye, and she dismissed it.

Tracey came to meet them, trailing a leash with Cinnamon bounding on its end. The goat now acted like a faithful dog.

Yolanda immediately told the girl about her lunch, and about her job. Tracey gave her an impulsive hug and the inevitable thumbs-up approval. "A boutique, eh? That's first class, Landa. Bet you'll get ten percent off whatever you buy, too."

Affection welled in Yolanda for this daughter of Alex's. Suddenly she felt sad. She had Tracey to mother, and that was a good thing. But there would be no babies for her and Alex.

IT RAINED THE REST OF THE WEEK. Sunday, however, dawned with only a light gray cloud cover, and by the time Yolanda and Alex arrived at the garden party, the sun was making teasing appearances in an almost clear August sky.

Government House was located on a slight hill just outside central Victoria, and as Alex parked and gallantly helped her out of the car, Yolanda had an overwhelming urge to head off down the hill at a run, away from the discreetly merry sounds coming from the acres of lawn surrounding the imposing stone mansion, the official residence of British Columbia's lieutenant governor.

What was a country girl from Votice doing in a place like this?

CHAPTER TWELVE

"EXPLAIN TO ME AGAIN, please, who this lieutenant governor is that I will meet, Alex?" She stopped walking and put a hand on his arm. Anything that delayed the ordeal ahead suddenly appealed to Yolanda.

"Alex? This lieutenant governor?"

He was thinking how beautiful she looked, and how he wished they'd stayed home. He didn't want to share Yolanda today. He studied her legs and answered absently, "He's the queen's representative. Canada is a member of the British Commonwealth, and we have a governor-general in the nation's capital, Ottawa, and a lieutenant governor in each of the ten provinces. The appointed official is actually a figurehead, giving token royal assent to any legislation passed in his area of responsibility."

"Have you met him before?" Yolanda was beginning to panic at what she considered her social debut among Alex's colleagues.

"Yes, several times. He's a rather stern man. I haven't met his wife. Come on, Gypsy. Let's get this over with."

Gazing at the splendor that was Government House, Yolanda wondered why she was here. Verdant lawns stretched for what seemed miles, separated by a wide semicircular driveway. Rock gardens planted with dramatic and delicate flowers bordered the lawns. Small white tables and chairs were arranged in tasteful groupings, but Yolanda could see

at a glance that the crowd was much too large to allow many
of the guests to be seated.

"Alex, this was a big mistake," she protested, but he drew
her forward. Women dressed in every shade of the rainbow
mixed with men in business suits, guards in dress uniform,
RCMP officers resplendent in their scarlet tunics, diplomats in the formal array of their respective countries. It was
a visual feast, a panoply of color and character. It was an
"event."

For Yolanda, standing frozen on the periphery, hesitating with her arm tucked into Alex's elbow, the scene was
knee-shaking, dry-mouth terrifying.

"Alex, do I look correct?" With trembling hands, she
smoothed the shimmery cinnamon-rust silk dress. Twisting
around, with Alex's amused eyes watching, she tried to casually check the sheerness of her hose for runs.

"You're lovely, relax," he whispered in her ear.

Actually, she had to admit she felt attractive today.

Yolanda said a grateful, silent thank-you to Ruth, who'd
helped her choose this dress for the occasion.

The dress was cut in a chemise-style, with the currently
fashionable emphasis on bodice and shoulders. Its dramatic color wasn't one Yolanda would have chosen, but
Ruth had insisted, and she'd been right. When Yolanda had
slipped it on, the warm cinnamon-gold with undertones of
fire played up her exotically tanned skin tones, showed off
her raven hair, contrasted with the clear blue of her eyes,
trapping shadows and mysteries in their depths so they
seemed to shimmer.

The dress was deceptively simple and wickedly sexy. It
slipped and slid over her body, enticing and revealing.

"Ruth, you are certain so much of my leg should show?"

One side had a slit that opened as she moved, revealing a
shocking amount of slender thigh.

Ruth snorted. "Fashion is knowing how much and where to uncover. Believe me, those legs should be uncovered, but discreetly. Now you see them, now you don't. Perfect."

Yolanda gave up and took her word for it.

Too much leg or not, there was no more chance for hesitation. Alex drew her smoothly along the plush red carpet laid on the lawns. It led to the receiving line where a majestic old man in tails stood beside a tiny, bejeweled woman, greeting each guest with a word and a handshake.

"This is my wife, Yolanda Caine. Yolanda, I'd like you to meet—"

The words were repeated again and again, and half her mind listened and registered names. The other half was mesmerized by Alex's deep voice announcing her to the world as his partner. Smiling, nodding, listening, she accepted a cup of tea and nibbled at a tiny rolled sandwich.

Alex introduced clergymen, RCMP officers, judges and members of the legislative assembly with whom he worked. And their wives. Yolanda moved from one group to another, one hand captured in his, her teacup balanced carefully in the other.

She lifted an eyebrow at Alex when he accepted a tiny glass of sherry from a uniformed waiter, and he gave her a comically pained look just as a male voice demanded, "Where have you been hiding this lovely creature, Alex?"

The speaker was a handsome, heavyset man in a navy suit, part of a small group of people standing somewhat apart from the crowd.

"Yolanda, this is Curtis Blackstone. Curtis is Minister of International Trade and Investment. We work together. Curtis, my wife."

Yolanda smiled politely, held out her hand, and found that Curtis was loath to relinquish it.

"I work, Mrs. Caine—may I call you Yolanda?—but I'm afraid Alex, here, simply circles the globe and calls it 'labor.' Where in the world did he find you?"

Yolanda told him, and the dancing brown eyes studied her astutely, feature by feature. "So you're new to Canada. Well, if ever you're lonely while Alex is away, you will let me know, won't you? I'd be most happy to fill in for him, and I'm sure Alex wouldn't mind, would you, old sport?"

"Yes, I would mind. Sorry, Curtis, she's off limits." Alex's straightforward answer amused Curtis immensely, but Yolanda was shocked. She thought the words had a deadly serious undertone, and she glanced at Alex in surprise. He was smiling easily, but there was a hardness in his eyes as he watched the other man's reaction.

Curtis simply threw back his large head and laughed heartily. "A pity you saw her first and married her, my friend. I assure you I'd have given you a run for your money."

Was there a trace of seriousness in the banter, or did these men always talk this way to each other? Yolanda didn't know, and there wasn't time to dwell on the question, because Curtis drew them forward to introduce a thin man, impeccably dressed in black suit and white shirt, with a plump little woman beside him.

"This is Sergio Markoff, and his wife, Vasha, from the Russian consulate. I've wanted to get you two together, Alex, because Sergio is here with a group studying reforestation, and with your background in the lumber industry..."

Sergio and Alex were soon deep in discussion. Yolanda had stiffened at the mention of the Russian consulate. Before coming to Canada, she would have reacted to meeting high-ranking Russian officials with frozen, horrified silence, followed swiftly by flight. But these people seemed so ordinary. Surely the shy, nervous little woman beside her could hardly be considered a threat of any sort. She seemed ill at ease, and Yolanda searched her brain frantically for a topic of conversation.

Chitchat eluded her. Vasha stood silently smiling, and Yolanda stood silently smiling back as the minutes lengthened.

"You must excuse Vasha, Madame Caine," Sergio apologized with a little bow, interrupting his conversation with Alex. "She is learning English, but it's slow, and she is shy about her mistakes. Our home was in a rural area, and these gatherings are a little hard for her, you understand?"

How well Yolanda understood! Under her brave facade, she felt the same as Vasha, a stranger in a foreign land.

When the men again were engrossed in a discussion about salmon fishing, Yolanda quietly addressed Vasha in what she feared was Russian grown rusty from disuse.

The effect was electrifying. Vasha's eyes filled with tears, and she grasped Yolanda's hand in both of her own. A torrent of Russian words poured from her, explaining her difficulties with the English language, the aching loneliness she felt for her homeland.

"The children, they make it easier for me; they help with my English," she confided. "You have children, Mrs. Caine?"

"A stepdaughter," Yolanda explained. "She, too, corrects my pronunciation all the time."

"Mine are the same—" Vasha laughed "—even though they were born at home, they speak much better than I."

Born at home.

Home was unquestionably Russia for Vasha, as Czechoslovakia was for Yolanda. Would it always be so?

Sergio overheard them, and he broke off his conversation excitedly again to ask Yolanda where and how she knew his language, and an animated conversation followed between Sergio and the two women.

Several other people joined the group.

A smartly uniformed military band began to play, and under the cover of the music, Curtis said quietly into Yolanda's ear, "Beautiful, and talented, as well. Alex is indeed a lucky man, my dear." Yolanda flushed with pleasure at his compliment.

When the music ended, conversation became more lively. More and more people gravitated curiously toward them, drawn by the frequent sound of laughter and the fact that many knew Curtis and Alex.

Yolanda translated quite naturally for Vasha, and soon found people asking both her and Vasha their impressions of Canada, the things about the country they found most interesting, the social difficulties for newcomers to a strange land.

Yolanda didn't notice Carrie Russell's unobtrusive arrival, or her keen attention at what was being said, for Yolanda had gradually relaxed. She was glowing with the effect of stimulating conversation, laughing readily at anecdotes Vasha and Sergio told of natural, but funny linguistic mistakes and social faux pas they'd made when they first arrived.

They prompted Yolanda to relate some of her own experiences, and she did so humorously, including the tale of the goat and the garden.

With a teasing glance at Alex, she told of Cinnamon's dance on the roof of Alex's beloved sportscar, and that story especially delighted Curtis Blackstone, who seemed to be hovering near Yolanda's elbow.

Warmth emanated from those around her. Sergio and Vasha obviously regarded her as a valuable friend, and

Vasha was blossoming shyly now that she understood everything that was being said.

Alex was involved for long minutes by an excruciatingly boring judge who wanted to discuss free trade, and when he finally escaped and glanced around for Yolanda, it was surprising how the group surrounding her had grown. His face grew somber and then wary as he caught sight of Carrie.

"What difference do you notice between women here and women in your native countries? Do you see injustices here that didn't exist back in your country?" The speaker's bleating tones were strong enough to drown out the more general conversation.

"Surely our social programs aren't half as efficient as those in the Eastern bloc," the petulant questioner continued.

Alex knew this unfortunate woman. She was the head of a local women's group and was noted for her radical and partisan views on whatever cause was current. She'd buttonholed Alex several times at social gatherings, and the last time it had happened, he'd deliberately insulted her. After that he'd tried his best to avoid her.

Alex resisted the impulse to hurry protectively to Yolanda's side. Such a move would be too obvious. Glancing at Carrie, who was taking notes, Alex cursed under his breath.

The obnoxious woman persisted. "Now, Mrs. Caine, not long ago I read in the newspaper what you had to say about food banks. Your husband is in government. Does he share your concerns about such matters?"

Alex tensed. Curtis had a wary look on his face, but there was little he could do. The woman was cleverly baiting Yolanda.

Hesitating momentarily, Yolanda finally shrugged and said casually, "Alex believes the necessity for such things is a big mistake. In such a prosperous country, there should be no need for social programs.''

He had said something to that effect, in an argument once with Yolanda. He just hadn't meant it to be quoted publicly. Disgruntled, Alex caught Carrie's eye and read the impish, eyebrow-tilted expression there.

Yolanda went on, responding to the other query as well.

''Instead of differences, I see much that is alike between women in Czechoslovakia and women here. Women all want the same things, I think. Home, family, career, and balance between all.'' The group had grown silent while she spoke, and charmingly she made an effort to lighten the serious tone the conversation had taken. ''And, of course, a goat that doesn't climb on cars.'' The laughter neatly deflected any more serious conversation.

Before Alex had a chance to move, Carrie was beside him.

''Your wife's not quite the little seamstress I was led to believe she was, Alex. More of a philosopher, wouldn't you say? How many other languages is she fluent in besides Russian?''

''English, French, German, Slovak and Czech,'' he confirmed coolly.

''But not proficient in political double-talk?''

He shot Carrie a really filthy look and stalked off to collect Yolanda.

Yolanda was still smiling when the flashbulb went off, and she turned in surprise to find a young man holding a camera just to her left. Alex suddenly materialized, almost shouldering Curtis out of the way.

''We're going home, Landa.''

ROCKWOODS SEEMED DESERTED when they drove in. The geese and chickens were safely penned, and Cinnamon was firmly tethered to a tree trunk at the far back of the property. The unsettled weather had surrendered to sunshine, and birds trilled happily in the silence when the car engine died.

Inside the house, Alex took the stairs to the second story two at a time. He was restless, and he wanted to get out of this bloody monkey suit. He'd already yanked his tie loose and undone his vest.

He felt generally uneasy with the way the affair today had gone, and he'd bet Carrie would make something of Yolanda's innocent comments in tomorrow's column.

Damn it, what was there about Yolanda that attracted attention and that managed to embroil both of them in publicity?

His mouth twisted with the ironic admission that today, at least people would have had to be blind or dead not to notice her combination of sultry, exotic beauty and unusual linguistic ability. Curtis certainly had noticed, far too much for Alex's peace of mind.

Beauty and brains. Yolanda was undeniably intelligent, just as Carrie had said. She simply had an uncanny knack of saying the wrong thing at exactly the right time.

He was passing Tracey's door. She was home, he knew, because rock music from her stereo was blasting loud enough to shake the foundations. He slowed, about to knock and tell her to turn it down when a pause came between tapes, and in the silence he heard the murmur of voices. One sentence sounded clearly, and Alex stood frozen in place.

"Please, Trace. I've told you I love you. You want it, too, I can tell," an agonized young male begged, then added petulantly, "Everybody else does it."

"Victor, I told you, I—"

Without a thought for the wisdom of his actions, Alex burst into Tracey's bedroom.

Tracey was sprawled across her bed, her clothing in disarray. Vic lay facedown beside her, one hand fondling her breast. He'd obviously been kissing her. Both of them were flushed, and their breathing was heavy.

Blood rose in Alex until he could feel his pulse thundering with rage. He'd smashed the door open with such force that it had banged into the wall.

Trembling, his fists balled, he advanced on the now-terrified Vic, who'd leaped up and was taking refuge behind the bed, his hands nervously tucking in his loosened shirt, checking the zipper on his pants.

That particular action brought Alex dangerously near to hitting the boy, smashing his fist into that too handsome nose.

He restrained himself—just—and bellowed, "Out, get out of here. And don't come back."

Vic, obviously terrified, still made an effort to explain.

"Look, Mr. Caine, it's not what—"

"Shut up." Alex was beyond reason. He made a threatening move, and the boy headed for the door and pounded down the stairs.

Tracey had leaped from the bed and was straightening her own clothes. Her face was scarlet, and a mixture of humiliation and rage showed in her trembling lips and sparking gray eyes.

"What the hell is going on in here, young lady?"

Alex's voice held all the impotent rage and fear and disbelief of a parent learning that his innocent child is not so innocent, and no longer a child.

"Daddy, you have no right..." Her voice was quavering. She cleared her throat and bravely met Alex's gaze with a defiant glare.

"There wasn't anything. I mean, we weren't doing anything."

Fleetingly Alex realized he was handling this situation badly. But he couldn't seem to make himself stop.

"Not doing anything? From what I saw," he barked at her, "you would have been in another few minutes. Why, you're a baby—you don't even know what the hell you're doing. That bastard of a boy... I've got a good mind to go over to Cameron's and—"

"Daddy, you wouldn't." Absolute horror was on Tracey's face and in her voice. "This is between Vic and me. It's not anybody else's business." Her chin shot up, betrayed by a quiver. "And I'm not a baby, either. I have the right to make my own decisions."

Alex snorted. "You happen to be fifteen years old. That's far too young—"

"It is not." Tracey's fragile control was starting to crack, and her voice had a hysterical edge.

"Fifteen isn't too young, even Yolanda says it isn't."

Alex felt himself grow still inside. Carefully he moved toward his daughter and caught her shoulders in his hands.

"What do you mean, Yolanda says it isn't? What's Yolanda got to do with this?"

Tracey stared back at him, her features rebellious. "Yolanda and I are friends; she talks to me. I'm not stupid, Daddy. She said if I needed, needed birth control or—"

"Birth control?" Alex felt dazed. "Birth control?"

Tracey lowered her eyes. "She offered to come with me. But I decided, well, I thought it over, and I decided not to, not to have an affair. And right when you came in, I was going to tell Vic, but then you burst in here like a maniac, and now..." Tears began to roll down her cheeks, and her voice was going up and up, out of control. "I'll probably never even see Vic again after this. Daddy, how could you? Weren't you young once; don't you remember?"

She was shrieking at him now, but her words were barely registering. What was reverberating in Alex's brain was the knowledge that Yolanda had betrayed his trust, had... She'd poisoned the mind of his daughter.

"We'll talk about this later, Tracey," he said abstractedly and turned to the open door. Yolanda stood just outside it. She'd obviously heard most of what had been said.

"Alex, please," she began to say quietly as he came into the hallway, and she reached out to place a restraining hand on his sleeve. "This is not what you think."

Roughly he pulled his arm away. He fixed her with a cold, narrow-eyed look, the kind of look he'd give an obnoxious stranger, and he went up the stairs to their room.

Yolanda stared after him, her stomach churning with apprehension. She must go and talk with him, try to explain Tracey's words. She glanced into the girl's room, and her heart melted with pity for the huddled ball of sobbing misery on the bed.

"Tracey, darling, don't cry so."

Yolanda, forgetful of the elegant dress, hurried over to the bed and took the weeping girl in her arms.

Upstairs, Alex wrenched his suit off, tossing it on the bed. A button flew off his shirt, and he cursed foully and tore the garment off over his head, flinging it on the bed, as well. Every moment he expected Yolanda to come through the door, willed her to come so the outrage building inside him would have a focus. He drew on jeans and a faded T-shirt. He was bent over, tying his runners when she came softly through the bedroom door and closed it after her.

He looked up, and she shivered as a tidal wave of apprehension swept over her. His eyes were icy, remote and hard.

"I understand you've offered to supply my daughter with birth control." His voice was edged with steel. "And that you fully condone a fifteen-year-old having an active sex life.''

She walked shakily into the room, trying not to let him see that his anger was frightening her.

"I discussed these matters with Tracey, yes, Alex, but not in the way you think." She made an enormous effort to keep her voice steady.

"The way I think? What way is there to think? Did you or did you not tell Tracey that girls of her age have sex?" He got to his feet, taking several steps toward her.

She stood her ground, but the effort made her tremble. Why wouldn't he listen to what had actually happened?

"Alex, Tracey is not the child you imagine her to be. She is a young woman, and I said she must make her own decisions. I told her only what I believed to be true."

He knew he was being unreasonable, knew hazily that his anger wasn't really directed at Yolanda, or maybe even at Tracey, for that matter. But a demon possessed him, a deep confusion that made him lash out viciously.

"You're not her mother, Yolanda. You have no right to act like her mother. Dixie would never have allowed this to happen."

The words were evenly spaced, lethally cruel. Her face, already pale and drawn under the healthy tan, seemed to whiten even more. She flinched, as if his words were a physical blow, and she wrapped her arms around her breasts as if to shield her heart. But she met his gaze evenly.

"No, I am not Tracey's mother. Just as I am not your wife, not in your heart, am I, Alex? I saw your displeasure today. I say and do the wrong thing—I am not perfect as your Dixie was." The hidden frustration and hurt and anger she felt boiled to the surface. "You want me here as a convenience, isn't that so? To fill the awkward spaces between you and your daughter, to satisfy the needs of your body. But your love belongs to that—'' She gestured illogically to the place on the nightstand where Dixie's picture had been and where Yolanda still imagined it to be.

"You belong to that dead woman, just as everything in this house does.'' She was trembling visibly, and she had to finish before she began to cry. Finish, and leave. He took a half step to close the distance between them, and she held her hand up to him, warning him away. If he touched her, she would never be able to say what was in her heart, and it had to be said.

"You use me as a shield between you and your daughter, and you use Dixie as a shield between you and me. You told me once I didn't know you well enough to love you. Now, I do know you, and I see how little understanding there is in your heart for Tracey, or for me. I wonder, Alex. Were you sensitive to this Dixie you love so faithfully, or does it only seem so because she is dead?''

Her voice broke, and she turned and fled. He heard her running down the stairs, heard the door slam, and he didn't move. He couldn't. Her words had hammered at him, each truth a separate blow. He didn't need to have her say the final words. He knew what they'd be. Now that she knew him, she no longer loved him. He swallowed again and again, as if he were choking on words that should have been spoken long ago.

Yolanda charged down the beach path, vaguely aware of the incongruity of her dress and high-heeled shoes, but too miserable to care. The heels of the dainty shoes sank deeply into the sand with every step, and when she came to the area where the picnic had been held, she sank down on the log where she'd sat beside Ruth and Sophia.

Loneliness and a dreadful anguish grew in her with excrutiating pain. Homesickness—longing for *babička*, the feeling of alienation she experienced so often in this country where she didn't belong—mixed with the things she'd refused to accept in her marriage, and which, today, she'd been forced to face. She didn't belong in her marriage, either. She clasped her body with her arms, rocking back and forth in agony.

Time passed. She gradually became aware of the sound of gulls, wheeling and crying over the ocean, and the stillness heralding evening's approach. Despite the sunshine, she felt chilled. The devastating pain had eased, but what she had to do filled her with another type of pain, a more lasting kind but just as agonizing.

She had to leave. Rockwoods, Tracey, the animals; the thought of leaving them tore her apart. It would be every bit as painful as leaving Votice had been. And Alex? The thought of leaving Alex made her feel as if she were dying. But if she stayed, now that the truth was acknowledged between them, she would die a different way, more gradually, without pride or self-respect, and still without his love.

Better to go now. Her lips twisted in a sad mockery of a smile. She'd heard *babička* lecture a neighbor woman once, saying sternly, "Be careful of pride. Pride is cold comfort in bed."

Yolanda suspected the months ahead would be cold indeed, and devoid of comfort.

CHAPTER THIRTEEN

ALEX WAS GONE when she finally struggled back up the path to the house that evening. His sports car was missing from the garage.

"Grampa phoned about the fishing trip they're taking, and Dad's gone over there. He said he'd be home late," Tracey mumbled, offering Yolanda some soup and a grilled-cheese sandwich, but avoiding her eyes.

"I caused trouble for you, Landa. I didn't mean to…I'm sorry," she finally blurted out. "I made you promise not to tell Dad, and then I did myself." Tears trickled in a woebegone path down her cheeks.

"Oh, Tracey." Yolanda drew the girl into her arms, feeling helpless. How would she explain the confusions adults made for themselves, when she didn't fully understand them, either?

Yolanda drew a deep breath. Tracey deserved an explanation.

"What we have here is one of these 'breakdowns in communication' you and I read about in those women's magazines, Tracey."

The weak attempt at lightness fell flat.

"We were both wrong in not involving your father in such important affairs in your life. He loves you so much, that's why he grows angry when he finds you are growing up. It's up to you to help him. From now on, you must go to him, confide in him," Yolanda persisted.

How to broach the other matter, the collapse of their marriage, such as it was? Sighing, Yolanda said heavily, "The problems between your father and me are most certainly not your fault. It would be ridiculous to think so. He and I—that is an entirely separate matter, private between us."

She bent her head over the sandwich that she couldn't eat, steeling herself against the pain of what she had to tell the girl.

"Darling Tracey, forgive me, but I have decided to live alone for a time."

Her announcement brought hysterical tears from Tracey, and it took all evening and as much common sense as Yolanda possessed to convince the girl that Yolanda wasn't disappearing from her life just because she would live elsewhere.

Then there was the problem of the animals to solve, as well, with Tracey going back to school. Thankfully, a telephone call to Ian Cameron provided the solution. He would "board" Cinnamon and the geese and hens, as long as Tracey came over daily to help with their care.

Yolanda couldn't help but be proud of the responsible way Tracey was behaving. But the girl was badly shaken, all the same, by Yolanda's leaving.

"Please, can I come and stay with you sometimes, Landa? Maybe when the men go fishing?"

Yolanda promised, her heart twisting with pain for the child-woman who felt she was losing still another person in her life. She slumped into a kitchen chair when Tracey finally went up to bed, feeling drained and exhausted.

When Alex's car purred into the driveway an hour later, a cold numbness settled over her. She must end whatever was left between them, and quickly.

When she heard his footsteps approaching, a hollow sickness filled her. His first words made her feel immeasurably worse.

"Yolanda, I'm sorry," Alex said contritely the moment he came in the door. He looped his jacket over the chair back and came over to where she sat in the dimly lit kitchen. She wanted to scream with frustration.

"There's a lot about this business you don't understand," he began, but it was too late. Whatever he said, she reminded herself, nothing had changed between this afternoon and now. The very fact that she sat in the kitchen, avoiding the areas where Dixie's order was evident, was enough to remind her of the silent but very real ghost whose presence lingered here in this house and in Alex's heart.

Fear mushroomed within her as he approached, along with a desperate need to keep him at arm's length. She could only do what she had to if he didn't touch her, if she didn't acknowledge the sadness and appeal in those green eyes.

"I have decided to move, Alex, as soon as possible," she blurted out. "My decision is final, so please, don't make it harder for me."

"Yolanda, we have to talk. There's so much I need to explain to you."

Not for months had she used the mask she'd worn so often in Czechoslovakia, the impenetrable mask of cold silence and indifference she'd used so effectively. She used it now, unaware that it brought painful remembrances to him of another wife, of problems always left unresolved, of guilt he never quite forgot. His anxious concern faded into a cold mask of anger.

He'd put a hand on her arm, and she snatched it from his grasp.

Her face was pale when she looked him squarely in the eye, but her huge eyes were devoid of expression.

"Can you tell me you love me, that you trust me to help raise your daughter? Can you promise the memory of your first wife is only a memory, that she will no longer be there between us? I see you cannot. So I have absolutely nothing more to say to you, except that what has happened between us has been a big mistake."

Her hard, indifferent tone stopped him cold. She got up, fighting the urge to look at him, and with all the dignity she could muster, she marched out and up the stairs, locking the door to the yellow room before the torrent of weeping began.

The following morning she packed her suitcase, stubbornly taking only the clothing she'd brought and the things Tracey had given her. She left the luxurious wardrobe he'd bought her hanging in his bedroom closet. It was simply another part of the fantasy she'd been living, and she had to leave it behind with the rest of the dreams.

In a side pocket of her suitcase she found the small box containing her father's wedding ring, which *babička* had given her when she left. She stared down at the golden band and viciously shoved it back in its hiding place.

Her father's loyalty had been to a dead dream. Alex's loyalty was to his dead wife. There was an ironic similarity to both of Yolanda's losses.

There was a final tussle with Alex, this time over where she would stay.

"I will find a furnished room," she insisted, and was unprepared for the vehemence of his response.

"You will use my apartment in Victoria, Yolanda." The words were a command. "It's empty, and I assure you I'll never bother you in any way, if that's what's worrying you."

Stubbornly she started to argue, but his next words came out harsh and full of pain, and she had to give in to him. "Please, Yolanda, do this one last thing for the sake of what

we've had between us. I can't stand the thought of you living in some dingy room, and anyway, you still don't have
your citizenship. It's safer this way. And there's room in the
apartment for Tracey to come and stay now and then. She's
already told me she's staying with you when we go on that
damned fishing trip Barney's so set on.''

Reluctantly she agreed, and he drove her into the city, to
the imposing apartment complex near the park. He un-
loaded her few belongings: the suitcases and a box of fresh
vegetables Tracey had insisted on picking for her that
morning. It was that produce that nearly destroyed the rigid
and fragile control she imposed on herself while Alex was
there. She remembered so vividly how much hilarity the
garden had brought them.

He gave her the keys and a list of things about the apartment services.

"You will let me know if there's anything you need?"

His faded jeans were snug on his narrow hips, and his
cotton shirt was slightly rumpled. He had dark circles under his eyes, and his jaw tensed and released in grim testi-
mony to the stress he felt.

*Alex, my husband, my lover. I need you, I need you, only
you.*

But the time was gone to confess her love. She ran to the
wide window to watch Alex drive away, feeling as if her
heart went down the street along with him.

After she'd been in the roomy penthouse suite an hour,
she realized that living there would be as bad as staying at
Rockwoods, if she wanted to escape reminders of Alex.

There was more evidence of him here than had been at
Rockwoods: books he obviously read, pencil sketches of
forest scenes, a scale model of a sports car. Most of all,
however, was the sense of quiet masculine opulence the
apartment exuded, the leather sofa, the huge oak desk in the

corner, the butcher block table and sturdy modern chairs in the space-age kitchen. If Rockwoods was Dixie, every corner of this apartment was Alex.

She put her belongings into the bedroom farthest from the one she knew to be his, vowing to find a place of her own, regardless of what Alex had asked. But for the time being she was simply too tired to do anything.

The apartment was well stocked with tinned and frozen foods, and Alex had insisted on having even more delivered that afternoon. It was evening before Yolanda forced herself to go for a walk, and bought a paper to take back with her to the lonely apartment.

She opened it and gasped. There, in the middle section, her own face looked out at her, smiling, animated, happy. She stared down at herself, unable to believe she'd looked that way just yesterday. How could a life change so quickly? Underneath, Carrie's column, "The Way It Is," was subtitled "Light a Tiny Candle."

Assistant deputy ministers don't often comment publicly on our government's social programs or their effectiveness—or lack thereof. So it was enlightening to have Yolanda, beautiful Czechoslovak wife of Alex Caine, state publicly that her husband abhors the need for such programs, believing they should be unnecessary in a well-run country. Could one of government's own sons be lighting a tiny candle in support of what many of us have long believed? Yolanda Caine, pictured above, also commented on the universality of women's aspirations everywhere. She—

Yolanda crumpled the paper, her hands trembling uncontrollably.

The column would be an embarrassment to Alex, the final straw in their relationship. She walked to the window to stare down at the pinpoints of light starting to illuminate the city, and she wished passionately, fervently, hopelessly, that she'd never left Czechoslovakia. She wanted to go home.

Instead she dragged herself out of bed the next morning and went to work.

Foofera was incredibly busy during these first weeks of September, and for that Yolanda was grateful. The demands of each moment mercifully delayed the inevitable hours when she was alone at night.

DAYS, THEN WEEKS, passed in a gray fog of wretchedness. Usually impervious to illness, Yolanda now felt sick much of the time, and she had trouble sleeping.

The only time the shop was quiet was first thing in the morning. Yolanda was grateful for this short respite from customers.

This morning she'd been racked by such acute nausea and weakness that she'd been tempted to stay in bed.

She felt even worse by the time she arrived at the store. Lili was dangling casually from her mother's arm, and milk from her most recent feeding bubbled from her tiny mouth. Dominique plunked the baby into Yolanda's arms and motioned to a chair.

"Sit now, and tell me what makes you look like this. Holding a baby makes one feel better, whatever is wrong, no?"

It was true. The fragrant, squirming bundle was wonderful to cuddle, easing the aching nausea in Yolanda's stomach.

"For the past days I have watched you, the tear-swollen eyes in the morning, the pretense that all is well. Now you look terrible enough to finally tell me what has happened to make you this way. Talk.''

Yolanda hesitated, not knowing where to begin. Dominique began for her.

"You moved suddenly into the city, and that handsome husband of yours no longer calls you at the store. You are separated, no?''

"Yes.''

"But you love your Alex?''

"Yes.''

"He knows that you are pregnant?''

If Yolanda hadn't been sitting down, she would have dropped Lili. She stared into Dominique's sympathetic eyes as if hypnotized.

Dominique gestured at Lili. "I remember those first months well; that certain look one has, the yellow cast to the skin, the sickness.'' She frowned at Yolanda. "Even the tears. Of course, I might be altogether wrong. But it is possible?''

Yolanda numbly counted weeks in her head. Seven had passed since her period. It was definitely possible.

Suddenly she remembered the doctor's examination, the probing questions she'd asked. And Yolanda had ignored the follow-up appointment two weeks ago. What was the sense, she'd reasoned listlessly, of bothering with birth control now? She hadn't bothered even phoning to cancel.

She stood like an automaton, placed Lili gently in her mother's arms and reached for the phone to call the clinic.

"Let it be so,'' she whispered feverishly as she found the number and dialed. She couldn't have Alex's love. By some miracle, could she have his baby? "Please, God, let it be so.''

And it was. Yolanda was able to get another appointment almost right away.

"I suspected pregnancy in its earliest stages when I examined you, Mrs. Caine," the doctor said as Yolanda waited breathlessly in her office. "The lab tried to contact you for samples, but there was some difficulty in reaching you."

"I have moved. This is my new number." Reciting the digits, Yolanda felt light-headed, as if her voice were coming from a great distance. Alex's child. She would have Alex's child.

"I'd like you to start a course of vitamins," Dr. Carlisle said slowly, studying Yolanda's pallor, the look of fatigue in her eyes.

"You're a very healthy woman, and twenty-nine these days is quite normal for a first pregnancy." She looked up at Yolanda again. "Are you suffering some particular form of stress, my dear? Working too hard, perhaps? You're a bit thin, although your blood count is fine. If it's your job, I would recommend—"

"No, no. I will be fine now. This baby, this pregnancy...it makes me happy. I assure you, I will take good care from now on."

The doctor smiled and pushed her large glasses farther up onto her nose.

"And your husband? You did come to the clinic in the first place for birth control. Will he be as pleased as you are?"

The words hung in the small room. The doctor somehow knew.

"I am no longer living with my husband."

"You will tell him, though, won't you?"

Yolanda hesitated. Then she shook her head. "He will eventually know, of course. But for now, no. I think not."

Dr. Carlisle didn't comment until Yolanda was leaving. Then she said, "You've chosen a difficult route, my dear.

You know, a great many men have negative feelings about becoming parents. In my experience, those men are often outstanding when they actually become fathers.''

Yolanda said quietly, ''My husband already has a daughter from a previous marriage. He's made it very plain that he wants no more children.'' Then she thought to ask, ''When do you think my baby will come?''

''May, early May. Let's see, about the tenth, I should think.''

May. The gardens would be sprouting green shoots in Votice, the meadows would be sprinkled with poppy shoots and the first blue cornflowers.

The cuckoos would be nesting in the trees by *babička*'s cottage.

A baby, in May. Alex's baby.

''Thank you, Doctor Mary Carlisle. I thank you more than I can say.''

WHEN THE PHONE RANG THAT EVENING, Yolanda snatched it up, certain that it was Dominique. She ached to tell someone about the baby, and there was no one else she could safely tell.

She had no idea what Alex had told the family about her moving out of Rockwoods; Barney and Robert and Sophia had each come to the apartment the first week she'd moved in, silently closing ranks and making certain that she was well cared for and that she had everything their money could provide. And their love. She had no doubts about their love for her.

They'd never asked her to explain her sudden decision, and she hadn't felt strong enough emotionally to offer one without an accompanying storm of tears. She cried so much these days it was a wonder she didn't dehydrate, and they'd looked at her swollen eyes and never probed. She loved them dearly for it.

"Yes, hello?" she said breathlessly, and the silken smooth voice on the other end announced, "This is Carrie Russell, Yolanda. I'm sure you must feel like hanging up on me. Please don't, at least until you hear what I have to propose. I've had a hell of a time tracking you down. Your stepdaughter finally gave me the number, but she practically made me sign in blood for it. She's very protective of your privacy."

Almost an hour later, Yolanda slowly put the receiver back in the cradle and rubbed her ear. It felt as if it were swollen, the same way her mind felt with the idea Carrie had outlined.

Briefly, the columnist had suggested a series of articles—interviews, actually—in which Yolanda would expand on the comment she'd made at the garden party about all women wanting the same things from life.

"I've never had such response to a column as I had to that one," Carrie had explained. "Women have been phoning and writing and even dropping by the news office. It seems you struck a common chord by underlining the sameness of women the world over. The public want to know more about you, about the background you came from, more about Czechoslovakia that isn't simply political. Women want to know what kind of lives their Eastern cousins have, what type of jobs they do, what kind of day care and wages they get."

She paused and with some embarrassment added, "This is ironic for me, Yolanda, because the first column I did about you was definitely mischievous." There was a long pause. "I had, oh, fantasies at one stage about a future with Alex." She gave a self-deprecatory laugh. "I had no basis for hope, except, of course, my rather lurid imagination. So it comforted me to present you as a sort of gauche immigrant. Then, the other day when I realized you were an accomplished interpreter with the charisma to attract crowds, I have to confess I was jealous. Until my good sense took over. Now I'm afraid I'm in the awkward position of hoping you'll accept my apologies and agree to work with me. I've already been approached by several women's organizations, church groups and others, begging to have you come and lecture. They'll pay, and I've got a go-ahead from my editor to offer you a hefty amount for the columns.'' She named a salary that seemed outrageous to Yolanda.

''What do you say, will you do it?'' There was an anxious note in Carrie's voice.

Yolanda was curled into a ball on the leather sofa by then, the receiver propped between her chin and ear. She hugged her legs and shut her eyes tightly. It was all too much to comprehend, too much in one short day. There were many things to consider, now that there was the tiny life growing inside her.

''Please, Carrie Russell, I would like to think this over. I will call you with my decision tomorrow.''

Reluctantly Carrie had agreed.

In the end, it didn't take long at all to decide to accept. The job offered a fair chunk of money, which would become important with the baby coming. More than that, the experience offered a chance for Yolanda to test her wings in her new country, learn about the ordinary people who lived here, begin to carve out a career for herself, a life for her and the baby.

The baby. Yolanda sang the words over and over, glorying in the sound. She forced herself not to guess what Alex's reaction might be to the news. She intended to tell him, but she wanted to choose the proper time.

She got up stiffly from the sofa and went to the kitchen to plug in the kettle for tea.

What issues would Alex raise, and how would he react? She put a handful of loose tea leaves in the stoneware pot and leaned against the stove waiting for the water to boil.

First he would be angry. She smiled fondly, remembering Alex's anger. He was a passionate man, with strong emotions, and they had often clashed. The smile faded as she realized that this time the anger would be deeper, colder. He would feel betrayed by her, just as he had felt in the fiasco over Tracey. He'd made his feelings plain many times on the subject of children.

He'd blame her, even though her pregnancy hadn't been planned. He would feel trapped by a situation he'd never wanted.

At the very least, Alex would insist on paying support. He was impossibly stubborn when it came to financial matters. Two delivery men had arrived halfway through her first week in the apartment, leaving several huge boxes. Inside was the entire wardrobe he'd picked out for her. A note was pinned on top.

"Keep these, or so help me, I'll feed them all to Cinnamon."

Instead of smiling, the scribbled note had made her burst into a storm of tears, with the reminder of the small, homey details of Rockwoods. She'd hung all the garments in the roomy closet, poignantly remembering expressions on Alex's face the day he'd helped her choose them, the laughter they'd shared at some of the more bizarre designs, the shy way he'd presented her with the bag of lingerie, wanting her to accept, afraid she wouldn't like his choices.

He'd wanted to give to her, wanted to buy her these clothes. From working in the boutique, she knew that they'd cost far more money than he'd revealed. She'd never paid him for the clothes, either.

In a sudden burst of understanding, she realized that he'd never intended her to pay. He had been so magnificently generous with his wealth. How was it that he gave money so freely and yet hoarded his love? She wanted to give him love in untold measure, yet she felt uneasy with material support. And she instinctively knew that Alex was unable to unlock the Pandora's box in which he kept his emotions, giving money in their stead.

Stubbornly Yolanda determined to earn her own money and support their child herself. If he couldn't give love, she didn't want money. She would take the job.

Carrie had assured her that the newspaper articles would be given final approval only by Yolanda, and if she objected to anything, it would be cut. An ironic smile tilted Yolanda's lips. So much trouble in her life had been caused by the press; it would be satisfying to use the medium for her own interests for once.

She drank her steaming tea, nibbled a digestive biscuit, then went to bed in the king-size bed in Alex's bedroom. For the first time since she'd left Rockwoods, she slept deeply all night.

She called in the morning to accept the job.

"Fantastic, fabulous," Carrie enthused when she heard Yolanda's decision. "How about having lunch together Saturday, ironing out details?"

"Sorry, no," Yolanda refused firmly. Tracey was coming to stay while Alex went fishing. Having time with Tracey took precedence over anything else, even this job. The girl had become her younger sister, her daughter, her friend.

Carrie made an appointment for the following week and rang off.

Yolanda replaced the receiver slowly, and her hands cupped her abdomen. It felt exactly the same as it always had, but she knew that the mystery and magic of life was going on in there at a rapid pace, and a feeling of serenity replaced the deep anxiety that had gnawed at her for weeks.

The anguish of leaving Alex was unabated, but having his child within her somehow eased that pain.

Another of *babička*'s truisms came to mind.

"One door never closes but another opens."

Strange how the same phrases that drove her crazy in Czechoslovakia came back now in Canada to bring her comfort.

ALEX DREADED THIS fishing trip. He'd tried to back out at the last minute, feeling that his utter dejection would throw a pall over the outing, but Barney and Robert ignored his excuses and insisted. As usual with these two, the trip began at the incredible hour of 3:00 a.m.

"No use wasting good daylight," Robert had commented like an echo of bygone years, and with the oft repeated remark, a peculiar sense of déjà vu overcame Alex.

How many times had he sat between his father and Barney in a truck like this one, leaving home hours before dawn, sharing a thermos of tepid coffee between them, just to arrive at the same stretch of deserted river shortly after daybreak?

They'd started taking him along when he was about four, he guessed. He remembered the excitement of those childhood days, so intense he couldn't sleep all the night before they were to leave.

He hadn't slept much the night before this trip, either, but excitement wasn't the reason. He hadn't slept well since the day Yolanda left. It had taken fifteen minutes alone at Rockwoods to begin missing her with a vengeance, and the days since then had been the most hollow of his entire life. Yet something kept him from going to her, making the promises he knew to be necessary. Why? he wondered miserably.

He tore his thoughts away from that painful subject, concentrating on his memories of those other fishing trips.

The trips had been yearly events up until his marriage. Then, he'd felt it wasn't right to leave Dixie alone on a weekend, and he'd reluctantly stayed behind.

Barney and Robert kept up the tradition, though, and they'd never stopped asking him to come along. And he'd never stopped wanting to go with them, until this trip. This was the last thing he wanted to do right now.

The trouble was that he didn't know just what it was he did want. He'd made a damned mess of everything, and he felt about as bad as he'd ever felt.

Tracey treated him with cold reserve, fastidiously cooking meals and keeping things in order with an efficiency that amazed him, for it seemed only yesterday he'd had to tell her to wash and brush her hair. The changes in his daughter's habits had to be Yolanda's doing.

On the other hand, she refused to talk with him about anything but the most superficial topics. She chatted politely about her new school when he asked, or about the need for milk or bread. But when he'd awkwardly tried to broach the subject of Vic, she'd quickly left the room. Alex knew she and Vic saw each other at school and also at Ian's, where Tracey daily cared for her animals.

"I don't care to discuss Vic, Dad," she would say with dignity. And if there was a way to make any woman talk when she'd decided not to, he sure as hell had never learned it.

Neither could he talk to Tracey about Yolanda. The aching, twisting loss inside him, the countless times he reached for her warmth in his sleep, the silence of Rockwoods since she'd left, unnerved him. He blocked her out of his thoughts as much as he could, and the empty ache inside him grew remorselessly, day by day.

"That's the turnoff dead ahead." Barney's deep voice interrupted his thoughts, and he saw the faint path leading off the gravel road that would take them to the campsite.

The clearing was a natural semicircle of flat land, ringed by an evergreen forest of Douglas fir, cedar and hemlock. The variegated greens were already interspersed with fiery sprinklings of autumn-painted maple. The campsite fronted the edge of the wide, shallow Cowichan river.

A few hundred yards upstream, a gravel bar formed a natural pool where the steelhead gathered. Today, the sunlight filtered sleepily down through the trees, falling like dust into the campsite. Jays, sparrows and robins called back and forth, and the smell of the fresh-turned mossy earth blended with the particular odor of the oiled-canvas tent as the sun's warmth released the tent's winter mustiness. The ever-present roar of the river muted the other woodland sounds, making them a counterpoint to the restful melody.

Maybe this was what he'd needed after all, Alex thought. Maybe the peace of this well-remembered place and the easy camaraderie with the two men he loved would help him hold at bay the images that haunted him.

"Get the rods, lad," Barney ordered when the camp was set up.

Lad.

Alex's heart constricted. Thirty-nine years old, and to them he would always be "lad."

Robert wandered down to the gravel bar, and Barney found his own favorite spot. As the sun lazily rose to its zenith and started to dip downward, Alex worked his way along the uneven riverbank, sending his line out and drawing it in the way they'd taught him long ago, until slowly the compulsive rhythm began to bring him a sort of numbed peace.

"Still using that Mitchell spinning reel, I see," Alex commented when he found himself casting near Barney. It was a reel popular thirty years before, an antique like the ancient canvas tent Alex had just set up.

"I think they might have improved those, Barney," he ribbed his uncle gently.

Barney had on the filthy old green cap he always wore for fishing, and under it his dark eyes crinkled with amusement as he expertly sent the lure and line soaring upstream.

"They may look a little different, but the basic pattern's the same," he said mildly. "New equipment isn't necessarily better. It's just newer."

Alex shook his head at this bit of folk wisdom, and then suffered the arch looks his uncle shot him as Barney hooked, fought and landed a magnificent steelhead. They fished side by side in silence after that, working their way aimlessly down the curved path of the river.

They'd rounded a bend when Alex spotted the deer. Half-hidden by a protected gravel cutbank and by their own natural camouflage, two white-tailed Island deer were drinking, spraddling their legs in an ungainly way among the river rocks, dipping and bending in a delicate ballet.

The men stood silently watching until the graceful pair, hardly larger than good-sized dogs, turned and scrambled daintily up the bank and disappeared into the forest.

Deer. It was deer such as these that had launched Alex's sex education. He'd been about five. He remembered Robert holding branches aside for him on that hike through the woods. His father's back had been reassuringly broad, and Alex remembered wondering if he'd ever grow that tall and strong. They'd reached a high knoll, and eaten the lunch from Robert's pack.

Alex begged to use the binoculars, and Robert carefully suspended them around his neck. Looking down into the valley, Alex could see little at first, until his father patiently showed him how to adjust the focus.

Then, the green world below sprang alive, branches and even far-off rocks showing texture. He panned clumsily back and forth, enthralled by the magic of bringing far-off things close. Accidentally, he saw the deer.

They were playing, he thought, two of them in a sun-dappled glade too far away to even see without the binoculars.

"Deer, Daddy. Two deer, I can see them." Excitement was making his hands shake. Robert was stretched out in the warmth with his eyes closed, and he gave a grunt of interest. Alex sat immobile, the glasses propped on his knees as he strained to see every detail of marking and color.

They were bumping each other; the male with the horns was trying to jump on the female. The glasses picked up the male's swollen penis, and Alex stared unbelievingly. Then, as he watched, the male suddenly mounted the female, and the act of procreation began, seeming so close and urgent that Alex still remembered the shock and the rush of heat he experienced, the way he dropped the glasses to his chest in confusion. The raw energy, the driving thrusts, the way the female stood wide-legged, head down—he'd thought the male was killing her at first.

"What is it, lad? What'd you see?" His father sat up, curious.

Robert took the glasses and seconds later lowered them slowly, meeting Alex's flushed stare with a level easiness.

"It's okay, son. That's absolutely natural."

He gulped, and it took minutes before he mustered the courage to ask, "But what are they doing, Dad?"

Naturally, and with words easily understood, Robert had explained the process to Alex, and finished it by neatly linking it to human reproduction.

Alex remembered the ensuing scene vividly, and his mouth creased with wry amusement. His poor father must have been heartily sick of the whole subject by the time his son's curiosity was finally satisfied.

One of the trickier points, he remembered now, had been to try to relate the number of babies produced by this fascinating process to the number of times the act was performed, and the astonishing information that humans did something similar.

"Is it called rutting, too?" he'd queried, plaguing Robert with questions about mothers and fathers and numbers of times and how it felt and why anybody wanted to do it in the first place.

He could still see Robert now, sighing, rubbing the back of his neck and tipping his face wearily up to the sky as the conversation went on and on. He'd answered every single question, though, as honestly, and openly as he could. Alex remembered that clearly.

It hit Alex like a hammer blow, the sudden connection between the conversations he'd had with his father, and the ones he hadn't had with Tracey. It would have been easy for Robert to ignore the subject that day, but he hadn't. He'd struggled through.

Alex was the one who'd ignored any openings Tracey had presented. He remembered that damned coy book Dixie had bought for their daughter. Why hadn't she told the girl about love herself? The sunshine dappled and danced in the water, nearly blinding him, and his hands stopped their automatic reeling.

Like a hammer blow to his gut, he realized fully for the first time what he'd done all along. He'd fobbed off the difficult task of parenting first on Dixie, then on the boarding school and relatives, finally on Yolanda. What had happened with Tracey that Sunday afternoon was unfortunate, a direct result of his detached attitude as a parent. He'd refused to recognize his daughter was growing up, perhaps because he'd delegated most of her care in recent years to others.

He swallowed, and a lump stuck in his throat as he remembered that final conversation with Yolanda. Full realization came as he stood in the sunlight, watching his line float randomly down the current.

He'd avoided his responsibility, and then blamed Yolanda for taking it on. How could he have done such a thing? He'd always prided himself on being a fair man. The things he'd said to her burned in his head now like fire, repeating over and over like a tape he couldn't shut off.

Alex reeled in his line. He felt suddenly sick.

"I think I'll head back to camp," he said weakly, and Barney gave him a peculiar stare as he walked off, his shoulders bowed with the ordeal of looking clearly at himself. He didn't much like what he saw.

The rest of the day played itself out on two levels for Alex. He joked with his companions, the automatic responses echoing other times like this. He laughed, and he must have sounded fine, because the other two men didn't seem to notice anything unusual.

The long day slipped placidly into evening as the sun made a spectacular splash of color over the western mountains. The turmoil inside Alex grew until he wondered how he would contain it. In his mind's eye, he watched scenes of his relationships, first with Dixie, then Tracey, and most painful of all, with Yolanda, like an actor watching himself on screen.

The tape went on and on, until he couldn't be sure that what he said aloud had no connection to his inner agony, and so he stopped talking.

He sat stupidly beside the dying fire, not drinking the steaming enamel cup of coffee Robert poured him. When the time finally arrived, he crawled into the tent, found his sleeping bag and pretended to sleep until Robert and Barney snored an arm's length away from him.

Crawling outside again, he realized he was trembling. He crouched to replenish the fire and sat with his back against a tree trunk. He still didn't understand all of it, but one fact hammered at him relentlessly. He had fallen in love with Yolanda, somewhere between Votice and here. That love had lain hidden inside him, locked behind barriers he'd erected.

Today, it had demanded recognition, even after he'd done his level best to destroy it.

He laid another log on the embers, watching as the flames glowed and licked at the branches. A loon laughed across the murmuring river, and the fire crackled as pitch dripped into the blaze.

He clenched his jaw muscles against the waves of pain washing over him. The hours of the endless night were marked only by the number of logs he placed carefully on the fire, and the number of times he recognized the agony of loss when he thought of Yolanda.

CHAPTER FOURTEEN

THE BIRDS HAD STARTED their morning chorus, and the dark eastern sky was beginning to streak with sunrise colors. Alex rose, stiff and drained from his nightlong reverie and emptied the dregs of the blackened coffeepot, then walked down to the river for water to make a fresh pot.

"Morning, lad. You're up pretty early, aren't you?" Barney's voice was deep and somehow comforting in the stillness of the early dawn.

Alex tried to keep emotion from his voice, but it was there, anyway.

"I couldn't sleep, so I figured I'd keep the fire going."

Barney didn't comment, instead tipping a generous amount of coffee grounds directly into the cold river water in the pot and setting it on the iron grill to perk. The look he leveled on Alex was intent.

"You remember Mary Ellen Moore?"

The question seemed senseless. Alex stared blankly at his uncle, and then he did remember, vaguely. Mary Ellen Moore had been the first girl he'd been interested in, back when he was . . . how old?

Fourteen. The experience had scared him nearly to death.

Barney adjusted the pot on the coals, and shook his head, remembering.

"I recall asking you if you were real fond of that Mary Ellen, and you finally getting around to telling me you were, but you felt real mixed-up about it all. That you wanted to be with her when you were with your friends, and when you with her, you'd rather be with them." He chuckled, pouring two fresh cups of the biliously strong brew, blowing on his own to cool it. When he looked up again, his gaze was piercing.

"Confused. Doesn't seem to me you've changed all that much over the years, lad. Seems to me you still aren't too certain what you want."

Alex met his uncle's eyes squarely.

"You're talking about Yolanda?"

The query was unnecessary, but he made it, anyway. It gave him time to steel himself for his uncle's reply.

"Yup. Your dad and I feel mighty responsible for what's happened between you and her."

Alex was silent. He'd never talked with either Barney or Robert about Yolanda, and he didn't know how much they'd guessed. Probably everything, he concluded. They were anything but slow.

"It was plain as day you two had fallen for each other, and we were happy for you, Alex. No need to tell you she's one in a million, that girl. And I guess we felt pretty sharp, arranging it all, seeing the difference she made in Tracey, and in you." He sipped his coffee thoughtfully.

"Now Yolanda's moved out of Rockwoods, Tracey looks like a thundercloud each time I see her, and you can't sleep. To say nothing about how skinny Yolanda's getting. Seems to us you're not happy, any of you."

"The whole damned mess is my fault, Barney."

There was a peculiar comfort in admitting it.

Barney drew a fat cigar from his checkered flannel shirt and made a business of lighting it. He glanced at Alex sharply.

"Might help to talk about it, lad. As I said, Robert and I sure as hell aren't blameless in this, either." He carefully

voided looking at Alex, tapping the glowing ash from the
igar into the fire.

"To be honest, we had high hopes all along that you and
er would, eh, well, that you'd hit if off. Guess we're turn-
ig into meddling fools in our old age." His expression was
rave as he studied his nephew. "This whole thing is be-
ause of your first marriage, isn't it, Alex?"

The question caught Alex off guard, and he sipped his
offee, stalling for time. In some confused fashion, Barney
vas right. His ambivalence toward marriage was rooted in
is relationship with Dixie. But exactly how or why, Alex
vasn't certain.

"No marriage is perfect, son—don't get me wrong. God
nows your aunt Sophia can drive me nuts at times with her
ntertaining and her going places. I'd like to stay home
1ore, but in a marriage, you compromise."

His cigar was slowly burning away, and he tapped the ash
ff absently, his expression introspective.

"I loved Dixie. We were married a long time," Alex stated
efensively. Every time he tried to examine why he felt as he
id, that single point seemed to be both the beginning and
1e end.

"'Course you did, no question of that. Seems to me,
1ough, you struck a bad bargain in that first marriage of
ours. No disrespect for the dead, but Dixie was as much to
lame for the way things were as you were." He nodded to
imself, not noticing the frozen look on Alex's face.

"See," Barney went on, gesturing with the cigar, "you
ever let her grow up, Alex. Never made her grow up," he
orrected. "She was what, eighteen when you got married?
nd you were twenty-two. I remember thinking it was aw-
il damn young for the pair of you. Then I watched you get
der than you should have, fast, while she stayed the same.
lirty, pouty, dissatisfied. Fussy for the wrong reasons.

Worst of all, I watched you turning your guts inside out to make her happy."

Barney shook his head sadly. "That's where you were wrong. Can't ever make somebody else happy, lad. They've got to do it themselves. Mind you, you can give them a shove now and then, like I did with Sophia. Like you ought to have done with your Dixie."

Barney paused for a moment to sip his coffee. "Don't know if you remember, but when Sophia first came here from Czechoslovakia, she wouldn't budge out of the house. Scared to talk to anybody. Wouldn't go anywhere without me." He chuckled and gave Alex a resigned look.

"Doesn't sound much like our gadabout Sophia, does it? Anyhow, I made her try. Made her start shopping, go to night school, learn to drive."

A peculiar look of pride came into Barney's eyes. "Now, I've created a monster. The woman's never home." His gaze centered again on his nephew. "But she's happy, and so am I. We're friends, adult friends, as well as being man and wife. We don't expect the other person to do everything for us, be everything to us."

He squinted earnestly at Alex. "I liked Dixie; don't get me wrong. But I love Yolanda. And I'm afraid you've got some cockeyed notion that one marriage might be like the other, that the whole responsibility for whether the thing works or not is on your shoulders. Yolanda's no child, lad. She's a woman, and all that that implies." He shrugged and lifted an eyebrow. "Even when it's great with a woman, it's not easy. It's just worth it." He grinned wickedly. "Know something? I bet women feel the exact same way about us."

"Barney, you ought to get a soapbox instead of a stump. I've been lying there with the sounds of your voice going on and on for well over an hour, and damned if you two haven't drunk all the coffee, too."

Robert joined them, and his teasing words were a cover for the anxious look he shot his son. Alex looked haggard. But inside, he felt relieved, for the puzzle pieces were painfully coming together. Barney had solved part of it for him. He had to figure out the rest himself.

Alex found the old iron skillet, and the eggs and bacon. "Guess you two are just going to sit around and give orders and watch me cook, so I might as well get it over with."

He had a lot of thinking to do, a lot of painful memories to review, revise and discard. He tilted his head back, squinting up at the autumn sky. It was lighter now, and the grayness and moisture in the air might mean rain. The fish would be biting.

There was no better place than a riverbank for thinking. He was sure Barney and his father knew that quite well.

"HI, DADDY. COME ON UP." Tracey's voice sounded cheery on the intercom. He'd buzzed from the lobby, catching sight of his unshaven face in the oval mirror by the elevators. The drawn lines around mouth and eyes were accentuated by the stubble, and his hair looked as if he hadn't combed it all weekend.

He probably hadn't. He badly needed a shower, fresh clothes, a shave, but he didn't give a tinker's damn how awful he looked.

He wanted to see Yolanda. He needed to see her, talk to her, with a hungry, desperate yearning born of the emotional battle he'd waged with himself and won in the past two days, and the clarity that had resulted from it.

It had become irrationally imperative for him to tell her that he loved her. After that was done, he could take the time necessary for the rest of the explanation he owed her. The elevator sighed to a stop, and he strode down the familiar carpeted corridor with a feeling of expectancy rising in his chest. Somehow, he'd manage a few minutes alone with his wife. Somehow, he'd begin to repair the damage he'd done to their marriage.

Tracey opened the door, drawing him inside.

Too late, Alex realized Yolanda had company. He tried to turn and leave, but Tracey was already pulling him into the room.

"Alex, hello."

In that first second—as always when she saw him—she was aware of no one else. Her heart gave its customary lurch, and she took in the bloodshot eyes, the look of exhaustion. What had happened to make him look this way? He was staring at the others in the room, so she couldn't read his eyes.

Awkwardly she bridged the silence.

"Alex, you've heard me talk about Dominique, and you remember her brother, Armand, from the restaurant?"

Armand, suave and impeccable in his casual slacks and wine-colored sweater, rose from his seat beside Yolanda and extended his hand, appearing to Alex like a host comfortably welcoming a visitor. An open bottle of white wine stood on the low glass-topped table. Its label was French, and beside it was a bouquet of violets.

There was only the slightest hesitation in Alex's response, but Yolanda noticed. The room was fraught with tension, even though he made a joking apology for the way he looked, and several comments on the fishing trip. He studiously avoided even looking in Yolanda's direction.

"Come into the bedroom and peek at the baby, Daddy. Her name's Lili, and I got to hold her until she fell asleep. She's so cute."

His tone was curt. "I'm not much with babies. Another time, Tracey."

"Dominique is going to get me to baby-sit. She says I have a way with Lili."

"Get your bag, please." The words came out gruffer than he'd intended, and Tracey shrugged and obeyed, rolling her eyes heavenward in exasperation.

Within minutes, Tracey had given Yolanda a ferocious hug, and Alex had coldly thanked her for having Tracey for the weekend.

Yolanda found herself standing alone in the entrance hall, staring at the door Alex had just firmly closed behind him and his daughter.

Her hands were trembling, and she felt dizzy from fighting the anguish that seeing Alex had caused. He'd been so remote, so cold to her, never meeting her eyes after that first split second. And he'd looked almost ill.

There was absolutely nothing she could do for him, she reminded herself. Alex had made it plain there was no real place for her in his life. What she had to do now was concentrate on the baby they'd started together.

"I'm not much with babies," Alex had said, and she'd felt pain knife through her heart.

She returned to the living room, grateful that Dominique and Armand had come by this afternoon so unexpectedly. The apartment would be unbearable with Tracey gone. The weekend had been marvelous, and the bond between her and Alex's daughter seemed stronger than ever. If only it might have been so with Alex.

"Armand has offered to give us dinner at Chez Armand, despite Lili's tendency to scream the place down and scare the patrons. I suggest we accept before he comes to his senses," Dominique said lightly.

"I accept," Yolanda agreed, bending forward to hide the sudden tears in her eyes, sniffing the violets Dominique had brought. She had made good friends here. It was silly and childish to long for her grandmother when she was a grown woman expecting a child of her own. Tonight she'd finish the determinedly cheerful letter she'd started, and mail it off on the way to work tomorrow.

She'd told *babička* about the baby. She just hadn't told her about leaving Alex.

TRACEY WAS QUIET all the way back to Rockwoods. Alex alternated between desperately wishing that she'd say something to indicate the nature of Yolanda's relationship with Armand Mollins, and desperately hoping she wouldn't.

It had never crossed his mind that Yolanda would begin seeing other men. He understood logically how ridiculous that assumption was—she was a beautiful young woman, and she was no longer living with him. He'd watched her charm Curtis Blackstone and every man in the near vicinity at the garden party. Of course, other men would flock to be with her.

Like Armand, for instance. Alex's hands tightened around the steering wheel until his knuckles were white, and he had to consciously keep his foot from tromping on the accelerator.

Logic had little to do with the blazing jealousy he'd felt when that Frenchman had stood to shake his hand. Alex had had all he could do to stop himself from driving his fist into the unsuspecting man's handsome nose. Wine, flowers. He'd had to get out fast. An icy chill made him shiver with suppressed emotion.

"Warm enough?" he asked Tracey.

She gave him a puzzled stare.

"It's real warm out, Daddy. Maybe you're catching a cold. You're sure acting funny, and you drove right past our turnoff."

They finally reached Rockwoods, and everything was icy and empty.

The house had the musty closed-in smell of disuse. How could it get that way in just a couple of days?

Alex had forgotten to buy bread and milk. He lit the wood in the fireplace in a futile attempt at hominess. "I'll help get dinner as soon as I shower and shave."

Tracey nodded glumly, throwing herself down on the dainty sofa and driving it back several inches along the carpet. One of the ornate feet broke off, and the whole thing tipped drunkenly to one side.

Tracey got up and scurried to recover the broken leg. She shot him an anxious, guilty look, obviously expecting a reprimand, but Alex just shook his head. He was irritated, not with Tracey but with the ridiculous fragility of such furniture.

He wearily climbed the stairs and impulsively headed straight for the bedroom phone. Yolanda wasn't home.

Out of desperation, that evening he came to a turning point in his relationship with Tracey. When he came downstairs again, she was still sitting despondently on the tilted sofa. She didn't say anything or even glance up when he passed her.

He went straight to the kitchen, reached for his best bottle of Scotch, poured himself a hefty drink and added ice. On an impulse, he filled an identical glass with Coke, added ice, and carried both glasses into the living room.

"Care for a drink with your old man?" he asked Tracey.

Things had been much more formal in the past weeks, and she looked surprised. She straightened and swallowed.

"Sure."

He settled into one of the few comfortable chairs in the room and took a hearty swig from his glass.

"You know, Trace," he began thoughtfully, "getting older doesn't necessarily mean getting smarter. I've been pretty dumb about being a father, and I need to talk it over with you and see if you've got any suggestions."

The silence was long, and he wondered if he'd made another bad move.

"What do you mean?" she finally asked cautiously, and he relaxed a bit. Maybe he was on the right track, after all. At least she wasn't saying she didn't want to talk about it, or walking out on him.

"I think it started when your mother was alive," he continued. "I'd grown up an only child, with Grandpa and Barney raising me. Ours was a masculine household. So when you came along, I didn't know how to treat you, and it was easy to rely on your mother. If she said this or that was right for you, I figured she knew."

He glanced over at her. He had her attention, all right. She was sitting absolutely still, and her eyes were riveted on him. The cola glass was clenched between her hands.

"When your mum died, I was completely lost, Trace. I loved her very much." More than he'd known then, perhaps, now that he was beginning to understand a lot of things. "I was also scared, because now there was just you and me, and Lord, what I didn't know about raising a girl would have filled a whole library."

"Girls aren't that different from boys, Daddy." Her voice was low and defensive.

"I know that now, kid. But I'm one hell of a slow learner."

"You never talk about my mum with me. I used to wish you would." Her wistful tone tore at his heart, and his voice was ragged when he answered.

"I didn't know what to say to you, and I figured I'd just upset you all over again."

"It's there inside all the time, anyway. Talking about it helps." She remembered her Coke and took a quick gulp. The she said tentatively, "Do you still love my mum, Daddy?"

He met her eyes squarely. "Yes, Trace, I do. But I'm still alive, and she's gone." It was a bald statement of fact, and he wondered what her reaction would be. It wasn't at all what he expected.

"You love Yolanda, too, don't you?"

Something in his chest constricted. He drank the rest of his Scotch without a pause. "Yeah, I do."

Her voice was accusatory. "Well, she's your wife now, and I think you should tell her and get her to come back and live with us. I really miss her, Dad. Yolanda's my best friend."

He drew in a deep, shaky breath.

"I think she's mine, too, and I intend to do exactly that, Trace. But first, I think you and I ought to make some changes around here."

He explained what he had in mind, and she agreed enthusiastically.

Getting to know his daughter wasn't the easiest thing Alex had ever attempted, and they had a few difficult silences that first week. But it was hard to stay quiet for long when the evenings were spent carting the old heavy furniture, which Alex remembered from his own youth, down from the attic and into the living room. Alex phoned a charity and offered them the entire contents of the living and dining rooms, including draperies, on the condition they'd come and take everything away.

"You can keep whatever you want, Trace," he offered, wondering if some things might remind her of Dixie.

"That little dancing horse and the photographs are all I want. You ever try dusting all this junk, Dad?"

The "junk" was packed into a box and sent with the furniture. Then the two of them started moving the heavy old pieces out of the attic.

Halfway down the stairs with an armchair that might have been overstuffed with lead, Alex pantingly suggested that Tracey give Victor a call and ask him over to help them before Alex ended up crippled for life.

Victor appeared twenty minutes later, and both the work and the conversation became easier after the first awkward few sentences.

They got through most of the moving that evening. Alex ordered in a pizza, and he was pleased to find that Vic knew a great deal about sports cars. Before the evening ended, Alex knew a great deal about Vic. The boy wasn't that bad at all.

Yolanda's final week of work at Foofera went quickly. When Friday afternoon arrived, Dominique gave her a check with a generous bonus added.

"Most boutiques do not require one to change and cuddle babies in between serving customers," she said firmly. Then she wrapped her long thin arms around Yolanda in a ferocious hug.

"We are friends, yes? And I want to watch this—" she patted Yolanda's tummy gently "—grow to immense proportions, on someone besides me this time." She pulled away and looked earnestly at Yolanda. "Raising a child alone is not ideal, believe me, my dear friend. You know, of course, that Armand is half in love with you. He is a good man, and he knows about babies, not entirely by choice," she added with a grin.

Yolanda could only shake her head. She sensed that Armand wanted more than just friendship, and she liked him immensely. He was amusing and gentle, suave and urbane. She'd also watched him clumsily caring for Lili, swearing softly in French under his breath, a concentrated frown on his handsome face as he struggled to put a miniscule kicking foot into a tiny bootie. He was a warm, caring, uncomplicated man, and she liked him. But there was room for only one love in her heart, and Alex was the one.

Sophia phoned.

"The men all have to attend a board of director's meeting in Vancouver Saturday, so I thought we could have an early dinner, just us women. I've invited Ruth, and I asked Tracey, but she's going with Alex to visit her grandparents."

"Thank you, Sophia. I'd love to come."

The Saturday luncheon meeting with Carrie went much smoother than Yolanda had expected. Carrie was friendly and professional, and after the first few minutes, Yolanda relaxed.

"I've already booked you for two short talks in Vancouver next week, one for a church group, the other for a Voice of Women organization."

Yolanda shivered nervously at the idea of talking to groups. "I will do my best, although that may not be so good," she said candidly.

"From what I've seen, you'll be a smash hit," Carrie lavishly reassured her. "Because the newspaper's based in Vancouver, I figured that's where we'd start." Carrie efficiently planned the trip, and they spent the remainder of their time discussing the subjects Yolanda would talk about.

"I prefer to avoid political matters completely," Yolanda decided positively, and Carrie nodded thoughtfully.

"I agree, but is that because of Alex? He doesn't have any objections to this, does he?" she inquired in her forthright way. Yolanda met the redhead's eyes squarely.

"Alex and I no longer are living with each other." If she were going to work this closely with Carrie, the facts had to be revealed.

Carrie's eyes narrowed, and she held the eye contact for a long moment. Then she put a long, slender hand on Yolanda's shoulder and squeezed comfortingly.

"I'm sorry about that, Yolanda. Doubly sorry if it has anything to do with those columns I wrote."

"Nothing at all," Yolanda managed to say firmly. "It is a personal matter between Alex and me."

Carrie nodded, and when Yolanda didn't elaborate, the matter was dropped. By the time Yolanda rose to go to Sophia's, Carrie and she were well on their way to friendship.

The day was chilly, and rain was falling in a steady drizzle by the time Yolanda reached Sophia's. The apartment looked warm and welcoming, and there was a fire crackling cheerfully in the wide rock fireplace. Sophia greeted her with a hug and reached up to plant a warm kiss on her cool cheek.

"You're getting far too thin, child," she remonstrated. "Promise me, no more of this dieting. Heavens, if only that diet had worked as well for me." She tilted her head and gave Yolanda another long look.

"You've changed, Landa. You hardly look like the same person you were when you arrived in June. You were pretty then, but now—you're absolutely lovely, dear, although your eyes are sad." She hesitated, then blurted out, "I know this is prying, but I had such hopes for you and Alex. Why, last summer it seemed as if at Rockwoods you were both . . . oh, I don't know!" Not knowing what to say, Yolanda followed her aunt into the comfortable living room and took the easy chair she indicated in front of the fire. She would have to tell Sophia about the baby, and soon.

"Sit there—I'll get some tea. Ruth will be along, but first I wanted you to read Mother's last letter. Have you heard from her recently, Yolanda?"

"Two weeks ago, but she didn't have much to say." *Babička* wasn't getting any better at letter writing. The last one had been only a few hastily scribbled lines, mostly about the harvest.

Sophia looked worried, and Yolanda suddenly felt anxious. "She's not ill, is she?"

Sophia frowned, and then shook her head no. "I don't think so. She mentions the flu, a cold, but nothing serious. I suppose I got used to getting long letters from you, with the occasional note from her, and now it seems strange to receive only the notes." She shrugged and took the letter with its colorful stamps out of a drawer in the desk.

"However, that's one reason I wanted to see you today, Landa. Barney is taking me to Czechoslovakia before Christmas. I want to go and see for myself that she's all right." She poured strong tea in a fragile cup and added milk for Yolanda. "I would so love to have you with us, darling. I asked Barney, but he says it would be dangerous to go before your papers are finalized."

Yolanda half listened as her aunt prattled on, reading the letter carefully. *Babička* wrote only of the vegetables she'd harvested, and the fact that summer was nearly over. Then, near the end of the letter, she abruptly added, "Soon, now, I am going to visit in the Tatras. Before winter comes again. Autumn was always beautiful up there."

"Did she say anything about this trip to you, Yolanda?" Sophia was asking.

"Nothing. She used to tell me she'd go someday, but she must have decided quickly, because she says nothing in my letter." Yolanda stared into the fire thoughtfully. "It's strange for her to decide to go now. She hates traveling, and winter's coming." Yolanda reread the message, a puzzled frown creasing her brow. "I think I will write a letter to Jenda, the neighbor across the road, and ask her about *babička*."

"Better tell her not to let mother know we're checking up on her. She'll give us both the sharp side of her tongue if she finds out."

They smiled together, knowing the feisty old woman. The intercom buzzed, announcing Ruth's arrival, and Yolanda laid the letter on the small side table, glancing at it now and then during the evening, wondering. The train journey to the Tatras would be long and complicated. It was out of character for her grandmother, this impulsive decision.

Yolanda greeted Ruth and was amazed at the changes in her. The rather prim hairdo was gone, replaced by a short, fluffy layered cut. She wore subtle makeup and a soft, very feminine pink dress.

She flushed prettily when both women complimented her, and shyly announced that Robert was taking her to dinner the following evening. Yolanda remembered the night Alex had called her a matchmaker and wished she could share this pleasant news with him. There were so many things about their relationship she missed, so many things they used to talk about. And so many things they never talked about, she realized sadly.

The afternoon and evening passed pleasantly until Yolanda's morning sickness capriciously decided to become evening sickness. She fought off the queasiness as long as she could, but the dreadful nausea increased until it overwhelmed her, and she dashed for the bathroom, heaving.

"You have the flu," Sophia said worriedly when she returned, pale and trembling. "I'll get you some tablets that might help."

Yolanda waved her back into her chair and made her decision. They would know soon, anyway.

"I'm pregnant. I am going to have Alex's baby," she stated calmly. "Alex doesn't yet know about it. He made it very plain, you see, that he never wanted a child. And we are now separated, as well." She drew a long, shaky breath. "It's very difficult, because you see, I want this child very badly, and I plan to tell him, but..." Yolanda felt the easy tears begin. "This pregnancy, it makes me weep all the time," she added petulantly.

Stupefied silence greeted her announcement, and then both women began to talk at once. A few moments after that, all three were crying, the older two with their arms around Yolanda. They were wonderful, warm and loving and supportive. They didn't pry or judge or lecture. They made her weak, sweet tea and fed her soda crackers and fussed like two hens with one chick between them.

Once, Sophia shook her head and said, "All those years, Dixie blamed Alex because she didn't have children. I always wondered if perhaps she..."

The comment lodged in Yolanda's mind. How ironic that when he'd wanted children with the woman he loved, he couldn't have them. And yet now...

Ruth drove her home. When they reached Yolanda's street, Ruth pulled her compact car to the curb and turned the key off.

"I won't come up," Ruth said. "I think you need a hot tub and a good long rest." She paused reflectively, then went on, "I knew Alex's first wife, too, and I much prefer his second. Secretary's catch a firsthand glimpse of their boss's lives, and from what I gathered, Dixie was not an easy person, for all her charming ways, and many times—well, who knows. She was childish, and I suspect Alex was too patient." She grasped Yolanda's hand in her own and held it.

"He's worth fighting for, my dear, even if he's acting like a blockhead at the moment. Now, one more thing. I wasn't fortunate enough to marry and have children of my own, and I've ended up with considerably more money than I'll ever need. I'd consider it a great favor if you'd allow me to be a surrogate grandmother to your baby, and open an account to help you through the next months."

Yolanda thought of that conversation as she bathed that night, luxuriating in the hot water. Dominique, Armand, Ruth, Sophia, Tracey, Robert, Barney—she had so many friends who made it obvious they cared about her.

And Alex. Would the time come when they, too, could be friends, when the tension between them would ease, when her heart wouldn't pound out of control just at the sight of him?

A spasm of pain replaced the smile. She had to tell him, and soon—before someone else did accidentally. The very next time she had an opportunity to talk with him alone, she would simply say it, just the way she'd told Sophia and Ruth.

"Alex," she rehearsed, "I am going to have your baby."

And what would he say?

Goose bumps rose on her arms despite the heated water surrounding her.

He would never admit it, but he'd secretly feel she tricked him. He would feel he'd somehow betrayed the memory of Dixie, and Yolanda would spend the rest of her life living in the shadow of a ghost woman, just as she'd spent the past few months.

She couldn't bear that. She couldn't stand having his compassion, being his moral obligation. She'd already done that, helplessly standing beside him in that hall in Votice, knowing he was marrying her because of family pressure, and she'd sworn never to be in that situation again in her life. She'd be his lover, his friend, his companion—but never again his duty. Never again.

The only thing left to do was to convince Alex she wanted their marriage ended, before he ever found out about the baby. That way, there could be no question about her intentions.

Grief, and a terrible longing for what might have been—what should have been for this child she carried, and for her marriage—made her press her hands to her face in anguish.

Sunday morning came. Yolanda had slept deeply, exhausted and emotionally drained. She got up carefully, anticipating the usual morning nausea, but she felt fine. She padded over to the bedroom drapes and tugged them wide to see the day, grimacing at the gray, misty fog outside the window.

She wrapped herself in Alex's old blue robe and went to the kitchen to make tea. Coffee seemed oily and thick now, and she could no longer tolerate even the smell.

The intercom's buzzing made her jump. She pressed the button.

"Yes, who is it, please?"

"Alex. May I come up?"

Panic seized her. She wasn't prepared for an encounter now; she was still groggy and half asleep, and she wasn't even dressed. How ridiculous to worry about how she looked. This man had seen her, kissed her, held her against his naked body, morning after morning.

Wordlessly, she released the door for him, and then he was standing in the entrance hall. She looked up at his beloved face. Perhaps the baby would be a boy and look like him.

"I didn't get you up, I hope." He was dressed in a business suit, and he'd loosened his tie as usual and undone the shirt's top button. Tiny droplets of moisture clung to his

hair, and his cheeks were ruddy from the cool air. His wonderfully rugged face with the square, strong chin and
crooked nose was so familiar to her, and the green eyes
seemed less guarded this morning.

"Good morning, Alex, I was already awake. Would you
like coffee, or maybe breakfast?"

Without a word, he leaned forward and kissed her, a
gentle kiss, the kind he used to give her after lovemaking.
His lips brushed across hers, lingered at the corner of her
mouth before she pulled away. He smelled of fresh air and
the outdoors. He smelled of Alex, and his kiss unnerved her.

"I have to talk with you," he said huskily, holding her
startled gaze. "I've just come from the ferry. I dropped
Tracey and her friend at McDonald's for breakfast. She'll
walk over here afterward."

His eyes devoured the way she looked, that special, di-
shevelled morning look, with her dusky hair wild and loose
on her shoulders, her blue eyes wide and alluring, her lips
softly, naturally pink. She was pale this morning. He wanted
to tumble her back into the warm bed, strip off whatever she
was wearing. It was, in fact, a voluminous old blue robe of
his. A thrill of pleasure coursed through him, a feeling of
pure male possessiveness that she should wrap herself in
something of his.

"Coffee?" she asked again, confused by his kiss, wary of
his warm eyes stroking over her. She turned jerkily into the
kitchen, filled the automatic percolator and found the fil-
ters. The kettle was boiling. She put a tea bag in the pot and
filled it with water. What now? He was lounging in the
doorway, watching her so intently it unnerved her.

"Tracey is well?" she asked awkwardly.

"She's great," he answered, moving to sit at the butcher-
block table. "That's partly what I wanted to say to you. You
were right, about my needing to learn to talk with her, get

to know her better. You were right about so many things.
I'm sorry I lashed out at you, Landa. The change in Tracey
this summer is entirely due to you, and I'm more grateful
than I can say. Forgive me for being an ass?''

"There is nothing to forgive," she lied briskly, turning
away and finding him a mug, trying not to gag at the strong
smell of coffee in the room. She must not be ill; she must
fight it. She swallowed hard two or three times and poured
her own tea.

She sounded remote, far-away, and Alex frowned. He
wanted things open between them, and he wanted to tell her
the things he'd rehearsed all week as he'd struggled with that
bloody furniture, struggled with the new knowledge of
himself he'd gained during the past eternity of days without her. He'd waited until he could be sure of the words he'd
use and the best way to explain that what had happened between them was his fault, but more important, that he
understood why it was his fault.

She sat with her eyes down, staring into her teacup. Why
didn't she look at him, receptive and eager, the way she always had before?

"Yolanda." His voice was harsher than he'd intended.
She poured him a mugful of coffee, found cream and sugar
and a spoon. "Will you stop bouncing around and listen to
what I've got to say?"

She sank back into the chair, meeting his eyes unwillingly, folding her hands over her rebelliously churning
stomach. If she didn't look at the coffee perhaps she might
feel better. The odor filtered through the room.

"I've done a lot of thinking about us. Things were so
good there for a while, and I know now what happened to
change them. I made a bad mistake, letting you believe that
my first marriage was perfect." It was hard to say these
things, more difficult than he'd expected. He cleared his

throat, took a gulp of hot coffee. "The truth is, I knew there was lots wrong between Dixie and me, but I resented her for it and blamed myself. I never really treated Dixie as an equal, you see, as a mature woman. Then after she died, I felt guilty about the whole mess, felt it was mostly my fault, that I was a failure as a husband, and also as a father, the way Tracey was turning out. So getting back into another marriage wasn't what I wanted or planned."

Yolanda sat still, listening, fighting the nausea, wondering what he was leading up to.

"Then you came along and forced me to examine what I expected of a wife, what a husband and father should be. And Barney said some things that made me see myself clearly. It wasn't easy or pleasant." He rubbed an anxious hand over his tousled head. He wasn't getting any better at this as he went along, and she was making it hard, damn it all.

Well, Caine, what did you expect? That she'd welcome you back with open arms? She's not the unsophisticated woman you married, not any more. A dreadful premonition built inside him.

"What I thought was," he finally blurted, "maybe we could give this another try, this marriage of ours?"

Her face had that total lack of expression again, and he floundered. He wanted to stand up, pull her into his arms with savage force, make love to her on the floor if he had to, force her to let him have another chance.

But this had to be a free choice for her. Up till now, it had been his choices they'd lived by. This time, it had to be hers, or it wouldn't work. He'd never given Dixie enough choices, and he couldn't make that same mistake twice.

To Yolanda, he sounded uncertain. She suspected he was doing just what she'd feared, feeling obligated to make the best of things. She'd been surprised to hear his comments about his marriage, touched by the vulnerability in his face as he spoke. She longed to throw herself into his arms and agree to try again.

Two weeks ago, she would undoubtedly have done exactly that. Now, because of the baby, there was no way she could. If he had once said he loved her, taken her in his arms, told her he couldn't live without her; then, she could have told him about the baby. As it was, it sounded to her as if all he was proposing was another trial, another attempt. Nothing definite. No forevers. And the coffee was making her sicker every moment.

The telephone rang. Alex watched her pick it up, heard her say hello, listened abstractedly as she spoke.

"That was Carrie Russell," she explained when she hung up. "Tomorrow I go with her to Vancouver to begin my new job." She outlined briefly what she would be doing, never quite meeting his eyes as she spoke. She had to conquer her reactions to him, force herself to do what must be done.

"It will be exciting, this new job, and a challenge for me," she said as convincingly as she could. "I am beginning a new life. Therefore, I believe—" she tried and failed to draw a deep breath into her lungs "—I think it would a big mistake to go on with," her voice broke, and she disguised it with a tiny cough, "on with this marriage."

She crossed her arms tighter on her midriff and looked pointedly away from him. "I think we should have, should get, divorced now, as was planned in the beginning."

The pain in her chest and the sickness in her stomach were one. Her glance slid unseeingly across his features, not registering the disbelief and then the pain there, before he masked all feeling.

Through the cold agony her words caused him, Alex knew what must be done. He had to let her go. He'd held Dixie back from independence, until it was too late for both of them. If he loved Yolanda, he had to set her free.

It was too late, he'd waited too long, and he'd lost her.

"If that's what you want, then I'll begin proceedings." The words were toneless, spoken from the well of anguish rising in his chest. "The divorce may have to be postponed until after your citizenship is final, but I can have a legal separation drawn up, if you prefer."

"I think that would be for the best." To her dismay her voice quavered, and she stood up hastily. "I have to, excuse me, I—" She raced to the bathroom, barely able to close and lock the door, turn on the muffling fan, before the wretched vomiting began. It went on and on, leaving her shaking and weak and strangely removed from what had just occurred.

When she rinsed her mouth and reluctantly ventured out, a note sat propped against the sugar bowl on the table.

"Decided to pick Tracey up at the restaurant. Best of luck with your new life. Love, Alex."

She took the note back to bed with her and held it against her cheek until she fell into a deep sleep. When she woke, Sunday was nearly gone, and it was still raining. She bathed and dressed, forced herself to have milk and toast, and then walked as quickly as she could to the Provincial Museum.

The stooped-shouldered guard in the blue uniform nodded and smiled at her. She knew most of the guards by now; she'd come here so often in the past weeks. She rode the escalator up, and soon she stood before the Dutch half door leading to the kitchen.

It was always the same. The smell of cinnamon rose from the pie pastry on the oilcloth-covered table. The pump stood over the primitive sink. The old iron range had a bucket of coal beside it, and a child's doll hung by the arm from a small rocking chair. The kitchen curtain blew in and out with a gentle breeze, and somewhere just outside the sound of horses' hoofs sounded, a dog barked excitedly, a man's voice called.

She closed her eyes, and finally was able to let the pain of the morning grow and grow, until it enveloped her, consumed her. When she could stand no more, she brought the room into focus, concentrating on the comfort it provided.

She'd thought at first the fascination here was the similarity of this room to the kitchen in Votice. Yolanda had always imagined Anna outside, chatting with the neighbor whose dog was barking. Soon, any minute, she'd come back in and put coal on the fire, ladle out the soup for supper.

Now, she saw it as Rockwoods. She'd stepped outside to meet Alex. The room symbolized children, laughter, love, all the things she longed to have with him.

The things she would never have with him. She gripped the wooden barrier, forced her fantasy back again to Votice, and *babička*. Home?

The breeze blew the curtain in and peacefully out again. It was the cottage.

It was Rockwoods.

It was neither. Was there no meeting place for the fragmented pieces of her heart, no tranquil, happy spot, filled with simplicity and contentment?

In Czechoslovakia, she hadn't really belonged.

In Canada, she didn't belong, either.

"Kde domov můj," the anthem asked. "Where is my home?"

The answer wasn't here. She turned and walked quickly away.

DURING THE TWO WEEKS THAT FOLLOWED, Yolanda became something of a minor celebrity in Vancouver as she tried to illustrate the universality of women. Her daily interviews appeared as she continued her simple, straightforward talks, and ever increasing numbers of people came to hear her. She avoided religion and politics and dogma. Instead, she spoke of the lives of ordinary women in Czechoslovakia, their dreams for their children, the traditions handed down from mother to daughter through recipes, and folklore, the methods of housekeeping and cooking one generation taught another, the simple kitchen gardens they planted and tended. She underlined the common bond of female experience, and in doing so she won the hearts of her audience and her readers.

"You're a natural, kid. I knew you would be," Carrie gloated.

Yolanda was quietly pleased, warmed and humbled by the affectionate response she generated, yet in her innermost soul, she was lonelier than she'd thought a human could ever be.

The only thing that gave her joy and comfort was the tiny life quietly growing within her, but even that was mixed with a deep sadness because she couldn't share its magic with the man she loved.

ROBERT'S PHONE CALL CAME EARLY in the morning, before Yolanda was properly awake.

"Yolanda, dear, it's Robert Caine. I'm sorry to wake you up like this, but Sophia had an accident; she's fallen and broken her hip. Now, don't get panicked...she's going to be fine. It happened yesterday afternoon. She was working, taking a dinner to an old man in an apartment with rickety stairs, and—well, the thing is, she wants to see you. Do you think you could come this morning? I'll arrange a flight for you."

Barely two hours later, Yolanda sat beside Sophia's high hospital bed, holding her aunt's hand tightly in her own. Robert had insisted that Barney go with him for lunch to leave the two women alone.

Sophia looked tiny and softly fragile. Her eyes and her fierce grip on Yolanda's hand signaled her mental distress, despite the blurring effect of the drugs she'd been given to ease her pain. She spoke in Slovak.

"Darling, I'm so glad you've come. There's nothing either of us can do, but I wanted to tell you myself. I phoned to Jenda yesterday morning, in Votice, because I was worried about Mother. I just had a bad feeling, and, oh, Landa, she's sick—she's very sick. Jenda said—" A sob choked Sophia's voice, and she raised a hand like a child to rub the tears away. Yolanda found a tissue, and with her own fingers trembling, tenderly stroked it down her aunt's finely wrinkled cheek.

"She's dying, Landa. She refused to go to hospital; she's so stubborn. The neighbors are doing what they can, but she has pneumonia. I arranged for Jenda to get her a nurse, but now I can't go to her. I want you to phone, make sure she has whatever she needs, anything at all, please, darling. Barney will see to it, but he doesn't speak the language, and it's so complicated arranging it from here."

Yolanda somehow found the right words to soothe and reassure her aunt. When Sophie's eyes began to close for longer and longer periods, Yolanda slipped away. After the initial shock, she felt calm inside, resolved about what she must now do.

Babička was dying. She was the last, the only link between this new world and the old. She was all Yolanda knew of home.

Yolanda must go to her.

It was that simple.

But how to make the arrangements? She couldn't ask Barney or Robert for help. They would forbid her to even consider such a trip. She was still, technically, a citizen of Czechoslovakia, without landed immigrant status in Canada.

That made going home dangerous, but it gave her the right to return if she desired. Carrie had handed her a sizeable check when she left Vancouver, and gave her a hug.

"If I can help in any way, let me know. And come back soon. The job is waiting whenever you're free." Carrie had become a good friend.

The check, plus what Yolanda had saved from her job at the boutique, would mean she had enough money to execute her decision.

Next, Yolanda considered contacting Sergio Markoff, the Russian diplomat she remembered from the garden party. His wife, Vasha, had come to the boutique several times afterward, and Yolanda had enjoyed a casual lunch with her one day. Not allowing herself time to be shy about asking a favor, Yolanda phoned, and within an hour Sergio had made the arrangements, pulling who knew what strings to get her a flight out of Vancouver the following day, with connections in Frankfurt to Prague.

"You have given this careful thought, Yolanda Caine?" Sergio asked her worriedly. "You realize, getting into your country is not a problem. But leaving again? I can be of help only one way, and I am concerned for you. You have discussed this carefully with your husband?"

"I am no longer married, so the decision is mine alone to make," Yolanda said evenly. "And I understand, yes. I am grateful, Sergio. Thank you."

She packed the same suitcase she'd brought with her, the old, battered leather case that had belonged to her father. Tucked into the zippered compartment, she found the ring once more, her father's wedding ring. It might as well go back to Votice with her. Like the wedding ring she still wore, it symbolized only broken dreams.

She tucked it back into the suitcase.

CHAPTER FIFTEEN

RUTH PUT THE CALL through from the Russian Consulate.

Alex, tired and preoccupied, tried to inject a note of heartiness into his voice as he picked up the receiver.

"Hello, Sergio...not at all...of course I remember." He nodded and observed the appropriate social amenities and then abruptly he leaped to his feet, gripping the receiver with enough force to crush it, with the same force that seemed to be crushing his heart.

"When did she leave?" He listened, feeling the blood drain out of his face, feeling stark and vivid fear snake through him.

"Sergio, my friend, thank you for telling me. No, believe me, it's not meddling. Yes, I know, I know it's dangerous. Thank you again—I'll be in touch."

Ruth came running at his mad bellow, and her face, too, grew pale when he told her the news.

"Yolanda flew to Prague four days ago. Barney's at the hospital with Sophia; I'm going there now. Get Dad to meet us, and tell him to hurry."

Ruth hesitated, wondering if she should breach Yolanda's trust and tell him about his baby, wondering if he knew. But by the time she decided Alex was slamming the door of the office behind him.

Barney was in Sophia's room, tenderly and clumsily brushing the tangles from his drowsy wife's tousled hair. He looked up and grinned when Alex entered.

"Well, lad, we didn't expect you this early today. Good to see you."

He doesn't know, Alex realized as he walked over and kissed Sophia, giving her what he hoped was a smile.

"She's just had a shot, so she's kind of groggy," Barney warned softly, but Sophia took Alex's hand and clasped it in her own. Her eyelids were heavy, threatening to close, but she smiled fondly up at him.

"It's nice, having my family here," she murmured fuzzily. "You brought Tracey last night, too," she rambled on. "She's turned into a fine young woman, Alex. She's going to be so thrilled about the baby." Her eyes filled with tears. "I only wish mother could have—" Sophia's eyes slowly opened, and she put a hand over her mouth. "Oh, oh, I wasn't supposed to say, was I? But Alex, you really should forget your differences. Landa loves you so, and now your baby is coming, but mother is... Yolanda said she would take care of every..." Sophia drifted off, her hand relaxing its grip on Alex's nerveless fingers.

For the first time in his life, Alex seriously wondered if he would faint.

"Steady, lad." Barney's arm gripped his shoulder.

Robert strode in just then, holding Ruth's hand in his own. His concerned green gaze immediately singled out his son, and slowly Alex felt strength and purpose replace the nauseous faintness.

Two aging knights and one apprentice. It was enough. It had to be.

"Old Anna's dying, and Yolanda's flown to Prague. Her papers expired a month ago. We have some planning to do, because I'm going after her," he hurriedly explained to the older Caines. "Come into another room, so we don't disturb Sophie."

"Well, guess we'll tag along this time," Barney said easily. "Now, here's what we're going to have to do—" The
door swung shut, and Ruth settled down beside Sophia's
bed. The Parliament Buildings could run themselves for a
while.

THE AFTERNOON OF Anna Belankova's funeral was unsea-
sonably warm for a day in mid-November in Votice. There
was a cool breeze, but the sun shone over the autumn landscape, and the air was pleasant.

There was no real reason to feel this icy cold, Yolanda
thought, shivering uncontrollably as she began the walk to
babička's cottage.

"Get in, Landa, we'll drive you," Jenda had insisted, but
Yolanda needed to walk. It was only a mile or so, retracing
the path down the twisting, rutted road leading to this cem-
etery where Grandmother had requested she be buried beside her Karel.

Not far from the raw, new grave with the heap of funeral
wreaths was Josef's grave. Yolanda stared at it through tear-
swollen eyes, and the old resentment toward her father surfaced.

If he'd made different choices, better decisions, if he'd
lived, her life would now be different.

She stood for a moment, thinking she had never, not even
in Victoria, felt so alone, and turned away.

Even her passing had been the way Anna Belankova, iron
willed and determined to the end, had wished it. She'd refused to be moved out of her tiny bedroom in the cottage.
She'd welcomed death like a friend for whom she'd been
waiting calmly and peacefully.

Walking slowly between the fir trees bordering the path-
way, Yolanda was aware of the wind, sighing through the
empty branches, reminding her of *babička*'s voice.

"I was going to the Tatras," she'd whispered petulantly to Yolanda, her voice whistling through the growing thickness in her chest. "To see my home again. Then it came to me; it wasn't the Tatras I wanted. It was Karel, my Karel." She had had to rest a moment, and then she had gone on, "You have your husband now, your home, so you understand, Landa, how I miss my Karel."

That final night, Yolanda had sent the fussy, annoyingly talkative nurse away, insisting that she could care for *babička* herself until morning, and in the deepest part of the night, just before dawn, she had realized that the old woman's last rattling breath hadn't been followed by another, and the gnarled hand she had held in her own had relaxed it's feeble grip. Yolanda had held her own breath, second after second, waiting, hoping—but finally, she had to draw a gasping lungful of air. *Babička* was gone.

"Alex!" Yolanda had cried out then. "Alex," she'd moaned, over and over in long, hopeless, lonely anguish. The plea had echoed through the cottage, the bedroom where she'd lain in his arms that first night, down the stairwell, out into the blackness of the predawn *vesnice*, losing velocity as it had risen through the cold night air. Votice was ten thousand miles from Alex. Yolanda was ten thousand miles from home.

Dully Yolanda noticed the bareness of the land, the stripped and naked look the fields had after harvest. It was the way she felt inside; it was appropriate.

To the west, the village huddled, naked without its blanket of softening snow. It would come soon, the snow. She would have to make warm maternity clothing for the coming winter. She would have to get a work permit, find a job. For the first time since she'd boarded the plane in Vancouver, Yolanda faced the probability that she would never be allowed to board the flight back. She would try tomorrow, but in her heart she knew the attempt would be useless.

Entering Czechoslovakia had been deceptively simple. The guards had examined her documents closely, and she'd watched them scrutinize her and make endless notations on their endless forms.

"Is your husband traveling with you?" The question had seemed so innocent.

"I am alone. My grandmother is ill—"

"Will Mr. Caine be joining you here soon?"

"I am alone."

They knew. No one, no one, came back before citizenship in a new country was assured. Even her marriage was no protection now. The separation papers must be through by now. Alex was free of her. He'd given her freedom once. His responsibility for her was over.

She couldn't stand to think of the others; Tracey, Barney, Sophia, Robert...Dominique, Armand, Carrie... her friends, her family. Would they understand why she had to return? Did she herself understand the force that had drawn her back?

She shook her head. It was *babička*, of course, she'd had to see *babička* this one last time. But was that all?

She stopped under a tree whose naked branches sighed in the wind. She wrapped her arms around herself, around the small, hard mound that pushed out against the front of her black jersey dress, and she recognized what she had done by returning.

She had jeopardized her unborn child. If, as she suspected, her departure tomorrow was blocked by the officials, her child would be born here, a native of Czechoslovakia, with all the problems that entailed. A great shuddering sigh escaped her.

Coming back had been more than a need to see her grandmother. It had been an odyssey, a journey in search of herself.

Home. Curtains blowing in the breeze, the smell of cinnamon. Home wasn't the cottage or Rockwoods. It wasn't Votice or Victoria or Czechoslovakia or Canada. Home was a place in the heart, and she'd learned this truth too late.

Coming here was something she had to do, but it could also be the greatest mistake she'd ever made. How could an action be wrong and yet right at the same time?

It came to her then, and the admission made her tremble.

She and her father, Josef, had made identical choices, doing what each of them knew to be dangerous. Josef had died for his choice.

She'd gone through her life resenting the course Josef had chosen, because it had drastically affected the pattern of her life. Yet by choosing to return here, she had made a similar choice for her unborn child.

She stood, cradling her stomach, staring unseeingly out over the desolate landscape, the clarity of her new understanding stark and terrible, until the healing tears, the gentle tears of forgiveness began to fall at last. Josef had only done what he'd had to do, just as she had.

"I'm sorry, I'm so sorry," she murmured wearily to her father, her child, herself, and Alex. Then, there was nothing left to do but walk back to the empty cottage.

Her head down, exhausted beyond thought, she was nearly in the lane before she saw the blue Skoda parked by the door, and her heart gave a tremendous lurch.

"It might be anyone—it could be anyone," she cautioned herself aloud, afraid to hope. Still, she started to run, and the cottage door flew open.

"Alex, Alex!" she cried unbelievingly, and he caught her, his arms clamping her so solidly against his body she knew he'd never let her go again. He swept her up in his arms and carried her inside, kicking the door shut behind them.

"God, Landa, I'm so glad to find you. You're freezing! Here—" He sank down with her on the old settee, loosened her coat, rubbed clumsily at the tears still wet on her cheeks, and then he became very still, holding her tightly. She could feel his huge body trembling.

"Don't ever leave me again," he whispered roughly, passionately. "I won't ever let you leave me again. You can have a dozen careers, run for prime minister if that's what you want, but with me beside you. I love you, Gypsy. Do you hear me? I love you. I need you as my partner, as my wife."

He cupped her cheeks with his hands, forcing her to look into his intense amber-flecked eyes, and he repeated relentlessly, "Do you understand? I love you, and you must promise me, Landa, you'll stay my wife. Tell me you will, tell me you love me." She drank in the craggy lines of his face, the hard shape of his mouth, the slightly crooked nose, and then she closed her eyes tightly.

"It's not so simple anymore," she choked out. "You see, I am having a baby, Alex. Our baby, and you said you don't want babies."

She gasped as his mouth clamped down over her own in a wild and scalding kiss that choked off the rest of her words. He drew away, and she stared up at him, bewildered by the fierce intensity on his face.

"I know about the baby, but that's not why I'm here. I'm here because of you, Yolanda. We have to settle this matter of our marriage before we get into anything else. I can't even discuss babies until I know you love me, that you want to stay married to me."

He kissed her again, more gently this time, and his voice was harsh and raw when he said, "All this is my fault, for ever letting you leave me in the first place, for not telling you how deeply I love you. Damn my stupidity."

His tone became determined. "Now, either you love me or you don't. If you don't, I'll simply spend the rest of the night showing you why you should. If you do, then for God's sake, say it. I've chased you half around the world to hear you say it, Landa."

Through the almost unbearable relief and joy his words created, she whispered tremulously, "Alex, of course I love you. I told you once, but you didn't want to hear. From the first, I have loved you, and will love you forever." The quiet, growing certitude in her husky voice satisfied him, and his lips once again came gently down on hers, lingered, then lifted. He looked at her carefully, noticed the drawn, pale exhaustion stamped on her clear features and the slight trembling in her body.

"Stay here," he commanded. "I'll stoke the fire and get you hot tea and some food." He slid his hand tentatively, shyly, to her rounded abdomen. "There's plenty of time to talk about this child of ours." His hand stroked upward making her shudder with pleasure as he cupped her breast, traced her shoulder and neck, then each smooth cheek with lingering tenderness. "I've got one hell of a lot to learn, and not just about babies." A roguish gleam came and went in his eyes. "I suspect you'll force me into it, one way or another, won't you?"

Yolanda's eyes brimmed with tears. "This pregnancy, it makes me cry all the time," she sighed in resignation.

"It's okay, I brought some Kleenex with me," he teased, but his heart was at peace, his voice full of compassion and love and understanding of all she'd been through. He sought for words to comfort her, to ease the loss of her grandmother, but nothing he could think of sounded right. At last he simply said, "If our baby's a girl we'll name her Anna."

DARKNESS DROPPED LIKE A BLANKET over Votice. In the tiny bedroom where they'd lain together on their wedding night, Yolanda lay in the arms of her husband. This time, their passion was a white-hot flame that seared and melded and healed with its intensity, binding them together, husband and wife, forever.

She fumbled in her suitcase, found Josef's ring and slid it on Alex's finger.

"This belonged to my father, and *babička* said to give it to the one I love."

They talked then, each baring their soul to the other, revealing fears and hurts and doubts. Alex spoke freely of his marriage to Dixie, and the complicated maze of emotions he'd worked his way through so painfully the past few months.

"It was hard to admit we'd both been wrong. I'd spent so long telling myself the problems were all mine, yet secretly blaming her for not acting like an adult, even when I didn't treat her like one. We weren't partners, Landa, and that's what marriage must be, a partnership you commit yourself to every day of your life." He cuddled closer in the darkness, "As Barney says, 'It takes work.' Sometimes it's easy, and sometimes it tears your guts out, but because you love each other, you do it."

He related anecdotes from his weeks alone with Tracey, funny and poignant blunders he'd made, unconsciously illustrating the new relationship he shared with his daughter. What kind of father would he be to this new baby? He relentlessly subdued his uncertainty. He'd do his best, but would that be good enough?

Slowly, exquisitely slowly, he explored all the changes in her beloved familiar body, made newly foreign by pregnancy. He caressed the full breasts with their swollen, tender nipples, skimmed the warm curve of her rounded belly with his palms, awed by the hard, determined bulge his child made beneath the satin skin. "When will she be born?" he asked, pressing moist kisses across her stomach, making her breath come fast and labored.

"May," she answered.

Suddenly he tore his hand away from the silken curls his fingers were exploring. "Maybe I shouldn't—"

But she laughed softly, found his hand and replaced it. "When the time comes, then I will tell you. But now, this is necessary. The doctor would agree, Alex; this is necessary for my health."

Neither of them spoke again, losing themselves in the sensuous, throbbing delight their love demanded. But after Yolanda had fallen into deep healing slumber in his arms, Alex lay awake.

The ominous and dangerous specter of the Prague airport with the guards and officials and documents, and the scene to be played out the following day on that stage, kept him from sleeping. The arm that locked Yolanda's relaxed form tightly against his body went numb finally, but still he didn't move. He tucked the goose-down comforter more securely around her shoulder and waited grimly for the dawn.

THE UNIFORMED OFFICIAL with the cold, shuttered eyes slapped the green passport down on the desk and shook his head. "Outdated," he pronounced once again in his heavy accent. "It has not the proper stamp. I am sorry, Mr. Caine. We require the proper authorization."

"But she's my wife, and I'm a Canadian citizen," Alex grated out, and the man looked bored and shook his head again.

"This is not Canada, and Yolanda Belankova Caine is not a citizen of your country, unfortunately," he replied in a brisk tone. "She must have the proper forms and the proper stamp. I am sorry, Mr. Caine."

Where were Barney and Robert? Alex could feel his blood beginning to boil with rage and frustration and anxiety.

This same scene had been repeated three times, up through varying ranks of officials. And three times, the result had been the same.

The flight to Frankfurt was only twenty minutes away. Alex glanced at the clock high on the gray wall, and he squeezed Yolanda's hand reassuringly in his, praying fervently that help was on the way.

Yolanda felt the tension building in Alex, sensed his muscles flexing at the mask of official indifference confronting them, and she laid a cautionary hand on his arm, keeping her own protective mask firmly in place.

Her panic and terror, her despair, were increasing by the instant. Her worst fears, her every nightmare, seemed to be incarnate at this moment, in this place, and she knew with a sick and final certainty that her situation was hopeless. Barney and Robert hadn't managed to work a miracle this time.

She would have to stay behind.

These petty officials weren't being malicious, she thought tiredly. They were simply doing a job, obeying orders by rote, rejecting reason and compassion and humanity because that was what they'd been ordered to do.

She turned to tell Alex so, when there was a commotion behind her, the sound of loud voices, laughter, and Barney and Robert were suddenly on either side of her, and behind

them, dozens of men. Official tags proclaimed them to be
engineers from the Caines' pulp and paper plant, and as
they crowded around, their Canadian accents echoed
cheerfully.

The official behind the desk now looked rattled. From the
corner of her eye, Yolanda caught a glimpse of two military policemen watching suspiciously, moving slowly toward her.

Barney shoved a folder full of what looked to be important documents across the desk, but the official was shaking his head, refusing to even look at them.

"There are irregularities," he insisted stubbornly. Robert stepped forward.

"This is my son and my daughter-in-law," he said pleasantly. "The gentlemen with us are our engineers from the
pulp and paper plant in Ružomberok—I'm sure you've
heard of it? It would be unfortunate if we should have to
recall these men because of some misunderstanding, shut
down the business, lay off the workers. Especially..." He
slipped a thick envelope from his jacket pocket and slid it
discreetly across the desk. "Especially when all these papers prove that Mrs. Yolanda Caine is not only part of our
family, but also has official status as a Canadian landed
immigrant. Right here, see?" He waved a form from the
stack inside the folder, and the official suspiciously glanced
at it. He inched the envelope toward himself and peered inside.

Yolanda could hear the military policemen ordering a
path through the press of bodies surrounding them, and she
felt herself growing dizzy. The clock on the wall showed
fifteen minutes until flight time...*fourteen*...

The envelope of money disappeared.

"What is the problem here?" The words were sharp,
staccato.

Yolanda's throat convulsed, and she could smell garlic on the policeman's breath; he was so near.

"No problem, simply documents to be affirmed."

A barrage of stamps banged down like gunshots. Impassively, the official handed her papers with the requisite stamp boldly visible across them.

Thirteen minutes, twelve— She could see the leashed dogs straining at their collars beside the policemen—Alex was half carrying her, with his arm around her, hurrying, but her legs wouldn't work properly. Out the door, deep breaths of cold air, across the endless tarmac, up the ramp. Black spots danced in front of her eyes, and in a red haze, she imagined the guns, the dogs, the cries of the guards. Alex's arm encircled her, and then she was slumped in a seat, the world was whirling, and the floor vibrated beneath her feet.

"Bring my wife some water. Hurry! She's feeling faint."

A rushing tunnel of blurred images passed outside the window, and a sense of weightlessness engulfed her. She sipped at the water Alex was holding to her lips, and the world tilted, straightened. Slowly, as if awakening from a dream, she looked beyond the circle of his protective arms.

The plane was airborne.

Alex's face hovered over her, tense and strained, but a kind of glorious rapture burned in his green eyes.

"That's my girl, that's my Gypsy, better now?" he crooned in her ear. "We're safe, my love, my Landa. We're free; we're going home."

Across the aisle, Barney and Robert frowned worriedly at her until she smiled their way. Then exuberant grins replaced the concerned expressions, and they each held up a thumb to her in Tracey's triumphant salute.

Yolanda turned to the window. The plane was circling high over Prague, and she watched the city below grow steadily smaller, until at last she saw only an innocent patchwork of green and gray and brown.

The sun pouring through the tiny windows made her eyes water. Alex was cradling her against his shoulder. She rested there, and when she looked outside again, the tragic and beautiful land of her birth had disappeared beneath the clouds. All she could see was blue sky and golden light, and the silver wing of the plane.

The strangest sensation made its way lazily through her stomach, a wavering flutter like a tiny sea creature stretching, rippling, inside her. She held her breath, and it happened again.

"Alex," she breathed in awe. "Alex, our baby is moving, here, feel."

She pressed his large warm hand to her abdomen. The ring she'd placed on his finger dug in a bit, and the flutter came once more, stronger this time.

He felt it, and the lingering uncertainties that had plagued him in the night slowly faded, replaced by an incredible joy and a sense of wonder. He'd been given a second chance at loving, and at parenting. This tiny, living being beneath his palm was a symbol of their union, a living part of each of them.

"I hope she looks just like her mother," he said, and reverently he bent and kissed his wife.

EPILOGUE

ONE WINDY AFTERNOON in early May, the skies over Victoria slowly cleared, and cornflower blue replaced the wet gray rain clouds that had hovered for days over the island city, disguising the fact that spring had settled in unremarked, hidden by umbrellas and dampness.

Curtis Blackstone, hurrying out of the Parliament Buildings that afternoon to keep an afternoon tryst with a lady he was courting, noticed the rows of Japanese cherry trees, hung with pearly pink blossoms glistening in the warm sunlight.

Robert Caine removed the cover from his pristine white Rolls-Royce, and drove Ruth Prentiss to Beacon Hill Park just to see the carpet of golden daffodils, rolling nearly down to the sea.

Barney stopped at a market on the corner and bought a purple hyacinth to celebrate Sophia's graduation from daily therapy.

Sergio Markoff noticed that the arbutus trees in his garden had finished shedding their bark, and now the trunks looked warm, amber-shaded, naked.

Newborn. He paused to touch one before he opened the door of his house. Vasha came bustling down the hall to meet him.

"Look, Sergio, what comes today." She spoke to him in English now. The children insisted on it.

"Came," he corrected automatically, giving her a noisy kiss and examining the hand-printed message.

> Rockwoods, 45 Sea View Road, May fourth
> Tracey Caine announces the arrival of her brother
> Karel Alexander Josef Caine
> nine pounds, fourteen ounces.
> Mother excellent, father recuperating, baby noisy.

Across the bottom in phonetic Russian, Yolanda had scrawled "Rosjhani doma." Vasha traced the words with a fingertip, translating slowly into English.

"Born at home."

Harlequin Superromance

COMING NEXT MONTH

#230 ONCE A STRANGER • Megan Alexander
Holly Jones is happy working at her pottery in
Oaxaco, Mexico, until her former husband,
renowned filmmaker Christopher Brooke, arrives to
make a documentary. Suddenly Holly's
determination to protect her heart begins to
slip away....

#231 A DANGEROUS SENTIMENT • Lynn Erickson
When Daphne Farway joins forces with Wes Leroux
to prove her fiancé's death was not accidental, time
is not on their side. Only three weeks remain for the
cookbook writer and the secret service agent to
uncover motives, to snare a traitor...to fall in love.

#232 SEE ONLY ME • Shirley Larson
Investigating Jessica Moore turns out to be the
toughest assignment Rourke Caldwell has ever
had as a corporate crime specialist. Every time he
stumbles on evidence that could convict her,
Rourke remembers that day seven years ago when
the blind farm girl had lovingly traced his features
with trembling fingers as they kissed in the rain....

#233 FINAL PAYMENT • Evelyn A. Crowe
What price will JoBeth Huntley have to pay for
getting the man she has always wanted? In the fourth
and final book in this series, Brandon DeSalva agrees
to marry JoBeth, but wedded bliss may cost them
their lives.

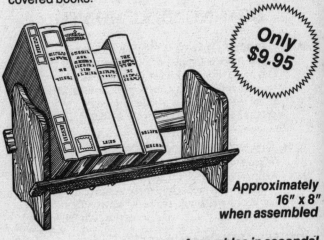

Take 4 books & a surprise gift FREE

SPECIAL LIMITED-TIME OFFER

Mail to   **Harlequin Reader Service®**

In the U.S.
901 Fuhrmann Blvd.
P.O. Box 1394
Buffalo, N.Y. 14240-1394

In Canada
P.O. Box 609
Fort Erie, Ontario
L2A 9Z9

YES! Please send me 4 free Harlequin Superromance® novels and my free surprise gift. Then send me 4 brand-new novels every month as they come off the presses. Bill me at the low price of $2.50 each—a 10% saving off the retail price. There are no shipping, handling or other hidden costs. There is no minimum number of books I must purchase. I can always return a shipment and cancel at any time. Even if I never buy another book from Harlequin, the 4 free novels and the surprise gift are mine to keep forever.

Name _____ (PLEASE PRINT)

Address _____ Apt. No. _____

City _____ State/Prov. _____ Zip/Postal Code _____

This offer is limited to one order per household and not valid to present subscribers. Price is subject to change.   DOSR-SUB-1RR

Violet Winspear

THE HONEYMOON

Blackmailed into marriage, a reluctant bride discovers intoxicating passion and heartbreaking doubt.

Is it Jorja or her resemblance to her sister that stirs Renzo Talmonte's desire?

A turbulent love story unfolds in the glorious tradition of Violet Winspear, *la grande dame* of romance fiction.